Tampa Heat

Thad Diaz

Cigar City Press

Contents

Acknowledgments

I could write no novel without the support of those closest to me.

First, I want to thank my wife, Melanie, and family for your patience and indulgence. Writing books takes hundreds of hours per book. And you have been nothing but supportive of me and these projects. I cannot thank you enough.

Dave Butler and Christopher Ruocchio, we pilgrims in an unholy land must stick together. Thank you for your support and encouragement through the years.

Aysha Rehm, these books would be horrible train wrecks without your hard, diligent work, and I would be lost without your help.

Merritt, JP, and B. Strenge, thank you for helping shape me into the firefighter and paramedic I became.

Earl Emerson for paving the way for firefighter storytellers everywhere.

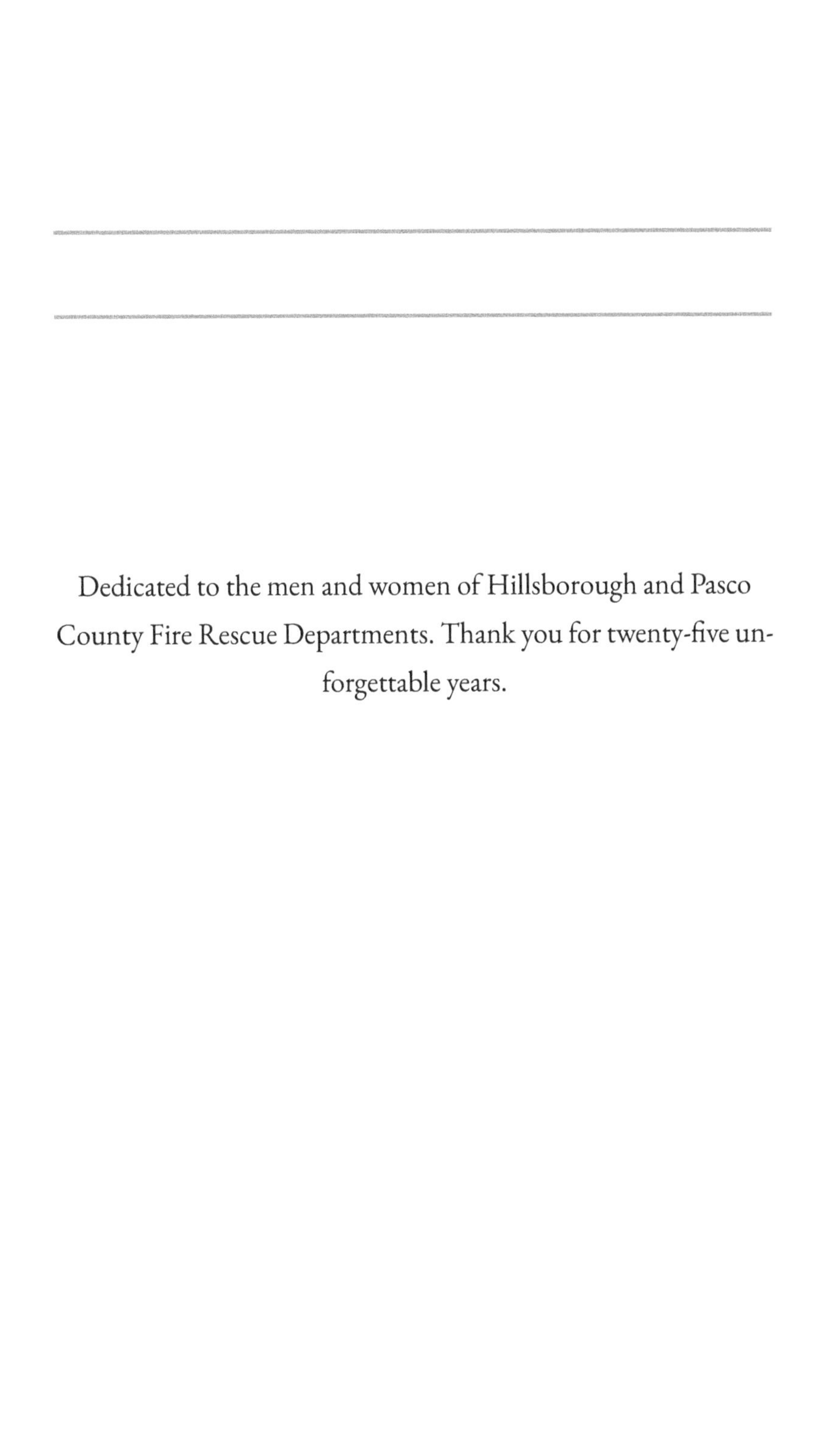

Dedicated to the men and women of Hillsborough and Pasco County Fire Rescue Departments. Thank you for twenty-five unforgettable years.

AN EASY COLLAR

Tampa has been accused of having more strip clubs per capita than churches. While far from accurate, there were neighborhoods doing their part to perpetuate the myth. Drew Park was such a neighborhood.

The tiny borough was nestled into Tampa International Airport's armpit south of Hillsborough Avenue and west of Dale Mabry Highway. Time had seen the names come and go, but the neighborhood's soul had stayed the same. It was still a place where machine shops and dirt path trailer parks sat side by side with strip clubs and adult toy stores.

My father, Martin "Marty" Walsh, and I sat in front of just such an establishment. We'd backed into a convenient parking spot in the TD Bank lot adjoining the Lucky Horseshoe Gentlemen's Club on the corner of Hillsborough and Lois. The Lucky Horseshoe had been the Prancing Pony six months ago and Lipstixx before that. Next month it would be Veronica's Playhouse or

Diamond Girls, but, like the rest of the neighborhood, even the superficial changes would be no change at all.

I gazed through the rain-speckled windshield, and the reflection of my weary sagging face with its three-day growth. A muted University of Florida Gator cap shaded my grey eyes and hid the coarse, black hair growing salty before its time. The pink and purple neon reflected off the still-steaming pavement, wet from the ten-minute downburst that left us hotter and steamier than before the storm.

"I told you; my info is solid on this. If he's not with her, she'll know where he is."

Pops shifted in the passenger's seat and winced, but voiced no complaint. "Well, if she's a bust, I'm out fifty grand."

I let the seat back and stretched my legs against the firewall. "He hasn't gone far. We'll get him."

His grunt had an if-you-say-so quality that suggested apathy and fatigue.

I glanced at my father across the gloom of the dark cabin. His once-lean firefighter frame was sliding toward frail. Taut bronze skin had grown sallow and sagged on a bony face that had been carved muscle when I was a boy. The dark eyebrows were always full, but they'd grown into a wild tangle of black and grey. His silver hair was a sparse covering for his liver-spotted head and getting thinner every day.

He caught my look. "What?"

"Nothing."

"That wasn't a nothing look on your face." I didn't answer, and he continued. "You have your own problems to tend to, Son. Val went to see a lawyer on Tuesday."

"She tell you that, did she?"

"The fuck do I do for a living?" He let that sink in. "She took the kids to a friend's house and spent the better part of an hour with a lawyer. A ..." He closed his eyes in recall. "Margorie Mimms, Esquire, on Collins. Nice brick building off Renfro."

"Tuesday was C Shift." My day job was a Hillsborough County firefighter. I was the C Shift captain at Station Twenty-five, a palatial country firehouse in the rural eastside. "Val called me on the station line that morning to talk."

"Couldn't have you coming home unexpectedly again."

The county drew my name for a random drug test four months ago. Union contract gave me the rest of the shift off, sending me home three hours into what was supposed to be a twenty-four-hour shift. The kids had been at school, but Val was there. She hadn't been alone.

I arrived at the house to find two sets of dirty breakfast plates and a pair of half-drank mimosas still on the table, breathy whispers and soft moans coming from the bedroom. I hadn't spent another night in our Plant City home.

"I'm sorry, Son."

"Who told you?"

"Lenny." Leonard Watts was one of Pops' sometimes trackers. "Why do you think I have you out so late on a B Shift?"

I sat up. "He's watching Val, right now?"

Pops tossed me a glance. "Sure. She went to see a lawyer. Next step is bringing Rockefeller back."

Rockefeller was Pops' name for Scott Marion. Scott owned Plant City Luxury Living, a manufactured home lot off I-4. Val had been his chief bookkeeper and accounting manager but graduated to courtesan, or perhaps things had happened the other way around.

"Maybe you should worry about your wife, Pops."

Familiar pain slid through his eyes. "Leave your mother out of this."

"Then leave Val out of it and stop following her around. We're trying to sort this out. She catches one of your stooges tailing her, and it'll ruin everything."

"Have it your way."

My anger ebbed. He wasn't the source of my angst, though I thought he was being as softhearted and hardheaded about his marriage as he thought I was about mine. But his failed marriage was an old wound, calloused and scarred. Mine was fresh and bleeding.

"You want something from the Circle K—"

He held up a hand and pointed across the rain-soaked parking lot. "Ssshh."

A woman had emerged, a pair of knee-high boots and fishnets covering her long, lean legs. The cuffs of her denim shorts rode higher than its pockets. The Oxford shirt she'd kept tied up hung loose at her sides and flapped in the wake of her rapid-fire steps. There was no sign of the glasses, but she shook out her platinum hair, setting it free from the hairpins that had given her the naughty teacher persona she'd sported when I dipped in to verify she was there.

"It's her."

Pops was getting on in years, but he'd bird-dogged skips for two decades. "No shit."

Crystal tossed her stuff into the back of a late model Prius without so much as a glance around the parking lot. It would be easy to think her nonchalant except for the Lou Ferrigno–wannabe filling the door to the club. She waved, and a smile broke across the swarthy face on his boulder head. He raised a fleshy hand that looked capable of crushing bowling balls and closed the door.

We held tight and let her climb in and search for her keys in the dark. She turned the motor over, rolled down a window, and struck a plume of flame to a cigarette. Whether it was tobacco or something more potent, I couldn't say. She blew a gust into the humid night and put the car in reverse. We waited, letting her back up and drive out of the lot.

A green-and-white TD Bank sign bordering the club's shared lot shielded us from view. The marquee stood higher than my car and offered excellent cover as long as we stayed dark until she passed. I started the car and brought the wipers to life, clearing the shed rain from the windshield.

I pulled from the slot as she was turning onto Lois, heading north toward Hillsborough. I flicked on the headlights and glimpsed a green intersection signal through the palms and oaks that bordered the northern edge of the property. Pops saw it, too.

"If she gets through that light, we'll lose her."

"No shit, Pops." I did a rolling stop onto Lois and floored the accelerator of my 2013 Toyota Corolla. She was still in the intersection when the light turned amber. I think I had broken the plane before the signal turned red, but there wasn't a camera or police cruisers to care. I slowed way down and tried to give her some lead time.

"Don't get too close!"

"Do you wanna do this?" He didn't answer, but I knew he did.

Lois Avenue transformed from a four-lane commercial avenue to a two-lane residential street in the course of a hundred yards. The wide, well-lit boulevard narrowed to a modest blacktop where the yellow streetlamps were the only light beyond the parking lot of Alexander Elementary. There was no traffic and no place on the empty street to hide. I slowed even more and hoped the distance would be enough to assuage any suspicions she might have of a car tailing her out of nowhere, but the air carried the sweet stink of burning ganga leaf, and I suspected I was getting some help with Crystal's situational awareness.

She crossed a wide, stocky bridge over a deep, trash-strewn furrow that more resembled a canal than the ditch it was and turned west on Henry. I passed the sleeping baseball fields, crossed the bridge, and came to a complete stop at the octagon. No one was coming, and I wanted to give her more of a lead before following at a respectable distance. She entered Henry's northern curve onto Manhattan, and a spark of nervous tension rippled through me. I'd have a splendid chance of losing her if she darted onto a side street before I made the curve, but the fears were misplaced. She was still riding north on Manhattan blowing out plumes of pot smoke when I broke free of the curve.

"She ain't acting like she's got a fugitive from justice hiding out in her home," said Pops.

"Maybe she doesn't. But my guy is clear. Bobby Lee was puppy dogging over her. He won't be far from her skirt."

Pops nodded at that. Crystal caught a red light at Sligh, and I backed off the gas to avoid sitting behind her. It didn't work, and we idled, watching her take hits off her blunt and listening to an obscenity that passed for music, oblivious to our presence. The light turned green, and I gave her a head start. We passed Leto High School, where a marquee proclaimed Welcome Back Students!

Crystal turned left into Manhattan Palms Condos. Broad Street was offset from the entrance to my right. I took that, made a quick three-point turn on the sleeping residential street, and watched her taillights recede over the low, sand-colored brick perimeter wall. The complex had a single drive between buildings of white-painted wood over sand-painted brick. A round Victorian turret capped the end of the main building facing the street, but it seemed the only one in the complex.

I followed through the ungated entrance, jogged past the turret, and passed Crystal getting out of her car. I slowed. Pops craned his neck and watched her make the climb. "Second floor."

I nodded and found an empty parking spot. It wasn't easy with all the residents home. I checked my belt for taser, ties, and gun and stepped into the muggy night. Pops did the same. He wore a tactical vest emblazoned with Bail Enforcement Agent in thick yellow letters, front and back. I wore a black Metallica shirt under a black-striped button-down that hung loose on my shoulders and arms. My distressed black jeans hung loose over the same black Rocky boots I wore at the fire station.

We glided up the stairs, quick and quiet. Horrific music boomed from the apartment on our left, and I wondered if Crystal hadn't brought the club home with her. I balled my fist and rattled the door with three quick overhand chops.

"Bail enforcement, open up!"

The music died, and hushed, worried voices echoed through the wood. I crouched and pressed myself against the brick that crowded my right. It was never a good idea to stand in front of the door, but this landing offered few options. I shared a nervous glance with Pops, staged halfway up the steps, his sixty-eight-year-old hand on his pistol butt. The deadbolt clicked, and the door opened.

A lean man in a beige wife-beater stood in the doorway. His sandy hair was long and greasy and he'd grown a beard, but I recognized his defeated face at a glance. "Hello, Bobby Lee. We've been looking for you."

A PLEA FOR HELP

Bobby Lee Kinsey rode in the back of our car, sulking in the rear driver's side doorjamb. But he recovered by the time we turned south on Dale Mabry and leaned forward, his hands zip-tied behind his back.

"How much money you getting paid for this?" He spoke with the twangy Florida accent that almost sounded foreign among the northern transplants and Latin immigrants.

Pops gave him an easy smile. "I'm gettin' my fifty Gs back from the man, Bobby."

Kinsey threw himself back into the corner, cursing and swearing, his grown man sobs filling the car. It was pathetic to behold, and I resented him for not taking his medicine with more grace. These tough guys, always the baddest of the bad until they got pinched. Then it was all crying to mother or God. I bit back a comment and banked onto 275 North. Traffic was sparse at 2:00 am, leaving bright, empty lanes.

"I never shoulda gone back to them, but they were on the way back up. I didn't think they would mind giving me a taste. You know?"

That was also a common theme. "I don't care how they got you to run dope, Bobby Lee."

He sat up, wet face angry in my mirror. "Man! Fuck you! That dope wasn't mine."

Another golden oldie. All us guilty people running around the cities free while the innocent lambs are locked up on false charges. "I suppose someone planted that shit. Right, Bobby Lee?"

Pops shot me a warning glance and smiled at Kinsey.

"Look, son." Kinsey was forty-two, but sixty-eight-year-olds could call almost anyone son. "That stuff is up to the jury."

"Jury?"

I glanced in the mirror. Eyes reflecting the desperation in his voice looked back at me.

"Jury? There's no way they're gonna let me live to see a jury. You gotta believe me. This ain't about a couple keys of coke."

"I put fifty thousand of my hard-earned dollars up for your bail. I have to bring you back, even if you had the fifty grand to give me. We're sworn court officers. We'd be dragged into the same Falkenburg pod you're headed to if we didn't."

"They'll kill me, man. Don't you hear?"

His feral, cornered screaming hurt my ears. "Who's gonna kill you?"

His eyes grew guarded, and he recoiled. Was he getting pale? It was hard to see in the mirror.

"Wouldn't you like to know?" His voice became graveyard quiet, and I wondered if he had psych history.

"Maybe I would."

We passed downtown Tampa, merged east onto I-4, and took aim at Ybor City.

"That secret is my meal ticket, man. I can only punch that card once. I ain't wasting it on you."

The change in demeanor gave me whiplash. I glanced at Pops. He shrugged. It wasn't like anything Bobby Lee could say was going to make a difference, anyhow. But I couldn't help myself. "I'm sure your supplier isn't happy over losing the coke, but busts happen."

"I told you, man, that dope wasn't mine. It took me years to get off the roxies ... cost me my wife, my kids. You think I'd want that shit around me?"

"I see." My voice was pure patronization. "It just fell out of the sky."

Pops shot another warning glance.

"Fuck you, tough guy. You're such a badass with these cuffs on my wrist. Why don't you let me out of here and we'll see who's the badass."

He had an inch or two of reach, but I outweighed him by twenty-five pounds. I tossed a dismissive glance into the mirror. "Thanks, but I value my license."

He withdrew to the doorjamb, mumbling about how he should have been smarter and how no one gave a fuck. I wondered if he was censoring himself. I'd read his rap sheet preparing for this trace.

It was clean, and forty-two was late in life for that kind of career move. Maybe he'd gotten desperate. Maybe he'd taken that one shot at Easy Street and gotten burned. It happened all the time.

I never once considered the possibility his babbling could be rooted in a deeper, darker secret that went back decades. Later I would tell myself there was nothing I could have done to change things, even if I had heard the truth in his panicked desperation. Those fanciful words might even have been true, but they didn't make me feel any better about myself.

We passed the giant guitar that was the Seminole Hard Rock and Casino and exited onto US 92 in tense silence. The two-lane highway was asleep at this hour. We passed a pair of Hillsborough County sheriff's deputies sitting driver's window to driver's window, their marker lights the only sign the cruisers were occupied. I turned south on Falkenburg, drove through the MLK intersection, and cast a glance at the sleeping fire station at Broadway.

Station Nine housed our HIT, or Hazardous Incident Team, and was one of the busiest in our department. I had never cared for hazmat incidents and had no desire to run the fifteen or more calls they pulled down every twenty-four-hour shift. My easy half dozen in the country was plenty at this stage in my career.

I pulled into the parking lot of the Falkenburg Jail and found a spot close to intake.

"We're here." I glanced at Pops, but he was glaring a hole in me.

Kinsey stood with my help, his body limp and resigned under the weight of his future. "Man, I would've cut you in. You just walked away from a fortune. Now I'm gonna have to cut a deal with the State Attorney … If them motherfuckers don't kill me first."

He spoke with the voice of a man who'd watched a winning lotto ticket burn before his eyes.

I guided him by the arm and closed the car door. "Yeah, you're a regular victim of fate, aren't you?"

Kinsey gave me a look of horrified fear.

A LONG TWENTY-FOUR HOURS

Pops didn't even let me get my seatbelt on. "This is the thanks I get for slinging you some under-the-table cash in your time of need?"

I glared across the dim cabin. "I didn't want to hear his 'I'm so innocent' routine. It gets old."

He chuckled in disgust. "Who are you talking to? These men are our prisoners. We have an obligation not to antagonize them, especially when you're compensating for the disaster that is your personal life."

Blazing anger burned my face. "What did you say?"

"Don't 'what did you say' me. We both know you beat on that poor bastard because of shit that has nothing to do with him."

"We haven't decided on divorce."

"No?" he said. "She's going to a family lawyer on a day you're at work and can't possibly show up by accident because she's so dedicated to working things out. Is that what you're telling me?"

I balled my fist at his sarcasm and counterpunched. "Well, at least a divorce gives me the chance to keep some of my dignity."

Pops's face sagged with sorrow, and he turned from my angry glare.

Regret quenched the fire that had burned there a moment ago. I extended a hand to his dry, liver-spotted arm. "Pops, I—"

He jerked his arm from mine and spoke in a husky voice. "No, you're right. I'm no one to be lecturing you on marriage. I was trying to... give you the benefit of my experience, but it's your life to live, your mistakes to make."

"Pops..."

But he looked out the windshield with glittering eyes.

I fired up the car and drove him the two miles to the stand-alone metal-faced building at Orient south of MLK. The place bloomed with bright safety lights and the red neon that proclaimed Pops's Bail Bonds. It wasn't a great location, but Pops did okay by word of mouth. He bragged about not wanting new clients, because his old ones went in and out of the joint enough for him to make a steady living.

The gravel crunched under the Corolla's tires, but the night's thundershower kept the dust tamped down.

"You wanna crash here?" Pops had lived in a converted storage room behind the office for most of the last decade while my mother burned through his pension and business earnings in New Tampa.

I glanced at the clock on my dash: 3:47 am. "Nah, by the time I fall asleep, it'll be time to get up and grab a shower. If I drive straight to Twenty-five now, I can get a good two-and-a-half or three hours before B Shift starts moving around."

Pops nodded and got out.

"Pops, I'm—"

He closed the door in my face.

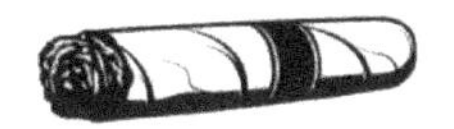

I entered the code into Station Twenty-five's keypad and slipped into the dayroom. The room was still. The TV and lights were off. A soft yellow glow overflowed from the kitchen to my right and from the captain's office, which looked out on the apparatus bay beyond the kitchen and the partition wall that separated it from the long corridor running the station. The low, familiar chatter of a radio mumbled from the room. Devin Phillips, the B Shift captain, enjoyed listening to that radio.

I glanced past the partition wall obstructing the captain's office and saw Rescue Twenty-five, our station ambulance, through the slit window of the exit door to the apparatus bay. Its big yellow-green form blocked my view of the engine and tanker beyond, but I guessed them to be there. I stretched out in a recliner and flirted with sleep, haunted by the wounded look on Pops' face.

The light hit me in the face. *"Beep! Rescue Twenty-five... respond to... traffic accident... located in grid LM8906."* The female voice was both soothing and robotic. I supposed the department intended her to be kinder and gentler than the klaxon she replaced, but the alert still sent my heart from sixty to a hundred in the span of a beat.

I opened my eyes and sat up. The clock above the TV showed 4:50 am. I'd slept forty, maybe forty-five minutes. I rubbed my face. The rustle of clothes and bump of flesh and bone on wooden doors echoed from the rescue dorms beyond the rear wall of the combination dayroom and dining room. The door opened. A tall kid with lanky features and a wild shock of unbrushed hair rushed into the room. The youth focused on clumsy hands wrestling with a stubborn belt, but he became aware of me and started. "Cap?"

I smiled. "Hey, Javi." Javier Gomez was the B Shift rookie assigned to the rescue.

"You're early."

"It was easier to come here than go home."

He nodded and motioned to the kitchen. "The coffee machine's full and the timer set, if you want some."

Coffee sounded good. "I might do that, thanks."

He smiled and moved through the short corridor to the same by the door through which I'd spied the rescue, the panic hardware making that low *thunk* against his body weight.

Javier was out of sight and the door to the bay had closed when the dormitory door opened again. A short, compact man in a pale grey T-shirt stepped through.

"I wondered who Javi was talking to."

I retracted the footrest and stood. "Just me."

Horace Drake didn't ask if the old lady had kicked me out. That joke had fallen flat the night it really happened, and he was too good-natured to twist the knife. Though that wasn't true of many of our colleagues. He pulled a black ball cap with gold HILLSBOROUGH COUNTY FIRE RESCUE letters over his thinning carpet of hazelnut hair.

"Javi tell you about the coffee?"

I followed him to the sliding window next to the captain's office. "He told me. Probably gonna get some."

Horace reached through the window and picked the paper from the printer placed there for easy access. I'd heard dispatch call it a grab-and-go, but us old-timers still called them tear 'n' goes from the days when the dispatch info was typed on one long ribbon of perforated paper and had to be torn from the top of the ream. He held the sheet at arm's length and read through bleary eyes. "Going to the interstate."

I hated interstate calls. "Be safe."

He nodded. "Get some coffee, Cap."

The diesel motor rumbled to life in the bay and the massive garage door rose on its rollers. Another *thunk* punctuated the early morning and the rumble of the motor filled the dayroom until the door nestled back to its jamb. The red and white strobes flashed off the walls, and the rescue eased out onto the apron. The garage door dropped behind it, and it was gone.

Nothing else moved. The timer shut off the lights, and I was alone again.

I flipped on a few lights and brewed the coffee. I was on my second cup when the first of B Shift's off-going crew staggered from the bunks, their eyes heavy with sleep and hair wild with bedhead. We exchanged greetings and did a rehash of how early I was. I smiled and sat at the foot of the dining table in the corner by the bunkroom door. Captain Devin Phillips stepped into the doorway leading to his office. He carried a shaving kit and wore a grin.

"Glad to see you."

I gave a tired smile. "Not so happy to be seen."

"Looks like you had a longer night than we did."

I nodded. "Ran down a skip by the airport."

"Tampa International?"

"Not Plant City." Plant City was a tiny town in east Hillsborough County. It had a small, local airport that played host to Cessnas and helicopters, but little else.

"No wonder you look like shit."

Another call came through for the engine. A fall injury on a familiar grid page. We both walked to the printer and read the address at the same time. "Alice."

Alice Kenmore pulled down better than three hundred pounds and called the fire department a minimum of once a week. She lived down a long, lonely country lane that usually required our 4x4 brush truck to get back there. I took the tear 'n' go from Devin's hand.

"I got it."

He didn't fight me. "You sure?"

"I'm sure." I glanced at Tracy Batts, Gavin's firefighter. She was tying her chestnut hair into a bun. "Alice Kenmore."

"I'll take the brush truck."

"Tighten that stream." My voice sounded tinny through the speaker on my facepiece, but it beat the garbled, muffled mess it was before we had the speakers. "Let the water do the work for you."

I reached down and turned the tip of the nozzle clockwise with my gloved hand, tightening the thirty-degree fog to a straight stream. "Open that bale all the way."

He held the nozzle at his hip. The reaction torqued his body. I shut down the bale and took the hose. I held it high, in front of my body and reached the bale with my fingers. I opened the valve with a slow, steady motion that brought the hose down and into me. "Get it in front of you and let the nozzle reaction push it into your weight."

The hose cradled against my chest, anchored by my two-hundred-plus pounds in full pack and gear. I played the stream back and forth over our heads, obliterating drywall and bringing chunks of ceiling and tufts of sodden insulation raining down with the streams of dirty runoff.

He took the hose I offered and repeated my actions. This time, the hose stayed put, and the stream was effective. "Flush it all out... anywhere the fire and heat might've touched the insulation. The fire's already done worse than we can do. The last thing we want is come back for a rekindle."

I looked over my shoulder, through the front room of charred furniture and blackened walls, at a figure beyond the front door. "Investigator's here. Let him have a poke around before we do any more damage."

Leo nodded, his body sagging under the weight of his wet gear and bulky airpack. "Yes, sir."

"Come on. Let's get you out of that shit for a while." I pointed at the holes in the front room's floor. "Steer clear of those. I don't want you breaking a leg on your first real fire."

Most Florida homes built before the days of air conditioning stood off the ground to encourage airflow, but that meant their floors could give under your feet if attacked by age or fire. Finding the joists under the decking was a bit of an art for men in seventy-plus pounds of protective equipment, but we passed through the front door and past the alligator-charred front porch.

A man in a black HCFR collared pullover stood at the foot of the porch. He was an inch or two shorter than my six feet, with skin and freckles like Morgan Freeman. He'd pulled a black HCFR ball cap over his eyes and wore a crooked smile that was equal parts joy and mischief. "Hey there, Lo."

I slipped my hand from the bulky glove protecting it and removed the regulator plugged into the snout of my mask with a twist, shutting it off with a nimble finger to the soft rubber button in the same motion.

"Dan." I gestured for Darlington to head off to rehab. "You lost? It's not B Shift."

"Overtime. Jenson is on vacation. Me and Richie are splitting his shifts." Oscar Jenson was C Shift's normal investigator. Richie Whalen was the A Shift investigator. We only had three, with no one to cover when an investigator was out. This meant the other two had to pick up the slack if we were to have twenty-four-hour investigator coverage.

Dan let me unclip and remove my helmet before speaking. "Chief says you were first-in."

I pulled the rubber mask over my head and wiped sweat from my face with a dirty hand, a habit I hadn't kicked in twenty years. "That's right."

He cast a discerning eye on the home. "Looks like the entire front of the house was rocking."

"Pretty much. We blitzed it with the deck gun before pulling the inch-and-three-quarter." The deck gun was the water cannon on the top of the engine. It could flow up to a thousand gallons a minute. The one-and-three-quarter-inch-diameter firehose was the standard attack line on most residential structure fires. It could do two hundred gallons a minute, but we rarely used over one-fifty.

"Was it poured?"

I redonned my helmet and led him back to the house, the caustic-sweet aroma of burned insulation hanging heavy in the humid, early morning air. "It has some suspicious holes by the front door."

Dan nodded and followed. He leaned across the threshold and played the beam of his Maglite across the floor. It swept over the fire damage lingering on the exposed sub-roof, which offered a view of twinkling stars in the predawn sky.

He killed the beam. "Looks like the worst of the damage is confined to the front room. No question it started here."

"Yeah. I tried to keep most of the overhaul ops in the hallway and front bedroom, especially after seeing those burn holes."

Dan's light was back on the floor, hovering on one of the irregular holes burned into it. Pour patterns of accelerant.

"It was occupied. Right?"

"It was. The homeowner was at the end of the drive, waving us down in nothing but a sheet."

"He say anything about how it started?"

I shook my head. "He kept yelling for us to hurry. We only stopped long enough to drop the supply line and lay in from the hard road. I did get him calmed down enough to tell me all the occupants were out, but I haven't had a chance to talk to him since."

"Didn't see anyone else?"

I smiled. "All I saw was fire... lots of it."

He smiled back. "You mind taking a little break while I talk to the homeowner and gather me some samples?"

"Don't mind at all." I left him at the front of the house studying the holes burned in the floor.

DEATH IN THE BIG HOUSE

I took an extra-long shower at the station, letting the hot water flow over my tired, aching body, weighed down by lack of sleep. The fresh smell of burning house flowed from my pores, competing with the lathered Dial soap I'd brought from home. I thought about Bobby Lee Kinsey and his pleas to be spared.

I'd heard it all a thousand times, but I had to admit, Bobby Lee put a new twist on it. "*Man, I would've cut you in. You just walked away from a fortune. Now, I'm gonna have to cut a deal with the State Attorney... If them motherfuckers don't kill me first.*"

Maybe it was the raw emotion. Maybe it was Bobby Lee's secretive, close-to-the-vest demeanor that drew my attention. Or maybe, despite the common nature of his pleas, I heard a ring of truth in them. Whatever it was, I hoped he was doing well and cursed myself for being so confrontational in the car.

I turned off the water, dried and dressed myself, and put my sweaty, smoky uniform in a tiny plastic trash liner I'd taken from the janitorial closet. The clothes were gross and sweaty, but they were also full of carcinogens and other contaminates. I would keep them bagged until washed.

I strode from the bathroom in the station's inner hallway, the same one that ran its length from the back door past the ten-by-twelve-foot captain's office I called home. The room had a built-in counter space that ran the perimeter. The workspace was crowded with a pair of desktop computers, an all-in-one computer/fax/print-from-any-location-in-the-world Ricoh, and our tear 'n' go printer by the sliding window closest to the corridor. The station radio took up more space by the tear 'n' go and a TV tuned to Bay News 9 mumbled at low volume in the left corner of the picture window looking out at the apparatus bay.

My bunkroom was the length and width of a walk-in closet. I tossed the bag of soiled clothes on the floor by the built-in desk and left my unmade bed for later. I walked back to the tear 'n' go. The printed times for our fire said they dispatched us at 02:17:53. The face of the clock above the bay window read 05:35:02.

Dammit, I was tired. I tucked the paper into the logbook on the desktop under the clock, got a cup of coffee, and returned.

I sat in the chair, found the next line on the ruled page, and scribed in red ink:

```
02:17 Structure Fire, 9225 Ryan Smith Rd, Grid
LL8890, #79854, E25,T25 (37-1285)
04:51—E25/T25 available. Working house fire.
```

The first entry was written in red ink and broken into two lines. The first line noted the alarm time, address, and map grid number. The second line of the entry noted the county incident number for the year, the suppression units assigned to the station dispatched, and the calls for the station by month and year. I wrote the second entry in black and indicated the time the units were available for calls and a brief description of the type of incident found. All times were written in the left margin of the page.

I'd hoped to turn this page over to A Shift with no red ink on it, but even a country club like Station Twenty-five had its nights, and it chose a hell of a time to have one. I logged onto the computer and wrote my report from behind bleary, bloodshot eyes.

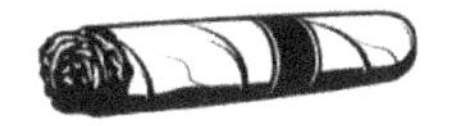

The station came to life and I stripped my bed to make way for A Shift. The clock read 6:10 am.

Gretchen Keigler, the lieutenant on the rescue, strode into the captain's office, coffee mug in hand. She barely cleared five feet and her cherub face held fast to a smooth, youthful beauty this business had a habit of ruining. She'd cinched a HILLSBOROUGH COUNTY FIRE RESCUE ball cap over her blonde hair and blue eyes.

"Morning, Cap."

"Hey, Gretch. You get any sleep after the fire?" The chief had released rescue more than an hour before the engine and tanker.

"Some." Her tone said it hardly mattered.

"Still better than us."

She smirked. "I guess."

Keigler sat at the work station to my right and started filling out her own green canvas logbook. "It beats a transport to the VA."

We both shared a grin at that. The James A. Haley Veterans Hospital was forty miles away in Tampa's University area. A Two O'clock transport there would cost as much sleep with twice the paperwork and encompass two hours of driving back-and-forth. The fire meant being up all night, but it was more exciting than fighting the hipnotic effect of streetlights on two hours' sleep.

The story on the TV changed and Kinsey's mugshot appeared. A banner underneath read Inmate killed in jailhouse fight. The smile dropped from my face. Anything Gretchen might be saying ceased to exist. Only the talking head had a voice. "*... orities have no comment on what caused the fight or whether any kind of weapon was used. Stay tuned to Bay News 9 for more information as we get it.*"

PROFESSIONAL COURTESY

I left as soon as my relief arrived, my still-dirty gear hanging on the rack, smelling of burning insulation and cancer. It was always a good idea to wash bunker gear after a fire to remove the carcinogens and other dangerous contaminants, but I would have to circle back. Too much was happening.

I sped across the county and pulled into the gravel parking lot, and stormed across the parking lot into front of his shop. Pops sat behind the greeting counter, staring at the TV to his left.

"I thought you might show up this morning." The speaker in the glass turned his voice tinny.

I glanced around the room. We were alone. "They killed him, Pops."

He glanced up from his programming. "Someone did; that doesn't mea—"

"He told us they would kill him. He said they'd never let him see a jury. Remember?"

His deadpan face soured. "I remember."

"We should have listened. We should have—"

"What? Let him go? Taken a fifty-thousand-dollar hit on his word and no proof? Did he ask to go to some state or federal investigator? If so, I must've fallen asleep, because I don't remember it that way. I remember you asking him what the hell he meant, but he said whatever he had was too valuable or dangerous to share. So, if whoever he crossed put paid his ticket, I don't see how that involves us."

He was right. I stepped over to the reinforced door, and Pops buzzed me back. The long, narrow vestibule of linoleum, vinyl walls, and metal-framed waiting chairs became a deep, wide office of shabby carpet, vinyl walls, and metal-framed office furniture.

Pops leaned back in his creaking office chair and returned to the Fox 13 coverage of the murder. He had muted the volume, but the scrolling, closed captioning kept us updated. A pretty, young spokeswoman from the Hillsborough County Sheriff's Office, variously known as HCSO, HSO, or plain SO, stood at a podium in front of the Falkenburg Jail, the summer breeze tugging at the few misplaced strands of her dark hair. The high, chain link fencing topped with razor wire provided a backdrop.

Spokeswoman: "We are still investigating possible motives and are not free to comment on that question."

She turned and pointed.

Reporter: "Can you comment on any weapons used in this attack?"

Spokeswoman: "We cannot, other than to say we did recover something from the scene we consider to be an instrument used in the attack."

She pointed again.

Reporter: "And what of the information that the assailant was a member of a local motorcycle club?"

I looked at Pops. "Motorcycle club?"

"You didn't hear? Iron Pirates ... at least that's the scuttlebutt."

I tried to recall Kinsey's history. "He have any known Pirate affiliations?"

Pops looked at the open file I hadn't seen from the customer side of the counter. "Nope. No priors, no criminal affiliations. I'd have never taken him otherwise."

I nodded. Bonds who had the support of criminal organizations often had the means to skip town or hide in safe-houses all around the county, making them a poor investment.

"So what's with the murder?"

"You askin' me? I know the same stuff you do. Kinsey ended up dead. Reporters say a Pirate did the deed. May or may not have been a mutual fight, but ole Bobby Lee didn't seem to be itching for conflict when we parted company."

Wasn't that the understatement of the year?

"I'd say conflict with a biker was the last thing he'd have wanted." I remembered how I taunted him and the horrified look on his face. "You were right. I was such an asshole to that guy."

Pops gave me a long, appraising look. "What? You had no way of knowing."

"But I had an obligation not to abuse our catch."

"Yeah, well. We all make mistakes. Don't we?" Pops held up a finger. "And so did he. If this is more than a coincidence, and he mixed himself up in some gang bullshit, he needed to tell us. That's a far graver mistake than a few mean words."

"Maybe, but I still mocked him and made fun of his cry for help."

He frowned. "Why do I think you're going to stick your nose into something that doesn't involve you?"

"Because you're my pops, and you know me so well."

He sagged in his chair and looked back at the TV. "Well, we can start calling in a few favors from the crews who ran the call. Maybe they'll give us a little professional courtesy."

My phone was already in my hand, and I was scrolling through my contacts. "Way ahead of you."

I pushed send and called Station Nine, the same station we'd passed that morning and the closest station to the jail.

"Station Nine, Cramer."

Joey Cramer was a longtime HIT tech and Driver Engineer. "Joey! It's Lo Walsh. How the hell are you?"

"Oh, you know, just another day as the chief's whipping boy. How you doing, Lo?"

Special Operations had once run HCFR, but our latest chief had a different vision for the flow of power. "Thanking my lucky stars I'm not in special ops."

He laughed. "You should be. We're going to the PSOC"—Public Safety Operations Center and HCFR headquarters—"to count Band-Aids at the warehouse."

Hillsborough County's PSOC was in Nine's first-due area, and Chief Reginald Price loved bringing them down to supplement our underfunded support staff. At least that was the excuse he gave. Most of us saw it as a way of establishing his dominance over the once mighty institution of alpha dogs.

"I'm sure you're in a hurry to get down there. Anyone from C Shift still hanging around?"

"Nah, they blew."

"Can I get a number from you? The Falkenburg stabbing was one of my skips, and I wanted to ask them about it."

"Oh, they didn't run that." He stretched out the words, and the rustle of paper passed through the phone. "They were on an overdose at the Rock."

The Hard Rock Hotel and Casino was deep in Thirty-two's area. "What the hell were they doing there? Thirty-two can't run their own calls?"

"It was one of those nights. HIT was on a nosebleed."

"A lot of that going around."

"Says the guy from Twenty-five."

"Is that jealousy in your voice?"

Joey laughed. "I only have myself to blame. I could've gotten out of here when Wiggins was still chief. Now..."

I knew what he meant. Another trend the new chief brought with him was punitive transfers. A person could get out of special ops, but decades of service to the county wouldn't earn a quieter assignment in the country or a nice suburban station in your golden years. The new administration had a way of sticking those people in the busiest shitholes in the department and had even transferred people out of bad stations to make room for the member who dared to opt out of the off-duty commitment, grueling training regimen, and a laundry list of Chief Price's honey-dos to hammer home the point.

"I'll try Thirty-three. Don't want to get you on Price's bad side."

"Yeah, as if." His voice carried a note of resigned sadness. "Take care, Lo."

THIRTY-THREE

Station Thirty-three was an unremarkable concrete block house with a two-door apparatus bay and tall hip roof. The single-story building sat on Falkenburg and Palm River, south of State Road 60. It was as far south of the Falkenburg Jail Complex as Nine was north, so they were the natural second-due. I pulled into the tiny parking lot at the rear of the station. The back doors were open, giving me a view of the big yellow-green engine's tailboard.

The rescue bay stood empty. It was a common sight in fire stations around the county, probably around the country. The apparatus floor wasn't air-conditioned and smelled of diesel exhaust. Sometimes you could pick out the sweet tang of burned fiberglass or the caustic smell of burned plastic, but not today. Thirty-three hadn't had a recent fire.

The door opened to Thirty-three's living quarters that would fit into Twenty-five's dayroom. A tiny water closet lay in front of me, a short hallway to the captain's office, kitchen, and dayroom lay to the right, and the door to the miniature bunkroom was to the left. The county had printed a giant map of Thirty-three's first- and second-due areas. It looked out from the wall separating the tiny aisle from the bunkroom, and a pair of computer workstations stood to my right. A familiar face in a blue HCFR T-shirt sat at the keyboard writing an incident report.

He stood and offered a hug. "Hey, Cap, what brings you here?"

"Hey, Ricky, good to see you... congratulations on making Driver."

Driver Engineers drove and operated the apparatus. They were noncommissioned officers and Ricky Baker could now work toward filling in for the captain when he was out.

Ricky nodded his appreciation and offered me a sly grin. "Thanks, Cap. Congratulations on Twenty-five."

"It's a lot nicer than this place." I looked around the tiny cubicle/hallway. "In more ways than one."

He laughed. "It's not so bad. We have a good crew, and that makes all the difference."

"Isn't that the truth?" It was common knowledge that a good crew could take the sting out of a thirty-call shift. But a mutant crew? They'd poison the best assignment, and Hillsborough County Fire Rescue had its share of mutants. "I came by to find out who was on duty yesterday. I wanted to ask about a call they ran."

"The stabbing?"

"Yeah."

"Well, 'C' Shift is gone, but Brooker is here on overtime."

Sam Brooker was always working overtime. "That whore."

"Right? He must get some nice paychecks. He's lying down right now. They had a tough night."

Sam had just worked a busy twenty-four, and his prospects of getting any sleep at this place were slim at best. I sighed.

"I'll call later."

"Okay, Cap. I'll tell him you came by."

"Thanks, Rick." I stepped back into the apparatus bay and was halfway across when the ka-chunk of a panic bar echoed through the vaulted garage.

"Hey!"

A bald, muscular man in a grey captain's T-shirt leaned out the door. "Where the fuck you going?"

I broke into a grin and strode back to him. He met me halfway across the floor, and we embraced.

"Don't you ever go home?"

Sam Brooker smiled. "Can't. The wife is still there."

I grinned at the joke but couldn't resist wondering if there was a note of truth in his words.

"Tell me about it." I gestured at his physique. "Still competing?"

He shrugged his bulky shoulders. "You know how it is."

I knew. His wife demanded he stop his body-building competitions after his second affair. There were plenty of loyal, dedicated firefighters who were faithful to their families, but those who gave our profession the often-deserved reputation as man-whores went the extra mile.

He moved his head. "Come in."

We passed through a grey wood and plate glass door that matched the one to the back corridor. His door to the station interior was closed; the lights dimmed. The desk lamp added its meager light to the flickering glow of the television obscured by the partition wall which separated the cramped quarters from an "office" that could only be called a workstation crammed into a pass-through. He gestured me into the computer chair tucked under the desktop of this workstation.

"Is this a fire station or a submarine?"

He smirked at my joke. "I try to look at the bright side; I'm almost never here."

I nodded at the truth in that statement. Thirty-three wasn't ever what you would call slow, but all the growth combined with limited station building turned it into a madhouse.

Sam sat on his bed. It was made but wrinkled. "So, what brings you by?"

I scratched an itch over my eyebrow. "I was hoping to talk to you for a few minutes about the stabbing last night."

"The jail? What about it?"

"Did you see the guy who did it?"

He smiled. "Oh, no. He was long gone. We did see the knife, though."

"Shiv?"

Sam shook his head. "Nah. Real knife... big fucker, maybe six inches." There were implications in that. Sam continued before I could ask a follow-up. "The brass was already there. Heads are gonna roll over this."

"Sounds like a real clusterfuck."

"And then some."

"So'd you see or hear anything about what went down?"

Sam narrowed his eyes and studied me.

I held up my hands. "Bobby Lee was a friend of sorts."

"Sorry to hear that."

"Thanks."

"No idea on how or why. A deputy said the patie—Bobby Lee—was sitting by himself and the guy just walked up to him and started stabbing."

"Was he a Pirate?"

"That's what the detention deputy said, but he didn't give a name or anything. Lou might be able to give you one."

Lou Ross was a captain on the other side of the county and an active member of the Iron Pirates Motorcycle Club. "I kinda doubt it."

"Me, too."

"Kinsey say anything to you?"

"Nah. He still had a pulse, but the Pirate got him good in the neck. Half the blood going to his brain was on the floor, the other half was in his airway. We called the trauma alert right away, but he coded,"—went into cardiac arrest—"by the time we got him packaged and through the gate. That's when Erica diverted to Brandon."

Erica Turner was the lieutenant on Rescue Thirty-three C Shift.

"I went and picked up Bryan and helped rescue clean up. That patient compartment was a bloody mess. We broke away to take a fall injury at Central Park."

Central Park Health and Rehab was one of many well-known and much-dreaded nursing facilities in the Brandon area. "Sounds like you need some sleep."

He offered a weary smile. "Sleep sounds good."

I thanked him for the info and left him to recline in his bed for as long as the fates would allow. I stepped out of the air-conditioned station and into the humid bay. The left front door clattered upward on its track. Rescue had returned. Only Thirty-three's north bay was a drive-through, and that was used by the bigger, less forgiving engine. I left the rescue backing into the south bay, the *beep-beep-beep* of their backup alarm chasing me out of the station.

My phone rang. "Hello?"

"Logan Walsh?" The voice carried a note of formality.

"Yes?" I was one wrong word from hanging up.

"I'm Sergeant Jack Donner with the Hillsborough County Sheriff's office. I'm investigating the death of Bobby Lee Kinsey. You were the bondsman who brought him in."

"I am."

"I'd like to ask you a few questions, if you don't mind."

"Sure. When and where?"

"I have some time for lunch... somewhere close to the jail?"

I looked across the street. "How about the Hooter's at 60 and Falkenburg?"

LUNCH WITH IA

The Hooter's patio offered a scenic view of the intersection of SR 60 and Falkenburg. It was a monster that grew in size every two years but whose volume increased daily, despite the Leroy Selmon and I-4 expansions. Tampa, it seemed, could find the cars to overflow its streets no matter how big or wide they got.

A Chevy Tahoe with dark tint and county plates pulled into a spot closest to the street. A tall, wide, linebacker of a man stepped out dressed in a bright blue Oxford and black slacks. He stood straight, closed his door, and adjusted his navy-and-gold argyle tie. He squinted in the noontime sun, accentuating the deep wrinkles on his weathered face. He'd been standing behind the HCSO spokeswoman at the Falkenburg press conference, though I hadn't heard him speak in the snippet I'd caught.

His pale eyes lingered on me in a way that suggested he knew who he was looking for. I took that to mean he'd read through my files and tried not to think that a bad sign. I hoisted my half-sweet-and-half-unsweet tea.

He held up a hand and strode over. He wore his Glock holstered to the right hip, but the only badge in evidence tacked the sections of his tie together.

I rose and offered my hand. “Sergeant.”

He took it in a powerful grip. “Captain Walsh.”

I got the feeling I was being schmoozed.

“I ordered myself a tea, but that’s as far as I got. I hope you don’t mind eating outside, but it’s full up in there.”

“No, this is fine.”

We sat. Donner ordered a sweet tea and watched our waitress Kee-kee walk away. It was a pleasant sight; I’d watched it when I’d first arrived.

He turned his attention back to me. “So, you’re a firefighter?”

“For twenty years.”

“Kind of a strange gig for you, isn’t it?”

“My dad owns a bail bonds business. I help him out when he needs it. Besides, most firefighters have a side hustle.”

That was true. Our twenty-four-hour shifts meant even the most grueling schedule was ten working days a month, and firefighters were accomplished at working on little to no sleep.

Kee-kee arrived with Donner’s tea. He ordered ten wings and blue cheese. I ordered a grouper sandwich and fries. We made the typical small talk of men in sibling agencies. I had twenty years. He would have twenty next year. How long did you plan to do? What are you gonna do after this?

We were almost done with the meal, and Kee-kee had taken our cards for payment, when he got to the point. “So, you’re the one who collared Kinsey.”

“Yes, sir.”

“Did he say anything to you about his life being in danger?”

“He did a lot of begging, but that’s not exactly uncommon when we drag someone back to jail.”

Donner’s smile was so good-natured I didn’t dare trust it. “But did he say anything to you about his life being in danger?”

I remembered his caged desperation and wondered who they were.

“No.”

I tried not to hesitate, to project honest sincerity, but the look in Donner’s grey eyes said I wasn’t successful.

“Do you... know something, Captain?”

I forced a smile. “He told me the cop planted the drugs. He offered to pay my father and I to let him go.”

“And did he say where this money was going to come from?”

“I assumed his drug money.”

Donner held me in that icy gaze. “So you don’t have any insights into anyone who might’ve had any beef with him?”

“I’m sorry, Sergeant. My orders were to chase Kinsey down and bring him back. That’s what I did. I’ve read less about him than you have.”

“But you’ve actually talked to him. You were one of the last to do so. I thought maybe he’d have said something to you in his desperation.”

There was a tell in that statement. Donner knew something or was working some kind of hunch. Otherwise, this was a dope mule getting his comeuppance for losing two keys belonging to the Pirates, or, as the rest of us would say, a day ending in -y.

My problem was simple. Kinsey knew he was in trouble. He knew he might go back to jail to be killed. He believed his would-be killers to be heavy hitters and ended up dead. Who had to turn a blind eye to let that happen? Who'd let a six-inch blade pass through security? Donner was probably asking those questions, too, but if he was trying to clip the loose ends...

"He did, but it was pretty standard stuff about his innocence and how he wasn't made for prison."

Kee-kee returned with our cards and receipts and asked if we needed anything further. We both shook our heads. I flashed her a grateful smile.

Donner didn't watch her depart. The pensive expression on his face said he was debating his next course of action. I saw the decision arrive but had no idea what it might be. He bent over his receipt.

"I was hoping for something of substance, Captain, especially from a fellow civil servant." He signed off on a five-dollar tip for a nineteen-dollar tab and extracted a metal case containing business cards. He offered me one. "Call me if you remember something."

I took the card and watched him stroll back to his SUV and head south on Falkenburg before setting up to make a U-turn short of the fire station.

Engine and Rescue Thirty-three were emerging from the bays, lights flashing. The engine laid on the air horn and siren first. It led the two vehicles north, and the pair screamed past Donner's waiting SUV.

I signed my check and watched the engine pass, a gleaming mass of yellow-green and black steel. The long, wailing moan of the engine's electro-mechanical Federal Q-siren roared its warning at the drivers, its long, air raid *rrraaarr* drowning out the warbling electric sirens. That sweet music still captured the imagination of firefighters everywhere and still filled me with a giddy excitement for the job like few things could these days.

Air horns from both vehicles added their voices to the cacophony, and cross traffic yielded. The two halted and made sure all lanes had stopped before banking a left turn on 60. They left my sight, but the wailing cries of their sirens still echoed back to where I stood.

Those scenes never failed to bring back memories of visiting the firehouse when I was a kid and watching Pops roll out on calls, the gleam of chrome, the flash of lights, and the scream of sirens blaring their warning. I returned to the Corolla ten years old all over again.

YOU GET WHAT YOU PAY FOR

Benson Roman Taylor, Esquire, had a luxury single-wide office/home in Seffner, a sometimes sleepy community north of Brandon known for its middle-class suburbia and semirural living. First responders knew it better for its low-rent motels, ramshackle trailer parks, and meth heads. In fire department circles, calling someone a Seffnerite had all kinds of subtext. Little of it was good.

Benny's facilities were in the latter camp. He'd set up shop on his brother Anthony's car lot on MLK east of Kingsway. A black-and-white board declaring BANKRUPTCY, DIVORCE, AND DUI was nestled under a lighted sign that said BUY HERE, PAY HERE. I passed below the fluttering red, white, and blue streamers and fell under the predatory gaze of a salesman on the porch of the main building, a two-story wood affair in desperate need of a cleansing fire. The thin, grey man wore a dingy white Oxford over blue jeans and was a poster Seffnerite.

His thin, wiry frame moved with the stalking grace of a Savannah cat, and he offered me a smile of four rotten teeth.

"Welcome to Tony's."

"Sorry, I'm here to see his brother."

A resentful scowl replaced the friendly smile. "His parking is around the side."

"I'll only be a minute."

He watched me walk across the face of his run-down office. A plump man with a dark beard, ill-fitting suit, and wraparound sunglasses watched me pass from inside the glass door. There was a note of challenge in his demeanor, as if he was expecting a rush of customers any second and my lone car would cost him that million-dollar deal.

I looked him in the sunglasses and offered a curt nod.

Discretion beat out his valor, and he decided that million-dollar deal might not be coming through right at this moment, after all. A footpath led me across the blazing lot to the back of Benny's single-wide office. It was a nice trailer, new and clean, with central air. I climbed the metal steps and passed through the backdoor marked Benson R. Taylor, Esq.

The inside was clean and well-lit. A hard-working central AC unit strained to keep the Florida summertime misery at bay, its frosty currents chilling my sweaty skin. The grey carpet was plush and clean, but it still had that new feeling, and I suspected a little wear might change that perception. A closed door barred the hallway to my left. Its black-and-white sign proclaimed: Employees Only.

The creak of a chair and swish of clothes drew my eyes right. Benny Taylor rose from behind the desk, sitting in the middle of what was normally a master bedroom. He'd pulled his long, grey hair into a greasy ponytail. His red Hawaiian shirt hung open to the nipple line, revealing a coarse patch of grey and white hair above a bulging belly that was out of proportion with the rest of him. Thick gold chains draped his neck, displaying medallions and other gaudy accessories. He wore both a crucifix and a Star of David. I imagined a crescent moon to be dangling somewhere among the stash, but his god was the golden calf.

We exchanged greetings, and Benny offered me a seat.

I pulled out my notepad and got right to business. "I guess you heard about Kinsey."

"I heard."

"I hear he was telling anyone who'd listen someone was out to kill him."

Benny raised his eyebrows. "Anyone, or you?"

"People I've talked to."

"Uh-huh."

"You know anything about that?"

"I know they busted him for running drugs. I know that often leads to undesirables."

"Like the Pirates?"

"Like the Pirates," said Benny.

"Did you know they might be connected?"

"When I took the case?" He spread his arms. "I look like I'm killing it as a mob lawyer, Lo?"

We shared a smile. "I suppose not. What about friends and family?"

"You have what I have."

"Humor me."

His face clouded with irritation.

"Please."

Benny turned to his computer, his labored breathing suggesting the typing and conversation were too strenuous for his neglected body. "You know about the ex-wife and the kids."

"I do."

"The job with the landscaper."

"It's how I found his girlfriend."

He shrugged. "You have everything. It doesn't help for me to hold out on a skip, you know."

I nodded and glanced at the file I had. "You talked to him more than I did. What was your impression of the man? Guilty? Inno—"

"Guilty as hell. They had him six ways to Sunday." He pulled a yellow legal pad from the file and started reading. "He worked with J&J Lawn Service. Construction was off the table because of his disability. Moonlighted as an after-hours handyman for his trailer park. He'd once had a drug problem... Roxies." Prescription drugs had been the street drugs for decades now. "But he was supposed to be on the wagon... TPD caught him with two keys of blow in his car."

"About that. A routine traffic stop?"

"That's what the report says."

"So these cops weren't the gang unit... no fed participation?"

"Nope."

"What was your plan?"

"For defense?"

I nodded.

"Plead. He went to rehab after the drugs wrecked his marriage. No criminal issues. I thought that could get him some consideration."

"How'd he feel about that?"

"Pissed. He told me how innocent he was and how he wouldn't spend a day in jail, but he ain't exactly the first to tell that story. You know?"

I knew. "He ever talk about any kind of leverage he might have?"

"Not to me, but I made it clear from the get-go I wasn't here to Clarence Darrow his ass. He didn't have the resources for a protracted legal fight. I invited him to take his case up with the public defender, but his retainer would be forfeit."

And lawyers wonder why we hate them. "So how'd the drugs get there?"

"Officially? They don't know who his supplier is."

"Unofficially then."

"Kinsey said the cops planted the shit."

"And you don't think so."

"Does it happen? Sure. But I'd say the Pirates putting paid his account suggests otherwise. Wouldn't you?"

I had to nod at that. "So, no drug debts. Gambling?"

"Not that he admitted to, but the next client to tell me the unvarnished truth will be the first."

"And this banty rooster routine... the whole I'm not going to prison... couldn't that compromise your case?"

Another shrug. "Maybe. But even if he did, it was his case to compromise. I mean, you get what you get. Right?"

And what you pay for, but I needed Benny's cooperation. "So, if he did have this mystery card to play, why run?"

"Because he didn't have dick. You've heard these shitbirds talk. None of this was their fault. It was the friend or the cop or God, but never them."

"And he ended up dead by coincidence?"

"It makes plenty of sense if you work on the assumption that his dope belonged to the Pirates."

"So you think they gave the drugs on credit and killed him when he got busted?"

"It wouldn't be the first time."

He was right there. "But how do they get their money back?"

The pandering glaze left Benny's eyes, and he straightened up. "What?"

"I mean, this is a business. He loses two keys in a bust that doesn't seem to be his fault and costs them... conservatively... forty grand?"

"Uh-huh."

"What purpose does killing him serve? How do they get their money back if he's dead?"

"Maybe this leverage he was talking about was to snitch on them."

"So he jumps bail and leaves the safety of the system and the protection of the police? Seems to me he was more afraid of the authorities than the bikers."

"Hey, man, there's no shortage of dumbasses in the world."

Or the legal profession. "I guess you're right."

Benny's expression implied he'd read my mind. "You call me if you think of anything else."

I folded my notepad and found my feet. "I'll do that."

THERAPY

Rachael Wood owned a therapy clinic run out of a strip center office on State Road 60 between Brandon and Valrico. My medical insurance covered her, and her office was close enough to each of our current residences to be middle ground. Her practice was one of several using the space. It was small, but comfortable, with eggshell walls and an industrial burgundy carpet.

Wood sat in a suede cream-colored high-back framed in dark wood. She gazed at us across a coffee table, empty but for a box of tissues. Her oval bronze face had the smooth, stiff look of surgical supplements and Botox injections. The color of her Peppermint Patty haircut was too even and grey-free to be natural. Even her full red lips were incongruous with her otherwise thin frame.

I liked the woman well enough, even considered her counsel wise and insightful, but I'd never fully reconciled taking life advice from someone so vain and insecure about her looks. However, I'd exhausted my vetoes on the six therapists before her, and Val was clear: we came to Woods or sought divorce attorneys.

"It's not like I'm out cheating." I thought of Sam at Thirty-three. "This is a tough job, and I'm working overtime and hustling to make money on the side. I always thought that's what I was supposed to do."

"Here we go. Lo, the hero." Val glared across the couch that represented a greater gulf than the three feet between us. "You were never home, never present. And you were nothing but a moody, sarcastic asshole when you were. What did you expect to happen?"

I leaned away with crossed arms. "I didn't expect you to bang your boss in our bed."

Val shot me a brown-eyed glare that made her thin, dainty features ugly. "I'm not saying I haven't made mistakes, but let's stop pretending there was any room in your life for being anything but a firefighter and hanging out with your firefighter buddies. Why do you think Christopher is so eaten up with following in your footsteps?"

"Love for his father?"

"You mean the hole in his life where a father is supposed to be? Maybe he wants to be a firefighter so he can get his dad's attention for more than five consecutive minutes."

The barb stung. I had missed a lot of birthday parties and holidays. "You knew what I was when you met me—"

"Parliamentary procedures." Rachael Wood's voice was quiet and even, but there was a stern, teacher quality to it. "Keep your comments directed at me and try to focus on *I* statements." Her gaze lingered on Val, but she looked back at me with a no-nonsense sincerity that broached no compromise. "We are here to sort out our feelings and to find a path forward. Right?"

I glanced at Val and thought about her calling me at the station on Monday. The good-natured conversation, the way she'd made me feel she was calling to check on me and keep the lines of communication open. It had been hard to trust her before. Now? Now I didn't know how I was going to find a path back to those days. Still, I said, "I'll do what has to be done."

"Good."

"Val has never once taken..."

Wood raised a stiff eyebrow.

"However, I feel like Val never takes responsibility for her behavior. She blames me." Another cautionary look. "I feel blamed for everything."

"I think," said Wood, "you're saying you feel blamed for things you don't consider your responsibility, including actions Val took."

I glanced at Val. "Yes."

"And Val?" She turned. "I think you were saying you feel abandoned and lonely. Did you want to say more?"

Wood refereed us for the next forty-five minutes and sent us away with homework. We each had to come back and explain what we thought the other person was feeling as we each made the decisions that brought our marriage to the brink of destruction. I pulled my card out for the copay, and Val headed for the door.

Wood processed it and returned the card. "See you next Friday."

"See you next Friday." I was already on my feet and forced myself to walk with the slow, deliberate gait of a man with nowhere in particular to be. But I put a spring into my step once her office door closed. I fast-walked past a woman and angsty-looking teen in clothes my generation would have called goth and out the front door to the parking lot. Val was opening the door to her 4Runner.

"Where are you going in such a hurry? Afraid I might talk to you?"

"I have to get back to the kids." But she loitered between her truck and a rusty El Camino in the next space.

I walked to the front of her vehicle but stayed on the sidewalk. "Thanks."

Val gave me an inquisitive look.

"For coming here, for agreeing to this."

She nodded. "Rachael is good at what she does."

"She is." I felt the danger in the next question on my tongue, but I didn't see how I could build trust without knowing where she stood. "I heard... that you saw a lawyer on Monday."

The half smile she was constructing fell from her face and the forced pleasantness in her voice turned to iron. "What?"

"I just want to kno—"

"Are you following me?"

The indignation in her voice was maddening. "Oh, I'm sorry. Blind trust in you has worked so well for me in the past."

She expelled disbelief in a grunting laugh and shook her head at the sky. "You really have some balls. You know that?"

"Look, I—"

"I'm not accountable to you, Lo. I'm not your property."

"I never said you—"

"I'll go where I want and do what I want."

"You certainly do *who* you want."

"That's real mature, Lo. You get that from listening to Christopher's high school pals?" Val stared at the awning that read Valrico Mental Health Group. "I don't think I'll be coming here next week. Have a pleasant night, Lo."

She climbed into the running SUV and backed out of her spot.

SLEEPLESS IN SEFFNER

I drove to my new place in Country Square Estates, a diamond-in-the-rough trailer park on a rural stretch of Sligh Avenue.

It was the cheapest residence I could find without needing body armor to go out at night, but it still put a strain on the budget. Two payments for lodging, two electric bills, two water bills, and Val not working since I demanded she break all contact with Scott made for some desperate financial straits. It was no wonder I had a string of late notice emails about everything from Val's 4Runner to both TECO bills.

I stepped out of the car, climbed the grated metal steps of the sand-colored single-wide, and let myself in. The afternoon heat lingered in the living room, accentuating the musty smell of my modest abode. I closed the front door, crossed a saggy wooden floor, and turned on the window shaker on the back wall.

The hot musty air became cooler musty air. The fridge was empty, but the kids had yet to visit my new castle. And while I wanted to see them, I was in no hurry for them to stay here. I glanced through the sheer curtains at the wood-framed home belonging to the owners, a Slavic couple who'd come over in the eighties. A Ninja motorcycle stood in the backyard overlooking the tiny dirty circle that made up the entire tiny park. The sign hanging around the neck of the handlebars proclaimed: FOR SALE.

I fixed a ham and mustard sandwich on stale bread that wasn't yet moldy, grabbed a bottle of Beck's from the fridge, and opened the laptop. There wasn't much to Bobby Lee's file. He did some under-the-table work for a lawn crew, but had no ties there once the cash changed hands. His daughter and ex-wife were distant acquaintances, and he didn't belong to any recovery group I could find. I found no friends beyond Crystal the stripper and that relationship felt more mutual opportunity than intimate closeness.

Lenny and Pops had kept the wife under surveillance for almost three full days but had blanked. Melissa Perez, formerly Melissa Kinsey, had made a social climb in the last decade of her life and didn't seem nostalgic for the bad old days. She'd told Pops as much when he called her from his stakeout spot on his second day of surveillance.

Now, I was going to be circling back after Bobby Lee's murder. That was liable to be a pretty awkward conversation. I dialed the number on the screen and waited.

"Hello?"

"Miss Perez?"

Suspicion darkened her voice. *"Yes?"*

"My name is Logan Walsh. You talked to my dad... about your ex-husband."

She didn't hang up, but I didn't know how long that would last. *"I remember."*

"I wondered if maybe you would be willing to talk to me for a few minutes."

"This isn't the best of moments for us, Mr. Walsh, and I'm in the middle of family time."

"I understand. Tomorrow, perhaps?"

"How about before work? It's my Saturday."

"I can be there early. Give me the location."

"Netpark."

"I'll be there."

She was gone.

I hung up the phone and considered calling Crystal, but the best way to hand her was with an unannounced visit. Later.

I'd returned to my research when the phone rang. It was Val's number. I checked the time on the stove: 7:30 pm.

"Hello."

"Hell-o!" a girl said in my ear. *"How are you?"*

"Better now that you've called."

She giggled at that.

"Did you have fun at your playdate?"

"Uh-huh. We played on the swing but Christopher kept throwing acorns at us." She spoke with that pouty indignation only preadolscent girls can pull off.

"He did? That wasn't very nice. Did you ask him to stop?"

"Uh-huh."

"And?"

"He kept doing it, anyway!"

A wide grin split my face. "Maybe it was his way of playing with you girls, of having fun with you."

"That's what Mommy says."

"Well, Mommy's pretty smart."

"I guess so."

"You do, huh?"

We laughed.

"I miss you, girl."

"I miss you, too, Daddy."

The sadness in her voice broke my heart anew. I blew a kiss into the receiver.

She blew one back.

The phone changed hands and my young man said, *"Dad! I was just playing with them! They were playing with my ball."*

"I'm sure, Son. You had fun with your sister?"

There was a long pause and the background noise grew more distant and softer. *"It was okay."*

Okay. I grinned again for different reasons. "You're a good big brother."

"Thanks, Dad."

"You be good to your sister. Okay? And look out for her."

"I will."

"I love you, Son."

Another long pause and his voice became a hushed mumble. *"Love you, too, Dad."*

His voice grew distant. *"Here, Mom."*

The phone went dead. I let out a long, sad breath, glanced from the dim yellow light of the kitchen past the darkened living room into the shadowy hall, and doubted this trailer was ever an emptier, lonelier place.

NETPARK

I crawled out of bed on five-and-a-half-hours of fitful sleep and drove to the Netpark office complex. The compound had once been Eastlake Square Mall, but it died when they built Brandon Town Center and stole the south and east county shoppers away from the aging mall. Someone later got the inspired idea of repurposing the building into office space and Netpark was born.

Many mall rebirths had a cheap, second-hand feel to them, and Netpark was no exception. The designers refinished the exterior in a crisp masonry with bright white paint they kept fresh and clean. Tall, thin palm trees stood sentry along the perimeter of the building, while shorter, stockier varieties lined the entrance and exit. The discerning eye could see the old mall construction with its general shape and anchor stores but it still felt new and revitalized for all of the superficial changes. I pulled into a parking spot on the building's east side and strolled past the smokers' perches into a clean, well-kempt complex.

The café and coffee kiosk were closed on Saturdays because so many fewer people worked the weekends than the other days. I'd been here on EMS calls and had even attended an infamous HCFR conference in the auditorium, but the odors of the place had never left me craving their food.

The inside was the same as the outside. Clean white drywall took the place of clean white stucco. The old interior display windows had been walled-in, but the familiar wide promenade that once hosted shoppers said this was not your typical office building.

The seven o'clock rush was a trickle on Saturdays, making it easy to find Melissa Perez sitting on one of the many collections of chairs and ottoman strewn across the canyon floor of the ground level. Her grey blouse and black polyester pants were loose-fitting, but did nothing to hide the curves underneath. Big, dark eyes and a bright smile framed by full, painted lips complemented her hazelnut skin. She rose at my approach, the gold hoops in her ears rocking. "Mr. Walsh."

I took her hand. It was dry and rough. This woman hadn't spent her whole life working in an office. "Miss Perez."

"Call me Missy."

"Only if you call me Lo."

"Okay, Lo."

We sat, and I drew a notepad and pen. "I appreciate you making time for me... and my condolences on your loss."

"Thank you. Bobby Lee was a... good man." Missy's tone suggested those weren't the words she'd been looking for, but she'd settle on them for now. She gestured at the round Formica table between our chairs. "I got you a coffee at Dunkin on the way in. I'm not sure if you drink it."

"Are you kidding? I have two jobs. Both of them require long hours of little sleep." I took the coffee and added cream and sugar. "My doctor has a line on my bloodwork for coffee content."

She smiled.

"Bobby Lee was the father of your daughter?"

"Yes."

I took a sip. It was bitter, but drinkable. "You probably knew him better than anyone, then. Do you know who would want him killed?"

"Killed? Wasn't this a random jailhouse fight?"

"Jailhouse fight, yes. But the randomness of the fight... that's more complicated."

"Just like that man from the sheriff's office."

Donner. "I don't work for the government. I was.... I met Bobby Lee right before his death."

"Did his bail bondsman hire you to track him down?" Her insightfulness surprised me. It must've shown. "I watch Dog the Bounty Hunter."

I shared her smile, but her comprehension didn't come from a TV show. "I understand you do medical collections with a firm here."

"Supervisor. A lot has changed since my Bobby Lee days."

"I see that. Good for you." We shared a smile. "So, did he have enemies? Did he run drugs? Or hang with a rough crowd?" I paused. "Have a taste for forbidden women."

Missy's face twisted with pain, and she chuckled at bitter memories. "I still hate thinking about it."

The vastness of the great promenade turned hollow.

"He blamed the drugs, you know... for the way our marriage fell apart, but I would have stuck by him for that. We had a daughter, and she needed a daddy." She paused again, and I let her take her time. "He was a foreman working for B&D Construction, throwing up homes as fast as he could. Twelve, sometimes fourteen hours a day. We never saw him, but the money was fantastic. You know?"

I nodded.

"Bobby was a hard worker. He did a good job for them and kept his crews on task and on time. They started courting him as a potential GC," General Contractor, "so he could oversee multiple sites. Things were crazy then. They couldn't put up homes fast enough."

I remembered.

"He... started going to parties sponsored by the company. You know, meet-and-greets. Bailey, was an infant then. so I stayed at home and took care of her."

A cold Deja Vu chilled my shoulders.

"We started fighting. I wanted him at home. He said this was all about making money and getting in with the muckety-mucks. He said it was for us, that his money helped me stay home." Missy paused for another five count. "Then he started coming home smelling of other women: perfume, scented body wash... other smells."

I didn't ask her to expound on that.

"We had been talking about another kid, a boy." Her smile was wistful. "But we were sleeping in separate rooms by then, and I couldn't bring myself to let him touch me. And that's when he got hurt."

"Hurt?"

"Yeah, helping with a roof truss or something. I was never a construction girl. But the accident messed him up, and no one at that company cared, not even a little. We consulted a lawyer. This was in two-thousand-four? five? Whenever. B&D held us up at every turn. Then the bubble burst in oh-eight. The company went bankrupt, and his hopes for compensation went down the tubes."

"Tough."

"It was, but he actually got a settlement payment from one owner, anyway."

My posture straightened. "After the company went belly-up? Who?"

"I don't know. He might've said at some point, but I was checked out by then. I filed for divorce, and we went our separate ways."

"And he went into rehab after that."

She nodded. "The great irony is: To this day he blamed the drugs, but him getting hurt and the struggles he endured in those months are the reason I stayed as long as I did."

I tried to imagine my marital situation compounded by disability and destitution. "Did you stay in touch? I assume he had visitation with," I reached for the name, "Bailey."

"Not at first. I wouldn't have it." Ghosts played across her face. "But once he put his life back together and proved we could trust him... Bailey was his daughter."

Her tone echoed Val's from the night before and bored a hole in my chest. I cleared my throat. "So, you know a little of the man he became."

She donned a poker face. "Some."

"But you don't think he was doing drugs?"

"No."

"Running with gangs?"

"Like gang bangers?"

"I was thinking bikers."

She laughed. "Did you meet Bobby Lee?"

I grinned. The question made me feel foolish. "How about drugs? Did he sell them?"

"No way. He would never see Bailey again, and he knew it."

"And he was still seeing her?"

"Some."

"What was their relationship like?"

"He was her dad. He loved her. She loved him, but they weren't as close as other fathers and daughters I knew."

I thought about last night's phone call and felt a pang of sympathy for this man. "Had you seen any changes in him lately?"

"You mean like drugs again?"

"Anything."

She thought. "Nothing new, but I did all I could to avoid him beyond custodial stuff."

I wondered again if I was previewing the life that awaited Val and I. "And you know of no links he might have to the Iron Pirates?"

"That motorcycle gang?" Concern touched her face and voice. "No way."

I pulled a card from my holder and offered it to her. "Here. Please don't hesitate to call if something comes back to you."

She took and gathered her stuff. "Thank you Mr.... Lo. But I really don't think I'm the one who has whatever you're looking for."

I couldn't disagree, but I offered my most charming smile. "Sometimes stuff comes up."

TWO PLUS TWO EQUALS FIVE

I sat among the dispersing crowd of workers. My coffee was getting cold, but I didn't mind.

My laptop hadn't even cleared its case when a pair of young women took Missy's seat and the one next to it. One was a Latina with a wasp waist and healthy bosom, the other a willowy blonde. They cackled with glee about a woman named Rory, or maybe it was a guy. I was too deep in Bobby Lee Kinsey's arrest report to notice.

It described the events: subject driving erratically, weaving off the road, and changing speed with frequency. The officer described his behavior as nervous and evasive. He ordered Mr. Kinsey out of the vehicle and placed cuffs on him for safety. The suspect granted permission to search the vehicle and signed a release. I scrolled to the form. It looked as if it was in order.

"No way!" said the blonde.

"I swear." The Latina held up her hand in a solemn oath.

The report described a package of powder taped in plastic found under the spare tire in the trunk. Pics of a black bundle accompanied the complaint. Pics of the bundle on the hood or trunk lid of a police cruiser showed it being weighed: 2.025 kilos. The report included pics of a field test. The test tube had turned a dark blue, a positive result.

I sat back. A fresh trickle of people moved over the floor, arrivals for later opening businesses. My coffee was gone; so were the magpies.

I read the sworn affidavits filed for the warrant to search Kinsey's home. They attested to the circumstances detailed in the arrest report. A Sergeant Diego Ortiz #13475 Tampa Police Department provided an electronic signature. The report detailing the search of Kinsey's home was sparse. It described arriving, contacting the landlord, and entering the home. It indicated the areas searched "in detail," but there were no pics and nothing listed on the receipt because they found nothing.

I scribbled another question on the notepad and scrolled down. The contact form listing friends and family in town and his Fourth Amendment waver were all that remained in the file. Nothing that added context to the search.

I took a deep breath and stared through the crowd. Benny's number was already at the top of my Recent Calls list. He answered on the third ring. *"Benny Taylor at Law."*

"Hey, Benny."

"Lo." There was a mental note in his voice to mark my number. *"What's up?"*

A man and woman walked hand-in-hand toward work and I felt a pang of jealousy. "I looked over the files again, and some things struck me. I hoped you could help with them."

"Shoot."

"My first thing is the search warrant. A search of his home turned up nothing."

"So?"

"So, a search of his car turned up nothing but a two-key bag of coke. No scales, no baggies, no cash. How the hell is he running a coke distribution center without these basic tools?" I let the line lay dead for a heartbeat. "And then there are the firearms."

"What firearms?"

"Exactly. Who do you know that rides around with forty or fifty thousand dollars' worth of coke in his car and doesn't pack? But Kinsey doesn't have one on his person, stashed in his car, or at his home."

More silence.

I changed direction. "And what about the warrant for his cell phone?"

"What about it?"

"What resulted from that? There's no report."

"I... think they delayed it in preliminary discovery."

"Delayed. Why?"

"It happens. Probably the phone company dragging its feet."

"Did the state attorney say that, or did they not find anything?"

"A lot of dealers use Tracfones these days, you know."

"And where was that? Not in his car, not on his person, and not at his home." I blew out a frustrated sigh in the face of his ongoing silence. "What about the body cam footage?"

"I was told there wasn't any."

"Wasn't any? TPD has body cams."

"Yeah, but the arresting officer was assigned to a special detail that didn't require them."

"What detail?"

"Honestly, I didn't ask."

I chuckled in disgust.

"Hey!" Benny found some indignation. *"You looked at those same files. It never seemed to occur to you until now."*

"I was looking over those files to get a feel for his history and places he might go. I was looking at him as a potential quarry to be run down, not as someone I had to defend as an attorney."

"I told you. He didn't have the funds for a trial."

"And that didn't set off alarm bells? A guy hauling around two keys of coke didn't have money for a lawyer?"

"It happens."

"Does it?" I let the tense silence stand. *"The report says this..."* I searched for the name. *"Ortiz called in patrol for backup and to handle the arrest. Can you get their body cam footage?"*

"How?"

"Discovery."

Benny's laugh was derisive. *"The case is closed, Walsh. It died with Kinsey."*

I frowned. He was right. "Do you think you could see what you could do?"

Another derisive laugh. *"Man, don't you have some balls? Call me up and imply I'm a shit lawyer, then ask me for a favor. You want it, you do the public records request, and tell your old man Benny Taylor is pulling him off the rotation."*

Benny hung up on me, and I listened to an empty phone. I didn't think any of my criticisms were implied.

I put the computer in the bag and headed for the door.

VIP ROOM

I used my Bluetooth to make a call from the Corolla.

"Pops's Bail Bonds."

"Hey, Pops."

"Logan, how did last night go?"

I thought about it and decided I didn't want to. "Not now."

The brief silence on the other end of the phone was heavy with concern, but Pops didn't press. "*What kind of favor you need?"*

"Look, I'm heading for another interview. Would you mind putting a public records request in for the body cam footage of Kinsey's arrest?"

"You on to something?"

I thought about all the pieces of his arrest that didn't add up. "I'm working a theory."

"Okay. I have all the info on file here. It'll only take a couple minutes."

"Thanks, Pops."

"*Sure.*" He hung up, and I placed the phone in the passenger's seat.

It took a full forty minutes to make my way through Hillsborough Avenue traffic and arrive at Manhattan Palms Condos. There were more available parking spaces on a Saturday afternoon than my last visit. I nosed into the one closest to Crystal's door, then went up and knocked. Nothing. I knocked again. Nothing.

No one was around. I considered the parking lot and only now realized Crystal's Prius wasn't in it. Some detective.

I knocked one last time, left a card in the door, and walked back to the Corolla. There was only place I had any hope of finding her. The Prius was in the same spot by the Lucky Horseshoe's dancer entrance. I parked my car and stepped into the early afternoon heat, tossing an appeal for relief to the cumulous clouds gathering in the bright blue sky. They remained mute.

"Welcome to the Horseshoe." A petite brunette with a red teddy pulled around her waist sat cross-legged on a stool. Her enthusiastic voice matched her bright smile and manic energy. "Twenty-five-dollar cover, hun."

I dug into my wallet and passed her the bills. She took them, slipped them into a register mounted next to her stool, and drew a red bracelet. She fastened it around my wrist, scraping my arm with her long, crimson fingernails.

Her voice took the same sultry turn her bright welcoming smile did. "Have a great time."

I nodded and tossed a glance at the Stone Cold Steve Austin clone behind her. The bald behemoth towered over me. His black SECURITY shirt strained to keep its hold on his python arms and hugged the contours of ample pecs and a washboard abdomen. We traded stern nods, and I turned my gaze on the club. It was busy for the early hour, but there was lots of floor space between patrons and plenty of tables to choose from.

The stage sat against the far wall in a bruise of blue light. White and yellow footlights lined its perimeter. A lean athlete of a woman twirled upside down on the pole to a pop song I couldn't identify. Her hair flowed in raven streams. Her stockings and garters clung to muscular legs and her breasts stood too tall and too proud amidst the centrifugal force to be natural.

I didn't linger on the thought and moved my attention to the floor in front of the stage. A handful of men sat in the front row, gazing up at the spinning dancer with expressions that traversed the scale from enraptured to bored with a few stops in between. Silver high tops hosted another ten or twelve patrons. Most looked on in interested silence, but at least one was eating. Tampa strip clubs did not have a reputation for their cuisine, but it was better than gas station sushi.

I chose a booth to my left and scanned the QR code on the tabletop with my phone. I found what I was looking for before the waitress in see-through lingerie stepped up to my seat. The

Horseshoe was an all-nude establishment. Tampa ordinances forbade them from serving alcohol.

"Can I get a coke and is Anastasia here?"

Anastasia was Crystal's stage name.

"She's up in two sets." The waitress shifted onto her right foot and slid her left foot in silent offer. "You want something in the meantime?"

I'd known plenty of men who came to strip clubs, knew guys on the job who preferred them to the complexity of family life and struggling through the balancing act of keeping a wife and kids happy while chasing death and tragedy for a career. But I'd never seen the attraction to the companionship these women rented one fifty-dollar lap dance at a time.

I slipped her a twenty. "Can you tell Anastasia she has a guest and see if she can trade dances, maybe with you?"

The girl frowned at the bill but took it. "Sure."

Crystal appeared from the beaded curtain leading backstage, her eyes fixed on my location. She didn't recognize me in the gloom, but that changed when she approached the table.

"You!"

I held up a hand and glanced at Stone Cold. He was looking our way, but he kept his station by the door.

"Don't you shush me with your hand. I—"

"I came to talk. I'm willing to pay for it. I'll need a lap dance–worth of time."

She closed her mouth and glared. I'd hit a soft spot. She wasn't working an extra shift because she was flush with money. "Two hundred."

"For a lap dance?"

She smirked. "Inflation."

I frowned. I could justify pulling some money from Pops's company funds for this, but I couldn't throw it around. "Okay, two hundred, but I get straight answers. No varnish. No bullshit."

Her eyes hardened. "Let's go."

The Horseshoe's VIP room was a closet-like partition in a wide corridor running the length of the building to the left of the stage. Crystal took me to the farthest nook in the back and closed the purple velvet curtain behind her.

"Who the fuck do you think you are coming here after what you did to Bobby Lee?"

"I don't like what happened any more than you do. If this whole thing was a setup, I want to know about it, because I don't like being anyone's stooge."

Crystal studied me from behind a pouty face, thumping music filling the air. "So, what do you wanna know?"

"How well did you know Bobby Lee?"

She leaned against the partition, her arms crossed. "Well enough. He was a regular."

"And you started dating?"

She glanced at the room behind me. "Look, Bobby Lee was a nice guy, okay? I... took him in."

"Like a puppy?"

Her face twisted with sardonic bemusement. “Something like that.”

I studied her streetwise face. “So, what was in it for you?”

I thought she’d feign outrage, but she said, “He was looking to come into some money.”

I perked up at that. “Money?”

“Yeah, he’d come in most every night, blow the cash he’d made in some side hustle, and tell me all about his mess of a life.”

I thought about that companionship sold one lap dance at a time. “Uh-huh.”

“Well, he’d bitch about it. You know? And I’d say shit like, ‘What are ya gonna do?’ and ‘Life’s a bitch.’ Ya know?”

I nodded.

“Then one night he comes in all happy. Tells me he’s done working for the man. Got some big plan to be set for life. Says he’ll never get on a Dixie Chopper again.”

“How long ago was this?”

The song ended, and the DJ said, *“Let’s hear it for Symone.”*

A muted smattering of applause rose from the front of the club.

Crystal gazed toward the curtain. “My set is next.”

“We’re almost done here.” The DJ fired up a Nicki Minaj song, and I assumed the next girl went to work. “How long?”

She thought. “I don’t know… three months ago? A little more, maybe.”

I scribbled notes. “And what did he think about that?”

“He was flyin’ high. You know?” She took in my unamused expression. “Talkin’ about how he’d eaten shit long enough and wasn't gonna take it anymore. Said he'd done so much for those rich pricks, and he was gettin' a little back."

"Rich pricks."

"Uh-huh."

"He say anything to identify these rich pricks?"

"No. Just that they were gonna pay."

I remembered what Missy said about a settlement after B&D went belly-up. I consulted my notes. "Is this the same guy who paid him a settlement in... oh-eight?"

"How the fuck should I know? I didn't know him then. Barely know him now."

"He tell you how much he was looking to get?"

Her hesitation was brief. "No, he didn't."

"But it was pretty good. Right? I mean, he was practically living with you."

"Bobby Lee was nice to me and gave me things, but he didn't live with me."

I decided not to push and moved to other threads. "You ever know him to do drugs?"

She shook her head.

"Sell them?"

"Nah, he hated all drugs. Said they ruined his life. Blamed them for taking his precious wife and kid from him. He could be stupid like that." She rolled her eyes.

I thought about Val and the kids. "Yeah, some men can be stupid that way." I stayed on point. "So, where'd the dope come from?"

"He told me he didn't have no dope. He says the cop planted it."

"What do you think about that?"

"It ain't like it don't happen. Besides, I told you; Bobby Lee hated drugs. Sometimes got weepy over that shit when they came up because it cost him his wife. He could be a real pussy sometimes. Don't see where it matters anymore, anyway. He's dead."

I wondered if she'd chosen the black teddy she was wearing as a mourning shroud.

"The sad thing is, no one believed him... not his wife, not his lawyer." She pinned me with another hard look. "Not his bail bondsman."

A shiver of guilt passed through me.

"I might believe him."

A harsh laugh escaped her throat. "Little late, don't you think, bounty hunter?"

It was a hard statement to dispute.

She glanced over her shoulder. "I gotta go. They'll be looking for me backstage."

I drew out the two hundreds and extended them between two fingers. She scowled at the bills like they were beneath her, but slipped them into her garter.

I let her get a head start, and she disappeared into a cubical behind the stage. Light spilled across the stage, casting a humanoid shadow on the otherwise dim floor.

An unholy blend of rap and pop music assaulted my ears. I considered stopping by the DJ booth and offering him a hundred bucks to play Gold Digger but decided against it. I had other things to do.

The door girl was still sitting with her legs crossed and breasts out. We shared a smile. Steve Austin still frowned from his spot on the wall, but he favored me with a stoic nod. I returned the gesture and stepped from the dim confines of the Lucky Horseshoe into the bright Florida sunshine.

CJ'S LUXURY LIVING

CJ's Mobile Home Park on Hubert was a stone's throw from the Lucky Horseshoe. Kinsey had called it home at the time of his arrest, and TPD had already searched the place with a warrant. The park was a tiny gravel drive on the west side of the road, nestled between a metal-skinned machine shop and an auto salvage yard. Weeds poked through the edges of the loose rock pavement. The one-car drive in front of Trailer Nineteen was empty, leaving plenty of room for the Corolla.

I stepped from the car and cast a glance toward the faded two-tone brown single-wide at the front of the private lane with the chocolate-painted sign proclaiming Office swinging in the heavy summer breeze. Someone moved behind a window screen that hadn't seen soap since the trailer was new in nineteen eighty. They didn't call out or come to investigate, so I turned toward Kinsey's front door.

Wood steps creaked underfoot. Black iron railing peeled paint at my touch. It was warm after basking in the Florida sun all day.

I knocked on the door, waited, and knocked again. No one came. I tried the handle, but it held fast. I peered through the diamond window in the door's aluminum hide, but saw nothing of the shadowy interior.

I retraced my steps, strode through the suffocating heat and knocked on the manager's storm door.

A rotund woman studied me through the glass. I guessed my clean-cut look wasn't the most common sight at CJ's.

"Hey, there."

"Yes?"

I produced my card and held it to the glass. "My name is Logan Walsh. I'm an investigator looking into Bobby Lee Kinsey's death."

"Again?" She shook her head. "You people came down to search his house after he got arrested and ask me all kinds of questions about his comings and goings. Then you show up yesterday asking me more questions. Now you're here again. I respect the law and all, but this is all a bit too much, you ask me."

I put all the understanding compassion I could fit into my smiling nod. "Yes, ma'am, I understand, but the wheels of justice turn slowly, and sometimes they have to cover the same ground. No other way to get it right."

She chewed on that and nodded in approval. "I'm Wilhelmina, Wilhelmina Hessler, the manager here. I supposed there's something to be said for getting it right."

"That's how I see it, Wilhelmina."

"You can call me Willie."

"Willie." I pulled out my notepad and pen. "You were here when TPD did the search?"

"I was. They came to me for the spare key to keep from having to break down the door."

"You still have that key?"

"Sure do." Willie reached toward the wall beyond my vision and produced a single key on a ring. She'd strung a tag to it. It read 19.

She pushed the storm door open and descended a pair of wobbly metal steps that shifted under her considerable weight. An unpleasant combination of stale cigarette smoke and unwashed human flooded from within the home. Her hand took a death grip on the rail, and the woman stepped with the care of someone who'd tumbled in the past. We set out for trailer number nineteen, Willie wobbling in that way the morbidly obese do. She was panting before we left the cover of her aluminum carport.

"It's a shame what happened to that man." She spoke between puffing breaths. "He... was never any... trouble." She let several steps go by. "And had that delightful daughter."

"Did you talk to him often?"

She stopped. We were almost halfway there. "I saw him at the mailbox sometimes."

The boxes stood in a row under a faded Old Glory, turning over in the breeze.

"You ever see any signs of trouble?"

"You mean like the drugs?"

I nodded. "Yeah, like the drugs."

A yellow-toothed grin spread across her plump face. She leaned close, the odor from her house enveloping her and her unwashed muumuu.

"I don't think there were any drugs." A rancid halitosis washed the house smell with an aroma of rotting meat.

I forced a tight smile and leaned backward in my stance. "You don't?"

"He wasn't selling them here, honey. I would know."

I glanced at the dirty screen that looked out at the lonely shale road. "I think you would."

Willie had caught her breath and started walking again. "But he might've been getting desperate."

"Was he having a hard time keeping up with the rent?"

"I ain't really supposed to say, but most people here are week to week."

I nodded.

Willie kept her eyes on the unpaved surface. An inopportune pothole could put her on the ground or in the hospital. "I understand he was expecting some money to come into his life."

"He ever talk about it?"

"Not to me, but I... overhear things." Her breath was getting short again.

I considered the proximity of the mailboxes to her home and nodded. "You know what kind of money, maybe where it was coming from?"

"He seemed to think a lot. But..."

"But?"

Willie put a hand out to support herself against the rickety stairs leading to Kinsey's place, huffing and puffing. "But I don't know about where—" She gulped down air. "Seemed like a lot of daydreaming." More heaving breaths went down. "See a lot of that in this place."

I bet she did.

"Here." She extended the key to me. "I'll be up in a second."

I leaned closer to her red face and put a hand on her heaving back. "You okay?"

She nodded. "Just a little winded. Don't leave that house much these days."

I watched her struggle to breathe and could hear her wheezing without a stethoscope. But she didn't need a lecture from me, so I climbed the steps to Kinsey's home. It had a deadbolt and a handle lock. I worked both with the key and the sour smell of garbage hit me in the face. I reached for a light switch. Nothing.

"TECO was out here last week," Willie said from the base of the steps. "Guess he didn't pay them neither."

I nodded and pulled the mini mag I kept on my keychain. It didn't turn night into day, but it pushed the gloom back a foot or two. The home was standard for its era. Foam ceilings with plastic moldings at the seams, pressboard walls, and grated AC vents in the floor. Dirty olive linoleum covered the decking, except for the kitchen to my right where the plywood lay bare.

"Did he come back here after the arrest?"

"No. I'm supposed to have already cleaned the place out, but Five is empty and ready to go, and I've been busy."

The couch was old brown tweed. The stuffing peeked through the cushions that still sat askew, and the heavy wood legs sat out of the linoleum divots that matched the diameter and spacing. An LCD television worth more than everything in the room gazed from the opposite wall. It stood on a particle board TV stand out of the seventies. A DVD player was on the lower shelf along with a Roku. Someone had stacked a collection of kids' movies on the counter between the kitchen and living room. Framed pictures sat stacked next to them. Someone had broken one of the glass panes.

I peeked into the kitchen. "The cops didn't mess this place up too badly."

Willie was in the front doorway, blotting out the sunshine. "No, they weren't here long."

The sink still held dirty dishes. The kitchen table and chairs were a mismatch of blond and dark wood. A box of Frosted Flakes sat on the counter, but the rest of the foodstuffs seemed to be in their places. I perused the cabinets and drawers.

"The cops let you hang out with them when they were here?"

"No. I had to stay at the office."

The whole search didn't take long, and the signs that the cops' passage before me dogged every step, from the one-by-one search of the DVDs and removal of the family pics to moving the heavy furniture to look behind and under it. I probed Willie for information along the way, but she either saw nothing or was keeping it to herself.

I suspected the former, since keeping anything to herself seemed beyond her power. I re-searched the bathroom and moved on to the bedroom. An unmade bed stood in the center of a floor covered in clothes. The closet was open, and a computer desk sat under the front window, monitor, keyboard, and mouse in place, but the tower in the mini-cabinet next to the chair was missing. I stepped over to it and shined my light. Dust covered the black polymer desktop, except for a spot on the shelf next to the monitor. The perfect rectangle testified to the recent departure of an object. Hard drive? Some kind of case?

I pulled case files up on my phone and read the affidavit requesting the search warrant. "Computer and electronic storage devices" lay on the items being sought list. I scrolled to the receipt and verified my memory from this morning. They reported nothing found. But it had been here. I looked out Kinsey's window at the single-road trailer park. Unless it was missing when they did the search. I looked back at the report. The house was intact, with no sign of break-in.

"Everything okay?"

Willie startled me. "Did anyone come here before they searched the place?"

"It's funny," she said. "The cop asked me the same thing when he returned the key. Something missing?"

I looked back at the computer desk. "Yeah, I think so."

"Well, I didn't see anybody, and I have a good view of everyone who comes and goes."

"Do you know if anyone else had a key to this place?"

"They weren't supposed to, not if they weren't on the lease."

"Do you guys have a camera?"

Her laugh confirmed my suspicions. "Why on earth would we do that?"

"They're pretty cheap these days."

Willie leaned close, assaulting me with her rancid breath. "Truth be told, I think Charlie's attitude—Charlie's the owner—I think Charlie figures the less he knows about what goes on here, the better it is for him, as long as the rent comes on time."

I weighed the possibilities and strode back to the doorway. Willie stepped aside, and I unlocked and opened the back door. The humid air was fresh on my skin compared to the stuffy, unair-conditioned trailer. I checked the door for pry marks, the paint for scratches, but it was clean.

I found the inch-and-a-half deadbolt locked. Any intruder coming this way would have destroyed the door defeating it. I sped through the home, checking the windows and screens for signs of prying or damage, but the dirt and corrosion were intact. The same was true of the front door. I returned to the back, where Willie gaped at me as if I'd lost my mind. I gazed out across the backyard, and through a thin line of saplings and blackberry bushes at a tilt slab warehouse.

"What is that place?"

Willie looked over my shoulder. "Don't even know. I never really leave the office much these days."

A VISITOR IN THE NIGHT

I gave Willie the key, thanked her for her time, and strode to the brush. I stood at the edge of the property and took in the manicured St. Augustine grass that filled in the edges of the tiny lot. A two-story tilt slab concrete building stood alongside a tiny paved car park that ran three-quarters the length of the lot. I stooped under a juvenile live oak branch and froze.

The track was old, but someone had left a tennis shoe print in the soft mud in the low ground between the properties. Time had eroded the mark and had done too much damage for any useful comparison, but its depth suggested the ground was soft when our subject passed through. The toe pointed toward Kinsey's trailer, but I found no suggestion of a return trip. This print didn't prove my theory, but it did nothing to damage it. I stepped over the mud and made my way to the glass door that faced south at the parking lot.

Decals on the door proclaimed the place Damien's Pool Supply and Service. Dark plastic domes of security cameras hung from under the soffits at the southwest and northeast corners of the building. A smile of victory touched my lips. I opened the door to blessed conditioned air hitting me in the face. The cleansing odor of concentrated chlorine and vinyl was a refreshing change from Willie's dirty muumuu and Kinsey's rotten garbage.

An electronic chime announced my arrival, but it wasn't necessary. A man of late middle age studied me with pleasant grey eyes. He stood with both hands flat on a glass counter displaying chemicals and skimming heads. His sales floor was sparse, but there were shelves of chemicals and treatments on one wall, floats and toys on another.

"Hey, welcome to Damien's."

"You Damien?"

He raised an eyebrow. "Depends on who's asking."

I offered my ID and told him I was helping with a murder investigation. His smile soured.

"Oh?"

"Yeah, I was searching the victim's home directly behind your property here."

"I see." The flat understanding in his voice suggested murder at CJ's couldn't surprise him less. "I didn't even know."

"It didn't happen there, but it looks like someone used your parking lot to stage a break-in days before the murder. I was wondering if I could sneak a peek at your footage from the night of June twenty-third to the twenty-fourth."

"Got a court order?"

"Do I need one?"

A smile touched his face. "I guess not. Come on. I'll see what we have."

He led me to an office in the back. Several screens looked out from behind his desk. Each carried the view of a different camera: two outside and three inside. He sat in the chair and reached for the mouse.

"So you're looking for June twenty-third to the twenty-fourth."

"Yes."

He pulled up the files and said, "We actually have markers."

"Markers?"

"Yeah, the motion trackers notify me of movement around the shop and marks the footage for me to revisit later."

"Awesome! Can we sneak a peek?"

"Already pulling it up." He watched the first couple of frames play across the screen and said, "Score one for your detective's intuition."

We watched the footage, and my elation turned to ash. It was a real Tampa gully washer. Lightning flashed and streams of water flowed from the roof. The walker strode out of the south, rain falling on his hooded poncho. He strode right down the center of the parking lot, head down and hands in his pockets. He disappeared into the brush at the edge of the property. Damien skipped almost fifteen minutes.

The same figure stepped back into view, leaning forward, head down. He had a cloth grocery bag in his hand but never looked around, never looked at the camera, and offered no identifying characteristic.

A car drove north past the store ten minutes later, an older Accord. The camera didn't catch a plate and even the color was hard to gauge in the lightning and rain. Gold maybe or green. Not that it mattered. There was no way to be sure this car belonged to the thief. I studied every frame of the car driving by. "What street is that?"

"Manhattan."

"I appreciate this, Damien."

"I'm sorry it wasn't more help."

"At least we know he used this entrance."

He grinned up from his chair. "Maybe your CSI guys can do something with it."

I chuckled. "I don't think so, but I'll tell you what. You mind holding onto this for a couple of weeks? Maybe we'll swing back to it."

"Sure, I can do that."

"Thanks, Damien."

I let myself out the way I came in, walked to the driveway entrance, and looked south. A long chain-link fence marked the east side of the road, and a wooded lot looked out from the west. The fence marked the edge of a truck pen. It was the kind of place with twenty-four-hour video surveillance. I walked down to check the pen's gate cam, but it opened at the southern edge of the property onto Alva. I snapped a pic of the number on the No Trespassing sign and went back to my car.

WAITING OUT THE RAIN

It was after five by the time I circled the block and got back to my car. I made note of cameras and addresses that might help me out, but few of them looked as welcoming as Damien had been, and I didn't expect to have an abundance of time in the next couple of days. Maybe Pops could do it, but I knew him well enough to know what he thought of all this. I was beginning to agree with him. Whatever was going on here, it was a lot deeper than I could dive.

I closed the Corolla's door, turned the engine over, and felt the blazing hot drafts turn cool after a few heartbeats. The white puffy clouds of noon were getting heavy with water by five. Bruises of grey streaked their cottony contours and swirled along their faces. Soon, the first rumble of thunder would start on the horizon and a ten-minute deluge would replace this tropical misery, completing the daily cycle.

I contemplated a course home but a constant as true in Tampa as any other big city of the age confronted me: There is no good way to get where you're going at five O'clock, even on a Saturday. My empty stomach rumbled, and I employed a time-honored strategy: layup and wait for the traffic to subside. I made my way back to Lois and then Hillsborough, where I turned east toward Dale Mabry Hwy. Dale Mabry connected Tampa with the oldest of its suburban sprawl: Carrolwood. The artery had once been synonymous with the traffic headaches that come with commuting. Now Tampa's suburban satellites stretched into Pasco, Polk, and, depending on how you were keeping score, Hernando Counties.

I passed under Dale Mabry's overpass in a stop-and-go marathon that churned my guts with impotent frustration. I'd made a practice of turning my thoughts onto more pleasant topics when in these situations and so turned to the matter at hand. This case was turning into something too broad and too big for a lone investigator poking around. There was little doubt in my mind Kinsey had told us enough of the truth to be "honest." I no longer believed he'd been running drugs. Either the cop had set him up, something I was having a hard time believing, or someone put the stash in his car and called in a tip.

They made sure he got busted and broke into his house that night to abscond with his computer and storage hardware before the cops could serve the warrant. That all made a certain amount of sense, but these people had to have a key. So, it had to be someone close enough for Kinsey to trust with one or to steal it. But stealing it didn't feel right, either. Was he going to make a copy and get it back onto Kinsey's keyring before he noticed? This was becoming Mission Impossible shit.

I thought of Crystal and her sudden change when she found out he might be coming into some money. I'd taken that for standard gold digging. But what if someone paid her to get close to him? I laughed at my paranoia. There wasn't enough here to draw any conclusions, and my theories were getting too fantastic to be real. The truth was always simpler. I had enough proof to convince me there was a lot more to Kinsey's story than I'd imagined, but there was no way to figure out what those things might be.

I pulled into a Cuban Sandwich shop on Jamaica and Hillsborough as the first plump drops from a threatening sky smacked my windshield. I put the car in park, stepped from the passenger compartment, and felt the storm hit. *Plop... plop.... plop-plop... plo p... plop-plop-plop... plop... plop-plop-plop-plop-plop...* until the drops became a constant roar of water falling all around me. A flash of lightning chased me into the cinderblock diner. The rolling, rumbling thunder didn't sound until I was inside, wrapped in the aroma of Latin cuisine.

The food was authentic and delicious and those embracing aromas also taunted me, mocked the ham and mustard sandwich I'd eaten over my computer. I drew a little more from the expense account.

"Welcome!" The woman behind the counter had a pleasant matronly face and plump figure.

I looked past the tiny dining room brimming with people. "Good afternoon."

"You got here, just in time."

I looked down at my shirt marked with raindrops. "I could have been a few moments sooner."

Another bolt flashed outside, and the *swish* of a hundred cars driving back-and-forth on wet pavement blended with the pounding rain.

She smiled. "Sit where you like."

A thunderclap, sharper and more pronounced than its lazing predecessor punctuated her comment. I found a spot by the window. It afforded me a good view of the passing traffic and the post office across the street. I ordered. Ropas vieja is a Cuban recipe for shredded beef. It means old clothes in Spanish, I assume for its appearance. But it could mean foot fungus, and I would proclaim my loyalty to toe jamb. I don't know what they put in that dish of delight to make it come alive in my mouth, but its inventor deserves a Nobel Prize in Cuisine for developing it.

I called Pops and updated him on my interview with Missy, Crystal and my findings at Kinsey's trailer.

"So, you think they set him up?"

"Somehow."

"Any theories on who they are?"

I considered my abortive brainstorming session under the Dale Mabry overpass. "Nothing that holds water."

"What are you going to do now?"

"I'm about out of options. Maybe I'll turn over what I know to Donner, the IA guy, and let him run with it. He has the resources to track this stuff down."

"Why don't you sound so convincing, then?"

"Because whoever these people are, they have connections, and I just don't know who's on the business end of those connections right now. On the other hand, I don't have the resources to run down all these leads."

"I see your point." No 'I told you so.' That was nice.

"You get that public records request?"

"Sure did, right after I got off the phone with you. Who cares if Seffner's finest had to languish in jail while I did it?"

Oh, the drama. "They tell you how long it would take?"

"No. It's an email request. You fill out your name, address, and email info, and they auto respond that they'll get it to you as fast as they can, which in government bureaucratic terms means before you retire."

I laughed, but not because he was wrong. "You gave them all that info?"

"I used the business. He was my skip."

"You can make those requests anonymously, you know."

That offended Pops. *"Anonymously? What do I have to hide? I'm doing right by my client. Aren't I?"*

I let it go. It wasn't like the cops would show up at his door just for asking. "Alright, I gotta call the kids. Catch you in a few."

The woman returned with a heaping plate of ropas vieja over rice with a side of fried plantains. "Here you are."

I beamed down at my meal. "Heaven on a plate."

She smiled but was called away by another customer.

I took my first bite of edible bliss and turned my gaze to the streets. Cars still *swished* by, but the fat heavy raindrops falling in sheets had become the scattered peckings of small, thin drops. The thunder and lighting had receded to flickers in the clouds followed by the long lazy rumble of a spent god. I tried to take my time and washed the food down with tea.

My mind wandered not to the mystery of who killed Bobby Lee Kinsey, but to the wife and kids who were slipping from my grasp. I had been a poor father in some ways, but I'd been doting and affectionate in others. How could you be a good, hard-working provider and home all the time? I drew my phone from the table and called Val.

Christopher answered. *"Hey, dad."*

"How's it going, son?"

"Good. Mom's taking us to Anthony's." Anthony's was a pizzeria in Brandon.

"Very nice. I'm eating ropas vieja in Tampa."

"Tampa? What are you doing in Tampa?" Tampa was a gorgeous city, but Christopher knew my penchant for staying away.

"I'm working on something for Pops."

"Hunting down a fugitive?"

I smiled at the excitement in my son's voice. "Just tying up some loose ends."

"Oh." He sounded crestfallen.

"Well, you behave for your mother, or you'll be a fugitive. You hear?"

His voice beamed with a facetious grin. *"Dad!"*

"I love you, son."

"Love you, too." The words came slower than they would have a year ago.

"Is your sister there?"

"Uh, yeah."

Squabbling came over the phone, and the sound of objects scraping the microphone filled my receiver.

"Hi daddy."

"Hey girl! I hear you're going to have pizza."

"Yep! Christopher says you're working."

I watched the traffic stream past. "I am."

"You should come home." Her tone took on a pouty quality that cut me to my soul.

I found my voice, but it was hoarse with emotion. "I know, baby. Maybe soon."

"We miss you, daddy."

I closed my eyes and turned my head so the patrons wouldn't see my grief. "I miss you, too, baby."

Sadie was gone.

I took a deep breath to inflate a blow-up smile and looked at the waitress. "Can I get a box?"

UNAUTHORIZED VISITOR

The aroma of ropas vieja filled the Corolla, but I paid it no mind. I thought of Val and her broken promises. The places in our lives where I neglected a marriage that I knew would always be there later, the shifts I worked to build a better life for the family, for me. Now, that future was here, and they were living it without me.

I climbed the steps, thinking about Val and Christopher and Sadie, searching for a way to break the cycle I was contributing to, but a wind gust pushed against my front door, ending my reverie. The door swung unlatched. My gaze moved to the keep in the jamb, and I saw warped metal, twisted and bent. Electricity pulsed through my nervous system, and I drew the snub nose .38 on my hip. The door eased open to the touch of my foot. The inside was a wreck.

No one had put things back where they belonged; my possessions lay strewn on the carpet. Couch cushions were on the floor, the drawers of my end table sat overturned on the linoleum. Even the kitchen cabinets were open, their contents pulled out. The bedrooms were the same: dresser drawers emptied on the floor, mattresses flipped over, and closets turned out. I touched nothing, only poking around to make sure the culprit was gone.

I let out a breath and retreated to call SO.

The sheriff's office took most of an hour to arrive. I waited in my car and exited when the deputy pulled up. The woman was shorter than I with silver-blonde hair tied into a bun on top of her head. She gripped at the collar of the white vest under her white uniform and pulled to let it vent in the summer heat. I brought her up to date.

"You touch anything?"

"Only with my feet."

"Anything taken?"

I thought about the mess. "No way to know until it's cleaned up."

"They trashed the place, huh?"

I nodded.

"Okay, give me a few minutes. I'll get back with you."

She climbed the steps to my trailer, destroyed the early evening gloom with her Maglite, and disappeared into the house. I swiped at the squadron of mosquitoes circling my head.

"Is everything alright?"

It was Rosalie Karuchminov. She and her husband, Pytor, owned the park and lived in the wood-frame house by the entrance. "Someone broke in."

"To your house?"

I nodded. "Looks like they pried the door. Did you see anything?"

She shook her head. "Nothing."

I figured. No one had called the cops. It stood to reason they saw nothing or didn't care enough to come forward.

"Are you okay?"

Someone had come in while I was gone and violated my home, rummaged through my things, turned my kids' room upside down. "I will be. Thanks."

The deputy appeared at the door, walked down the steps, and back to me. "I'm gonna call a supervisor and the crime scene unit. You have someplace to hang out?"

"He can wait with me and Pytor," said Mrs. Karuchminov.

"No," I said, but her stern look said this wasn't up for debate.

"It is better than being eaten by these, these. How do you say ... komaps?"

I grinned. "Mosquitoes?"

"Mosquitoes!" Her eyes brightened, and her Slavic tongue butchered the pronunciation.

The deputy smiled, too. "Well, I'm going to wait in the safety of my car. You should probably find safety, too."

I accepted her shelter but declined her offer of food. We sat on the screened-in porch that looked out at Sligh's lonely rural asphalt.

I sipped at the coffee she'd offered, wondering if I would sleep tonight and cursing my instinct to call SO. I was on duty in the morning and liked to go in with fresh batteries because I never knew how my twenty-four hours would go. This investigation would cut hours out of that recharge time.

Another SO cruiser pulled into the lot.

Rosalie was talking about how terrible it was that no one looked out for one another anymore. She didn't tell me about how it was in the old country or criticize her new homeland by comparison. She chose another path. "I think it is God. Too few people in this world put God in their lives anymore. Even fewer put him first."

I nodded in mute acknowledgement.

Pyotr looked over his reading glasses. "You listen to what she says." He held up a finger for emphasis. "My Rosie is a smart woman. The world would be a better place if we all submitted to Him."

I nodded again. Many believers traveled my circles, but I abstained from the matter. Maybe I'd stooped over too many dead kids to believe in a kind and just god. Maybe I'd seen too many senseless tragedies to believe in some grand purpose behind it all. But there were times I envied my religious brethren for the carefree way they trusted God to see them through it all. This was one of those times.

I tried to change the subject. “How is Frankie?” Frankie was their twenty-year-old son.

“Frankie still no work,” said Pytor. “He sell his motorcycle.”

I remembered seeing the bike looking out at the interior of the trailer park. The red Kawasaki Ninja 250 was an early 2000s model. They were asking $1500. It was a little steep, but automotive prices were going through the roof these days. “I had a bike like that when I was young.”

Rosalie gasped. “You rode such a thing?”

“I sure did. Val made me get rid of it when she got pregnant with Christopher.”

“Yet you stayed a...” Rosalie searched for the word.

“Firefighter,” said Pytor.

“Yes!” she said. “Firefighter.”

“I figured that was enough danger. I could spare the bike.”

The couple shared my smile, and a flashlight beam played across the dark lawn. A thin, grey sergeant came up the path to the screen door and tapped on it. The couple waved him inside. Our eyes met. “You the complainant?”

“That’s me.”

“Firefighter?”

“For the last twenty years.”

“You wanna chat in private for a minute?”

I followed him into the mosquito-infested night. “I see you’re a bail bondsman and PI.”

"It's a side hustle."

"We see a lot of burglaries. And these guys can be as ballsy as any other criminal, but most of them are opportunists. They get in. They get out. And they make a hundred or two on whatever is lying around the house. Right?"

I nodded.

"But these guys, they turned your place upside down in broad daylight." He took a breath and let the crickets and the distant whoosh of I-4 traffic fill the silence. "My point is, they came here looking for something specific, and they took a hell of a chance doing it. I'd like to know what that is and whether or not they got it."

I was now certain calling SO was a mistake. "I don't know what they were looking for. Or even who they are. I won't even know what's missing until I clean up that mess."

The sergeant studied me for long moments. "We have a witness who saw an older gold car pull up around 1:00 pm. Mean anything to you?"

I thought about a green or gold Honda Accord and shook my head.

"No perp description. No plates." The sergeant looked over his shoulder at the entrance. "I didn't see any cameras here."

"There aren't any."

He nodded. "That was my recollection, too. The crime scene folks are a few minutes out. Once they're done, you can have the place back. A burglary detective might be in touch in the next day or so."

I nodded and let him get back to his work.

AN URGENT MEETING

The SO crime scene folks didn't leave until almost midnight, and I hadn't been able to get comfortable in a space that no longer seemed my own, even with the crushing fatigue. I managed a couple of hours of fitful sleep and woke up at 5:45 feeling like someone had beaten me with a Billy club. Fresh water on my face and ultra mint toothpaste on my teeth put some life into me, and I resolved to find a coffeehouse that would finish the job.

The Corolla smelled of ropas vieja, and my heart broke for the waste. I tossed the forgotten leftovers in the trash, and mourned the ten bucks I might as well have set afire. The Ole Tampa Cubans shop was open, and I picked up a café con leche. The brew helped liven me up and started my day with a bang. I got to the station by 6:50, an hour and ten minutes before the official start of my shift.

The day passed without incident, and I stuck to my routine. Twenty-five had a small workout closet that doubled as our safe room. Exercise equipment filled it to overflowing with a treadmill, an all-in-one home gym, a pair of benches, and a rack of dumbbells against the far wall. A window shaker kept the room icy cold. I was in my fifteenth of a twenty-minute circuit drill when the factory ringtone replaced *Life in the Fast Lane*. I put down the twenty-five pound dumbbells, took a few deep breaths, and looked at a number I didn't recognize.

"Lo Walsh."

"Mr. Walsh?" The female voice on the other side was pensive and shy.

"Yes?"

"It's Missy Perez."

"How are you?" The question was rhetorical. Her terror was palpable through the phone.

"Been better. Can you meet me tomorrow morning before I go to work?"

"I'll do the best I can. I'm coming off... from my regular job. Will lunch work?"

"No. I need to see you in the morning. You know the Steak 'n Shake in the parking lot? On the Hillsborough Avenue side?"

"I know it."

"Can you meet me there at 6:00?"

"Mmmm, 6:30 ?"

"Okay, 6:30. Thank you."

She was gone. I hung up the phone and had arrangements to make.

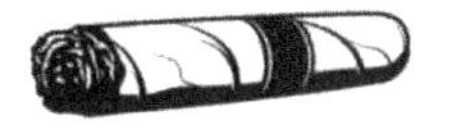

I arrived at the Steak 'n Shake at 6:40. Mike Bennet, the A shift captain, had promised to relieve me at 5:30 but arrived closer to 6:00. However, I didn't dare complain. He was doing me a favor, and I was happy to get out of there without having to run a call that would have ruined all my timing.

I changed out of my uniform into a Tampa Bay Storm T-shirt and jeans over hiking boots that wanted to be Timberlands. The pale blue shirt was faded and worn, but it had been shot to me at halftime in the middle of the team's final season in 2017. I just couldn't let it go.

Missy was in a booth in the rear, her back to the wall. Worry morphed the features that were so carefree two days ago. I took a seat next to her.

She looked at me with perplexed apprehension.

I hoped my smile allayed her concerns. "I don't want my back to the door, either."

Her fear dissolved into a wry smile. "You must think me paranoid."

I thought of the two break-ins I'd been witness to. "Just because you're paranoid doesn't mean they're not out to get you."

That got a chuckle. "Well, they just might."

She slid an oversized manila envelope with bubble wrap lining across the bench to rest against my right hip. It bulged with something heavy.

I didn't pick it up. "What's this?"

"It was sitting on my porch when I got home from work yesterday. This was inside." She handed me a note.

> *Missy,*
>
> *I'm sorry for all my mistakes. Please hold this until I call you, or get this to a cop you trust if something happens.*
>
> *Bobby Lee*

No one in the restaurant looked our way, and the parking lot was empty. I moved the open mouth of the envelope. My body tingled with excitement. "A hard drive?"

"Yeah."

I thought of the break-ins again. The thief at Kinsey's place, disappearing into the night with his computer and electronics. This is what he was looking for. "You look at what was inside?"

"I did."

"And?"

"A video. That whole damned thing has just one little video. A shitty one at that." She reached for her coffee with trembling fingers.

"What's on this shitty video?"

Missy shook her head. "A conversation. Not that it matters. There's no sound."

I stared at the parking lot, daring someone in a gold Accord to be out there, but he was a no-show.

"Do you think they killed Bobby Lee over this?"

I offered her a glance, my body cold with certain knowledge. "I'm starting to."

"Well, get it away from me. That fucking idiot. Why would he send something so dangerous to me, to our child?"

"Maybe you were the only one he could trust."

"It's in your hands now. I have a new life and kids. I can't get mixed up in Bobby Lee's craziness."

Missy rose.

"You still have no other insights to add?"

She hesitated and came to a decision. "The one person in the video I recognize is Doug Ardendorff. We called him Ardie. He was Bobby Lee's supervisor during the B&D days."

"Oh? You know anything about him?"

She glanced at the front of the diner and back. "I didn't know him well. He came over for beers a few times and sometimes watched college football on Saturdays they weren't working... which was rare."

"I don't suppose you know where he is now."

"No." Missy hesitated and looked back at me. "It's the damnedest thing. I never gave the thought much credit, but I'd always assumed Ardie was the one to get that settlement for Bobby Lee when he needed it. You know?"

I opened my mouth to speak, but MIssy was halfway across the floor. She climbed into a Chrystler 3000, backed out of the curb, lights glaring, and drove away. I realized she'd stuck me with the check and smiled at my reflection in the dark glass.

A CLUE TO DIE FOR

I pulled into the gravel parking lot of Pops's Bail Bonds and skidded to a halt in the spot closest to the side ramp. The steel door at the top was a private entrance for employees. I opened it with my key and crossed a short corridor onto the main floor. A thin industrial carpet covered the slab, which was enclosed on all sides by easy-to-clean linoleum walls that had faded from white to yellow when Bush Jr. was in the White House.

A squad of old-school filing cabinets stood at attention on the opposite wall, still guarding records older than the yellowing linoleum. I'd brought our record keeping into the twenty-first century, but I wasn't looking forward to converting the old stuff.

The back door to my right led to an old storage room that had served as Pops's efficiency for most of two decades. The main reception counter stood to my left. It looked through the same bulletproof glass I'd spoken through to Pops the morning of Kinsey's murder. The reinforced security door I'd used that morning was mag-locked and had to be buzzed open from one of three stations: the front desk, the main office, or Pops's apartment.

Loretta Hill sat where Pops had that morning, pecking away at her computer. Her Dunkin' Donuts coffee and a half-eaten donut rested on the lower counter. Six monitors showed the parking lot, the front and back of the building, the office from two angles, and the employee entrance. No one stood at the counter. No one sat in the metal chairs we'd placed in the tiny reception room beyond the bulletproof glass, but walk-ins were rare. We got most of our business through referrals or the almighty internet.

"Sometime," I'd told Pops more than once, "you're gonna have to close this place and save the overhead."

He never liked it when I said that, and I was sure he would keep the office open until the day he died.

"What's going on, Lo?" Loretta was a thick black woman with dark skin, ample buxom, and a cherub face that always smiled. She didn't look up from her screen full of QuickBooks.

"Not much, Lo." It was a game we played. "How them kids doin'?"

"Oh, you know." Her voice was weary. "Raisin' hell."

"Any different than mamma at their age?"

She shot me a glance over her shoulder that was equal parts indignation and mischief. "What the hell is that supposed to mean?"

I smiled. "Don't you know?"

She laughed.

The walls of the office muffled Pops's voice over my left shoulder. "What brings you by so early, Son?"

I leaned against the doorframe and held up the envelope.

He looked half asleep behind his metal desk. “What the hell is that?”

“Kinsey’s wife got this special delivery yesterday.”

His fatigue evaporated behind apprehensive curiosity. “What is it?”

“Apparently, a video.”

“You think it’s his meal ticket that was going to make him rich?”

I glanced at Loretta. She liked to wear an earbud in one ear while she worked, but you never knew when she was listening. “And that probably got him killed? Yeah, I do.”

His gaze shifted toward Loretta’s station, though the walls of his office obscured his view. “Let’s take a look.”

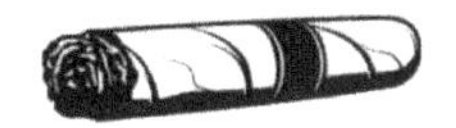

Pops’ attached efficiency was Spartan: a single bed made to military precision with a grey wool blanket, a nightstand with a brass lamp, and a wardrobe that did its best wooden imitation of a high school locker. An old picture of the family in happier times stood under the lamp’s spotlight. We took it on Clearwater Beach. The old colors were fading, as if the reality was dissolving with the years and would someday cease to have ever been anything but a dream.

I shifted my gaze to the print hanging on the inside of the painted cinderblock wall. It depicted a nineteenth-century firehouse. Someone had cast the doors open. A firefighter slid down the pole.

A team was harnessing the horses. It was the kind of print that hung in firehouses all around the country. And I thought, not for the first time, how much this place felt like a fire-station dormitory.

"What are we supposed to do with this?" Pops took his seat in front of the computer and looked at me with a lost face.

I smiled, took the package from the envelope, and had everything up and running after ten minutes of trial and error. A washed-out scene played out over the screen. The point of view was high, looking down on dirt that was churned by large industrial tires. Some kind of stacked wood, possibly trusses, touched the upper-left corner. A construction permit box sat left of center in the frame, looking left at a street that was beyond our view. A bright sign that might've once been red gazed out from it. None of the words were visible, but I'd read many like it. Warning Construction Site, No Trespassing.

A man stood in the frame, his back to the camera. He wore a dark bandana patterned with white, his hands jammed into the pockets of his leather jacket. His weight shuffled from booted foot to booted foot. The camera's perspective offered an excellent view of the patches on his jacket.

Most were indistinguishable thanks to the age of the video and the limitations of the original technology, but the big one on the back was easy to discern: a silver skull holding a dirk in its teeth with the crossed handle bars of motorcycles creating a Jolly Roger effect. A rocker over the top read Iron Pirates. Tampa filled the rocker underneath. A tiny square with the letters MC stood to the upper right of the skull.

Pops and I shared a worried glance. The presence of this Iron Pirate was no coincidence.

Another pair of men appeared from the upper right. Both wore hard hats, but that's where the similarities ended. A short, fire plug of a man wore dirty blue jeans over battered work boots and a tool belt under a reflective vest and denim work shirt. His clothes and skin were sweaty and covered in dirt.

The other man was taller and wide-shouldered. He wore a crisp white button-down over brown pants and dress shoes that were more suited for court than a work site. He'd tucked a tie the color of dried blood into his shirt.

The shorter man carried himself with dangerous hostility, his head down and fists clenched. The taller man moved in a noncommittal stroll that suggested flexibility.

Hot words flew, complete with hand gestures, pointing, and flying spittle. Fire Plug took a few angry steps, but his partner halted him with a hand on the shoulder and said something. Fire Plug retreated the way they'd come, sullen reluctance on his red face. Cooler words passed between the pair for another forty seconds. The partner extended his hand. The biker received it with all the eagerness of a groom at a shotgun wedding.

The biker offered us a profile of his face. It was hard to see on the transferred data, but a long slim nose was visible over pronounced lips and a strawberry blond goatee that grew wild. His eyes were hidden by wraparounds, though the slanted light and condition of the construction worker suggested it was close to sunset. The image faded to black.

A heavy silence filled the room and dropped the temperature. I was sweating despite it. "Well?"

"Who's the Pirate?"

"No idea. You see the logo on the fancy dress shirt?"

Pops nodded.

"B&D. Kinsey's old construction company."

"I figured."

"Apparently the fancy dresser is a man named"—I consulted my notepad—"Ardendorff. He was some kind of management."

"Upper management from the looks of things."

I nodded. "Missy Perez says he may or may not have been the one who paid Kinsey off for his back."

"After they were bankrupt and in the clear?"

I nodded.

"That means he paid with his own money, too."

"Either that or he embezzled it from B&D. Either way, it was an odd play to make after running the clock out."

Pops looked back at the screen. "I'm not thinking guilty conscience."

I stared at the screen, now black. "No. I don't think he was at all concerned about Bobby Lee's back."

"You suppose he blackmailed this Ardendorff the first time and got killed for trying the second?"

"Maybe the second time he went to the Pirates."

Pops winced. But his death at the hands of a member was suggestive.

I leaned forward. "Let's watch it again and see if we can't get some screenshots."

IN OVER MY HEAD

We finished watching for the third time. I'd pulled some screenshots that showed the players. Pops sat in his chair, a hollow look of worry on his face.

I clapped his shoulder on my way back in with the printed pics. "You okay?"

He turned his head with slow, deliberate fear. "You telling me you wanna keep looking into Kinsey after this?"

I glanced at the black screen, thought about Val and the kids and the life I was trying to put back together. "No. I don't think I do."

"Okay, so what's the plan?"

"Donner."

"The IA guy?"

I nodded. "Yeah, Kinsey's TPD arrest stinks, and the Pirates got a knife into the HCSO jail. That leaves him as our first, best actor... unless you wanna call the FBI?"

"No, thanks." He motioned at the printouts in my hand. "So, what's with the pictures?"

I could have tried to lie. "Keepsakes."

"I thought you said we were out."

"We are. I just want to hang on to a few of these as insurance." I didn't tell him I was uploading a copy of the video onto his computer. "Besides, once the video is in the hands of law enforcement, we become irrelevant."

Pops scowled with suspicion. "And what if law enforcement does nothing with this video that proves nothing and probably isn't admissible in court if it did? What are you gonna do with a couple of stills?"

I sat on the corner of his bed. "I don't know. Find the last reporter with ethics and drop it in his lap."

His harrumph said I should go out drinking with the Easter Bunny while I was at it. "And in the meantime, you're just gonna sit on your hands and let this case slip by?"

"Sure." Inspiration struck me. "You want me to prove it? I'm gonna put my name on the OT list for tomorrow." Hillsborough County Fire Rescue filled its staffing shortages by moving its extra people around the county, but, once they were out of people, they hired overtime from a list of volunteers. The department could and did mandate overtime, but only when necessary. Those necessary days were usually the big holidays no one wanted to work. "Forty-eight hours of no Kinsey."

"Uh-huh."

"But first." I produced a business card and reached for the phone. "Gotta call Donner." His line went to voicemail. I left one and followed up with a text asking he call me. "I guess you're staying here?"

Pops leaned back in his chair. "I reckon."

"You?"

"Library."

"Itching to read the latest Patterson?"

I grinned. "Something like that."

Brandon Public Library is a tall, two-story structure on Vanderburg where it curves east into Parsons. The two-story dark glass face gazed out at the street, a look that gave it more age and gravitas than its nineteen ninety construction date. I carried my laptop bag through the automatic doors, past the checkout counters to my right, and up the long ramp to the books and resources on the second floor. I found a table, whipped out my computer, and plugged it into an outlet on the floor.

I preferred libraries and coffee shops to a stuffy office or trailer. There was more to see and a chance to walk around and take in the sights: people, scenes through the windows, or any of the thousands of books. But I had no interest in those things today. There were burning questions to answer.

I searched all kinds of databases and even accessed the library's newspaper archives. I'd gotten a picture of the highlights by afternoon, but it was a superficial understanding. B&D had spearheaded much of the urban renewal seen in the Seminole and Tampa Heights area north of downtown Tampa in the nineties before building a number of subdivisions in the north county, an activity that continued through the early aughts. It went out of business in '09 after the bubble popped and the economy went into a tailspin. Kinsey worked for the company during the early days of the expansion, building homes in the bulldozed orange fields in what would become New Tampa.

I pulled corporate charter filings with the state and permit applications, writing names as I found them. It was monotonous work, boring and unsexy. It was also a great example of why someone like Donner needed to take this project off my hands. I was in over my head. I worked for four hours and sagged from fatigue, hunger-induced weakness, and mind-numbing monotony dragging me toward sleep.

I closed my eyes and opened them—thirty seconds? ten minutes?—later. The dull pattering roar of rain echoed from the library roof. Cars swished by in the deluge beyond the floor-to-ceiling window. It had gotten to be 3:00 pm. I'd done all I could do and started gathering my gear. The cloudburst stopped in the five minutes it took me to pack, and I walked down the ramp and onto an asphalt parking lot heavy with the soupy afterglow of the downpour. Sweat beaded on my forehead and slicked my back, and I wondered again why I didn't live in Tennessee.

My phone rang. I didn't recognize the number, so I had a guess who it might be. "Walsh."

"I see you called." It was Donner.

"Yeah," I hesitated. I'd become possessive of this case and my commitment to turning it over to a stranger, no matter how qualified or appropriate, wasn't total. "Something has come to my attention that you might want to look at."

"Oh?" He sounded curious. "In the Kinsey thing?"

Would I be calling you about anything else? "Yeah, I… I received a package… important stuff."

"What kind of package?"

"The kind I'd like to hand over to you and get out of my life."

"But you don't wanna tell me about it."

"Not on the phone. You need to see this."

"I'm in Orlando for another two hours. How about I get it tomorrow?"

"Sure. When?"

"Morning, maybe I'll bring breakfast."

"Sounds good. You know where the office is?"

"I do."

I remembered the OT shift I signed up to work and cursed my rashness. "I'll tell Pops. He'll be expecting you."

We hung up, and I debated pulling my name from the OT list, but I let it go. Money was tight.

I called Pops on my way to pick up the kids and told him about his appointment.

"It'll be my pleasure."

Pops had never been happy about this case, and I couldn't blame him. "Well, it's SO's problem now."

"Uh-huh. Where you been all day?"

"Doing research on B&D."

"I'm shocked."

"Well, I've concluded that my talents definitely do not lie in this direction, and there is way too much digging for me to do it. Besides, people are dying over this."

"You noticed that, huh?"

I smiled. "I'm headed to get the kids. Catch you later."

"Catch you later."

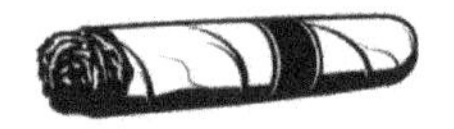

Val opened the door to the Plant City home we once shared. "I thought I was taking them to your trailer."

I considered its condition and withheld news of the break-in. "I was in the area. Thought I'd save you a trip."

"Oh, thanks."

"You wanna come?"

"Is that a joke?"

I glanced past her at the empty stairs. "Look, I'm sorry, but this..." I paused to keep my composure. "This is killing me."

A malicious light flicked through her eyes. "Is that why you keep calling me a whore?"

A flare of anger went off in my gut, but I held back.

Christopher came charging down the steps. Sadie was right behind him.

We embraced, and it amazed me how much comfort such tiny arms could hold.

I slipped into the car. "Two weeks till school starts. You guys excited?"

They were not excited. I had planned something closer to home, but I read the kids' moods and saw an opportunity. We drove to Brandon Town Center, the same sprawling closed-air mall that had ended Eastlake Square's existence. The place's ability to clog the surrounding streets was legendary, and it belied the notion that malls were a dying breed around the country. Strip centers and stand-alone restaurants enveloped the whirlpool of commerce, feeding off the commercial giant's leavings with the eagerness of Remora.

I chose a different view of the hated traffic and made the most of the time. "So, you got you a girlfriend, Christopher?"

"Dad! Stop!"

I looked in the mirror. "How 'bout it Sadie? He got a girlfriend?"

Sadie struggled to hold back a smile.

I squinted my eyes. "How about you? Any boys I need to be running off?"

I got a giggle from the backseat.

"Maybe I need to have Pops put some of his people finders on you two."

Christopher smiled at me. "You're a people finder, Dad."

Val's words about his fascination with firefighters being a compensation for the hole in his life cast a pall over his proud tone.

I forced a smile. "You wanting to be a people finder now?"

Christopher shook his head. "Unh-uh. I'm gonna be a firefighter."

Both faces beamed in the mirror, and I savored the moment. "Well, you need to finish school first, and I figured we'd do some back-to-school shopping while we're here. What do you think of that?"

Sadie sat up. "Really?"

"Sure." I wondered if this wasn't akin to bribery, and if it was a healthy way to deal with the trauma of our imploding family. But shopping was a distraction, and this was the happiest I'd seen them since I'd moved out.

Most of the traffic was branching east on the mall access road, a vain attempt to outsmart the logjam of cars moving inland from Tampa. I bore west, to get away from the crowd and parked by the Books-A-Million. The kids and I dismounted and walked through the open courtyard between the Cheesecake Factory and California Pizza. We entered the west entrance, passed the carousel, and followed our noses to the food court.

Everyone split up. I got Chinese BBQ, Christopher got Sbarro Pizza, and Sadie got Chick-fil-A. We shopped for an hour and a half, joking with each other and laughing. It had been a while since the kids were so loose and carefree around me. I watched them joke with each other in Hollister and fight over which character was best in the Disney Store. We made it all the way back to the food court, where they perused Hot Topic for the second time. I held the bags and stood in the door, happy to have brought some joy into their days, instead of the turmoil that always brewed between me and their mother.

My phone rang, and I recognized the number. "Chief! Got some OT for me?"

Vinton Hayes's Southern drawl warmed the phone. "Evenin' Lo. Gotcha a couple of options. Need captains at Forty, Thirty-two, and Sixteen."

The short list of bad choices told me I was farther down the list than expected, but I also saw an opportunity. "I'll take Thirty-two, Chief."

His voice responded with a hint of surprise. "Thirty-two it is. Have a good shift."

"I'll do my best."

Thirty-two was a busy house notorious for its night runs and nonsense. It also ran a lot of violence and fires. I was no fan, but it was first-due to Pops' store and would give me the hope of sitting in on the meeting with Donner. I glanced at my phone: 7:45. I had a lot to do before bed and sleep was not in the cards at a place like Thirty-two. "Come on kids. Get something if you're gonna get it. We gotta go."

FIRST-IN

Station Thirty-two was a behemoth four-bay firehouse off the north side of Hillsborough Avenue. It was home to our Heavy Rescue Team, a crew trained in everything from enhanced vehicle extrication and confined space operations to building collapse and high angle rescue. Everyone assigned here had to be trained and certified. Non-qualified outsiders could staff the engine. So people were jerried in or hired for engine spots to backfill team members who needed to staff the technician spots on the truck and the heavy.

It was 7:02 when I pulled in, and it did not surprise me to find most of the units gone. It did surprise me which unit was still in quarters: the engine. I nosed into a spot toward the rear of the parking lot and lugged my gear out of the trunk and along the back of the massive station. The bedding, toiletries, and spare clothes could keep until I was situated.

"Mornin' Cap."

"What's up, Ron?"

Ron Diehl was hosing down the engine for the shift-chamge wash. He was a brand-new driver. I took his presence to mean he was on overtime. "You coming or going?"

I was hopeful. Ron was good people and one pitfall of OT was the threat of a mutant crew.

"Off-going. John'll be happy to see you, though."

I glanced at the black helmet with the red shield on the doghouse, the motor cowling between the driver and captain. "Johnny Miles?"

Diehl smirked. "Yep. He was on EOT yesterday and needs to get to Twenty-two before someone gets the bright idea of using him in the Third Battalion."

EOT is an exchange of time, one person working for another. It allowed the person taking the day off to do so without burning his sick or vacation. The person working didn't get paid, but was now owed a shift for when he needed a day off. The department did nothing to enforce paybacks and doing an exchange could be a risky proposition if the other person didn't want to return the favor later.

"He inside?"

Diehl nodded.

"I'll find him." I left my gear in a pile by the right front of the black-cabbed yellow-green fire engine and strode across the cavernous bays. Johnny Two-step was leaning on the kitchen counter with a coffee cup in hand. He was tall and lean, with chiseled arms and chatted with Michelle Hernandez, one of the on-coming B Shifters. The smile on his tanned face bloomed into full excitement. "There he is! I didn't know if you were coming from home or another station."

"I wouldn't do that to you."

It was good manners to call if you expected to be late relieving someone, but it had fallen out of fashion in recent years. Now, it was nothing to find out your relief was inbound from another station on the other side of the county at rush hour, ten minutes before 8:00. I was a traditionalist and always called ahead when I knew I would be delayed.

"Where is everybody?"

"Chief ran with the truck and heavy to an extrication on the west side. They came available about twenty minutes ago, but it'll be a few."

I nodded. "Anything I need to know about?"

"Not a thing I—" The lights above us came on followed by a slow *beep!* that stretched out over a long second or more. A soft, feminine computer spoke from the overhead speakers, her tone coaxing, even pleading for us to run this call. *"Battalion Chief Three and Truck Thirty-two and Engine Thirty-two, respond to, structure fire. Located in Grid LL-5520."*

I walked to the printer, my heart running at a cantor, and read the paper. My eyes always went to the comments noted at the bottom of the page. This was a good indicator if we were running a smell of smoke from an AC or something more severe. MULTIPLE CALLS/ REPORT OF FLAMES AND SMOKE. BELIEVED TO BE OCCUPIED. DISPATCHING A WORKING ASSIGNMENT.

A working fire brought two extra engines, a rescue, and a batt chief. I walked to the truck with purpose. Diehl had tossed the garden hose used to wash the truck aside and fired up the motor. He shouted through the cab. "I got us going."

A good driver would do that for you. I waved, put the tear 'n' go in my mouth and started climbing into my gear. It takes a little time to make all that happen and even the best of us get tangled on occasion. But I was in my Nomex hood, unbuckled pants, boots, and open jacket in under thirty seconds. John stepped backward out the cab, dragging his gear across the wet pavement and out of my way.

I threw my helmet and mask bag onto the doghouse, set my station boots on the floorboard, and climbed into the engine. I closed the door, took my first look at the address, and couldn't speak. The dispatcher came over the radio. "*All units responding to Orient and MLK, this is reported to be Pops' Bail Bonds. We are getting a report of an intruder alarm at the same location. Units stage at your discretion.*"

I looked at Diehl, but he spoke before I could. "That's your old man's place, isn't it?"

I nodded.

"We ain't fucking staging then."

I was incapable of movement until we reached the end of the long drive and were turning east on Hillsborough. My hand trembled on the switch to the electric siren, but the selector knob turned and the siren wailed at the congestion before us. I slipped my seatbelt over my shoulder and started the cumbersome task of buttoning my pants and coat in sixty tons of steel doing forty-miles-an-hour. I added doses of air horn and Federal-Q siren at Orient. We turned south and passed the Hard Rock on our left.

I put thoughts of Pops on the side and focused on the problems and challenges I would face, and how best to accomplish our tactical goals. Engine Thirty-two cleared the I-4 overpass and a dense haze spread across the road beyond the canopy of oaks ahead of us. This was common in Florida. The dense humidity pushed down on the smoke, forcing it to collect along the ground rather than climb unfettered into the blue sky.

The Mobile Data Terminal mounted on the dash by the doghouse showed me all the units and their location. It was helpful when issuing tactical assignments and approaching intersections other apparatus had to traverse. I put the headset over my hood and adjusted the mouthpiece. "Nine is coming west on MLK, but you got 'em beat by a quarter mile or so."

"Copy." The speakers put Diehl's voice in my ear canal. *"Any plan on how you wanna play this?"*

I glanced at the road ahead for signs beyond the smoke, but we were still too far away. I willed the truck to move faster, but Diehl was doing a good job. Manhandling this beast in traffic was dangerous, especially when running emergency. We hit Orient and MLK with a flurry of light and noise, and I got my first glimpse of flame through the thin line of trees on the northern border of our property. I tightened the straps of the airpack I hadn't yet checked or logged into.

There was a lot of smoke. If Pops was in there...

We got a good look on final approach. Flames billowed out the side door and into the eaves. A white-and-green deputy's car was parked in the center of the lot and was probably going to suffer some paint and plastic damage, if it didn't catch fire itself. The deputy stood at the edge of the street, flailing his hands and pointing, as if we could somehow drive past the conflagration without seeing it.

Diehl took me past the front of the building, popping the brake only after I'd gotten a three-sided view of the structure. Smoke stained the front windows and door, but they stood intact. What wind there was blew out of the southwest, pushing the smoke across Orient. The roof was still holding together, but that would change, and soon.

"Two-and-a-half to the door on the Delta side." That would put the crew in motion while I worked the radio. I touched the transmit button on my headset and kept a tight rein on my voice. "Engine Thirty-two, EDC."

Emergency Dispatch Center.

"Engine Thirty-two."

"On scene with SO, single-story combined occupancy, heavy flames and smoke. Engine Thirty-two will be operating in the offensive mode, stretching a two-and-a-half to the Delta side to facilitate rescue. Let's go ahead and set up Orient Road Command. Accountability will be at Engine Thrity-two on the Alpha side."

A crowd gathered on the sidewalk at a blue-top hydrant across the street. The color told me I could get fifteen hundred gallons a minute or more from the plug. That should be enough, but there were plenty of hydrants here, if the need arose. Loretta's face in the crowd eliminated one rescue concern but stressed another: Pops wasn't with her.

The dispatcher repeated my size-up, and I undid my seatbelt, wove it around the bulk of my gear, grabbed my mask and helmet, and dropped from the cab. I slipped on my helmet, reached under my coat, and turned on the portable radio hanging there. The channel selector knob *clicked* once then twice, putting me on Tac-3.

It was always a good idea to take the long way around a burning building in order to get a three hundred and sixty degree view. I strode west to toward the back of the structure, then north to the side lot to better judge the conditions of the building. It didn't look promising.

Heavy smoke pushed out of the eaves on the leeward side, suggesting the fire had at least partial possession of the attic and was attacking the overhead roof supports. The volume of fire at the door and smoke-stained front windows said there was plenty of fire waiting on the main floor. They also painted a grim picture for anyone still inside. Pops!

Quint Nine's screaming Federal-Q split the morning air, its sharp horn punching at the drivers too busy gawking at the blazing building to pay them any mind. The deputy ran up. "They say the owner's in there. We got an intrusion alarm. But this..."

I nodded and grabbed the portable handset dangling by a cord out of my jacket's throat. "Command, EDC."

"Command."

"Get me a second alarm." They acknowledged, and I transmitted again. "Command to Quint Nine."

"Nine on final."

"Gonna enter the door on Delta. There are living quarters on the Charlie side. We'll do the fire attack with the two-and-a-half, if you'll do a search."

"Copy."

I arrived at the employee entrance door at the top of the ramp, reaching back with my right arm to turn the knob on my air bottle and charge my airpack. Jimmy Krauss was crouched before it, facemask on and plugged into his air supply. A long, angry tongue of yellow flame rolled out and over his head, spreading into the attic. I pushed the door closed and knelt next to him. Someone had pried at the latch and it wouldn't stay shut. The flames boiled back out and Nine pulled behind Engine Thirty-two on the street. This gave their aerial-capable apparatus the front of the building and the best reach for its seventy-five-foot stick.

Diehl was behind us, stretching out the two-and-a-half-inch-diameter hose so it played straight into the building. It would help keep the monster from getting snagged on the lead-up to the doorway, but the gesture would do nothing to make it lighter. I stuck a finger in the air and twirled it like I was gonna throw a lasso, the universal sign for water.

He nodded and followed the hose toward the engine. I doffed my helmet, pulled the mask over my head, and cinched the straps until the rubber seal rested snug against my face. I replaced my helmet, clipped the strap, and pulled it tight. The regulator clipped into place next, pushing cool air over my face with my first breath. My hands wiggled into bulky gloves, and I was leaning into Jimmy's back before the water arrived.

The hose lumbered and jerked in his hands. He turned his body left. I shifted right, and he opened the bale, releasing a loud hiss of escaping air. Water mingled and then flowed from the smooth tip nozzle's throat. The reaction tugged the hose, trying to wiggle free of his grip. He shut the nozzle, squared himself, and put the first drops on the fire less than ninety seconds after our arrival.

Davis Carlyle, a hazmat captain from way back, knelt at my side. I leaned close. "There's a door in the back wall. He has a chance if it's closed."

He nodded without taking his eyes from the straps of his facepiece. The mask went over his head, muffling his response. "We got it. You just keep that fire off our ass."

I nodded. The heat had warped the steel door, but the column of water had knocked down the fire, sending a plume of steam and smoke out of the mouth and blotting out most of the blue sky. "Let's go!"

The two-and-a-half was a three-person hose. But with Diehl running the pump and Nine trying to effect a rescue, it was just me and Jimmy. He tried to pull the hose with him, like he would our smaller inch-and-three-quarter hose, but this line just laughed.

"Pick it up." I pulled my webbing out of my coat pocket. It was a one-inch-wide-by-fifteen-foot-long nylon strap with the ends tied together to form a loop. It had many uses, including firefighter rescue and wrestling heavy hose. I fed one end under the hose, lay the other over the top, and pulled the bottom through to create a sling I could put over my shoulder. I lifted with my legs and drove into the building.

Jimmy wrestled it with his arms, got the hose looped over his shoulder, and we dragged it into the blinding heat. He crouched at the end of the short hallway where I'd chatted with Pops twenty-four hours ago. Thick black smoke dimmed the flames, but I could see them everywhere. He opened the nozzle, hitting the fire with two hundred and sixty-five gallons a minute.

I patted his head and pointed right. Fire burned the spare desk and chair in the corner and Pops's heavy wood door was still on fire. Jimmy turned the stream on it, blackening the flames and clearing the path for the rescue. He hadn't lined this angle up with the weight of the hose and the reaction pushed hard. I leaned into Jimmy, bracing him against the powerful water jet.

We shut down and repositioned, wrestling the hose into alignment. I pointed up, and Jimmy played the nozzle across the ceiling. The solid column of water sliced through the acoustic tiles, sending them to the floor in pieces. The space above flashed orange and winked out into hot white mist that bowled down on top of us, raising the temperature at the floor and heating my ears and neck through the Nomex.

The surrounding room was alive with sounds: the *whoosh* of water, the *pop* and *snap* of superheated substances being cooled, the rapid, rythmic *hiss* of two hardworking firefighters on positive pressure regulators. But there was very little to see beyond the grey-black mist of smoke and steam.

Two lumbering shapes pushed past our right into the blackened fog. I kept my eyes moving and detected a dangerous flicker rising from our left. Fire was rolling out of Pops's office and along the ceiling behind us to the fresh clean air outside. I tapped Jimmy's helmet and pointed. He tried to bring the nozzle to bear, but firehose, especially two-and-a-half-inch firehose, doesn't bend that way.

"Shutdown, shutdown," I shouted into his ear. "Stretch into the room so we can turn." He nodded in the humid gloom.

I loosened my webbing and moved back to the entrance. I cinched it down and leaned with all my might, dragging the two-hundred-and-fifty-pounds-per-hundred-feet firehose. My muscles ached, and my lungs struggled to draw the air from the tank on my back. The rapid in-and-out *hiss* of my regulator filled my ears. I pulled with all my strength. The hose came in fits and starts, resisting my fatigued muscles. Chuck Waters, Nine's driver, saw me struggling and picked the section up in the middle. He helped feed the hose and allowed us to advance it.

I nodded a thank you, loosened my webbing, and rejoined Jimmy at the tip. He'd stretched eight feet into the room and had plenty of hose in front of him. He wheeled left. I manhandled the hose right, trying to bring it around in a gentle bend that left a section straight enough to align with the nozzle flow, while not kinking. This technique used the weighty hose as a base to counter the nozzle reaction of slinging the better part of three hundred gallons a minute through an inch-and-an-eighth opening at fifty pounds per square inch.

Jimmy opened the nozzle, and I resumed my position behind him, my body pressed into his arm across his back. The flames *hissed* out of existence, spitting more scalding steam at us. He leaned back and played the stream through the ceiling. Less scalding steam came down to meet us, but pieces of broken acoustic tile and hunks of fiberglass insulation did.

A *whomp* drew my eye. The office fire had flared back to life. Jimmy didn't need my instruction. He redirected and quenched the revived fire. Visibility was improving. The ceiling above was dark. So was the back of the room. The telltale glow of flame and rolling smoke from that section of the attic indicated the presence of fire, but we had beaten it back. I chose to wait and let Nine get out from underneath there before I brought the ceiling and hundreds of gallons of water down on them without warning.

The door below moved, and a beam of light cut through the acrid haze. A murky form in bulky gear appeared. The helmet was white: Carlyle. I hadn't even noticed his firefighter. Whoever it was, they were dragging a body between them. Pops.

AFTERMATH

"*Command to Engine Thirty-two.*" Chief Max Bartlett had arrived and assumed the command I started. When had that happened? I couldn't say if I'd been too busy fighting fire or if our notorious radios had failed us again.

I fumbled for the mic, still dangling from my collar. "Thirty-two."

"*CAN report.*" Condition, actions, needs.

I surveyed the scene and gathered my thoughts. "We have a good knockdown, but there is one stubborn section of fire in the Charlie-side attic space and in an office on the Delta side by our point of entry. Need smaller hand lines and fresh crews."

"*Repeat?*"

I did.

"*You're very broken up. I have Four and Fifteen coming to relieve you and Truck Thirty-two coming to do a secondary. You need anything else?*"

Secondary searches were slower and more thorough than the fast and dirty primary. A unit other than the one who did the primary always performed these searches, often using a different pattern.

I depressed the transmit button and got a low *boop*. I rolled my eyes. The President could watch Navy SEALs take out targets around the world from the White House, but I couldn't talk to a battalion chief a hundred feet away. "Negative."

Jimmy and I stepped from the gloomy, burned-out structure into the sunny summer morning. The bright blue sky and shining sun was a different world than the smoky, claustrophobic environment from which we'd just departed. Jimmy was down to half of his forty-five minute capacity and was required to leave the interior for rehab. I had a few minutes before hitting half, but protocol demanded we stay together as a unit. So, I left with him.

I stripped a glove off and pulled the regulator from the front of my facepiece, thumbing its valve closed in a single, practiced motion. The acrid smell of burning plastic and insulation flowed into the hole left behind, stinging my nostrils. The other glove came off, and I plopped them both at my feet. I doffed my helmet, drew my hood back, and removed my facepiece in three quick pulls. Experienced hands removed the rest of the gear with the same practiced motions, loosening belts and slipping from straps.

I piled everything at my feet and reported to the CP on the edge of the parking lot in an open coat and pants.

Max Bartlett stood at the rear of his F-250. The back door stood open to reveal a grease board propped next to his rear mobile radio. Department brass surrounded him, and a morose shadow hung over his features. We were right down the street from the PSOC, and the admin chiefs weren't shy about turning up at fires in the neighborhood, especially multi-alarmers. I turned my radio down to prevent feedback from the CP. He saw me and said, "*You* are on Thirty-two?"

I nodded, and he hugged me in his clean button up. Max was a good man. He held me at arm's length. "Four trauma alerted him to Tampa General. That's all I know, right now."

The tears almost broke, but a voice pushed them back into their place.

"We are so sorry, Captain Walsh." Fire Chief Reginald Price was what we firefighters might call a truckie-type, tall and wide, all brawn and power for the work required of firefighters assigned to ladder trucks. It would be easy to think the oversized, almost oafish, face that looked out from his massive football player's body belonged to a simpleton or fool. But it didn't, and I think this was a strength of one of the least popular chiefs in Hillsborough County Fire Rescue's history, at least with the rank and file.

"Thank you, Chief."

He gestured at the man to his right. "Chief Myers will give you a ride to the hospital so you can be with your dad during these trying times."

If there was a more unpopular man in the department than Chief Price, it was Shift Commander Wilson Myers. He had many nicknames: Salesman Myers, the Little Napoleon, and others. My favorite was Slick Willie. Myers had always been the greasy, political type and had once been the president in our own union, charged with representing our members in disciplinary matters. Then he resigned one day and took a seat at the right hand of Fire Chief Price the next. Myers went from necessary evil to Judas Iscariot before the sun set, and there were firefighters who swore they wouldn't hit the brakes if that bastard stepped in front of their car.

"Thank you, Chief, but a simple ride back to the station and my car will be plenty."

"Nonsense," said Price. "I don't want you driving at a time like this. You've been through too much."

"Yeah, Lo." Myer's Florida twang rippled down my spine. "I'm already headed that way. It's no problem."

Neither was taking me back to the station, but I read the message between the lines. "Okay, let me stow my gear."

I walked back, bent over the pile of equipment I'd left on the gravel parking lot, and a hand touched my shoulder.

"I got this, Cap. You tend to your dad." It was Diehl.

"No, it's fine, I..."

"Driver's job, Cap. I got this."

His job was to take care of the truck and its equipment, not my gear, but I understood the bigger gesture and wouldn't snub it on selfish principle. "Thanks, Ron."

I got another heartfelt hug and wished I could pile into Thirty-two and ride up there with the boys. But the smoke still curling out of the eaves and the two inch-and-three-quarter hose lines that now joined the two-and-a-half we'd pulled suggested there was a lot of work left to be done, and Thirty-two would have to stay to do it. I picked up my helmet and gloves and walked to the cab of the engine. I stripped down out of my gear and slipped my unzipped station boots over socks soaked with sweat.

"You doin' okay, Lo?"

I glanced up from my boots. "Hey, Dan. I didn't see you."

He smiled and looked over his shoulder. "Well, it's easy to hide in the glare of all that brass."

I chuckled and started to hoist my nasty bunker gear into the floor, but I hadn't even rinsed it off. I left it on the ground. "You know anything about Pops?"

"No, man. I'm sorry."

I nodded. "I guess he had a pulse. That's something."

"Yeah. Looks like you boys did a hell of a job."

I shrugged. "It was kinda hectic there for a few minutes."

"Uh-huh." He hesitated, and I knew what was coming. "Look, Lo, I hate to ask at a time like this, but you were first-in, and all."

I nodded. "It was ripping when we got here. SO parked in the way and waving us down."

"I saw the cruiser; melted the lights and blistered the paint."

That didn't surprise me. "I didn't see anyone suspicious when we pulled up, but somebody forced that side door. And that first office to your left was poured."

He looked up from his notepad. “Poured?”

“Poured. We knocked it down with a two-and-a-half and it came right back on us. It was poured.”

He nodded. “Alright. One last thing, and I’ll let you go. Your dad have any enemies?”

I thought of the external hard drive and the appointment he had with Donner. And how this guy had showed up hours before.

“Lo?”

I met his probing stare. Donner might be here already. Dan would find out anyhow, but Donner or someone in his circle could be the reason I was here now. “No. Not that I can think of.”

He didn’t like my answer but nodded. “Thanks, Lo. You take care of your dad. Tell him we’re all praying for him.” Dan turned and walked back toward his investigator’s truck beyond the CP.

I reached into the cab and pulled a clean T-shirt from the bag that held my mask. It was good to keep one in case I found myself in public after a hot training or dirty call.

I wanted to find Davis Carlyle and thank him, but there was no sign of the man. He was probably inside, pulling ceiling and searching for hidden fire. That would take a while.

“Yo, Walsh.” It was Myers. “C’mon, let’s go see your dad.”

THE GENERAL

The heavy silence mixed with the musk of sweat and the acrid-sweet scent of burned building. I leaned against the door, glaring out the window. He hadn't wanted to do this; I told myself. He'd said it from the beginning. "Stay out of it." Hell, even that slug Benny Taylor had the good sense to steer clear of this. Only I, the man with a crumbling family and an insatiable desire to fix the unfixable, couldn't—no, wouldn't—let it go. Now Pops was lying in a bed in TGH with a reservation to the burn unit, if he lived that long.

"He's a tough old bastard." Myers drove with his left hand at the twelve o'clock position, his right on the armrest. He glanced at me with those measuring eyes that were legendary when he was the local's junkyard dog. I didn't like their look half so much now that he was on Price's leash.

"What's that?"

"Your old man." He turned his eyes back to the road. "He's a tough old bastard."

"I hear Jenn was the medic." Jennifer Strauss was the A Shift lieutenant on Rescue Four.

"She was."

There were people on this job who I knew would give their patient every chance at life through knowledge, competence, and pure talent, and those who conducted a macabre comedy of errors in their patient compartments. Jenn was one of the former.

I nodded, and Myers took that as an invitation to continue. He added a fake chuckle of remembrance. "One time, we caught this church fire down in Ruskin... I was his rookie on One-seventy and—"

"I really don't wanna chat right now, Chief." Pops hated Myers for what he'd done to the union, and I didn't want to hear this prick reminisce about him to cement some fake bond with me.

His faux smile faded into angry discomfort in the window's reflection. EDC sent Engine Six and Rescue Thirty-eight to a stroke. Engine Seven went out of service mechanical. The buildings on State Road 60 changed from the metal warehouse and run-down construction of East Tampa to the brightly painted tilt slab and rehabilitated brick of South Ybor that seemed to have sprouted out of the ground while I wasn't looking. The new appearance gave this stretch of Ybor a fresher, cleaner feel that felt a little too contemporary for one of the oldest sections of the city, but it did give the place new life.

I turned my thoughts from Tampa's rejuvenation boom. There were bigger concerns. Someone broke into Pops' store hours before he was to hand critical evidence over to HCSO and burned my father in his home and business. In what world could that be a coincidence? Not the one I lived in. But what could I do about it?

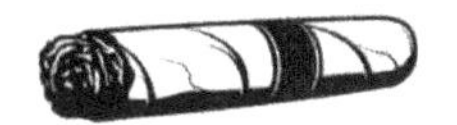

Tampa General Hospital or "The General" stood on Davis Island in Tampa Bay, an island that was actually three islands, known for its old money and exclusivity. The mismatched hospital of pastel-painted tilt slab, poured concrete, and old-school brick looked north at the scenic Bayshore Boulevard and east at the Tampa Convention Center, its reflection shimmering in the rippling blue-green waters of Hillsborough Bay, a tiny maritime offshoot of its big brother, Tampa Bay.

Myers followed the service road along the west side of the building and up the ambulance ramp to a tall, covered drive-thru ER drop-off. Rescue Four was at the head of the line. The patient compartment doors stood open. I glimpsed a navy-blue shirt working in the back, cleaning equipment, and readying the truck for service. Jenn was probably inside, writing her report.

"Thanks, Chief. I've got it from here." I pulled the lock and opened the door before he'd come to a full stop.

"Hey!"

I closed the door on his words and walked to the back of the rescue. The blue shirt looked up at my approach. She was tiny, thin, and young enough to have ridden a school bus to work. "Hey, Cap."

"Morning." I didn't recognize her, but I didn't recognize most of our people with a badge number north of a thousand, and I would bet hers was north of eighteen hundred. "Jenn around?"

"She's right here." A lean woman in a grey HCFR T-shirt and black ball cap with gold lettering had emerged from the automatic doors to my right. She carried a Toughbook cradled in her left arm and a paper cup in her right hand.

"Hey, girl!"

She wrapped her free right arm around my dirty, sweaty body. "I'm so sorry."

I had a moment of emotion that threatened to break out, but the moment passed, and I swallowed the fist of sorrow in my gullet. "Me, too."

She took in my appearance. "Were you there?"

I nodded. "I'd just walked into Thirty-two on OT."

"Jesus." She glanced into the patient compartment. "Hey, Cher, this is Captain Walsh. That was his father."

"The patient?"

Jenn nodded. "Cap, this is Cheryl Anne Kennedy. My new partner."

"New partner" for a lieutenant like Jenn meant rookie.

We exchanged "Good-to-meet-yous" over a handshake, and I turned back to Jen. "How's he doing?"

Jenn held my gaze, her expression grave. "He had some burns and smoke inhalation, but he'd taken a beating, too. I RSIed him." Rapid Sequence Induction was the medical procedure of sedating a patient to place a breathing tube in her trachea. It protected his airway from vomit, swelling, or other threats. "He had soot on his face, but his airway wasn't swollen. It went off without a hitch."

"That's because you're one of the best in the business."

We both turned to Chief Myers, and I glanced past him at his car, still sitting on the ramp.

"Thank you, Chief." Jen's voice could never be called disrespectful, but the pleasant joy it held when aimed at me was absent.

Myers glanced into the compartment. "Looks like your unit's all cleaned up. EDC was asking for rescues."

EDC was always asking for rescues.

"We'll go available, Chief." Jenn looked at me. "Let me know if you need anything."

I thanked her and said goodbye to Cheryl.

Myers and I passed through the ambulance entrance. I didn't recognize the nurse behind the desk, but it had been a decade or more since I rode rescue like Jen.

"Help you?"

I opened my mouth, but Myers answered. "We're here about Walsh."

She furled her brow, and said, "The fire casualty. Of course. He's in Trauma One. I can check, but I don't think he's talking."

"He's my father," I said.

The nurse looked back with wide-eyed horror. "Oh my god! I had no idea."

I nodded my understanding. "You didn't know."

"Why don't you guys wait in the EMS room? I'll make sure Doctor Zabrat knows you're here."

The EMS room was an oversized office that was the designated workspace for paramedics to work on their patient care reports in private. State law required we leave a completed report with the ER staff before the crew left. In practice, they got a paper cover sheet with few details, but the system sent a completed document when the report was closed out and sent to the county server. Most medics tried to get their reports banged out in the time it took to put the unit back in service for three reasons: the memory of the call was fresh, it was a break from the relentless beatdown to which HCFR rescues were subjected, and letting reports pile up was a good way to wipeout what little downtime a crew might get later.

The room was stocked with chips, fruits, and drinks. A pair of stainless-steel coffeemakers stood on the counter against the far wall, a sleeve of paper cups leaned against the one with the orange dispensing handle. I drew a Mountain Dew from the fridge underneath. Myers sat at the table, playing with the volume knob on his radio. He was on Tac-3, listening to the tedious hunt for dying fire.

I took a seat in an office chair left over from the days when Tampa kept a computer in every hospital so their crews could do their reports on site before leaving. We sat in semihostile silence for a half hour before the door opened. It wasn't the doctor.

Fire Chief Price's white-and-gold-clad body took up the doorway. The smile he offered had all the warmth of an arctic plain. His fire marshal, Brenda Mason, and Chief Fire Investigator Robbie Stewart filed in behind him. Mason's smile looked genuine, but I'd seen enough of what lived on the other side of that expression to know of the rot underneath. Robbie wore a deep frown. Whether it was from Pops' situation or something deeper, I couldn't say.

I spied Dan Warren on the far side of the door as it closed. A guard?

Myers jumped to his feet with the alacrity of a recruit. "Chief!"

The men shook hands and shared a hushed exchange. Price's measuring eyes fell on me. "How you holding up, Captain?"

I glanced at his entourage. "I've had better days."

Sorrow filled his phony eyes. "Terrible what happened. And you being first-in on overtime. Tragic."

I was getting a picture of what was happening and held onto my silence.

"Astronomical, really," said Mason.

"We should thank the good Lord you were there," said Price. "Captain Carlyle says you directed him right to the victim."

Mason nodded in solemn reverence.

Were these people serious?

I glanced at the cross he wore on his lapel, the not-quite-regulation display of religious affiliation. "You know what they say, Chief. God provides."

Something flickered across his features, leaving an irked smile in its wake. "And so he does."

"The press is already making a fuss about this story," said Mason.

"That's true," said Price. "Did you happen to see them before you left?"

"I saw them." News trucks frequented the fireground, especially multi-alarmers.

"It's gonna be quite the tale when they find out the first-in captain was the son of the victim," said Mason.

"That's true," said Price. "They're gonna be looking awful hard at this one."

He pulled a chair and sat across from me with more grace than most men his size. "Tell me, Captain. Is there anything I need to be aware of about this fire?"

"Like what, Chief?"

His warm, sympathetic smile invited me to unburden myself and tell him what he needed to know before the media took matters out of his hands. "Are you and your dad doing well?"

I glanced at Mason and Robbie, surprised they weren't conducting this interview. "Are you going somewhere with this, Chief? Because I don't even know my father's condition or prognosis, and this feels a lot like an interrogation."

Hard anger settled in his hickory eyes, but he held on to his smile. "Just looking out for the department, Captain. You know? My job."

I smiled at that and remembered. "You were an investigator back in your Tampa days, weren't you?"

His smile cracked and twisted. "I was the fire marshal."

I nodded. "Well, I don't know how my father ended up here, but you can be sure I had nothing to do with it."

"Warren says you told him the place was poured." It was Mason.

"Of course I did. We knocked down the main office with a two-and-a-half and it flared back up in that way poured fires do.

Understanding that makes me an experienced fire officer, not an arsonist."

Price and Mason exchanged glances.

"Do I need union representation here, Chief?"

The question changed the tenor of the room. "Only if you have something to hide."

"So only guilty employees have rights? Is that in the handbook somewhere?" I rested my gaze on Robbie. He diverted his eyes. I tried to surmise if he was ashamed of me or of being part of this circus. I decided it was even odds. "I don't think I like having this conversation."

Price leaned over me, his meaty hands resting on my chair back. "Listen, Captain, I have the family member of an employee burned in a fire in which that employee happens to work on overtime. You were first-in, no less."

"I'm here for my dad."

"He directs the search crew right to the victim and comes out of this looking like a hero. I want to get ahead of this if there's something to get ahead of. You understand?"

I could see the logic in his concerns, but it didn't stop a cold rage from settling in my gut.

"Perfectly." I rose and pushed past him.

"Where do you think you're going?"

I kept my hand on the door. "To take a piss. You wanna hold it?"

"Is that how you talk to me?"

"That's how I talk to a man who just accused me of trying to kill my father."

He had no response.

I opened the door, came face-to-face with Dan Warren. He glanced over my shoulder and stepped aside. I went down the hall toward the controlled chaos of the ER.

MOTHER

Tampa General had a fully functioning McDonald's. It took a few minutes, but I followed my nose to it. I was still munching on my double cheeseburger when I stepped out of the west entrance toward the Ford Fiesta sitting under the concrete overhang of the hospital's main entrance.

"Where you goin', Lo?" Dan Warren leaned against the wall next to the entrance, arms crossed, his brown eyes obscured by aviators.

I finished chewing and swallowed a mouthful of meat purported to be beef. "Dammit! It's almost like you're some kind of investigator."

"Chief ain't gonna like this. You're technically on duty, you know."

"Am I? I'm here checking on my father. As far as I'm concerned, I'm on emergency family leave."

His nod and shrug said that was one interpretation. "Okay, he still ain't gonna like it."

I glanced into the open mouth of the automatic doors. People moved to and fro, but no one in fire department clothes. He'd come alone. "Well, I don't care for being called a would-be murderer."

"Fair," he said. "But you have to admit, it's a hell of a coincidence."

It was. "I'm no murderer."

"I know that."

I remembered him taking up station outside the door instead of coming in for the interrogation. "And you told him that, didn't you?"

"You running ain't gonna make me look good."

"I don't guess it will. You gonna stop me?"

He gave a slow shake of his head. "Nah, not sure I wouldn't do the same in your position. Just don't do anything illegal. Okay?"

I grinned. "Deal."

The Uber dropped me off at Thirty-two. I slipped into my car and out of the parking lot before anyone had time to know I was there.

I drove north into New Tampa, a section of north Hillsborough County that was annexed by the city just as it was about to undergo an explosion of development. Most people shrugged and turned the page in the paper. Pops had been livid. The county fire department stood to experience similar growth with this development, and Pops was looking to get up there and work closer to our family home in Lutz. But the city had gobbled it up.

Now, they sported not less than four stations in the area and gave us static for running calls along the lonely stretches of the county that fell outside their jurisdiction of million-dollar homes and lucrative commercial occupancies. It was galling to those in the know, but just another day in municipal politics.

Tampa Palms Golf and Country Club, and its multi-million-dollar clientele, were in this acquired jurisdiction. The immense resort stood on the southern leg of Tampa Palms Boulevard's circle of tropical paradise. Palm trees lined the clubhouse drive, while giant live oaks provided shade closer to a main building that could have been the seat of government for a third-world monarch. Crisp, gold paint covered the proud building's walls, unsullied by the fading effects of the Florida sun. Unblemished white columns stood along the face holding up the veranda that formed a shallow U around the traffic circle to the main entrance.

The white 2016 Cadillac Deville in the sparse northwest parking lot said I had chosen well coming here first. I slipped into a spot under an oak and climbed from the car. My shirt was clean and my pants and socks had dried, but I was still in desperate need of a shower.

I found her on the cushioned wicker furniture on a rear verandah that looked out at the lush, manicured golf course. Her feet rested on an ottoman. She gripped a highball in one hand and the knee of a man almost half her age in the other. The white skirt and sneakers under her broad white straw hat said I'd caught her after tennis but before bedroom gymnastics. The man attached to the knee she groped wore an ivory smile across his bronze face and an erection in his white shorts.

"Isn't it a little early for booze, Mother?"

The smile she wore fell, and she pursed her lips, her eyes hidden by sunglasses.

The expression on her partner's face said, *"Mother?"*

A thick curtain of vibrant honey hair flowed down the back of her head, spilling over slender but firm shoulders and a lean, cut body. She looked good for any age and could have passed for a distinguished thirty-five.

"Logan!" Her tone expressed both surprise and consternation. "What are you doing here?"

"Came to talk."

"Horatio and I just finished a vigorous tennis match. He's quite good."

This man could be my brother. The thought sent a shudder of disgust through my body.

"It did take five sets," the blond-haired Jimmy Connors–wannabe said.

I didn't take my eyes from Mother. "You should be proud. Beating up on a sixty-five-year-old woman."

The victorious smile creeping up his face fell with the weight of an anchor.

Mother's bronze face gained a rosy hue, and she spoke through clenched teeth. "That is not funny, Logan."

"It's kinda funny." I looked at Connors. "It's also true."

Connors sat straighter and placed both his sneakered feet on the floor, pulling his knee free from her grip. "I'll... give you a moment."

"You do that."

She waited until we had the porch to ourselves. "Are you satisfied? I have a reputation for being half my age, you know?"

"Don't worry, Mother, that's not the most important part of your reputation."

Her eyes flew wide, and the pain they reflected cut me.

"I'm sorry," I said. "I thought you'd want to know Pops is at Tampa General."

Her hurt anger became worry, and I wish I could say it was about Pops and not the income he represented.

"Yeah. He'll be bound for the burn unit, if he lives long enough."

Her face curled with confusion. "Burn unit?"

I nodded. "There was a fire at the store today."

"Fire?" Her voice became small and fragile, the bearing of her face faraway and wistful.

I put an awkward hand on her shoulder. "I don't know how bad it is, yet. I... came here to tell you."

She nodded, looked at the highball she'd forgotten, and emptied it with three gulps. "What happened?"

"The investigation is just getting ramped up. We won't know anything official for a while."

She looked at my uniform. Maybe she picked up my scent. "You were there."

"I was there," I said. "But I didn't see Pops. The crew who took care of him were good people."

She nodded, knowing how sparing we firefighters could be with such praise. "I, uh… I need to get home."

"You want me to take you?"

"No… I… no." Mother wasn't the weepy, vulnerable type.

I nodded. "Just be careful driving."

"I just had the one."

I knew damn well she'd had courtside mimosas between sets, but didn't contest it here. Besides, she was an old pro at doing everything drunk, and she had a short drive ahead of her. The official Walsh "palace" was one of the smallest in Tampa Palms, but it was in the Palms.

"Okay, Mother. Just remember. The last thing you and Pops need is a DUI to pay for."

Fire flashed in her eyes. "Are you my son or nag?"

That was Mother, all warm goo in the middle. "Just be careful."

ATONING FOR FAILURE

I strode back through the extravagant clubhouse, past its plush bar and through its windowed foyer, and back to my car. Mother was probably still sitting on the veranda, looking out at the distant golfers, wondering how she could patch things up with Horatio. The look on his face said she'd be better off moving to her next target, but she could be stubborn about her vanity.

I started driving and called Val.

"Hello?"

"Hey."

"*Lo, spare me the 'I'm sorry' routine. I—* "

"Pops is in the hospital." It was the first time genuine emotion had slipped into my voice. "There was a fire at the shop and... He's hurt, bad."

Her silence stretched to my southern turn onto I-75. *"I... How hurt is bad?"*

I checked my blind spot and merged. "Bad enough to kill him."

"Lo, I... I'm sorry."

"Thanks. Me, too."

"I... don't know how to deal with this with the kids."

Another silence stretched over the line, this one more contemplative than shocked. I filled the void. "I was thinking of holding off telling them until we had something of greater substance to report."

"Yes, I think that is a good plan. Are you okay?"

It was the first time she'd asked about my well-being in months. The realization conspired with my repressed grief and almost broke my dam of self-control. My voice strained against the pressure. "I'm hanging in there."

"You know, Lo, you don't have to be the big, bad superhero. Be—"

"I said I'm fine." The words came out sharper than I'd intended.

"Right." The warmth that had infiltrated her voice vanished.

My guts churned with regret. "Val, I—"

"I'm in the middle of stuff here, Lo. You take care of yourself."

I moved my mouth, searching for the right words, the right tone to tell her I hadn't meant to be short. I hadn't meant to cut her off. But she was gone. I thumbed off the phone and tossed it across the passenger compartment with an angry flick of the wrist.

"When are you gonna learn to watch your big fucking mouth?"

I missed my exit at I-4 and got off at MLK, blocks from Station Nine. I considered stopping by to thank Carlyle and his crew for what they did for Pops, but I was feeling a little too fragile to get into another emotionally charged conversation. Later would be better.

The back roads added a good ten or fifteen minutes to my trip, but I pulled into Country Square Estates and recognized the black pickup with black-and-gold striping backed into my spot. Dan sat in the white plastic chair I'd placed in front of my steps to watch life go by. He focused on the grey Toughbook computer in his lap and didn't seem to hear me pull up.

I stayed in the gravel circle, taking care not to block him in. "Don't I know you?"

He didn't smile, didn't look up, and didn't sound pleased. "Chief sent me to bring you back to the PSOC as an atonement for my failure to stop you when I had the chance."

"They figured you out, eh?"

"Security cams caught the whole exchange, sans voice."

"So, if I run now..."

He looked up from his computer. "I'll chase your ass down."

I didn't ask him under what authority. A heart-to-heart with Chief Price was inescapable. "Okay if I shower?"

He looked me up and down and wrinkled his nose. "I insist on it."

LONG NIGHT OF QUESTIONS

Hillsborough County Fire Rescue's Public Safety Operations Complex was on Columbus Drive. It was around the corner from both Station Nine and the Falkenburg Jail and combined the department's once far-flung support divisions onto one campus. Dispatch, training, and logistics were now under the same roof as the headquarters staff and could look across the parking lot at vehicle maintenance.

Dan took me through the monitored gate to a parking spot in the rear, along the building's north facing. He led me through the back door, passing with the fob in his photo ID. Shift Commander Adrian Muñoz stood in the pass-through corridor, a deep frown beneath his thick mustache. "Captain."

"Chief."

He glanced at Dan. "I have it from here. I think they want you in the front conference room."

Muñoz led me through the headquarters, weaving us through training's cubicles and following corridors with walls covered with framed messages of inspiration and poster-sized photos of HCFR on street calls. The hallway opened up into an anteroom where the executive assistants sat. Muñoz exchanged pleasantries with one woman and was told to go right back.

I smiled and nodded. Suspicion muted her return gesture.

Muñoz rapped on the door and stood by to let me pass. Chief Price's office was spacious, even grand. Chief Reginald Price stood with his back to me, stooped over his desk of polished oak, coffee cup in hand. He was studying a frame that held two pictures. Him in his Class A dress uniform with coat and glossy-billed cap next to an American flag, and him standing in front of an altar in religious regalia that suggested rank. I remembered stories of him being a deacon at the First United Methodist in Plant City.

I stopped halfway between the door and the desk. Price didn't turn until Muñoz closed the door behind me and assumed a wide stance with arms crossed. He cast a disapproving eye on the grey dry fit pullover I'd worn in place of the button-down uniform shirt with badge and brass trimmings he preferred, but that was hanging in my locker at Twenty-five. "That was quite the stunt you pulled at the hospital, Captain."

"I had things to do and didn't want my mother notified by an impersonal call or a visit by some deputy."

"It is a good thing they kept your father sedated. I can't imagine how he'd feel had he awakened to find you weren't there."

I pictured him waking up surrounded by department administration. "I think he'd have understood."

Price's eyes narrowed with scorn, and I knew he'd pulled that picture from my mind. "I could come after you for abandoning your post."

"What post was that, Chief? A hospital waiting room? Are you saying you didn't hire another overtime captain to ride Thirty-two for the balance of the shift?"

His glaring silence was answer enough.

"I'm sorry for the misunderstanding, but as I told Investigator Warren, I thought I was on emergency family leave. I still consider that my status and don't expect to be at work tomorrow. Are you seeking discipline in this matter? Do I need union representation here?"

"No." The disappointed resignation in his voice mingled with a dangerous confidence. "But Fire Marshal Mason wishes to see you before you leave."

I followed Muñoz through the same dark corridors to the front conference room. Every florescent was lit, contrasting the the dim, intimate lighting of Chief Price's office. Plastic tables sat in four rows, with chairs that faced the whiteboard and projection screen at the front of the chamber.

Familiar faces looked out from the front row. Fire Marshal Brenda Mason sat in the center. Robbie Stewart sat to her left and Jack Donner to her right. Fatigue held court over all their features, but they wore it well. Robbie's black shirt and BDU pants betrayed none of the grime or muck from the fire scene he surely helped work. Donner's shirt showed wrinkles, but mucking around a fire scene wasn't his bag.

Mason was a different story. Her white button-down was wrinkled from a long day and had a streak of soot below her large breasts. More stained the cuff of her left sleeve, a sign she had likely poked around the store's ruins since I saw her last. Full lips pursed in severe disappointment on her heart-shaped, mocha face. "Captain."

"Chief Mason." Though she was the department's fire marshal, her official rank was Chief of the Prevention and Investigation Division.

She didn't offer me a seat, and I didn't ask.

"I was hoping to get your memory about the fire on the record."

I told the story as it would soon appear in my written report. She nodded as if she'd already read it. "I listened to the radio… it sounded very smooth and controlled."

That was one of the highest compliments you could pay a fire officer. I would need to be careful. "Thank you."

She glanced at Donner. "I was looking for more of the stuff that wouldn't be in your official report."

"Like?"

"You were supposed to turn something over to Mr. Donner. You're aware of that."

I nodded. "My father was, yes."

"And what was this item?"

The compulsion to lie was heavy. "A hard drive."

"What was on it?"

I glanced at Donner. Pops's place burned little more than twelve hours after calling him. "I really don't know."

She tipped her head. "Are you telling me you don't know why you called Sergeant Donner?"

Donner regarded me with the calm confidence of an alpha predator. Robbie might've been a college student listening to his professor.

"I called him because I got a package in the mail. The attached letter implored me to give it to the most trusted law enforcement agent I could find."

"And you didn't look at it or open it?"

I shrugged. "It was delivered to the store. Pops told me about it and asked me if I could think of anyone I trusted. Sergeant Donner came to mind, so I called him. He"—I motioned toward Donner with my chin—"can tell you I called him much earlier than 4:00 pm, and he was out of town on business I know nothing about."

She didn't look at him for any kind of confirmation. I assume because they had already discussed that fact. "And you just happened to work overtime at Thirty-two the morning of the fire."

"Truth be told, it wasn't pure coincidence. I was hoping to swing by there and see Donner or have him swing by Thirty-two for follow-up, calls permitting, of course."

"You mean you set yourself up to work your second job on department time?" She said it as if every firefighter with a side hustle didn't take or make business calls on department time.

"No, I intended to cooperate with the lawful authorities in their investigation of a homicide. I didn't think I needed to secure permission for such action."

She frowned and turned back to her notes. "Investigator Warren says you found the door forced."

"That's right."

"And Captain Carlyle says you directed him straight to the victim."

"It was a purely tactical insight. I saw the heavy fire and smoke coming from the Delta side door and the smoke-stained windows across the storefront and knew the only survivable space would be in Pops's back bedroom, and then only if the door was closed."

Her sigh sounded disappointed. "Do you and your father have remote camera data storage?"

Pops was never a fan of tying our cameras to the internet. *"If I can peek in anytime I want,"* he would say, *"so can they."*

"No."

The look on her face confirmed what I'd already known. The fire was most stubborn in the mass of melted plastic that was Pops's office. That room to make sure the electronics got destroyed.

It went like that for hours, with the trio taking turns asking the questions. The same questions phrased differently. New questions that tested my consistency on related facts were introduced. Mason asked me point-blank if I'd burned the place down. Donner asked me if I could think of any connection with the Kinsey case.

"You mean besides the fact we were about to give you what I assumed to be some kind of critical evidence the same morning, and the arsonist targeted our computer hardware? No."

He glared at that.

Door Dash delivered Chinese at 9:00 pm, and they started on me again.

Robbie drove me home after midnight. I didn't speak until he pulled in front of my home. I opened the door and looked at him in the yellow dome light. "You didn't ask any questions."

"I didn't have any questions."

I smiled and stepped out of the truck.

EIGHT O'CLOCK BEERS

I got a good six hours of sleep, but still hurt when the alarm went off. I climbed into the car with a coffee in my right hand, a cold paper bag tucked into my pit. It was turning 7:00 am. I pulled out into traffic and made the official call to the station.

"Station Twenty-five, Phillips."

"Hey, Devin. You sound suspiciously awake."

"Lo?"

"Yeah."

"We caught an MVA on the interstate." Motor Vehicle Accident. *"Thirty cancelled us. I heard about your dad. He doing okay?"* The fire department was a nuclear-charged rumor mill. Word on a former member being pulled out of a fire by his on-duty son would be known by every on-duty and three-quarters of the off-duty personnel by dinner.

"He's holding up. I'm heading over to see him now. I wanted to make my absence official."

"Family leave?"

"Yeah. I'd have called yesterday, but things were hectic, and it was after midnight by the time I broke free."

"Don't give it a second thought, bro. We all knew. Besides, Muñoz prehired me." The department filled the known vacancies the evening before, the same way I had been the night before the Pops' store fire.

"Well, be safe."

"You, too, bro. And call if you need anything."

"You know I will."

Official visiting hours started at 8:00 am, but it took an hour and ten minutes to cut through the traffic and another fifteen to find a decent parking spot in the hospital's garage. Pops wasn't in the burn unit, but an ICU bed. I found his doctor in his room making rounds. She was a short, slender woman with dark brown features and black hair that implied South Asian heritage.

"You are family?" she said when she saw me.

"Son."

"I am Doctor Rajagopal. I am on the team taking care of your father." She gestured at her gaggle of ducklings. "These are medical students learning with us today."

The bright young faces smiled from above notepads and tablets.

She explained to me how Pops's burns were minor, and they were more concerned about his head injury. He had facial fractures and bleeding on his brain. They had relieved pressure by removing part of his skull and were keeping him in a medically induced coma. I frowned at his bandaged head.

"Brain injury." I think I would rather him be a little burned. "What are his chances?"

"We really do not know that. Your father is holding out, but he has factors working against him."

He'd been trached and put on a vent. This fucker beat a sixty-eight-year-old near to death and set out to burn his place down around him. I clenched my fist and nodded with emotion I hoped looked more somber than enraged. "How long before we know something?"

Rajagopal's smile was compassionate and friendly, a trait not found in every doctor. "There is no way to know that, either, I'm afraid. Whenever the swelling goes down is the best answer I can provide."

I nodded. "And his burns?"

"Minor smoke inhalation and some partial thickness burns on his neck and right arm."

I nodded and tried to put that together. Was he close to the fire when it started and crawled away, or had his assailant left him for dead after beating him to a pulp and then left the door closed out of ignorance? Who could say?

"Thank you, Doctor."

She shook my hand again and led her class to the next specimen for their consideration. I pulled the curtain behind her and sat in a chair next to the bed. I slid the wheeled tray table so it rested above his abdomen. The Budweiser six-pack wasn't cold anymore, but my coffee was. "Eight O'clock Beers, Pops."

Pops had a tradition with his crew: Eight O'clock Beers. They would leave the station together on shifts that had been long or stressful, buy a six-pack at the first convenience store they came to, and split it at the nearest park or other convenient location. It wasn't healthy, but after two decades of death and tragedy, I understood the reasoning.

I hadn't come to exorcise anything. I brooded on the horror of this crime, how Pops had not wanted to follow this path. The danger I had assumed for both of us. The price he was paying for my stubbornness. And the way this prick was getting off scot-free.

They murdered Kinsey in a locked jail, surrounded by Hillsborough County deputies. I had gone to IA with our evidence and been burned... literally. My department suspected me of being involved with this crime. And I was out of people to trust, out of people save one. I tipped my coffee against the closest can of Bud.

"I'm gonna find who did this to you, Pops. And when I do, I'm gonna burn the bastards to the ground." I looked at his unconscious form. "Right to the fucking ground."

THE SCENE OF THE CRIME

I stood in the smoke-stained side doorway to the shop, the steel door creaking in the gentle breeze. Rust covered the exposed metal: oxidation from the angry flame. The smell of burning building wafted from the hole, fresh and caustic in my nose. The inside was dark, contrasting with the bright, hot sunshine in which I stood. A flashlight playing over the interior cut the gloom.

I stepped over the yellow scene tape that was pulled down and eased into the hallway, my .38 snub nose in hand. I peeked around the corner and smiled. "Aren't you off duty?"

Dan Warren knelt in the office, studying the bare concrete floor. The imprint of fire had burned a scour mark on the concrete left behind after they cut the carpet away and took it for evidence. He glanced at me. His dark eyes lingered on the hip where I was holstering my gun.

"Gonna shoot me, Lo?" He wore a helmet over his black collared shirt and fire boots over his black cargo pants.

"I didn't know who was here. That's not a county vehicle out front."

His helmet bobbed with his nod. "Richie did the initial process because Mason thought I might have a better rapport with you, so I had to go to the hospital. Then I had to chase your ass down, and Nineteen had a worker at dinner time. So, there went my day."

"So, you're here on your time off?"

He rose from his squat, his voice straining. "Yep. You think you could run me through the whole scene from your perspective? Since you're here."

I did. It was the fifteenth time I'd told that story in the twenty-eight hours since I'd pulled up on the street outside. I took him outside, telling him about the conditions upon arrival, and led him to our setup location. I pointed to the warped door and told him how I tried to close it to cut off the fire's oxygen while we finished dressing, only to have it open in defiance. The whole story took under ten minutes to tell.

Dan studied the heavy-duty jamb. "That's a hell of a door to force."

"That bothered me, too." Steel doors were notorious forcible entry challenges. "He'd have needed a specialty tool to get through there."

"Yeah." He turned to the door and took a long hard look at the crumpled section of heavy steel just above the locking mechanism. "I was thinking something akin to a Halligan Bar for a while, but this morning"—he shook his head—"the pattern isn't right."

Halligan Bar was a specialized forcible entry used by firefighters and police agencies the world over.

"And the noise!" said Dan. The Halligan had to be set or driven into place by another tool. Firefighters used flathead axes, cops sledgehammers. Either way, it wasn't a quiet operation. "The bedroom is pretty well-preserved. Your old man had a panic alarm right there on his bed, and a pretty badass door he could close and lock."

"And a Walther 9 mil in the nightstand."

He nodded. "We found it in the closed drawer."

I shook my head.

"But." Dan studied the jamb and door for fine marks. The fire oxidized anything that had been there into oblivion. "The uniform pattern of five inches is consistent with some kind of specialty tool. Like a..."

"Rabbit Tool." The Rabbit Tool was another specialty device used in fire and police departments. It was a portable tool with a five-inch jaw powered by a manual lever. The lever operated a hydraulic pump similar to a floor jack. One person could wedge it between the jamb and the door and generate eight thousand pounds of pressure with a few strokes. More than enough to pry our little security door.

"And ain't a whole lot of folks running around with a Rabbit Tool in their pockets. I pointed that out to Mason in front of Price, and he drew the line to you." He averted his eyes. "Sorry."

"Don't worry about it. Price didn't need you to zero in on me."

"I tried to argue that you had a key and would never cover your tracks with a tool you were likely to have access to."

"What about a robbery crew?" I didn't believe it, but I wanted his thoughts.

"Some of the high-end guys use hydraulic entry tools like that, but for your dad's place?" He shook his head. "Too high-risk for too little reward. Plus, there's the fire. There's enough accelerant in there to get a rocket into orbit. No crew in the state uses that MO or we would know it."

"So our perp was more interested in destroying what was in there than getting it out."

"Or at least willing to settle for that," Dan agreed. "We think your father's desktop is in that heap of twisted plastic and metal, but there's no way to be sure. The perp could have taken it with him."

I nodded and looked past the car lot to our north toward the state fairgrounds only blocks away.

"What are you thinking, Lo?"

What was I thinking? I tried not to laugh. A skip I'd taken in was killed in SO custody hours after he told me it would happen. A member of the Iron Pirate Motorcycle Club killed him with a knife smuggled through SO-controlled choke points. I was on the verge of turning a video clip featuring a member of that same club over to law enforcement when someone broke in, took that clip, and burned Pops' business to the ground, sending him to ICU. And the only person who knew that was the SO sergeant who was supposed to take custody of this clue less than an hour after the fire. Now, Dan and I discovered evidence that the perps used a tool exclusive to fire rescue and law enforcement circles. "Not good things, Dan. Not good things, at all."

Dan waited. Perhaps he knew what I would say before I did.

"Look. I wanna tell you some things, but it has to stay out of your report. Pops is in the ICU over this, and I don't know where it's coming from. Until I do..."

"Where what's coming from?"

"I'd like your help. I'll feed you what I have. You're welcome to follow up on it any way you like."

"I hear a 'but' coming."

I smiled. "But you can't source me, and you can't use some of my evidence in the file, at least not yet."

"That's not how this works, Lo. I'm a sworn law enforcement officer."

"And I'm willing to work with you as a pseudo-informant. But I can promise you this. You could spin your wheels for months and not get to what I have."

"I'm listening."

I told him everything, leaving out only Missy Perez and her role.

"And you hid this from Donner because of the timing of the fire."

I nodded.

Dan rubbed the scruffy stubble that had overgrown his face. "I'm in," he said. "As long as I can back out any time I want."

"Same for me."

"Deal." We shook hands.

STAYING BUSY

I returned home and started cleaning my wrecked trailer. Pyotr Karuchminov fixed the door, but everything else seemed as the burglar left it, and I wasn't sure where to begin. I decided on the floor. I put the big stuff back where it belonged: straightening and righting furniture, picking up items dumped out of drawers and knocked off shelves. They took a family pic from the wall; the back taken out, and the picture pulled apart. Thorough sons of bitches.

I picked up the pieces, found the glass broken and the cardboard backing bent where careless feet had trampled it. I tried to straighten the wrinkles in the picture. It was the four of us on the deck I'd built with Nick Rawlins, a driver engineer who was assigned with me at Ten during my firemedic days. We'd hosted a cookout for the crew with hamburgers and hot dogs. The kids ran through the grass, playing in the sun and frolicking in the sprinklers. It was getting late in the afternoon when we finally wrangled them for a pic. They were wet-headed and rosy-cheeked, with matted hair, but their smiles were the pure, unconcerned exaltation only children can manage. Even Val put aside her normal disgust for my friends for a quality afternoon.

I don't know how long I stood there, smiling through the tears, but I looked around the house and decided I hadn't the strength to put it back together. I sat at the kitchen table, haunted by my failures, and did what I always did in these times: found something to occupy my mind. My computer bag still sat at my feet. I pulled the pad with my notes and flipped through pages of my long, messy scroll until I found the background I did at the Brandon Library. Only two of the names I'd pulled from the company records were still in town. I could make both if I hurried.

North Park Professional Center was on the northwest corner of Dale Mabry and Pinecrest Manor. Aaron's Realty was on the north leg of the complex. There were only a hundred or so empty spots to choose from. I found one and turned off the car in the middle of another political ad telling me how Monte Silver was good for Tampa and how he would be good for Florida. The pic of my family together and happy on the deck gazed up from the lower-right corner of my dashboard display. I took a long look and stepped into the grueling Florida heat.

The tiny office had a décor more suited to a travel agency than real estate. A framed poster to my left showed a woman lounging on a tropical beach with white sands and an isolation that said

Caribbean rather than anything anywhere in Florida. Sweeping letters scrolled across the bottom read: "Get away from it all." The trademarked logo of a cruise line punctuated the phrase. Another poster showed off old buildings with a Mediterranean feel to them, but an airline sponsored this ad. The same themes echoed in the smaller, unframed pics pinned to the partition in front of me: skiing and mountain climbing. A chair creaked and a man with greasy blond hair peeked from behind a partition with a print of snow and rock on it.

"Help ya?"

"Yeah, I'm looking for an Aaron Duran."

The middle-aged man popped up, stepped around the partition, and offered me a damp, pale hand that was warm enough to make me wonder where he'd been keeping it. "That's me."

"I like your place. It has an exotic feel to it."

He looked at me the way a hungry jackal might a lame gazelle. "Yeah, my sister Kim and I share the space, but she's here most of the time, so she gets to decorate. She runs a travel agency."

Chalk one up for my detective bona fides. I glanced at the window.

He laughed at my unspoken question. "The signs are nonadhesive. Whoever's using the place puts their sign in the window. You're lucky to catch me. I'm usually on the road."

"My name is Walsh. I'm doing some research for the NTR Historical Society."

His smile fell into a confusion. "NTR?"

"New Tampa Residents."

The smile returned. "Oh, yeah. Well, I haven't sold a house out there in forever."

"Right," I said, "but you were the sales manager for a B&D Construction and Realty during the boom. Yes?"

His face lost its hungry predator look. I was losing his attention. "That was a long time ago."

"The corporate filings list you as manager of sales."

"That was my technical title, but I was really a glorified salesman. I mentored some of the new guys and helped keep the paperwork straight. But Mandy was the one who held it all together."

"Mandy?"

"Drexler."

Her name went onto my notepad. "She was your boss?"

His eyes narrowed, and he made a grab for my notes. But I was too quick.

"Hey." I spoke with more harshness than I'd intended. "Don't touch that."

He glared through narrow slits. "Who are you?"

"I told you, I—"

"No. I mean, who are you really? Because you sure ain't working for some historical society."

I held the pad

to my side and squared my stance. "I need a few questions answered. That's all."

Aaron was a few inches shorter and fifty pounds lighter. "You some kind of cop? Got a warrant?"

"No, but I am looking into Bobby Lee Kinsey's death."

"Who?" His face held no trace of recognition, and the question came out with such natural speed, I couldn't believe he faked it. "I don't know no fucking Kinsey, and I'm done talking to you, snoop."

"This Mandy Drexler. She still in town?"

"You're the one investigating. You figure it out."

I frowned and pushed back into the Florida sun. On to the next stop.

AN OFFICE WITH A VIEW

Traffic couldn't be called bumper-to-bumper, but it was no swift current, either. I took the better part of thirty minutes to cover the six miles or so from North Park to I-275 and another fifteen to reach the Ashley Street exit. The one good thing about the late hour was that it made parking downtown easier. I pulled into a spot darkened by the magnificent building's shadow and looked up at the thirty-one stories of the Rivergate Tower. The high-rise was also called the Sykes Building, because it housed the international headquarters of Sykes Enterprises and because it sported their name in red across the brow of the building's cylindrical form.

I strode through the glass face and found an elevator that carried me to West Coast Real Estate and Investments on seventeen. Giant polished oak doors the size of football fields opened into a cavernous waiting room of marble-tiled opulence. The hardwood furniture looked to be more for style than comfort, and a tiny electric fountain babbled from the table in the corner. The receptionist sat at a dark wood counter that felt more like a judge's bench than a greeting station. She was talking to a woman in a skirt suit in hushed tones.

I gave them their privacy and took a moment to review the pictures on the barn-red walls. They were an eclectic bunch in expensive, dark wood frames, and featured men who could only be generations of the same family. Tall, proud figures with strong faces, deep-set grey eyes, and distinctive, politician's smiles filled a variety of scenes with a common theme: power. Their hair started out a sandy blond, but greyed with distinction and without a hint of cosmetic dyes. These men wore their wealth with a casual grace seen only in old money. No ostentatious suits or gaudy jewelry. These men might own a Ferrari or Lambo as a personal toy, but they wouldn't try to impress you with it. Their status was a matter of course.

The other people in the pics were all different but kept with the common subtext. There wasn't a Susie Homemaker or Walt the Window Washer among them. Jon Gruden and Tony Dungy posed with the current generation in clear digital photos I could almost reach into. Older, faded pictures of previous generations smiled alongside greats like Lou Piniella and Tony La Russa. There were pictures of the dour-faced John McKay in his orange-and-white canvas fedora and a smiling Burt Reynolds from his Bandit Ball days.

But there were others as well, mayors and senators. One with President Clinton and each of the Bushes. Jeb was on the wall, too, along with a dozen other politicos and Chamber of Commerce–types I couldn't identify. Our current mayor and candidate for the governor's mansion, Monte Silver, was in this crowd, but it was an older picture from his first term in the late nineties. Two brothers of the current generation smiled from either side of the man, each towering over his sub-six-foot frame. They both had less grey in their hair than they did in more current pics, and Silver was half a man thinner with a full head of hair compared to the plump, balding figure he'd become today.

"Excuse me?" The woman in the skirt suit had disappeared, leaving me as the receptionist's sole focus. Her expression told me I couldn't afford it, whatever it was.

"Yes, ma'am. I'm here to see Mr. Richardson."

"Mr. Richardson." Her voice sounded as if I'd asked her to produce the President of the United States. "Do you have an appointment?"

"No, but I'm willing to wait."

She smiled at the quaint notion. "Mr. Richardson doesn't see anyone without an appointment. Mr....?"

"Walsh. Logan Walsh."

"Mr. Walsh. It's quite impossible. He's just too busy."

I forced a smile. "Can you please call him?"

"I'm terribly sorry," she said in a tone that wasn't. "But he's a very busy man."

I tossed a disgusted glance at the frosted glass wall and doors behind her. "Thank you."

She picked up the phone on the first ring, and I had a grip on the gold handle to the exit before she called after me. "Mr. Walsh?"

I stopped and looked over my shoulder.

She spoke into the receiver, her servant's voice subdued. "Yes... Yes, sir." She turned back to me, her voice carrying every bit of the stunned shock I felt. "Mr. Richardson will see you."

I glanced around the room searching for the cameras but failed to find them. This was too classy a place to let you know you were being spied upon.

"Through the doors, turn right. Last office on your left."

I strode down the corridor of frosted glass to a frosted glass door. A. Richardson, President and CEO was etched into its surface. My rapping knuckles made a high-pitched tink-tink-tink.

"Come."

I pushed the door on its hinge and beheld a view of the city that beat all my forty years of experiences. The Hillsborough River stretched from beyond my right shoulder, cutting the cityscape in the foreground and flowing into the bay. The top-down perspective somehow made it both larger and smaller at the same time. Three bridges crossed the ribbon of water that shimmered silver in the afternoon sun, the Leroy Selmon Expressway dwarfing the older Brorein and Platt Street bridges. The guitar pick of Davis Island stood delta-like in the river's mouth, Tampa General's new, fresh-looking face gazing north across the river's mouth at me.

Built-up high-rises framed the river's left bank, and I glimpsed the Tampa Convention Center beyond the concrete parking lot that serviced it. A couple of mid-rise condos stood on the right bank, but the concrete jungle of the city gave way to the green of trees as the landmass stretched to the west. Hillsborough Bay became Tampa Bay somewhere on the southern horizon, where a fleet of sailboats moved in a loose formation that brought to mind a school of fish. A yacht cut the water around Davis Island, and a pair of University of Tampa crew boats paddled south on the river.

Andrew Richardson slid from his workstation and posed in front of the window. He held a bottle of water I didn't recognize with soft, manicured hands. His grey eyes were greener in person than the lobby pics. His taut, sun-blessed skin was showing its first wrinkles. It contrasted with the bleached and starched Van Heusen shirt that was still buttoned and tied, though he'd shed the jacket that was certain to be lurking here somewhere.

"Mr. Walsh?"

"Yes."

He rounded his desk and met me halfway across the floor. "Drew Richardson."

My callouses scuffed his soft palm, but his grip was firm and skin dry. "Thank you for taking the time to meet me, Mr. Richardson. Your receptionist told me how busy you are."

He laughed and gave a dismissive wave of his left hand. "Please. We have them tell that to all our unexpected guests. The truth is, this place runs itself."

I took the offered chair and let him make his way to his before speaking. "I'm sure you had many busy days getting here."

His smile never faltered, but I got the feeling I'd set off a tripwire. "You know the old song. It's a long way to the top."

"I can only imagine. I was looking into your New Tampa boom days."

"Oh! Yes! We built half that place, you know. Maybe more."

I nodded.

"Of course, we were B&D back then, building and selling. Now, I just sell 'em. Less risk that way."

"More money in the other, I'd bet."

"We couldn't help but make money back then. It was hand over fist. Land that far out of town was cheap. And the demand for new homes! The banks couldn't lend money fast enough. But all good things must come to an end."

"Yes. Did you know a Bobby Lee Kinsey?"

His eyes narrowed. "Bobby Lee?"

"Yes."

Richardson shook his head. "No. Should I?"

"He worked for you building houses."

"So did several hundred others, plus subcontractors. Would you like to quiz me on their names, too?"

A cloud moved across the sun behind him, and all pretense of this being a friendly chat about the history of his company evaporated.

"This man ended up dead, murdered in jail."

Richardson leaned back in his chair and tilted his head as if considering how I would taste with garlic cloves and wine sauce. "The man from the news. The one killed by the biker gang. Wasn't he dealing drugs?"

"Bobby Lee stood accused but not convicted."

"And you think it has something to do with me." It wasn't a question.

I went for a reaction. I handed him one of the hard copy pics printed from Kinsey's video. "Bobby Lee had this. Do you recognize any of these people?"

Richardson took the picture, looked at it, and looked at me. "Where did you get this?"

"A video he sent me."

"He?"

"Bobby Lee," I said. "Do you know any of these people or not?"

"I've never seen the man in the leather jacket in my life. I assume the guy in the jeans and vest was one of mine, but I don't recognize him. The man in the shirt is Doug Ardendorff. He ran B&D's construction division. He must've overseen hundreds of homes. Maybe thousands."

"You know his whereabouts these days?"

"Sure don't." He handed the picture back. "So, what does this have to do with me?"

"Well, that is one of your construction sites, and that is an Iron Pirate in the picture."

"And?" He leaned forward on his desk. "For all I know, Ardendorff or this other guy were ordering blow for a company party."

"B&D have many drug parties?"

"We held company parties to celebrate accomplishments and goals met. Some of the staff brought favors. It was... technically verboten but..." He gave a what are you gonna do shrug.

Or maybe they let the staff bring their own to protect the company officers if they ever got caught.

"You looked over the lobby, the pictures. The Richardsons are an old family stretching back to this town's days as a backwater." He said it as if being from an old, powerful family precluded him from doing anything salacious.

"I'm sure."

He pointed at the door in a chopping motion, using all five fingers. "Now, I really am busy."

I left without another word, glancing at the pictures of him and his family yucking it up with Tampa's rich and famous on my way back through the lobby. *"The Richardsons are an old family stretching back to this town's days as a backwater."*

THE RIGHT PATH

I drove home and climbed the metal steps to my trailer, plastic Publix bags dangling from the wrist of my right arm, my computer bag in my left hand. I opened the door and elbowed the light switch, casting a sickly yellow glow across the pre-evening gloom consuming my home. The mess on the floor was still waiting for my healing touch.

I fired up the window shaker, set the bags on the table, and opened the fridge. It was just as empty as it had been when I spent my lonely night thinking about the kids. I emptied my bags, but a pack each of ham, bologna, and chicken thighs filled less than half of one shelf. A small ketchup, mustard, and mayo went into the door shelves, where I found an errant can of Mountain Dew hiding behind an almost-empty thousand island dressing. I snatched it up, popped the top, and took two glorious gulps of its sweet goodness.

The Publix cheddar slices fit into the empty drawer, and the pair of tuna four-packs sat alone in the pantry with the BOGO bread and twin tomato soup four-packs. I stood, admiring my handiwork, weighed the disparity between my income and expenses, and wondered what I would do when that ran out. Go on a diet was the only answer I could think of.

My phone rang, sending my heart into a gallop. It was Val.

"Hey." Her soft voice projected a wary probing.

"Hey." I tried to keep mine loose and relaxed. I failed.

"How are you with... everything?"

"Oh, I'm... I'm holding on." I gave her the latest on Pops.

"I know how close you two wer... are."

I loosened the vise on my throat with a long gulp of Mountain Dew. "Yeah." I was pretty close to you, too, but I left the words unspoken.

"Look... um... I... I'm sorry about last night."

I smiled and felt something like hope stir inside me. "I... understand. It's been a tough time for all of us."

"Yeah. I wondered if, instead of taking the kids somewhere on Saturday, have dinner here."

"Dinner?" That stirring hope became a bursting rainbow.

"Yeah. The kids would like it, and I think... it would be nice."

"It would."

"I'll buy some steaks, and you grill them?"

That iron grip seized my throat again, but I managed to speak. "That sounds great."

"Just dinner," she said.

"Just dinner."

I chatted with the kids and teased them about the looming school schedule. Neither was looking forward to it, but we joked and talked and laughed with fewer barriers than we'd had in weeks. Hanging up was bittersweet, and I stared through the window past the Karuchminov house and out at Sligh Avenue. It was bereft of traffic, but a man in a ball cap and shades stood at the end of the drive.

He took a pic of the park sign and walked west beyond my view. I frowned, my joy forgotten. Something about him felt wrong, or perhaps familiar. He was the height and build of the guy in the Damien's Pool Supply video. Did they have the same gait? I couldn't say from the little I saw. Plus, how well could I see from this distance in the fading sunlight?

I shrugged off the impulse to go out and dumped a can of soup into a saucepan. There was no milk, so I had to mix it with water. I'd also forgotten the butter, so I "grilled" my cheese sandwich in the toaster oven. I stepped away from the stove and stooped for a good look out the window: nothing. He was probably taking a pic for a friend looking for a place to stay. I put my meal in front of the computer and pulled out my notepad, eating as I read.

I tore into the sandwich, swallowing half-chewed mouthfuls, taking the next bite before the former had hit my stomach. It was doing terrible things to my GI system, and made it hard to keep the weight off, but two decades in the fire department encouraged speed-eating that would make a piranha envious. The sandwich was gone by the time the computer had warmed up. The soup was gone before the first Google search was done.

I didn't think I'd have much trouble finding the Richardsons. Andrew Richardson had described his family as dating back to the city's birth. That was truer than I expected. His great-great-grandfather, Argus Richardson, sold oranges and beef to the Confederacy and was still here when Henry Plant's railroad arrived in the eighteen eighties. He helped W.C. Brown and W.B. Henderson woo Vicente Martinez Ybor from Key West via Tampa's port. His son, Marcus, later sold cattle and oranges to Cuba and all manner of goods to the US Army during the Spanish-American War.

Later, they diversified and bought into a number of cigar factories through their connections with the Ybor family. The most recent generations got into construction and land development and turned their own ranches and orange groves into subdivisions, cutting out the middleman and generating more profits for themselves. They were instrumental in the Ybor and Tampa Heights revitalizations during the nineties and early aughts, converting old cigar factories into upscale flats and run-down bungalows into middle-class family homes.

I leaned back in the chair and stared out the window, seeing only my reflection in the dead of night. I thought about the influence required to kill Kinsey in his jail cell and decided the Richardsons were the kind of influential family who could call in such favors from government and criminal alike. I was on the right path. I could feel it, and it ran right to Richardson's Ashley Street doorstep.

The question was, where to from here? I reconsidered my notes and read through the first interview of the day. A name jumped from the page: Mandy Drexler.

NEVER LET 'EM SEE YOU SWEAT

Mandy Drexler set Hyde Park Realty up in a quaint two-story building with white stucco over white brick. It looked west across Dakota at the Goody Goody Burgers and the Hyde Park CinéBistro. The storefronts had all changed since I haunted the place as an awkward teenager come to see how the other half lived. Back then, the CinéBistro was an AMC, and we walked to Bennigan's for our food.

Asphalt had replaced Dakota Avenue's brick surface, and the shops up and down Swann were still upscale, albeit with makeovers that brought them into the twenty-first century. They had the clean, crisp look of freshly painted facades and newly framed windows. I recalled my days of youth and decided the new look was a step backward. The gleaming paint and fresh stucco lacked the character and refined elegance the block had during my days running here. Or maybe I was nostalgic for those days and anything that reminded me they were gone was to be loathed.

I crossed the street and finished my journey. An electronic bell announced my presence with a three-tone ring. Cold air that smelled of paper and brewing coffee slapped me in the face, chilling my sweating skin from the humid 9:00 am air. Her office had a different feel than Duran's repurposed travel agency and Richardson's projection of wealth and power. This place was cozy and chic, with just the right combination of comfortable furniture and empty space.

A denim-blue poly cotton blend couch rested against the saffron wall to my right. A coffee table with wrought iron feet and a glass surface sat at the foot, a collection of real estate mags and a plastic card holder posed on its tabletop. Floor-to-ceiling windows looked out at the sidewalk running along the building's north face and up the Dakota's paved surface, where it turned into a treelined lane of the wood-framed bungalows that dominated the city before air-conditioning.

The *clack! clack! clack!* of Mandy Drexler's heels on tile gave her presence away before I saw her. She emerged from behind a simple blond wood desk that sported a single stand of pamphlets and a business card holder next to a tall, woody-stemmed plant with drooping, glossy green leaves.

I wore the same jeans and T-shirt under an open short-sleeve button-down ensemble I'd wore in the day before, but felt none of the judgement I'd seen from the receptionist at West Coast.

"Hello!" Her voice was bright and bubbly and made me feel as if she'd been waiting for me to arrive all morning. She had the look of a woman who both took care of herself and had the help of judicious surgical supplements. Her pageboy-cut blonde hair was too perfect not to be from a bottle. Her tan was a perfect contrast to the woman's bright, straight smile. Even the tight hourglass figure under her grey skirt suit belonged to a woman half her age.

I'd looked over everything I could find about her over breakfast. She didn't appear on the later corporate filings of B&D, but she was on some of the original documents I had missed on my first look. Executive Vice President of Sales and again as CEO and President of B&D Realty when it became a subsidiary. This made her Aaron Dugan's boss during the housing boom of the late nineties but gone before the gold rush of the early aughts.

"Miss Drexler?"

"Mandy, please, Mister...?" Drexler stepped up to me, head erect, blue eyes glistening with welcoming confidence. She offered a slender hand with ruby nails.

I took it. "Logan Walsh. My friends call me Lo."

She nodded from behind appraising eyes. "Okay, Lo. It's a pleasure. How may I help you?"

"I'm a reporter, doing a history piece for the New Tampa Residents Historical Society."

Something flickered across her perfect, golden-brown features. "New Tampa."

"Yes, our records show you were on the B&D Realty management team."

"For a while, yes."

"And what did you do for them?"

"I... isn't this a little granular for a 'days of yon' puff piece?"

I smiled. "I'm a thorough guy."

She returned the gesture, but it had lost much of its energy. "I only worked there a few years."

I consulted my research. "You're listed as the Executive Vice President of Sales for the B&D realty division. Isn't that right, Miss Drex... Mandy?"

Her tan lost some of its color and her voice grew sharp. "I admit the name is a cutesy idea, and I was flattered at the time, but flattery is all it was. I wasn't even a proper partner."

"But you were an officer."

"On paper."

"In practice?"

"A glorified sales manager."

I nodded. "And the construction company was under a man named Doug Ardendorff?"

"That's right."

"Do you know him well?"

Drexler gave me a long suspicious look that said she didn't believe my journalist story for a moment, but she answered. "Did. He was there before I was."

"You both worked for Andy Richardson. Right?"

A smile broke over her face, but a fond memory did not inspire it. "That's right."

"How did that come to happen?"

"I'd just gotten my real estate license and got hired to sell for Bay Area Realty, another Richardson company. I was quite the looker back then, but I was good at my job," she said with a desperate urgency in her voice. "I earned my numbers. Drew... Richardson saw that and offered me a senior sales position with his new company B&D."

I nodded and scribbled.

"We were selling off parceled lots from his daddy's orange groves and cattle ranches in north Hillsborough and south Pasco. Ardendorff built the homes."

"And the two were a package deal."

"Right. We had several floorplans buyers could choose from with various trim and exterior options. We even had landscaping packages."

It was a common arrangement, but Richardson was profiting more than his contemporaries. He didn't have to purchase the land that had been in his family for generations, and he owned the construction company that did all the work. I flipped back through a few pages of my notes. "And then he made you VP in charge of sales."

Drexler smiled. "Sure."

"Sure?"

She shrugged. "It was a title. I was a glorified sales manager. Drew made all the decisions."

That tracked with my read of the man. "And so you made hand over fist until you left in..." I consulted my notes. "Ninety-nine?"

A cloud crossed her face. "I left in June of ninety-eight. Dre—Richardson kept me on the books until the next filing."

"Was that standard practice?"

She shrugged, her bronze skin paling. "I don't think so."

"So it ended on bad terms?"

Drexler smiled, but it was so forced and broken I thought she might cry. "This is hardly fluff piece material."

She had me. "You're right. I'm... a detective."

"Private?"

"I'm technically a bondsman, but I hold both licenses."

She had a decision to make. "So who do you work for, or is that confidential?"

I decided to play it straight. "The memory of a... client."

"Memory?"

"The name Bobby Lee Kinsey mean anything to you?"

"Sounds familiar." I showed her an old pic from his construction days. "I knew Bobby. He was one of our foremen. He had a good rep with the management. Was a bit of a womanizer... got around at the parties."

The mischief in her eyes and voice suggested she knew firsthand.

"Nothing illegal?"

"With him?"

"In general."

Drexler shook her head.

"You know someone murdered him recently."

"What? When?"

I told her and took her shock to be sincere.

"Did you ever know B&D to be harassed by local gangs?"

"Like the mafia?"

"Bikers."

"No. Never." She trembled. "And you think that has something to do with B&D?"

"He worked for them."

"Twenty years ago."

I pulled the still from the video. "You know these men?"

She glanced at it, swallowed hard, and handed it back as if it had bitten her. "Where did you get that?"

"Bobby Lee got this off a B&D construction site security cam."

"They weren't my locations."

I held the pic out and pointed. "That's Ardendorff. Right?"

Drexel studied the pic and nodded.

I fingered the biker. "And that guy right there? He's a member of the Iron Pirate Motorcycle Club. That mean anything to you?"

She shook her head, offering no voice to her denial.

"You're not a very convincing liar, Miss Drexler."

Anger ripped the shock from her face, leaving a sharp glare. "You listen to me, detective. I'm telling you what I know, what I remember. I don't have to do that."

"Look, I—"

"That was almost twenty-five years ago... I really don't remember what you want me to."

But the feral fear and rage in her eyes said she did remember. It also said, *"Push on at the peril of your life."* She'd given all she was going to for now.

I slipped her a card. "Call me if you think of anything."

Drexler said nothing but took the card.

I stepped out onto the Hyde Park sidewalk, cursing my butcher's cleaver technique. The temperature had risen during my visit, but it was the humidity that made the air so oppressive. I slipped Oakleys onto a face already damp with sweat and glimpsed a lone figure in the Goody Goody across the street. He sat at a high top, looking out at Dakota Avenue. The contrasting shadow of the restaurant obscured his features, but I was certain he'd been staring at me. His gaze was back on the menu before I let mine sweep up the street to a fresh sight that chilled the humid Florida air. A gold Acura TSX sat at the curb halfway up the block on Dakota.

The TSX was an Accord clone, and it wasn't there when I gazed through Mandy Drexler's north window. The sun's glare on the windshield denied me a glimpse behind the steering wheel. I checked my left. Traffic flowed on Swann, but nothing came my way. I stepped into the lane and looked back to my right and north up Dakota. The driver still wasn't visible, but the shape of the interior suggested someone sat behind the wheel. I strode onto the curb, looking at neither the man in the restaurant nor the car and slipped into the oven my car had become.

No cross traffic awaited me, and I did a rolling stop out of the parking lot and pulled to the red light on Swann. The Acura eased from its spot and approached at a crawl. I had no view of the man in the Goody Goody, but I suspected he was moving, too. The question was, would he hop in the Acura or did he have his own car? I would've bet the latter. Sharing a car in a stakeout was good for companionship, but being able to switch out lead cars and take alternate routes to get ahead of your quarry was the best plan in case of red lights or other traffic conditions.

The light changed. I banked a left, turning east toward Bayshore and Davis Island. The Acura made the light and fell in behind me. I played it cool and let him think I hadn't noticed.

AN INAUSPICIOUS VISIT

I strode down the hospital corridor, past the Intensive Care waiting room, and glimpsed a familiar face in one of the hard, plastic seats, looking down at his phone: the Jimmy Connors–wannabe from Tampa Palms.

My anger boiled, and I upped my pace. I rang the phone by the locked entrance doors and identified myself. There was a brief pause. "Come on back."

The nurses watched me approach from their seats behind the counter. I forced a smile onto my angry face, but it projected a meanness not directed at them. The apprehension they reflected suggested they expected trouble.

I found Mother in the chair by Pops's bed. She was talking, telling him something in her cooing, maternal voice that could be so assuaging.

I leaned in the doorway and crossed my arms. "I see you didn't come alone."

"Horatio was nice enough to bring me."

"Something wrong with your car?"

"You know how I get at times like this. My spells."

I knew all about her spells. "So you hitch a ride to your injured husband's bedside with one of your bunkmates? Man, you can't make this shit up."

Her eyes narrowed, and she spoke hushed words through clenched teeth. "Your father might be able to hear us."

I frowned. She was right. Many patients had awoken from comas able to recount conversations and the names of loved ones who'd visited. "He's limited to one visitor. I only have time for a quick stop."

She rose, tears in her eyes. "I should have stayed away. Clearly I'm not entitled to visit my stricken husband."

I thought of my argument with Pops in the car and of his feelings for her. "No, Mother. This is for Pops, and I think he would like you being here, even if Horatio drove you."

Her smile was equal parts victory and vindication. "I'm glad you see it that way. I'll go down and get a bite and come back up. Would you like to join us?"

I couldn't tell if she was that unaware or if she was gloating over her victory. "No. I have a lot going on today. Have you coordinated with Jeff?"

Jeff Mills had stepped in to take over all our pending contracts. Mother was still part-owner and was supposed to coordinate this. "I... haven't talked to him."

I rubbed my head. "Well, did you at least talk to Loretta?"

More silence.

"I don't have time for this. Call both of them on your lunch break, Mother."

"You know, Son, you could—"

"I'm very busy," I told her. "There is no way I can do this. Earn that highfalutin life you lead, or you won't have it anymore."

"Excuse me." It was the nurse.

"Don't worry." Mother didn't look at her. "I'm leaving."

She stormed down the corridor toward the exit and the waiting room.

I offered an apologetic smile but got a stern look of reproach. She passed into the room and checked the monitors.

"He needs peace and quiet." Her back was still to me. "So do the rest of the patients here."

She gave me a sharp nurse's gaze. "I like him having visitors, but not at the cost of stressful drama for him or the other patients. Understood?"

"Won't happen again."

She nodded. "Do you have any questions or concerns?"

We discussed Pops's condition. She explained they were still keeping him medicated, and his condition was unchanged.

"Thank you," I told her. "And I'm sorry."

She favored me with a warm, sincere smile. "I understand. We... know about her... friend. But I'm deadly serious. You pull a stunt like that again, and I'll ban you."

We parted as friends. I walked to the window and looked down on a view of the graveled roof and seagull poop.

"Sorry you had to hear that, Pops."

Only the rhythmic *hiss* of his vent answered.

"Mother and I. You know?" I sat by his side and leaned close. "Val called. She wants to have dinner, a family dinner. Maybe things are turning around." I thought of her betrayal. "Maybe you and I aren't so different."

My giddy excitement filled the room, and I hoped he could hear me. He gave no sign, and the moment passed. "I could really use you now, though. I think I'm onto something."

I told him everything: about B&D Construction and Realty, my interview with Richardson and Drexler, the tail I seemed to have picked up along the way. "I know my next move, though."

And I didn't expect it to get me very far.

TWO MASTERS

Hillsborough County Fire Rescue Station Thirty-one sat on Memorial Highway north of Hillsborough Avenue. It hid behind a 7-Eleven on the Sweetwater River. Most of the through traffic followed the Sheldon Road bend two hundred yards south of the station and probably didn't even know it was there.

The two-bay white firehouse with red doors was a carbon copy of Thirty-three and old Thirty-two, signaling the shared era of their construction. I pulled into the tiny parking spot on the north side of the station under a live oak and slipped through the side door.

It didn't surprise me to find all the lights off and the crew vegged out in front of the TV. The hours between lunch and time to prep dinner were called nap-thirty for a reason. I'd taken more than a few siestas in those big faux-leather recliners during the heat of the afternoon and couldn't fault them for doing it now.

A head popped up at the sound of my entrance. The face was foreign to me. I swear, the department was getting so big, I soon wouldn't know anyone who worked here. I held a finger to my lips and pointed at the captain's office to my right. He waved an acknowledgement and went back to resting his eyes.

Captain Lou Ross lounged in his bunk watching TV in the dark. He'd pinned his long iron-grey mane to the top of his head. A thick mustache drooped over his lip, hanging past the corner in a fashion that pushed the regs. It did nothing to hide the delighted smile that broke out beneath it. He leapt from the made bed onto sock-covered feet and embraced me. "Hey! Lo! No shit! How are you, my man?"

Lou was always pleasant around the firehouse and one to press the brotherhood aspect of the job, but the fire department wasn't the only fraternity to which Lous Ross belonged. A leather jacket with a silver skull and crossed chopper handlebars for crossbones hung from his open locker door. Rockers above and below the sigil read *Iron Pirates* across the top and *Tampa* on the bottom. The square with the *MC* was there, too. His scuffed, worn riding boots stood on the floor at the open mouth of his locker.

"How you been, Lou?"

He leaned close. "Sorry to hear about your old man. Marty is good people."

I knew he meant it, and I knew he would not like this conversation. But it had to be had.

"Actually, he's the reason I stopped by." I gestured toward the parking lot beyond the room. "You mind?"

We stepped from the air-conditioned sanctuary into the humid cauldron, making small talk about assignments and how his day was going. We cleared the rear bay door and paused at the north edge of the station's tiny parking lot. The river snaked east and then south around the station and flooded every time we had a hurricane.

"I'm looking for the guy who burned out my old man."

"Aren't the cops looking into it?"

I thought of Kinsey's murder and the setup that killed him. "I don't exactly trust the cops right now."

Lou nodded with gleeful enthusiasm. "Fuckin' A!"

"You know the guy who put Pops in the hospital might have connections to the Pirates."

The smile he was wearing fell from his face as if shot.

"What?" The happy-go-lucky voice of a long-lost brother firefighter took on a grave defensive edge that warned me to take care with my words.

"Pops and I had just taken a fugitive back to Falkenburg. The man was... concerned for his safety. One of your boys killed him in less than twenty-four hours."

"Hey, bro. I don't know shit about shit, but if Leon did that man, he had it coming."

Had it coming. A flicker of rage brought heat to my face. "Well, he killed him with a fucking knife, Lou. A knife, not a shiv, a knife brought into the jail through SO security. That sound like a spur-of-the-moment killing or a planned hit?"

"That ain't how we roll, man."

"No? Tell that to Big Al Krauss." Big Al had been a member of the Iron Pirates before St. Pete PD found him in the mangroves on Fourth Street, most of his head removed by a shotgun.

"I don't know what you're talking about."

"Wasn't he one of yours?"

"He was a fucking narc, man."

Lou's voice echoed off the station wall two hundred feet away. I gave him a second, and he took a step back toward the station. My hand found his wrist. The man who turned on me wasn't Captain Lou Ross anymore. It was "Ironman" Ross, Pirate enforcer. "Maybe you should leave it with Mason and her people. You're in over your head."

I pulled a printed image from my pocket and shoved it into his face. "This is from a video the asshole who burned my father was after. I have nothing but these pics left. You understand? They burned the rest up. My skip sent this video to me... the same skip who told me he'd be dead and was killed by your boy, Leon, hours later."

Lou studied the pic, rage leaking from his expression. He shoved it away, stubborn defiance replacing his anger. "I took a blood oath."

"You took an oath here, or did you forget about that one?"

"This is different. You want me to be a narc."

"I want you to back up all those comforting words about how sorry you are about Pops."

The sting of guilt touched his eyes. "You're asking me to betray my brothers."

"I'm asking you to step up for your brother, the one laying in a TGH hospital bed."

The babbling of the Sweetwater and *swish* of distant traffic filled the red-faced silence between us.

A long beep echoed from the apparatus bay. The female robot spoke in her soothing tone. *"Engine Thirty-one, respond to, fall injury..."*

"You can't serve two masters, Lou. Eventually, you have to make a choice."

"I gotta go. Don't be here when I come back."

Lou crossed the lot, went through the yawning rear bay, and closed the door behind him.

I walked back to the Corolla and fired it up. I beat the engine to the mouth of the parking lot, but the door was coming up. They rolled out onto the tarmac fifty feet from me. The engine paused to drop the door. Lou gave me a hard stare. I stared back. The driver stepped on the air horn and Federal, breaking the spell. Lou reached for the overhead console between him and the driver, turning on the electric siren without taking his eyes from me.

The black-cabbed yellow-green engine went south on Memorial toward Hillsborough Avenue. I watched them go and glimpsed a gold Acura in the rear parking lot of the Publix across from the 7 Eleven.

TAILED THROUGH RUSH HOUR

Memorial Highway stretched south across Hillsborough Avenue before winding back to the east through the southern reaches of the expansive Town 'N' Country neighborhood. It bifurcated again, continuing east toward Eisenhower Boulevard, a road running north along the western edge of TIA or curving southeast on Independence Parkway. I called the kids from this bifurcation, the gold Acura in my rearview.

"Hi, Daddy."

"Hey, Princess! How are you?"

"Good. Mommy says you're coming for dinner on Saturday."

I followed Independence back to the southeast and toward the on-ramp to merge with the Veteran's where it ceased to be a toll road on its course to become the southernmost section of Memorial Highway. "Sure am. I wouldn't miss it."

The Acura behind me didn't say so, but I didn't think he'd be missing it, either. I frowned.

"We have a surprise for you."

"Oh?" Traffic was heavy but flowing, and I had to be careful which lane I took or I'd be on the road to Clearwater. I stuck left but kept a close eye on the signs and traffic. I'd need to take a right ramp soon. "What surprise?"

"It's a surprise." She spoke with that childish gloat of "I know something you don't know."

I grinned and made my turn. A monster plane came in for a landing, its rumbling engines piercing the passenger compartment. "Oh, well, I can't wait to find out what it is."

Her giggle grew my smile two sizes. "Love you."

"Love you."

"Let me talk to your brother."

"Hey, Dad."

"Hey, Son." The traffic stopped at the 275 North on-ramp, and I knew it was stop-and-go from here. "Enjoying your last days of summer?"

"Yeah, Pete and I have been gaming."

I frowned. "You can go outside, you know."

"Dad."

The whine in his voice irritated me, but I didn't push it. I had five minutes and wouldn't waste it fighting. "Okay, it's your summer break. Maybe we'll throw the ball or something when I come by."

"Okay."

"I'm holding you to it. Is your mother there?"

"Yep."

"Lemme talk to her. Love you."

"Love you, Dad."

"Hello." Val's voice was soft and sweet.

"Hey, how are you?"

"I'm good. How's Pops?"

We moved ten feet and stopped. I glanced in my rearview. The Acura was several lengths back, but he could afford to be in this gridlock. "Unchanged. I saw Mother, today."

"How did that go?"

"The usual."

"I hope you weren't too harsh." Val always thought I was being too hard on people.

"I'll be more careful in the future."

A silence stretched between us, but I couldn't qualify it. Doubt? Uncertainty? Judgement?

I broke it. "You okay?"

"Yeah." But her voice was different.

Panic replaced the serenity and hope I'd clung to. I was messing this up. "Look, Val, I'm sorry. I just..."

"Look, I have to go."

"No! I mean. Shouldn't we... I just wanted to explain."

"I don't want to do this right now. Okay?"

It wasn't. But what was I supposed to say?

"I'm hanging up now. Goodbye."

She was gone.

I looked into the mirror at the car now six lengths back. "Gonna have to deal with you, fuckhead."

I ground my way past downtown and through the interchange. The plan had formed before I was on I-4, but I couldn't get to the bank before 4:30 pm. So I came up with Plan B. I stopped at the ATM and used the business debit card to pull the maximum five hundred from its account. It wasn't what they were asking, but I had a plan for that.

I pulled into the trailer park with plenty of daylight left. My prize was still there, and I smiled at the Acura pulling past the entrance to continue west on Sligh. I stepped out and walked to the mailboxes at the driveway entrance. I stayed focused on the mail, but saw where he'd taken up a location on the north side of the road facing west. He was surely watching me in his mirror. I opened my mailbox, pulled the letters, and went through them one at a time.

The screen door to Missus Karuchminov's clapboard home was feet away. I stopped on the return trip and knocked. The action sent an icy shiver of understanding through me. The man I'd seen last night, the one I'd imagined taking pictures for his friend, he wasn't taking pictures for a friend. He was checking to see if I was home. I willed myself not to look west at the Acura and smiled through the screen door at Miss Karuchminov.

"Afternoon, Miss Karuchminov."

"Mr. Walsh! Is everything well?"

"Sure, sure, everything is wonderful. I wondered if I might come in and discuss something with you."

She opened the door. "Of course! Come!"

I stepped inside, strode past the chairs where we had waited for SO to process the house the night of the burglary, and into the gloomy confines of her home. She offered me food and drink. I declined.

I pulled the envelope out of my pockets. "Is that Ninja still for sale?"

She eyed the packet. "Yes! Yes, it is. Are you wanting to buy it?"

"I am, but I sorta need it tonight, and I could only get so much cash. Would you take five hundred down and the rest tomorrow when I can get to the bank?"

Rosalie frowned at the envelope. I thought of the concealed place they kept this bike for sale. "Or, I could rent it for a couple of days."

She looked at me.

"Will this get me a month?"

"Yes. A rental." She tried the word on and decided she liked it. "A rental. Yes."

"Good. Now, can I trouble you for a helmet?

THE HUNTER BECOMES THE HUNTED

The rain came as it always comes in summer: all at once. I listened to the roar and glimpsed the mouth of the driveway. It was barely visible in the grey veil of the deluge. Now was the time. I'd returned my bedroom TV to the dresser; a crack marred the screen, but it worked. I turned it on, set the sleep timer for three-and-a-half hours, and stepped out the back door.

The rain wicked off my slicker. It was county-issue, but I'd scraped off the black HILLSBOROUGH COUNTY FIRE RESCUE written across the back. There was only one driveway in and out of Country Square, but there was a footpath traversed by school kids and vagrants that ran behind a neighboring trailer park to a paved street called Barbara.

I pushed the bike through the gloom of thunderstorm, the canopy of oak and palmetto trees only providing limited protection from the cloudburst. The mucky, rutted trail wove through the vegetation. Discarded booze bottles and cigarette packs that could be from either kids or vagrants littered the floor of the wooded lot. A flash of lightning turned night to day and the cracking boom of thunder gave me second thoughts about being out in Mother Nature's temper tantrum.

Neither the rain nor the lightning did anything to assuage the clouds of mosquitoes that descended on me as I struggled to push the street bike through the mud of the trail. I reached Barbara and turned north on the block-long street, where I found a convenient pine tree to lean the bike against and looked west at the Acura still sitting in its place, five or six hundred feet west of where I'd popped out.

The rain slackened, but the light was bad. The windows had fogged up, and the occupant rolled his down. A hand wiped the mirror. He was having trouble seeing. I smiled, then remembered my reflective fire department–issued jacket and shed it. I doubted he would look for me where I was, but he wouldn't see me at all in my AC/DC shirt and black jeans.

The door opened, but the car's interior light stayed off. A slim man in dark clothes and a dark hat pulled low over his eyes emerged. He crossed the lonely country lane with his head down and that same purposeful stride. His hands stayed in the pockets of a windbreaker or hoodie protecting him from the drizzle.

He passed the entrance to the park. I missed the glance he must've shot down the drive, and he continued his stroll east, straight at me. My heart galloped, and I weighed my options. If someone else was in the car, and he left them to mind the front while he walked the perimeter...

The man stopped, shifted to take a peek between mobile homes along the eastern edge of the circle, and went back the way he'd come. He was much less subtle about his gaze on the return trip, but he continued to his car. The dome light stayed off, and he sat in that same spot, waiting for the better part of two hours. I rose from the bike and stretched my legs. I tried to walk off the cramps building in my back, but there was nothing to be done for them.

I was bent forward, touching my toes to work the stiffness out of my lower back, when the Beemer zipped west past my outpost. The red of his brake lights smeared the wet asphalt in crimson. My instincts said this guy wasn't coming to Country Square and didn't have friends on Timmons Road.

He pulled up next to my babysitter. They sat side by side, the newcomer's bright brake lights glaring in the middle of the street, the Acura dark on the roadside. I heard none of their exchange from my vantage point, but whatever they had to say lasted half a minute or more. The Acura's brake lights flared to life, and the motor turned. The white reverse lights flashed as he put the car in gear, and my babysitter eased into the street in front of his relief.

I thumbed the Kawasaki's starter switch with my left hand, but nothing happened. A brew of icy fear and flaming outrage broiled in my chest. I hadn't test-started the bike since I rented it. I slammed the handlebars with a fist, took a calming breath, and thought.

The frustration ebbed. I opened my eyes and looked down at the console. The key! It was still in my pocket. I almost laughed, whether out of relief or at my foolishness, I couldn't say. I drew it from the pocket of my wet jeans, slipped it into the slot, and turned it. The starter brought the motor to life, and I was in business.

My quarry went north on Timmons. He could play this two ways: turn around and come back up Sligh or loop north on Timmons. Either way, he would end up on Black Dairy. I gave him a ten count after he disappeared around the curve and eased the Ninja east to Black Dairy. The road was an empty tunnel of country night enhanced by a thick canopy of hundred-year-old oaks reaching their heavy interlaced branches from both sides of the road. No car could traverse its pavement without the headlights betraying it. I made the direct sprint in seconds, it would take a minute or two for my quarry to weave his way back to civilization, not that I would call Black Dairy Road civilization.

I swung the Ninja into a tight U-turn. I stopped short of the Sligh stop sign and started looking in my mirror. It didn't take long. The Acura rolled through the stop sign on Russel Drive, his headlights turning my way.

I eased the bike to the stop sign on Black Dairy and Sligh, made sure no one was coming, and took a long look at the Beemer. It had assumed its predecessor's spot on the north shoulder and was dark. I lamented not following the Acura up Timmons to get a glance at this driver, but such a move would have been riskier. The Acura could have made a U-turn at the end of Sligh and taken the quick way back or gotten suspicious when I appeared in the middle of nowhere and followed him out in the dead of night.

No, this was the more prudent course. I went east on Sligh and raced to the Flying J. The Acura surprised me. It pulled in behind me and drew up to the gas pumps. I took up station on the far side of the semi truck fueling stations. It was a conspicuous place to loiter, but I didn't dare get close enough to be recognized. I dismounted and sat with my back to him, my gaze on the phone in my hand. I used the camera to watch him over my shoulder without turning my head.

He pumped gas for almost two minutes and walked into the store, where he disappeared for six. I was back on the bike by this point and ready to follow. He pulled from the pumps, out onto CR 579, and down the west I-4 on-ramp. I gave him a lead in the moderate traffic and followed him onto northbound I-75, hanging back to give him plenty of distance. One advantage to tailing someone on a motorcycle at night was that I had great visibility but was so hard to pick up in a mirror, especially if I hung back. My single light would blend in with the forty or fifty headlights behind me, and the target wouldn't know I was there.

I practiced this for the four miles from I-4 to Fletcher, hung way back on the cloverleaf, and suffered a moment of panic when I came around to find the left turn light for Morris Bridge Road to the east yellow, turning red, and no gold Acura in sight. I gave the Ninja gas and flowed through the right-hand turn. If he wasn't on Fletcher Avenue, running west, I'd make a U-turn and see if I could catch him on the dark, lonely ribbon of Morris Bridge.

But fortune was with me; the Acura came into view. I got caught by a red light at Telecomm Parkway, and my prey's taillights shrank beyond a tiny bridge that crossed the Hillsborough River. The well-lit roads were empty, no cops were visible, and there were no red-light cameras. I took one more glance at the lonely taillights making the slow northerly jog beyond the bridge and dropped the bike into gear.

The lights grew closer, and I had to keep a tighter grip on our way through Temple Terrace and Tampa's university area. We passed Fifty-sixth Street and continued west, riding into a dense collection of low- and mid-rise student housing and the tallest nursing home this side of Canterbury Towers on the right and the University of South Florida campus on the left.

I gave him more space at Bruce B. Downs and let him turn north at the old University Hospital, and he wove a westerly course onto Bearss and then back to the north on Nebraska and east on Crenshaw Lake, where his brake lights disappeared onto a side street. I sped up and had to keep my handlebars straight at the last minute. He was waiting for a community gate to open. I passed him, his view of me obscured by the same hedges that offered me no warning of his presence.

I hit the brakes, downshifted, and brought the bike into a slow U-turn. I could have spun this thing on a dime when I was younger, but too much time had passed and too many of my skills had eroded over the years. It all worked out. The gate was just closing when I got back to the entrance, and my quarry was gone. The bike slipped past the lumbering gate, and it jerked back to open, the metal NO TAILGATING sign rattling against the sudden motion.

I glimpsed taillights on the first cross street and followed them to my right. The street, with its black lampposts topped by yellow globes placed in regular intervals, gave the neighborhood a quaint throwback feeling that made me want to look for Wally and the Beave. But Wally and the Beave never saw homes like these.

The sleeping neighborhood was one of vast, manicured lawns that spoke of professional services and paving-stone driveways with enough bricks in them to build a neighborhood of plebe houses. Tropical landscaping was the theme, and banana plants and rare palmettos drooped in the planters of most homes, forming jungle hedges that would require a machete to navigate if not for the brave work of the landscapers.

One home had a low, wrought-iron fence circling an acreage that would make some national battlefield parks jealous. A column of red brick stood every thirty feet and flanked the concrete path from the street to the front door and the matching driveway. Another home sat so far back from the pavement, I thought it must be on a different street, but the driveway running from its detached six-car garage to the large gate on my right said otherwise.

My quarry had vanished, but I glimpsed the glow of his brake lights on a driveway down a side street to my right. I took the turn, stopped on the corner, and killed the motor. I put the bike in neutral and backed it under the shadow of a gigantic oak, shielding me from the glow of the nearest streetlamp.

The man had parked on the far left side of a driveway in front of a three-car garage. The interior light stayed dark when he opened the door, leaving his face a shadowy profile. He walked across the front of the house in my general direction and ice slipped through my guts. There would be no playing this cool if he looked up at this tree and saw me.

But he kept his hands in his windbreaker, his eyes down, and walked through the amber glow leaking from under the palmettoes and liriopes in the flower beds. I lost him in the tropical foliage that flanked his door, but a wedge of light shined, casting his shadow across the lush lawn. The silhouette stepped out of frame to its left and the wedge shrank into nothing, leaving me alone in the dark.

He didn't reappear after more than an hour, and I drove past his home. The street curved right and then back to the left, following the edge of a retention pond that faced his home. I set up camp where the curve flowed back to the left, leaning against a slim oak a hundred yards down the street. This vantage point offered me a decent view of his place while putting the bulk of my bike behind a ground-level transformer shrouded by hedges.

I checked my watch. It was barely past 11:00. I rested my head against the tree and waited.

I'd always been blessed with the capacity to sleep in odd places. It's not always healthy and not always safe. But it was a god send in a career where the capricious needs of the public dictated the course of your day. I woke with a start when a car drove past.

My gaze went to the vehicle on the pavement seven feet away, but the window tint obscured my view. The driver took his time, and I got the impression he was giving me a hard look from his side of the glass. There was no way to know what he would do about it, but his Infinity Q50 kept moving.

The sky was already a pale grey with oranges and pinks showing from the far side of the pond. Songbirds were tweeting their early wake-up notes and the low, close-in whine of mosquito wings filled my ears. I swatted at one beast making a meal of my hand. The slick wetness and bloody smear said she wouldn't be making a meal of anyone else, but more low whining and the gentle brush of insect legs on my neck and face said my efforts were futile.

A dull, stiff ache that promised to make itself known for most of today or longer made it hard to turn my neck. I had vague recollections of a fitful sleep, of my helmeted head rolling off the tree and snatching me awake, of me removing the helmet and dropping it on the ground by the bike, and of waking up with mosquitoes descending on me. It was after 6:00 am, almost 7:00. I'd wondered if I slept through my quarry coming from his home, but I figured he'd likely sleep in and keep me tied up here until afternoon.

However, he had other commitments and, ten minutes after I'd decided I could take a piss break but seven or eight before I did, my quarry appeared. He didn't come from the jungle around his front porch, but from the garage. The door rose, and a vehicle slipped under. The sight almost took me from the Ninja in a fit of shock and fear. A Tampa Police Department cruiser backed out onto the street and drove away, turning left at the stop sign toward the exit.

I don't know how long I stared. Five minutes? Ten? But I knew with cold certainty everything had changed.

I waited another half hour and kept getting dirty looks and curious stares from travelers on their way to the office and retreated. I paused long enough to break federal law and checked my quarry's mailbox. If he was single or if his wife was as inattentive, maybe I'd get lucky.

I did and read the name on the first envelope that didn't say "Resident of." It was a TECO bill. I looked up from the mail at the house. "Hello, Mr. Diego Ortiz. I can't say it's a pleasure."

STALKED BY A HERO

I awoke to the pounding of rain on the metal roof of my trailer and the distant rumble of thunder in the sky. The house was looking better. I hadn't picked everything up, but I was doing it in phases and could now walk on the floor without breaking something precious. I started coffee and flipped open the computer.

An F-250 had replaced the Beemer sometime last night. I'd almost missed him parked in the grassy lot of the church across the street but glimpsed him when I made the turn onto Barbara. He still sat there when I made a fake run to the mailbox. I was an important guy.

I Googled Diego Ortiz's name. What I found sent me into a panic attack. He appeared on a PR release hailing his 2018 Officer of the Year award. The release called him a decorated officer who advanced through the ranks.

I read on. *Officer Ortiz survived an assassination attempt in August of 1998. He received the Purple Shield and the Medal of*

Honor for keeping his senses and taking the assailant's life. A bona fide hero was stalking me. Fantastic.

Digging up info on cops is hard to do by design, and I was getting nowhere when Dan called. "Late lunch?"

I weighed his offer. "You got TPD friends out there?"

"No one I'm really tight with."

"How about an acquaintance who'll shoot straight and keep his mouth shut?"

"Mouth shut about what?"

I told him about my evening adventure the night before. He whistled into the phone. "You sure don't do half measures when it comes to trouble, do you?"

"Apparently not. You got anyone?"

"Let me make a call and I'll let you know."

He called back in four minutes. "Bring Brocato's for three to Thirty-fourth Street, ASAP."

The Tampa Fire and Police Training Center's campus squatted at the extreme south end of Thirty-fourth Street and looked out at McKay Bay. It was a collection of single-story brick buildings unchanged from my days as an aspiring firefighter. It said Tampa fire and Police on the sign, but this facility had educated cops and firefighters from all over the state, probably the country. Hillsborough Community College once had a contract to train all its fire and police academy folks here, but they moved to a more modern facility up the road, relegating the training center back to the city.

I slipped out of my car and looked past the rows of portable classrooms that had sprouted up in the last twenty years and the four-story concrete tower where I had climbed and run and performed evolutions in my training days. Flocks of seagulls filled the sky beyond the perimeter, their shrill caws calling other birds to the feast that was the McKay Bay Scalehouse or, as the rest of the world called it, the city dump. The smell was especially fetid on humid days when the heavy air pushed down on the rising stench, spreading it across the ground and into our noses, and was our constant companion as we marched up and down the tower, learned to lay hose from a hydrant, and stretch it from an engine.

"The hell you been, man?" Dan sat at one of the concrete benches on the building's south side. "It's two O'clock. I called at 11:30."

"It was closer to noon and Brocato's isn't known for its short lines or limited wait times." Brocato's might've been the busiest Cuban sandwich shop in Tampa and had a well-deserved reputation as one of the city's best. It was a favorite among the firefighting community, and I'd paid for it with company money.

Dan turned to the woman sharing a bench with him. "Lo, I'd like you to meet Sergeant Tammy Schultz. Tammy, this is Lo."

Schultz was a petite woman with tanned skin and dark hair. She wore a midnight blue TPD uniform with a silver shield and offered me a hand. "Nice to meet you."

"Same." I handed her a sandwich.

"Any man who brings me Brocato's can't be all bad."

We all smiled, and I took a seat where I could look at her and Dan. "So, how do the two of you know each other?"

"Tammy was my academy instructor when I came through."

I took a bite of sweet ham and spicy pork and was so grateful I lived in a town with real Latin cuisine. The two of them reminisced on their time here, and we did the cop/firefighter shit talking that often arises between the two groups. It was Tammy who got us down to business. She looked at me. "So, you have some questions?"

I swallowed my bite half-chewed and wiped mustard and mayo from my mouth. I would have to tread with care. "Yeah, I was wondering if you ever worked with a Tampa cop named Ortiz, Diego Ortiz?"

Her curious face shrank into something suspicious, and she tossed a glance to Dan. "I know a little about him."

An open book these cops, but firefighters could be a tight-knit, protective crowd, too. "I think I'm on his bad side."

Tammy addressed herself to Dan. "This got something to do with an open case?"

Dan shrugged. "Might. We just wanna know if he's on the level. What his rep is like?"

The look that passed between them suggested this might be their last lunch date for a while. "Depends. He's well known, but his popularity is very hot and cold. Cocky to a fault, but backs it up when it matters."

I offered a smile as a peace offering. "Women want him, men want to be him?"

"More like he ain't the kinda guy you fuck with." She shrugged. "He's cool enough. I've seen him doing the bar circuit, always got a smile, always got a story, bangs badge bunnies two at a time. I'm sure you know the type."

"But?" I said.

"He's vain and arrogant and, even if he is *that* good, we get tired of hearing it. You know?"

"I know," I said.

Cops, like firefighters, need healthy self-confidence to step into the situations they did, but there were plenty on the job who took that confidence too far. These ultra-alphas also had other characteristics in common. "Personal life?"

She laughed. "What personal life? He *is* the job, man. From the moment he wakes up to the moment he goes to bed, he is nothing but a cop... and pussy hound."

"Don't forget lush," said Dan.

She smiled. Maybe they would have that lunch after all.

"So he's eaten up with the job?"

Tammy took another bite of her Cuban and talked around it. "Oh, yeah! Done all the bigs: QUAD, SAC, ROC." I gave her a quizzical look. "Tip-of-the-spear street crime shit. High risk, high adrenaline. They're also notorious prima donnas and dicks."

I thought of our special ops division and realized for the hundredth time how similar our cultures could be. "He ever get into any trouble?"

"I told you, I only know his name in passing, seen him at bars after big functions. I know nothing about his record."

I glanced at Dan. "So, one of the most notorious alphas in your department, and you want me to believe everyone doesn't hear about it when he gets taken down a peg or two?"

She held my stare for a moment. "This is courtesy shit for Dan. I don't know you, and I don't like being asked these questions by a firefighter trying his hand at police work, especially when he's asking about a brother officer."

There was danger in her eyes, but I pushed the issue. "This guy is running surveillance on me, looks like on his own time, and I gotta ask. Should I be worried? You can understand, right?"

She sighed. "You know about his Purple Shield?"

I nodded.

"The official narrative put out by the mayor's office was informant who tried to kill his handler, but got the tables turned on him."

I remembered the article. "A patrolman was this informant's handler?"

She didn't meet my eyes. "Word is he got into a beef with the informant over an off-duty issue, but the mayor's office covered for him because of some task force work he'd been doing at the time."

"And if it came down to believing the word of a cop or a street informant accused of trying to kill him..."

"Tie goes to the cop," she said. "Especially when the informant is dead."

"What kind of issue?"

She shrugged. "There was lots of speculation. But it was all rumors and suppositions."

"Like?"

"Like maybe I don't feel comfortable speculating, and don't really buy any of that bullshit, anyway. Ortiz had a bullet in him, you know. At least that's the story today."

"The incident hurt his career?"

She shrugged. "It was before my time, but since Mayor Silver is back, so is Ortiz. They made him Officer of the Year and sergeant in the same quarter."

I thought of Chief Price and the lackeys he'd promoted. "Politics matters. You think Silver'll win governor?"

"Can't say I'd hate to see him go, but I never really loved any of these shithead politicians."

"Some are definitely worse than others."

She shrugged and offered me a smile. "So, he's chasing you around, huh?"

"Apparently." I took a bite of my Cuban.

"I'd wondered why I hadn't seen him around here."

I stopped chewing. "Hadn't what?"

"Seen him around here. I told you. He *is* the job. He teaches it all: personal defense, firearms, breaching techniques, you name it. I'd see him around every now and again, teaching in-services in the portables."

In-services were classes taught to uniformed on-duty personnel. The topic could be anything from street skills to new reporting software. I didn't imagine he taught a lot of computer classes. "So he taught here off duty?"

It was common among firefighters and cops to teach on the side.

"That's right."

"How long ago did that stop?"

"Probably the last year or eighteen months." She looked past me into the covered courtyard surrounded by the campus classrooms and offices. "I should be going."

I nodded. "Thanks for everything."

"I hope I was of some help, but mostly I hope I haven't gotten anyone in trouble." She rose and pinned Dan with a stern brown gaze.

"You've been a big help," I said.

She forced a smile and walked inside.

I waited until her footfalls stopped and a door beyond our view opened and closed before speaking. "I hope this doesn't cause a problem for you."

Dan laughed, his white teeth dominating his face. "Nah, man. We're good. She might be pissed off for a little while, but there are other fish. You know?"

I nodded.

"I, uh, didn't want to interrupt your interview, but I do have some additional info you might find interesting."

"Yeah?" I cast an eye over my shoulder to the covered walkways and bricked in classrooms. "Maybe we should go over it in the truck. What do you say?"

"I say that sounds good to me."

"I've been doing some thinking ever since I found this guy out."

"Uh-huh." Dan pulled a file from an accordion folder while the AC struggled to bring a measure of cool to the broiling heat of the closed vehicle.

"Ortiz was Bobby Lee Kinsey's arresting officer. He was the one who found the two keys of coke at a traffic stop. But," I looked at Dan. "He's also the guy on the video who broke into Kinsey's home before the search. His walk and mannerisms are perfect. Plus, there's the Acura that conveniently passes by minutes after he's out of frame."

Dan gaped in disbelief. "A 'walk' and a vehicle that passed by minutes after this 'walker' left the frame. That's what you're going with? The State Attorney wouldn't twitch on that kind of evidence."

I frowned at his sarcasm. "There's what we know and what we can prove. Agreed?"

Dan nodded.

"No forced entry means he stole the key off the ring at the scene and broke in before the warrant could be served. Presumably to secure this video. Right?"

"Right."

"But it's not there, so he gets onto us somehow, hears I'm nosing around, and breaks into my home one night and burns down

Pops's shop the next morning. He teaches forced entry. He'd have access to a Rabbit Tool, either with the police department or from his training gig. His teaching credentials would give him contacts in multiple agencies like SO when he needs a knife smuggled between the lines. Or a couple of bad cops willing to run surveillance off the clock."

"You're being paranoid."

"Let someone break into your shit and burn your old man down after killing a snitch behind bars, and you tell me you wouldn't be."

Dan took a deep breath and let it go. "Well, I'm afraid I'm not gonna to do much to set your mind at ease. Tammy's rumor, the one about the shooting?"

"Yeah."

"Pretty accurate." He handed me the file, and I perused it as he filled me in. "He didn't just kill an informant-turned-assassin. He killed Tony 'Downtown' Townsend, a patched member of the Iron Pirates Motorcycle Club."

I shot him a glance and caught the victorious smile on his face.

"That's right, patched."

I searched for Townsend's pic and found it. The thick beard hung under a long, thin nose and dark angry eyes. His curly walnut hair a was a tangled mess from where they'd removed the headgear. I tried to compare him to the man in the shades with the bandana on his head.

Dan was ahead of me. "The quality of the picture and other factors make it impossible to know for sure if he's the mystery biker from your video, but the general appearance is right."

I sighed. "Him and every other biker this side of the pond."

We shared a grin.

"True," said Dan. "Got some details on him, though. Several counts of assault and battery, resisting with violence, domestic. He's the person of interest in a couple of arsons."

I flipped up the rap sheet and kept reading. "Anything special about the arsons?"

"Girlfriend shit, and a bar that threw him out after a fight conveniently burned a week later, but you know how it is with those things."

I nodded. Proving a fire is arson is rarely a problem. Proving who did it without the physical evidence destroyed in that fire was a very different matter. Scorned lovers who committed their crimes in a fit of blind passion was the only subset I'd ever known to be caught on the regular. Even people caught on video had to be filmed in 4K with hoodies down or hats off to meet the beyond a reasonable doubt standards of American courts.

"So, in nineteen ninety-eight, this... Townsend goes to a construction site to hassle Ardendorff. The security cameras catch it. No audio. But Kinsey gets ahold of it and keeps it and uses it, according to his ex-wife, to get some settlement money out of Ardendorff ten years later. But no one ends up dead then.

"Now, he suddenly sees this opportunity to get rich quick, even brags to his girlfriend about it, but he gets shanked at Falkenburg before he can cash in. So what's the story here? And why whip that old video out now? What, twenty years later? Why not keep pushing it when he was getting paid? Or anytime since?"

The full-blast whoosh of the AC blended with the muffled calls of the seagulls until Dan said, "A lot of unanswered questions there. Heading up to see Ardendorff?"

I nodded. "Back on duty tomorrow, but I'm leaving for Coleman as soon as I get off."

I'd found Ardendorff incarcerated in Coleman Federal Prison in central Florida for running an internet pyramid scheme.

Dan nodded. "Probably the best next step."

"Where are you guys in all this?"

Dan snickered. "Still looking through your old bonds, trying to find anyone who might hate your dad more than the average criminal. Mason liked you for it, but the closed circuit shows you in Thirty-two's parking lot seventy-two seconds after the intrusion alarm tripped at your father's store. Now, she's leaning toward robbery."

"With all those burned-up computers?"

He shrugged. "Destroying the video evidence of the crime."

"And Donner's going with that?"

"Donner's concentrating on the Falkenburg angle. Policing cops is where the glory is these days. I'm not even sure he's sold that these crimes are one big package. Of course, I don't get much contact with the man."

I tossed him a quizzical look.

Dan held up his hands. "All out-of-agency communications must go through the office of the fire marshal."

"Mason?"

"Technically Robbie's the contact, but Mason keeps him under her thumb."

I nodded. "So the big question is, what is the glue that holds all this together? What's the common denominator? And why go through all this now, over twenty years after this damn video was taken?"

Only the taunting calls of the seagulls deigned to answer.

YOU DON'T WORK HERE, ANYMORE

"You don't work here anymore." Captain Wayne McMasters was not one of our most popular members. The way he sat in my chair with his sock-covered feet resting on the counter of my office didn't help.

I gazed past him at the empty apparatus bay through the panoramic window behind him. "What the hell is that supposed to mean?"

He shrugged without taking his hands from atop his head. "Just what I said. You don't work here anymore. Been transferred. They hired me on overtime."

I clenched my fist, my mind trying to deny what I already saw with 20/20 clarity. "Bullshit."

McMasters gestured at the phone. "Feel free to call the battalion chief."

I did.

"Sorry, Lo," Battalion Chief Jed Winters said over the line. *"I just found out myself."*

I looked at McMasters' shit-eating grin and resisted the urge to curse. "But, Chief, I don't have any paperwork in, no disciplines."

"I know."

"McMasters is here. He can—"

"Lo, spare us both. I'm told this comes straight from the fire chief's desk, and we both know duty assignments are—"

"Management rights," we said together.

I offered a disgusted sigh. "Where do I report?"

"Forty-five."

A parade of outraged curses passed through my head but giving voice to them would make a bad situation worse. "Yes, sir."

I replaced the handset.

"Where you headed?"

"Have a nice shift, Wayne."

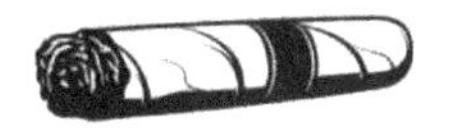

The black-over-yellow-green engine was returning from a call when I pulled into the lot.

"Fuck this place." Kraig "Dooley" Dawkins was a Driver Engineer at Twenty-one in Thonotosassa who'd ridden captain the day before.

"Tough night, huh?"

"Tough night? Tough twenty-five hours. You know there's no squad here."

I knew. Hillsborough County had once run a handful of pick-up trucks staffed by firemedics—firefighter-paramedics—to take medicals in busy areas in order to keep the engines free for fires and traffic accidents. Forty-five was surrounded by more nursing homes and medical facilities per capita than any station in the department, but administration had cannibalized the squad to staff a transport-capable rescue. It was a noble, if painful, sacrifice for the station.

"Twenty-three calls." He tossed his coat from the cab, followed by his helmet and bagged airpack facepiece. "Almost twenty of them to nursing homes."

"Well"—I stayed back to let him get his gear out so our stuff didn't get mixed up—"at least it's over for you. My sentence is more permanent."

"Yeah." Kraig reached for a canvas bag on the doghouse, straining his voice. "Well, gotta do it all over again next shift."

I smiled. "Coming back?"

He grabbed his boots. "Sure am."

"What did you do to Henson?" Ted Henson was his battalion chief.

He chuckled, glanced over his shoulder at the empty bay, and leaned close. "Speaking of chiefs, the word is Garrison has a hard-on for you."

I nodded and looked over his shoulder. "Good to know."

I let him get clear before placing my equipment, checking my pack, and signing into it with my fob. The county was working toward an electronic accountability system that would someday track us by our packs, know where we were, who we were with, and how much air we had. It sounded like a great idea, but cutting-edge tech was expensive, and we were still years full realization. I'd settle for radios that could broadcast from inside a building.

"Beep. Engine Forty-five, respond to, fall injury ..."

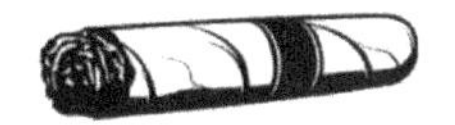

We got two more calls before returning to the station and found the chief and rescue gone when we made it back. I conducted our morning meeting in the cab on the way to the store, telling the crew a little about me and listening to their stories. I knew Driver Engineer Darnell Rhodes from my travels, but Firefighter Carlie Harris was a serving-since-oh-eight-hundred rookie. We agreed that training was important and committed to finding the time at this busy station to make it a priority.

It wasn't until the sun was down, the dishes were washed, and Battalion Chief Paul Garrison's staffing for next shift was done that I found a modicum of time to follow up on my leads from the Kinsey Case. I logged into the county wi-fi with my VPN and started surfing the net.

I was trying to make heads or tails of Ardendorff when my cell phone rang. "Walsh."

"Hey, brother. How's it hanging?" The voice was morose, but familiar.

"Dan?"

"Yup. I just wanted you to know they took me off your father's case."

"What?" Cold fear danced across my shoulders.

"That's right. Someone saw us together at Thirty-fourth Street and narced us out."

"Are you... okay?"

"Am I in trouble? Not so long as the union has a say, but the staff meetings are liable to be a little cooler for a while."

I nodded, even though he couldn't see me. "Well, thanks for being there."

"It's what we do, bro. It's what we do. You watch your ass. I heard Chief put the hex on you."

"Tell me about it. They moved me to Forty-five."

"Hush your mouth!"

"Oh, no. I'm serious."

"On C Shift that's..." I let him do the math between the three shifts. *"Garrison?"*

"The one and only."

"Je-sus. You'd better grow eyes on your back."

"I know. Sorry if I—"

"Don't. I'm in the union, bro. They can't touch me. I just can't do any more."

"I understand."

We said our goodbyes. I hung up and thought about the situation.

Who had ratted us out? Tammy? She didn't seem put out, but cops were trained interviewers. She could keep things close to the vest. I thought of the courtyard and the potential for echo in the space surrounded by brick and mortar. I tried to draw lines from Thirty-fourth Street to our headquarters, but the possibilities were endless.

Chief Price was a Tampa fire chief long before he was a county one. He must have a hundred connections to the old department, to say nothing of people he could reach through intermediaries. But why? Why this? Why me?

"Whatcha doing, Lo?"

I started and closed my computer in a manner I hoped looked casual. "Some surfing."

"On your PI case?" Battalion Chief Paul Garrison was a young, pleasant-faced man with a disarming affect. He'd dressed down into his plain white T-shirt with the HCFR logo on the left breast. He combed his thick hickory hair straight back. It was still wet with deep comb marks cutting through it.

"I'm looking into my father's injury."

He smiled, stepped into my tiny bunkroom, and closed the door behind him.

"You know, Lo." His voice took on the patient note of a fifties sitcom father. "When Chief Myers called me and told me you were coming, I was delighted. 'Bring him on down,' I said. 'We need good people in the First Battalion,' I said. And when I heard you on the radio, training up your new crew on day one?" He winked and clicked his cheek in approval. "That was good stuff."

"Thank you, sir."

"The thing is, Lo, I need to make sure you and I are on the same page. You know? I mean, the chief, he's worried that you might be getting distracted with stuff outside the job. He brought you here to restore focus."

Focus! I said nothing.

"'Well,' I told him, 'Chief,' I said, 'You don't get better people than ole Lo Walsh.'"

I nodded in pretense.

"I told him I would work closely with you and make sure we keep our focus where it needs to be. A battalion chief's station is quite an honor, you know." He was mostly right. Captains at chief stations were all supposed to be on the promotion list so they could ride as chief on his days off and take care of the paperwork necessary to keep the battalion running. It was a chance for candidates to show their potential and grease the wheels of advancement. It could be a punishment in other circumstances, an opportunity to put the offending captain under the thumb of an oppressive, eager-to-please, sycophant battalion chief. My assignment was clearly the latter.

"Most chiefs would be pissed that they couldn't pick their right-hand man in their own station, but I'm delighted to have you. You work with me on keeping your nose clean, and the chief'll need a horde to get through me to you."

The lights came on and the tones blared to send me to a traffic accident. I slid my computer and the papers from the counter into my bag, followed Garrison out, and closed the door. It was better than an hour before I returned. When I did, my computer bag was where I'd left it. I drew out the computer to get back to work and noticed something missing. The pics I'd held back. The last of the pics I had from the video were gone.

The station radio sent Engine and Rescue Four with Quint Twenty-six to an overturned vehicle on I-4.

I cursed in silence. Garrison.

The lights came on, the tones went off, and I strode to the printer.

The radio dispatch was a moment behind and a human dispatcher said: *"Engine Forty-five, Rescue Eleven respond to difficulty breathing in Grid..."*

HOT TIME

Val had always been annoyed by how easy it was for me to fall into conversation with a total stranger who worked "the job." We could be at the grocery store or mall, but if I saw an FDNY shirt or Hawtucket Kentucky Volunteer Fire Department hat, I could strike up a conversation, and we could talk like long-lost friends. And if it was a member of my department? Forget it.

Most people assume that bond firefighters share rises from the dangers inherent to the job and the need to depend on each other in tough situations. I suspect there is certain to be truth in that. But I never thought that explained the ability to fall into instant and engrossing conversation with people from around the country or around the world. The reason I thought most firefighters could fall into immediate conversation was the shared experience I lived that first morning at Forty-five.

I sat at the table, the entire station smelling of Cuban coffee and disinfectant. Darnell stood at the stove over an industrial-sized espresso maker, staring at it with the wasted longing of a punch-drunk alcoholic. Darkness still owned the window that looked out on Oakfield beyond and the trickle of traffic at this early hour.

I rubbed my sagging, bloodshot eyes, the green canvas logbook splayed open to a sea of red ink in my scrabbled hand. Five calls after midnight, six if you counted our 11:45 jaunt to Brandon Health and Rehab. Kraig Dawkins's words of twenty-one hours ago came back to me. "Fuck this place."

"Booch, Cap?" Darnell's eyes drooped, but his voice held onto its vigor.

"We got any milk?"

"Café con leche?"

"Extra sugar?"

He laughed but didn't tease me about my manhood for watering down the elixir that kept Tampa Bay's fire departments running.

"You need any help with those reports?" All our calls had been medical, meaning my only responsibility was to keep up the logbook. It was the driver medic's job to keep up on the reports.

"Nah." He waved a hand. "Two of them are Unit Assists. For the others, I showed Carlie how to do the demographics and upload the data from the monitor. I just have to clean it up a little and add a narrative. Besides, I like to let traffic die down, and if I can't get a little HOT time for six reports after midnight, we need to disband the union."

I grinned and rose from my seat. Hold Over Time was negotiated into our contract. Labor law allowed firefighters to be paid straight time for up to fifty-six hours a week. That was eight hours past the normal forty-eight Hillsborough County firefighters averaged. But our contract required we be paid time-and-a-half if were held up beyond our normal shift because of lack of relief, late calls, or other department needs.

"Milk's not hot," said Darnell.

I crossed the floor and took the carton from his hand. "I got this. Your relief'll be here soon."

"So will yours."

"We can only hope." I motioned at the tiny espresso cup. "That chief's?"

"Yeah."

"I got it from here. You worry about the engine."

The engine had to be washed and swept out for the on-coming shift, and that was the driver's responsibility. But Carlie would pitch in.

Darnell grinned. "Alright, Cap."

I mixed my milk and coffee, heated it in the microwave, and carried the booch to the chief's office. HCFR's official shift change took place at 8:00 am. Most people reported before 7:30 am. Most chiefs were in station by 6:45 am. It was just shy of 6:30 am, but Ken Borges was already standing in the doorway, talking about some fire he'd had.

He saw me and made room. "Lo! How are ya?"

Ken was the A Shift captain, but the timing of his arrival, his presence in the chief's door, and the white button-down he wore said he was acting today.

"Chief! Good to see you. Want some?"

He held up a RaceTrac coffee cup. "Maybe in a few. Right now I have fuel."

Garrison was still at his desk, his perfect hair a mass of dark tangles. The light to his adjoining bunkroom was on, and his bed stripped of linens. He met my bleary eyes with bleary eyes of his own. But his bleary was different; it belonged to a man who'd just awoken from a long night of sleep and was still adjusting to the waking world. Mine was soul-crushing fatigue from pronounced sleep deprivation.

"I hope we didn't keep you up and running all night, Chief."

He leveled a sardonic smile over the cup he took from my hand. "Not even a little."

I nodded and considered confronting him about the missing papers from my bag, but the conversation I'd rehearsed kept coming back to evidence I'd withheld from a potential murder investigation. The same conversation might be loitering in his thoughts.

"Got something on your mind, Captain?"

I held his gaze. "No, Chief, just tired."

My relief showed up at 7:15 am. Connie Haskins was a lean, strong woman with a pleasant smile and an excellent reputation both as a person and as a firefighter. I greeted her with a "Fuck this place."

We shared a grin, and I told her everything that had transpired in the last twenty-four hours, starting with our six after midnight.

I changed into jeans and Doc Marten knockoffs. I'd forgotten to add a shirt to my bundle, so I stayed with the grey HCFR captain's T-shirt and walked out to the parking lot, dreading my long drive to Coleman.

Robbie Stewart was leaning on the Corolla eating a pastry out of a white paper bag. "Mornin', Lo."

"Chief."

He pointed the bag's mouth at me. "Guava pastry?"

I shook my head.

He rolled it up and held it at his side. "Need you down at PSOC."

"Am I being held over, Chief?"

"This is a follow-up interview related to the Orient Road incident. So, yeah, I'm authorized to pay you, if you insist."

"I insist."

He wanted me to ride with him, but I insisted on driving myself. I had stuff to do, and I didn't have time to be shuttled back and forth across the county. He led me into the same back parking lot Dan had brought me to the day of the fire. We went through the same back door, past the Shift Commander's office and training into the front conference room.

Mason sat in her familiar spot, but she was joined by Chief Price and Chief Myers. Robbie left my side and sat on the end of this parade of brass. Myers was leafing through papers, making a show of holding some of them out and reading others. He looked at me over the tops of his reading glasses. "I thought you told us you had no insight into why anyone might burn your father's shop."

"That's right."

Myers nodded as if I'd confirmed some deep-held conviction. "And you know nothing about anything that's going on with the investigation. That right?"

I nodded again.

He showed the paper he was perusing to me. "Then what the hell is this?"

It was one of my missing pics from the video.

I suppressed my rising anger and withstood the disconcerting gazes being leveled at me by a panel that controlled the fate of my career with all the courage I could muster. "Looks like some kind of photo."

Myers glared, his Florida twang filled with anger. "A photo you were carrying around, a photo found in your possession, along with notes detailing interviews and research." I recognized my hieroglyphic scrawl on other sheets he brandished. They were photocopies of my notepad. Garrison could've had a career as a Cold War spy.

"Is it against the law for me to want to know who tried to kill my father?"

A long pause stretched through the room.

"Our concern," said Good Cop Mason, "is that you'll poison the stew, damage lanes of investigation."

Is that why you took Dan off the case? Is that why you control all communications between your division and other agencies? I glanced at Chief Price's five-gallon head, trying to see some kind of tell on his features, but he sat straight with his gold shoulder boards. Robbie stared past me, even when I looked to him.

"Where did you get this?" Myers again.

It was a jarring technique, and I was past being intimidated. "I don't know what you're talking about."

Myers's face pinked, but it was Mason who answered. "We recovered this from your office last night."

She read my expression. "The facilities belong to the county and are subject to search anytime we desire."

I imitated Myers's knowing nod from my entry. I gazed at Chief Price. "Is that your official position, then? You can go through my personal effects anytime you like? Tell me. Were any pics taken as to the location of these alleged documents you say you found? Were there credible third parties present to bear witness to the veracity of the location and contents of these documents? Do you have the chain of custody logged to show where these documents were obtained, and who's touched them along the way?"

A broiling hostility burned away what trepidations I'd had.

I turned my gaze back to Myers. "Would County HR approve these methods?" I looked at Mason. "Would the union?"

No one answered.

"Because I really hope this administration didn't just admit to sending a designee of the fire chief to sift through the personal effects of an employee in some targeted, off-the-books investigation that violates both county policy and the Firefighter Bill of Rights." This was the name given to the statute that set out the parameters for how investigations into uniformed firefighters were to be handled. "I've received nothing in writing. No one's told me why I'm being investigated, offered me union representation, or assigned me a case officer."

I looked back to Chief Price. "In fact, when I asked about needing a union official present in our first conversation about this case, I was expressly told you weren't seeking disciplinary action, and you told me your interview was part of an ongoing fire investigation."

I pointed at the sheaf of paper before Myers. "I'll have that back, thank you, and you will destroy any copies of my personal notes, or I'll put Local 2294 on the case and you'll be explaining yourself on the six o'clock news."

Myers opened his mouth to speak, but Price spoke first. "Give us the room."

His three stooges searched among their faces to make sure they heard that right.

"Please." Price's voice was quiet, but iron hard.

The trio rose and filtered out.

Price waited for the door to close. "That was quite the performance, Captain."

I tried to offer nothing.

"Some of what you say is true. Some rules were bent by well-intended parties acting on their own initiative, and, perhaps, this," he waved his hand as if searching for the words. "query we conducted here could have come across more heavy-handed than intended."

I couldn't resist a begrudging admiration for this man's cunning. He was cutting Garrison loose and would burn his entire staff rather than take the fall.

"I just want to head off this problem before it becomes messy. Before some intrepid reporter discovers you're investigating this on your own and starts speculation that might damage the department."

You mean you. I didn't dare say it.

"Surely you can understand how it might look to the public to find out one of my captains... who isn't even law enforcement... is running around this city like Dirty Harry? Conducting his own investigation and poisoning the well not just for us, but our partners at HCSO. And if it came out that same captain, a respected and trusted member of the community, had held back evidence from both this agency and the sheriff's office in an effort to protect this vendetta." He gave me a helpless, innocent shrug. "It would be on the six o'clock news for a week, with periodic follow-ups. The Board of County Commissioners would demand answers, call on me to take action I would rather not." He leaned forward, his ugly giant's face full of concern. "Maybe sic professional standards on us all."

Professional Standards was a section of human resources. They had a bullpen of ex-cop investigators who operated with a free hand and broad authority. They were renowned for being both thorough and relentless. "And there would be nothing you, I, or the local could do about it."

He sounded concerned for both of us, but Reggie Price only cared about Reggie Price.

"I'd like my papers back."

Price sagged and frowned in a way that suggested both resignation and annoyance. He stepped over to Myers' seat, sifted through the papers, and handed me the thicker stack. I knew what I would find before I looked: it was the copy of my notes. "The pics?"

"You can formally request them in writing, entailing what's on them and where you got them, so I can forward that to... the appropriate authorities." He flashed a victorious smile, and I left the room, bound for the Coleman Correctional Complex.

COLEMAN

Coleman Federal Penitentiary was a mass of bleached concrete on a verdant plain of Florida grass surrounded by twelve feet of concertina wire. I passed through what they purported to be medium security and felt echoes of my many service calls to Falkenburg Jail. I never enjoyed being locked up, even if it was only a voluntary submission scheduled to last a few minutes.

I took the chair on my side of the wired glass. A sign read Conversations Subject to Monitoring. The man on the other side of the glass had changed since his days as the construction manager at B&D. The segments of his sandy hair that hadn't fallen out had turned grey. His lean frame had gone willow thin and taken on a frail look that bordered on elderly. He sat, folded long, thick fingers together, and leaned forward on his elbows.

"Do I know you?" he said from behind quizzical blue eyes.

"No. I'm looking into a fire in a bail bonds office in Tampa."

"Yeah? Well, I was here. Been here since twenty sixteen."

"I know that, but your name and face keep coming up."

The smugness left Ardendorff's features. He glanced at my shirt, then back up at me. "You a firefighter?"

I'd forgotten I was still wearing the T-shirt but went with it. "That's right."

His face shrank in the glass, and his baritone became a hoarse whisper. "I don't know anything about any fires."

"I'm not here to ask you about the fire. I'm off duty."

"I said I know nothing."

"Look, man, I just want some background into B&D—"

"That was a long time ago. I don't know anything about any fires."

I slipped a paper out of my coat pocket and pressed the business side against the glass. The stills from the video were gone, but I had Townsend's mugshot next to Ortiz's city ID photo the papers had run with after he won the Purple Shield. I tapped Townsend's side. "I have a video of you talking to this guy. Not too long before this guy," I moved my finger to Ortiz, "killed him."

Ardendorff had been about to call for the guard, but he stared past the picture at me, cornered terror glittering in his eyes.

I tried to keep the momentum, get him to say something, anything. "You paid Bobby Lee Kinsey to sit on this video thirteen years ago, and someone else killed him for it now. Why?"

But the words I'd hoped would unsettle Ardendorff had the opposite effect. He chuckled and shook his head.

"Man." He stretched the word into three syllables. "Man, you have no idea what you're digging into. Do you?"

He leaned back and stared at me through the strands of wire running through the glass. "You think I'm gonna talk to you about something like that? You'd better bring a federal prosecutor and sweet, sweet terms before I even think about it."

Fatigue tore at the back of my eyes. My head was a swirling cauldron of ill-tempered frustration and poor judgement. I slammed my fist into the glass. He flinched. The guard on the door behind him focused his gaze on me.

"I need something to work with... anything."

A hand touched my shoulder. "That's it. You're through."

I glared up at the guard and recognized his stance. Left foot forward, right hand on his belt behind him, a promise of imminent violence in his dark eyes.

I nodded. "Just a—"

"Now!"

Ardendorff said something, but they'd killed the mics and speakers that passed sound between the glass. I saw "Mr. Off duty" cross his lips, but it was useless. I put the pic back in my pocket and rose.

The guard walked me to the exit and said, "I could cite you for that, misdemeanor disorderly. There are plenty of guards or supervisors who would. Pull that shit again in my presence, and I will. We clear?"

I held the big man's stern gaze. "Crystal."

I drove home in a rage, trying to make this all make sense. Ardendorff, Ortiz, and Townsend had to fit together somehow, but even if they did, what was the angle with Richardson and B&D? I considered the possibility that Richardson had nothing to do with any of this. That he was a victim of coincidence.

After all, Ortiz had ties to both his LEO contacts through his job as a cop and an instructor and the Pirates through Townsend. Maybe he was the brains, running some kind of bent cop racket I couldn't see. The notion had appeal. It might even be true for all I could prove, but I thought of those pictures on Richardson's wall and the abject fear in Mandy Drexler and Doug Aredendorff.

No, Richardson was in this up to his ears. I just had to figure out how.

My phone rang. "Hello."

"Captain Walsh?"

It took me a second. Garrison. "Yeah."

"Gotta deny your EOT request."

I'd made arrangements with Haskins before I left. "Connie acts captain."

"Now, see," said Garrison. *"That's what we were talking about before. Your focus is not where it needs to be, Captain."*

The friendly, "the chief will need a horde" protector was gone. The stern, uncompromising taskmaster had taken his place.

"That's fine, Chief. I'll take it up with the union. Also, never go through my shit again, or I'll go straight to HR if it gets us both fired. You hear me?"

Several light poles went by before he answered. *"I don't know what you're—"*

"Price already told me. He also made it clear that if I filed a complaint, he would deal with any overzealous supervisor who acted upon his own initiative and exceeded his authority. So you might need someone to stand between you and his horde."

Another long silence, and he was gone.

A ROADSIDE CHAT

I crossed over the headwaters of the Hillsborough River on North US 301, jamming to Slow Hand and *Lay Down Sally*. The lush, undeveloped landscape crept right to the edge of the two-lane ribbon, held back by guardrails in some places, barbed wire fences in others. I wrestled with the hypnotic glare of the sun across my windshield, resisting its soothing urge to close my eyes for just a moment.

I jerked them open, took a deep breath, and noticed the car behind me closing fast. Its general shape and low-profile light bar spoke of law enforcement. I watched for a tense moment and sagged when the lights flicked on. My speedometer next to the rumpled pic of my family said fifty-eight in a sixty-five. What had I done? Driven erratically? Crossed the center line in one of my moments of near slumber? I had no clue.

The guardrail gave way to another fence, and I saw the chance to get over. But the shape and look of the car struck me as off, and I felt a wrongness. I continued another hundred yards. He gave me a welp of his siren as a blue-and-yellow Sonoco sign came into view. I breathed a sigh of relief, signaled, and eased into the parking lot.

A pair of cameras mounted under the fuel pump awning looked out over the tiny lot. I parked at an awkward angle to reach their field of vision. The right side of the cruiser came into view during my turn; the familiar two-tone blue racing stripes ran its length, the words on its door distorted by the angle but suggestive of my fears: *Police City of Tampa*. I placed my phone in the cup holder, rolled down the window, and cast a level gaze across the top of my steering wheel and out my bug-speckled windshield.

It was him. I caught a glance in my mirror and tensed at his approach. Was I getting too close? Would I be going to Falkenburg from here? I remembered the feeling of passing into Coleman, the cold walls of the prison trapping me in away from the rest of the world and shuddered. He stood back from the door, a bronzed hand resting on the butt of his gun.

"Afternoon." His masculine tenor was pleasant, almost chipper.

"Officer." I didn't look at his face.

"License, registration, and insurance."

I willed calm into my body and fought the tremors in my fingers. I pulled the first two from my wallet and eased my hand toward the glove box for the third.

He took them and read, as if he and his friends hadn't parked outside my house for days. "Clocked you doing seventy-two in a sixty-five."

"I showed fifty-eight."

"It was seventy-two."

"I don't think so."

"Tell it to the judge."

"I will. I'll also tell him this isn't your jurisdiction. New Tampa ends a few miles west of here."

He studied me through his mirrored shades.

"Unless you wanna call an authority with jurisdiction for backup. If you're lucky, we'll get a trooper. I'm sure a city cop effecting a traffic stop on his highway for the terrible crime of driving seven miles over the speed limit won't put him out at all."

A car whooshed north and a tractor trailer rolled south in the time he took to mull over my words. "Maybe you and I should have a talk. I think there might be some misunderstanding here."

"About the purpose of this traffic stop?"

"About a lot of things. You wanna follow me—"

"Not happening," I said. "You wanna talk? Let's talk. Right here."

His roving gaze fell on the cellphone in the cupholder. The glow of the screen reflected on the seat behind it.

"I'm livestreaming this for posterity." That wasn't true. I could only record with the reception I was getting, but he couldn't take that risk.

The jaw of Ortiz's lean brown face bulged with tense muscles, and he'd have flushed had he fairer skin. He handed me my paperwork. "I'm gonna let this go with a warning."

Ortiz took his first step toward his car before I said, "Officer?"

"Sergeant." His voice was cold steel.

"Sergeant," I corrected. "Do you have a card? In case I want to have that talk later."

He studied me for tells, but relented and produced a card from a black case. It had his info, including his email.

"Thanks."

Ortiz didn't speak, but strode back to his cruiser. He climbed in, killed its lights, and pulled past me, heading south on 301. I watched him disappear and tapped the corner of his card against the steering wheel.

He was gone for a full half minute, then a minute, before I put the car in reverse and backed up to the pumps. I filled my tank and walked inside to buy a Mountain Dew to keep me awake. The man at the counter was South Asian. He smiled at my approach. "Bad day?"

I glanced out the window at the highway. There was still no sign of Ortiz. "Had worse."

I thought again of Sergeant Ortiz's business card in my console. "Could I ask you for a favor?"

We stood in the tiny office in the back of the store, stooped over a cluttered desk crammed against the wall. An LCD monitor stood above the mass of paper receipts and invoices. Five different camera views looked out from the split screen: three interior and two exterior. I picked the camera angle that showed our traffic stop. "Can I get that video right there?"

"Of course." A few keystrokes turned the five-panel display into one big view of the east side of the building. I had not parked as well as I'd thought.

I watched the video, and my face twisted in disappointment. My car was visible, but the camera focused on the doors and the fuel pumps and didn't get a good look at the plate. Worse, was the position of Ortiz's cruiser. The camera glimpsed him getting out of the car and making it over to me, but the top of the frame cut his head off. Also, his plate, like mine, was at a poor angle for reading. There were no identifying numbers on the front or rear quarter panels, nothing to set this City of Tampa police cruiser apart from the rest of the fleet.

But that changed when he returned to his car and pulled away. The instant before he left the frame, I got a good look at his vehicle number and city license plate. I grinned and pulled my phone from my pocket. "Can we run that one more time?"

Ten minutes later, I was in my car swigging Mountain Dew and uploading the videos from the CCTV and my phone to a cloud file. It took forever out here in the country, but my patience paid off. I sent the link to Ortiz's city email. I put *"Thanks for the Visit"* in the subject line and wrote, *"In case you try to give me the*

Bobby Lee Kinsey treatment, this visit will be immortalized by state Sunshine Laws."

I waited five minutes, then ten, for a response, but I didn't get one. I found a song on my phone that reflected my mood, took a swig of Mountain Dew, and headed south on US 301 to Steve Miller's *Take the Money and Run.*

UNION BUSINESS

The International Association of Firefighters Local 2294's union headquarters was a grey-trimmed white building tucked behind a pair of oaks on Fifty-ninth and Powhattan. The assembly hall's concrete and tinted glass both blended and contrasted with the no-frills metal-and-block buildings of the neighborhood.

I pulled onto the lot and lucked into a shady spot under a tree in front of the office, killed the Corolla's motor, and strode through the warm, humid air that promised another day of brutal temps. The union hall was cool and quiet first thing in the morning, though I could hear Jamie Dreyfus's voice from the president's office. His baritone spoke, paused into emptiness, and spoke again in a way that suggested a phone conversation.

"No," he said. "No, I know exactly what you mean."

Pause.

"Yeah."

Another pause.

"That's what I told him."

I followed the smell of coffee and sound of movement to the breakroom. Manny DeSoto stood before the coffee pot. He wore a blue 2294 collared shirt on a muscular frame and took Goliath bites out of an oversized apple fritter. He sensed my presence and turned his broad, swarthy face to me. It lit with genuine joy, and he gulped down most of what was in his mouth.

"Lo Walsh!" He spoke around the rest and wiped his thick black mustache. "What the hell are you doing here so early?"

"Hoping to catch you." We grasped hands the way Roman centurions might've and embraced. "They say it's a busy time for you guys."

Our union officers did a lot of campaigning during election season. Doing favors to help get officials elected so we could call those favors in when the Local needed help from the board or other organization. "Yeah, you wanna come along? Run with the big dogs?"

I laughed. "Nah, I'll leave running with the big dogs to you."

His smile eased into a frown. "Sorry about what that prick Price did to you, especially after your old man. How is he?"

"A day at a time. I'm headed out to the hospital now. I thought I'd stop and chat about this EOT bullshit Garrison is pulling."

He studied me. "Come on, let's take this to my office."

I grabbed a can of Dew and a bag of chips from the stash they kept for union meetings and followed. Manny's vice president's office was a modest affair, but it had a window that looked out at Fifty-ninth. The blinds were closed, but light spilled through it into the room. He sat at an orderly desk, backdropped by a poster-size newspaper. The headline read: TAMPA FIREFIGHTER KILLED IN OVERNIGHT BLAZE! The picture featured a burned-out wooden bungalow tied with crime scene tape beyond the nose of a Tampa fire engine.

Manny's desk featured fire department mementos. An Ahrens-Fox ladder truck clock flanked by an old-school brass nozzle and a paperweight shaped like a Ben Franklin fire helmet. A steno notepad with a fire hydrant stamped onto the paper stood at the top of his workspace. Even his pens were 2294 swag.

He leaned back in his chair. "So, what's going on with you two?"

"I don't know, Manny. I really don't know." We discussed how I thought Pops's injury was related to one of our skips and how I'd taken it upon myself to look into it. I steered away from the details of the case but told him about both the meetings on the day of the fire and the most recent one the morning before.

"So, now," I said, "not only am I transferred, I can't get any EOTs approved, either."

Manny listened to it all and let several seconds tick on his Ahrens-Fox clock before speaking. "You only come to me with this now?"

"The first time they interviewed me was hours after the fire, and they did it under the auspices of the investigation. The second time, I stopped it as soon as it became clear they were actively investigating me. That was yesterday."

Manny asked a few more questions about the meeting and who said what. What my responses were. “So you don’t want me to pursue these papers?”

“You can try, but I think Price is deadly serious about turning me over to the law if I push it.”

“Alright. I’ll see if I can back him down, but you really should have called me on day one.” Manny held out his golden-brown arms. “You can’t unsay your words, you know.”

At least it was a toned-down lecture. “You’re right, Manny. Sorry.”

“Jamie went to see him, your dad. We’re all pulling for him.”

“Thanks. That means a lot.” I rose. “I’ll do a better job of keeping my mouth shut from here on out.”

“No matter how good you are, you’re always giving something away.” It was his famous admonishment to new recruits. Hearing it aimed at me rankled, but I probably deserved it and hadn’t come to fight.

I looked over his shoulder at the glass-encased newspaper and the burned-out bungalow. I’d seen that pic a dozen times. Manny kept it in tribute to his brother. The fire hadn’t killed him, but it had left its mark on him. And something held at bay by the morass of my fatigue-laden brain punched through: Ardendorff looking at the Maltese on my shirt, how he kept saying *“I don’t know nothing about no fires.”* Not fire, but fires.

I stepped around and Manny’s desk and read the date I had never paid attention to: June 25, 1998.

“Everything okay?”

He said *"fires"* not fire.

"This is your brother's fire. Right?"

"That's right."

"Wasn't there a big controversy around this?"

"You mean the Seminole Heights arsons? Yeah. The city had a torch running free for eighteen months." He motioned at the front page. "Chelsea Street was the last of the bunch. The fire caught my brother and his firefighter in a flashover. It killed the firefighter. Ralph... never recovered."

"I remember my dad talking about it." He'd taken it pretty hard, but I didn't get it at the time. I was still a punk kid. "Didn't they catch the guy?"

Manny chuckled. "The very next week. They caught a drunk-off-his-ass vagrant with lighter fluid in an abandoned home on Taliaferro, right around the corner from the fire. Why the interest?"

I thought of the research I'd done into B&D. Sure, they had made crazy money in New Tampa and the unincorporated counties, but they'd cut their real estate teeth gentrifying Seminole and Tampa Heights.

Bobby Lee: *"That secret is my meal ticket, man. I can only punch that card once. I ain't wasting it on you."*

The video of Ardendorff, the man who would one day pay Bobby Lee his settlement money, and Townsend, a suspected arsonist, chatting alone, just the two of them.

"I don't know anything about any fires."

I tingled with excitement. "Do you think I could chat with your brother or someone from Tampa who'd run those fires?"

He studied me. "Is this related to the case Chief Price doesn't want you pursuing?"

"If I said it did, would you refuse to help me?"

"No."

"Then yes."

"You'll hear from me."

A SHARED PAST

I drove to TGH and found a crew from Rescue Thirty-eight visiting Pops. They asked how he was doing, and I thanked them for coming by. The nurse let them stay, but after ten minutes of reminiscing, she told us one group had to leave. We said our goodbyes, and they left to start their long journey back to Town n Country.

I told Pops about my visit to Coleman and my conversation with Ardendorff. I told him the same cop who'd arrested Kinsey pulled me over in the county. "They're getting desperate, Pops. Very desperate."

The words still hung in the air when someone knocked on the metal frame of the open door. Doctor Rajagopal was peeking around the corner, straight black hair framing her brown face. "Mr. Walsh?"

I jumped to my feet, wondering what she might've heard. "Yes?"

"I was doing my rounds. I thought this might be a good time to update you and answer any questions you might have."

"Yes. How is he?"

"He looks the same, but his swelling is going down. There are tests we can perform to gauge his brain function and other benchmarks, but we won't know how he's going to do until we try to wake him up." She paused. "And even a best-case scenario means months of rehab without pre-incident levels of recovery."

"Yes."

"His white blood cell count is elevated, so we put him on IV antibiotics to prevent this from becoming global."

I glanced at the labeled IV bags hanging from the pole.

"They are going to take your father to CT soon. You might want to stay in the waiting room, and they will let you back inside when he is done."

"Sure." I squeezed his hand and smiled down at him. "You're gonna be back with me real soon."

I shared a smile with Rajagopal and left.

I grabbed McDonald's, returned to the ICU waiting room, and started my deep dive into this arson angle I was trying out. A Google search only touched on events in the last decade, so I dove into back issues of the Tampa Tribune by date and started finding story after story. I gnawed on fries and a cheeseburger as I read.

The headlines read *Abandoned Home Destroyed in Overnight Inferno* and *Blaze Keeps Fire Crews Busy Late into the Night*. Sometimes I found them in the Metro section, sometimes on the front page, especially if they had a flashy photo to go with it. They shot one pic across the tailboard of a Tampa engine, yellow supply hose trailing out of the bed. Flames poured from a front picture window. Another told of minor injuries to a firefighter who stepped through the floor, another cut himself on glass.

The stories evolved from the all-night house fire to multiple fires blocks apart raging at the same time. I read about a pair of firefighters transported with heat exhaustion after rushing from one working fire to a second and wondered how long they went in their gear and airpacks before they couldn't take it anymore.

A map next to the column on the inside page showed a fifty-square-block section of Seminole Heights. One orange flame appeared on Osborne east of Fifteenth, the second west of Fifteenth on New Orleans. The articles changed from reporting the fires as individual stories to a broader narrative with headlines like *Seminole Heat!* and *Fire Terrorizes Local Neighborhoods*. They wrote of the human toll and the fear the residents of this poor community faced.

Residents were interviewed, people who said they wanted to move but couldn't afford it, and others said they didn't care and were getting out. The property value plummeted, and those willing to sell either couldn't find a buyer or had to take bottom dollar. It went on like this for hours until I came upon the front-page headline that read *TAMPA FIREFIGHTER KILLED IN OVERNIGHT BLAZE!*

The accompanying picture showed a firefighter in a white helmet with a red stripe on its crown taking a knee in front of the extinguished home, powerful spotlights turning night into day. The captain bawled with his face in his hand, grieving a lost friend and brother. The sight touched a nerve of grief.

I swallowed a lump and read. *A Tampa firefighter was killed, and another rushed to Tampa General Hospital after a fire in an abandoned house overnight. The fire took place at 698 East Chelsea Street in Tampa. The call for help came in at...* The story concluded with *Authorities refuse to speculate as to the cause of this fire or if it is in any way related to the spate of arsons seen in the Tampa, Seminole, and Ybor Heights area over the last year-and-a-half.*

A grainy black-and-white pic of an engine and ladder truck parked nose-to-nose with the burned home in the background. There was front page coverage of the funeral with the headline *Hero Laid to Rest*. The picture looked past rows of firefighters in dress uniforms facing off across the narrow lane of Memorial Gardens in East Tampa. The faces were somber. Unshed tears dampened eyes. Blue Florida sky looked down from beyond the heavy oak branches thick with Spanish moss.

I touched the screen and felt a two-decades-old loss pass through the connection. Grief's icy hand took me by the throat. I tried to put a leash on the runaway emotion and pressed on. *Tampa Fire said goodbye to one of its own today in Memorial Gardens...*

It talked about Jason Acres spanning back to his high school days when he turned from a future of athletics to one of public service. His employment picture was on the back page: a dark, unsmiling black face gazed out from above the pale blue uniform shirt of the Tampa Fire Department. The article quoted then Fire Chief Brandon Finch calling Acres a *"fireman's fireman"* and praising the youth for seeking busy assignments like Station Ten in College Hill. Today, College Hill was the site of some renovated, modern-looking government housing. Back then, it was the most notorious ghetto in the city.

A footnote in the article mentioned that Driver Engineer Ralph DeSoto continues to recover from severe injuries in Tampa General's burn unit. I supposed he didn't rate high enough for his own article because he'd had the temerity to survive. I frowned and renewed my search for updates.

It didn't take long: *Arrest Made in Tampa Heights Arson.* The arresting investigator sent my brain into a tailspin. He was younger, had a thick mop of dark hair, and his body, while still muscular, was leaner and harder. But, in the event I'd misplaced him, the captions read *Tampa Fire Rescue investigator Reginald Price takes Elias Walker into the Orient Road Jail after authorities caught Walker in an abandoned Tampa Heights home with suspicious items.*

"Motherfucker!"

I checked the date: July 6, 1998. Nine days after they put Acres into the ground and not quite two weeks after the Chelsea Street Fire. I went back, Googled Reginald Price, and found that the mayor appointed Price to fire marshal in October of ninety-eight, after his predecessor retired. The article speculated the previous fire marshal, a Mark Vinman, had left in disgrace after botching the investigation into an arson spree that culminated in the death of Tampa Firefighter Jason Acres. The articles made no mention of Ralph DeSoto's months in TGH.

I went back, sifting through article after article, and came to a new one. *Ybor Untouchables.* The story of the Tampa Heights Arson Taskforce. It was the story of an amalgamation of fire department investigators, police detectives, and a hodgepodge of support volunteers who accepted reassignment for the extent of the emergency. The article was long on praise and short on substantive info.

I took a cursory glance at the grainy pic with washed-out color before moving on and made the second startling discovery in fifteen minutes. One of the TPD patrolmen on the extreme left of the formation was a young Diego Ortiz. He stood less than six feet from Price.

They knew each other. Chief Price and Diego Ortiz knew each other. I tried to absorb that new information, figuring out how it all related to each other, and my cell phone jarred me back to the present.

Manny. *"Don't know who you pissed off, but the chief is backing Garrison."*

I looked at the pic of Price standing four people over from Ortiz. "I do."

"Well, it's an obvious violation of the contract, but I can't advise you to be insubordinate. If he tells you to be there..."

"Be there."

"Right."

An awkward paused filled the line, and Manny said, *"I have this political thing with the union tonight that's likely to go long, but my brother says he'd love to meet with you, if it has something to do with the people who lit that fire. Can you head down there this afternoon?"*

"When and where?"

CHELSEA STREET

Wellswood was a quiet community bordered by Hillsborough on two fronts. The avenue ran along the community's north boundary, and the river meandered along its east. The neighborhood was one of the oldest developments in the city. Its modest ranch homes sat on lawns that varied from weekly landscaper and horticulture treatments to "I cut it on the weekends, be glad I edge it."

Tall pines and heavy oaks that had seen the first Tampa settlers stood proudly in the spacious yards, sometime looming over the road in short tunnels of heavy oak and mossy beards, other times stepping back to give the place an open, expansive feel.

Ralph lived on Beacon, a street that sliced southeast from Hillsborough Avenue to River Shore Drive. River Shore was the exclusive section of the neighborhood and, as the name implied, the only street to have riverfront access. Ralph's single-story ranch stood behind a pair of short sentry palms, but they were nothing like the foliage at Ortiz's place. I pulled into the drive and decided he was more the "you're lucky I edge it" crowd, but the yard was well kept, even if it had a few weeds and a patch of blue-green crab grass.

The skies had kept their peace today, leaving the heat unchecked, but rain was only water on the sauna rocks, so I considered its absence a wash. Ralph's white door needed a coat or two. So did the entire house, but it was clean and otherwise maintained. I rapped, and the door opened with such speed, I decided Ralph had watched me cross his lawn and waited.

I don't know what I was expecting, but whatever it was, Ralph DeSoto wasn't it. He was taller than his younger brother and gaunt. Sullen eyes gazed from behind a drawn face. Silvery-white bristles too short to be a beard covered his jowls. Splotches of angry pink scar tissue climbed up the right side of his neck, disfiguring his ear and pushing the hairline by his cheek back an inch. It wrapped around his throat in choking fingers that reached across better than two decades. He looked eighty-five, but I knew him to be closer to sixty. A vapor cloud of whiskey fumes engulfed us, and an intoxicated luster muddied his maple eyes.

"Ralph?" I said.

A warm smile of relief creased his aged face. "You're... Logan, Manny's friend."

I nodded and took a warm, moist hand that was incongruous with the sallow paleness looking back at me. "Lo. Only my parents and the law call me Logan."

"Alright, Lo." Flammable breath washed over me. "Come on in."

He stepped out of my path, allowing me into a foyer of immaculate white tile and wood-paneled walls that smelled of citrus. Custom shelves full of old family mementos and pictures filled the wall to my right. Black-and-white images and early twentieth-century dress suggested the nineteen twenties, maybe teens. It showed the age progression of two families. The pictures formed two columns on the shelves, his and hers. The older pictures stood on the top shelves. The pics moved through the middle of the century to the early seventies, ending on a sideboard with a large-framed picture of a family standing in a front yard, a Caprice or Impala as a backdrop. A man in his mid-thirties with a woman in her twenties smiled at the camera, a baby in her arms, a toddler son between them.

"Yeah." Bittersweet adoration filled his voice. "Our folks, God rest them."

"You and your brother?"

"I was almost four. Manny had just come into the world."

It was a sight: pics dating back to the youth of grandparents in mismatched frames that represented every decade of the last century, and the aching love on Ralph's scarred face as he stared at the shrine. "Was your dad on the job?"

His mesmerized gaze sagged from his face. "No. He did work for the city, though. Accounting."

Ralph led me into a house that was a portal in time. The furniture was immaculate and straight out of the seventies. So was the white shag rug between the oak living room set and the white tile floor that was as clean as the foyer flooring. The cushions were denim blue with a pattern of white specks that couldn't be called polka dots. The love seat matched, and an oak end table stood at their intersection where a brass lamp glittered in its own yellow glare.

The entire scene was showroom perfect, no stains, no wear. There wasn't a scratch or a watermark on the top of the oaken coffee table and nothing short of battery acid was getting through the ten-gauge plastic cover protecting the seating furniture. The feature that most impressed me about the scene was the complete lack of dust on anything: tables, lamp, even the plastic coverings were clean.

Ralph led me to our left through a kitchen that was clean but not museum quality and out the sliding glass doors to his living quarters on the patio. The screened room looked out on a lush yard with a centuries-old oak as its centerpiece and a row of banana trees lining a sun-beaten privacy fence at the back of the property. A worn couch rested against the exterior cinderblock wall under the kitchen window. Two pillows lay piled on the far armrest, and a blanket and sheet lay entwined on the cushions. A bottle of Jack and an empty highball glass stood among discarded food wrappers and dirty plates on a battered coffee table that bore no resemblance to its better maintained counterpart in the living room. A TV playing Sports Center hung from a support column to my right.

Ralph strode to the wet bar beyond the couch. "Drink?"

"Got Mountain Dew?"

He gave me a look.

"I'm driving."

"Suit yourself." He reached under the bar, poured himself three fingers of Horse Soldier Bourbon, and gestured me to a metal-framed patio chair.

"Nice place."

Ralph nodded. "My grandfather bought it in fifty. Been in the family ever since."

The distant humming bursts of rubber tires crossing the metal decking of the Hillsborough Avenue Bridge carried across the neighborhood; the pitch and cantor of each vehicle was almost musical.

He handed me a can from behind the bar and leaned on the couch. "I hear you're looking into the Seminole Heights fires from the nineties."

"I am."

"Man, that was a crazy time. You know? Fires, I mean fires all the time. We were running one or two a week, sometimes in the same shift. And all a year after that pirate Silver gutted our budget and mothballed Four and Nine." Stations Four and Nine were the Ybor and West Tampa neighborhood firehouses. They had both seen their aerial (ladder) trucks put out of service to cut costs. Nine had since been restored, but Four was gone for good.

"I can't imagine."

Ralph sipped his bourbon, exposing more pink scarring on the back of his forearm. I tried not to focus on it, but he saw me notice and modeled the burns. The horror of what happened in that bungalow cut through twenty-four years and his alcohol fog. "Yeah, got these that last night."

I nodded, but had no power of speech.

"I was acting at Five. Wasn't even a promoted captain." He smiled and shook his head. "It had been a pretty good shift up to that point, and we had gathered in the dayroom watching a movie we'd rented from Blockbuster. Some Schwarzenegger bullshit. It was wrapping up, and I was thinking about turning in when the bells dropped. Rescue was out, so we were on our own.

"We pulled up on a balloon frame with heavy smoke." Horrified focus settled onto his still face, and his voice took on a faraway note. "A woman was freaking out on the roadside. She said..." Tears welled in his eyes. "Said there were kids in there, that she'd heard screaming."

He took long, loud breaths through his nose to rein in the emotions bubbling to the surface. "I heard nothing, and I didn't think anyone could be alive in there, but if they were closed up in a bathroom or something and gone unconscious..."

His pleading look begged for understanding. I tamped down my own emotion and nodded.

Ralph continued. "We pushed in the front, and it was hot, fucking hot. Couldn't see shit. The torch had poured it in the back, so we made our way across the floor. I don't know how far in we were when the black turned to orange, but the entire room blew up." He closed his eyes and tears rolled down his face. "Thank God for Rex. He was on Seven that day and pulled a two-and-a-half as a backup line. They were setting it up just as everything went to shit, or I'd be dead, just like Jason."

Ralph didn't give voice to it, but the self-loathing and guilt dominating his features suggested he had a bipolar view of that. I reached across the table and placed an awkward hand on his shoulder. "We don't have to have this conversa—"

He held up a hand and took thirty seconds to answer. "No. No. I thought… I thought I could talk about it after all these years, but… I'm good now."

I nodded and gave a squeeze to his shoulder.

He regained more of his composure. "I couldn't even make it to the funeral. I was his driver… his captain that day. I was… it was my decision to go in."

I tried not to imagine Carlie Harris laying in a coffin, put there by a decision I had made. "And the trapped kids?"

He shook his head, sniffled, and wiped tears. "Nothing. Who knows what that lady heard? Kids on the far side of the house. Dogs howling. Maybe even our sirens."

Stress caused people to see and hear things all the time, but you had to take them seriously. "You didn't have any choice. The lady said she heard screams."

He stared through me, his gaze traversing the years.

I decided no good could come from wallowing in these horrific memories. "And that was the last of the fires?"

Ralph rubbed his mouth with the palm of his hand, the crunch of bristles filling the silence. "Yeah. A week later they caught the hobo with the lighter fluid on Taliaferro."

"About that." I flipped through my notes. "Chief Price, he was an investigator back then?"

Ralph's face lit up, a lopsided smile pushing some of the grief from his features. "Oh, yeah! He was hot shit after that arrest."

"He had juice with the chief?"

"He had juice with someone."

"What do you mean?"

"He got to bring the bum in. His face was all over the TV and front page of the newspapers. Finch made him fire marshal less than six months later."

"So he didn't catch the guy?"

"He might've been there, but PD made the grab."

Inspiration struck me. "Routine patrol or one of the task force guys?"

His face screwed up in concentration, but the sun of recall dawned on his face. "It was a task force grab. They were patrolling the hood and caught the hobo, supposedly in the act."

"Supposedly?"

"I don't know. I never liked him as a suspect. We knew the guy. He was a regular. This homeless schizo alcoholic who was usually too drunk or DTed-up to stand was our master arsonist, who kept the police and fire departments stymied for eighteen months? That sound right to you?"

"No, it doesn't."

"He got off, anyway."

"What?"

"Yeah, they got him for criminal trespass and loitering, but all the arson shit?" He shook his head. "Didn't even make it to trial."

My research hadn't gotten to that part yet. "And they wanted him to go down for it?"

"Hell, yeah, they did. Jason's family... I... There was a lot of pressure... a lot of pressure."

"Thanks, Ralph. You ever wanna get out of this place and see the city..."

He smiled. "You're alright, Lo."

I nodded and searched for something to say, some way to take the burden from this man, but I left him in his misery.

NO RAT

It was another tough night at Forty-five, and, as much as I hated to do it, I went home for some sleep. I toppled into my bed at 8:45. The blissful embrace of sleep was putting its comforting arms around me when the clattering roar of motorcycle pipes shattered the tranquility. I cursed and rolled over, annoyed some asshole would come rattling into this tiny complex at such an hour.

But my eyes opened wide when the motors stopped outside my trailer. I was still trying to make sense of what I'd heard when a knock that threatened to cave my door in thundered. I eased myself from the bed and crept to the window. Three horses of iron and chrome leaned on kickstands behind the Corolla. I recognized the black bike with high, long handlebars and black tassels as Lou Ross'.

A pair of hard men in leather and denim stood watch. One looked at me through the window. No one in the neighborhood seemed to take notice, but a squad of troopers fast-roping out of a hovering Blackhawk would be more subtle than this crew.

The front door pounded again. “I’m coming. I’m coming.”

My footfalls echoed on the hollow floor, and I opened the door to Lou Ross standing on the metal steps of my abode. He glared at me. “I’m here.”

I glanced at his posse. They hadn’t moved. I stepped aside and let him pass. His boots were heavier on the plywood floor than my bare feet. He waited till I closed the door.

“Coming at me that way was fucking stupid.”

“Nothing I said was untrue.”

He glared. “Man, I ain’t ever been nothing but good to you and your father. Sent lots of work his way.”

That was true. Pops didn’t take Pirate bonds, but Lou knew plenty of people with potential to end up on the wrong side of an indictment. “You did, and I appreciate that. But Pops is lying in ICU after being piped in the head and set on fire. It revolves around a video of one of your guys talking to our murdered client’s coworker. I need to know what the connection is.”

“There is no fucking connection, at least not to us.”

“And if I told you I’ve since found out your brother-in-arms might’ve been part of a crew torching homes in Seminole Heights in ninety-eight, what would you say to that?”

Lou’s eyes narrowed. I’d provided him with info he hadn’t had when he set out for this place. “Well, he sure as fuck wasn’t doing it for us.”

“Well, he was one of your sold—“

"I said, he wasn't doing it for us." His booming words echoed off the thin trailer walls, leaving the room in silence. "And he was no rat."

That sent my head spinning. "What?"

Lou stepped closer. "He was no rat."

"Bullshit. I—"

"He was working a hustle on your cop."

"What?"

Lou glared, his voice low and threatening. "Downtown was trying to turn the pig into one of ours."

"Bullshit."

"That's so hard to believe? The oinker thought he was getting Downtown to do his dirty work, but Downtown was keeping score."

I considered this. "You were gonna extort him with it, get him to do your bidding."

Ross shrugged. "The pigs do it all the time. Why not us? Then Townsend got himself killed."

Ross glared at the door over my shoulder. "Shit went sideways. I tried to find out what I could, but my man wouldn't tell me. I just wanted you to know this pig killed our people, too."

What had Tammy said about Ortiz? *"... the mayor's office covered for him because of some task force work he'd been doing at the time."*

"He killed Townsend because Townsend killed a fireman."

"What?" Ross gaped at me.

"Yeah. Your brother Pirate killed a brother from Tampa. Put another in the burn unit. That was the hustle they were working.

Townsend was burning the locals out of their homes while Ortiz's buddy Richardson bought them up for peanuts and rebuilt them for an obscene profit. That was the dirty work Townsend was doing. Ortiz must've known about Townsend's penchant for arson and recruited him, but when Acres died, Townsend had to die, too."

"Bullshit." But it wasn't bullshit, and he knew it.

"Figure out how to live with that, Lou."

"Fuck you, Lo." He strode across the tiny living room, opened the door, and left.

RECONCILIATION

"Your father's swelling continues to go down, but now he's fighting an infection. We've upgraded his antibiotics and are rethinking his steroids." The compassion and warmth on Doctor Rajagopal's face blended with her quiet competence to project a perfect combination of humanity and talent I rarely saw. Or maybe me being on the receiving end for the first time fostered a gratitude I could only now appreciate.

"Thank you, Doctor. I mean it. You've been nothing less than amazing."

Rajagopal nodded, her dark hair bobbing with her head. "It is my pleasure, Mr. Walsh. We are doing all we can."

A fresh certainty Pops was going to die knifed me in the gut, and I watched her stroll through the ICU pod, past the nurses' desk. I coughed and wiped my eyes. Maybe it was Rajagopal's words. Maybe it was my general mood, but he looked so weak, so frail, and so close to the edge. Memories of him coming home smelling of acrid-sweet smoke and telling sanitized tales of firefighting that angered my mother blended with the fishing trips, teaching me to drive, and being there and the pride on his face when I graduated from the academy.

His skeletal hand was cold in mine and that knife twisted. "How are you, Pops?"

Beeps and *hisses* were the only answer. I offered a sad smile and let a few tears stream down my cheeks. We spent hours talking about the case, the Seminole Heights fires, and Chelsea Street. I went on about my dinner plans and my hopes to start putting my family back together tonight. I searched his face for a smile, an acknowledgement that he understood, but there was only the automatic droning of his monitor, low grind of his IV pump, and *swish* of his vent to answer me.

"I miss you, Pops, and I need you to find your way back. I'm not sure what I'm going to do without you."

The words were ridiculous. Losing a parent was a part of life, and Pops might not be as old as some, but he wasn't young. I'd always thought the specter of death would lose its teeth as we got older and the natural, inevitable order asserted itself on the loved ones who'd lived long, full lives. But I understood now it only gave them a bigger piece of our lives to take with them. I wiped my eyes, dried my cheeks, and left my father to the tender mercies of his antibiotics.

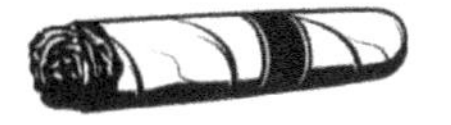

"Daddy!" Sadie ran full steam and piled into me, washing away the loss and worry I felt over Pops's deteriorating condition. I placed a gentled hand on her tiny back and squeezed. "Hey, little girl. How are you?"

She looked up with bright eyes. "I'm glad you're home."

"Me, too," I said.

"Hey, Dad." Christopher was more standoffish, caught between showing his emotions and being the tough, grown-up man he wanted to be.

I held out a hand and welcomed him into an embrace that brought us all to the edge of tears. I gazed up from Christopher's sandy blond hair and beheld Val. She stood next to the stairs in a loose-fitting Buccaneer's jersey over jeans that were less so, and brown hiking boots around her delicate ankles. Her hair hung loose with braided tresses that ran back along her temples.

"You look amazing."

She held back the smile, but glimpses of the woman I had loved and with whom I'd made a family shone through.

"The kids have something to show you."

I gave her an inquisitive look, but she offered an enigmatic smile. "Close your eyes."

I did, and the kids took me by the hand, leading me into the living room to my left. I let them lead me, stepping down where I knew the floor dropped. They led me half a dozen steps.

"Okay. Open your eyes."

I beheld the open passageway from the living room to the dining room. A homemade banner hung along the top of the doorway. It was white and covered in painted-on balloons I first took as polka dots. It proclaimed in bright crimson letters, We Love You Dad!

A smile cracked my face, and my throat grew tight with emotion. I gripped the kids and squeezed, breathing in as much of their hair as my lungs would take.

The afternoon rains held off again, giving way to a sticky afternoon that was almost as uncomfortable in the shade as in the sun. I stood on the wooden deck Micky Rawlins and I had built when we were at Ten together, flipping burgers and sipping Macallan. The kids intermittently kicked a soccer ball and threw it at each other in a modified dodgeball. Sadie squealed in delight and raced around the wooden play set I'd built for them when Christopher was four.

"They still love that thing. Both of them." Val sat on the bench we'd built into the banister along the edge of the deck. She sat with her denim-covered legs crossed and a glass of wine in her hand.

I sipped at the Scotch's oaky sweetness and smiled over my tumbler. I'd worked three shifts of OT to afford that play set. "They always did like that thing."

Memories of all the parties missed and afternoons lost to the uncompromising twenty-four/forty-eight of the firehouse schedule tainted my recall. Val read the sadness on my face. "They understood. You were keeping watch over us even when you weren't here."

The words made the loss more acute.

I nodded, fighting back against the darkness that always cast the fringes of my soul in shadow. "It seems they grew up without me."

"Well, you were always working two jobs, catching overtime." Val left off the charity golf tournaments and fishing trips. She didn't bring up the union meetings or the time I spent as the slowest receiver on the HCFR football team in the Firefighter Olympics. I loved her for that.

I closed the lid. "Maybe. But money isn't everything."

Her smile was self-conscious. "Can't change the past, but we can make today a happier time."

I reined in a hunger to kiss her and offered the lip of my tumbler.

She clinked the mouth of her beer bottle against it. "How are those steaks?"

"Oh, they're good." A broad, contented smile spread across my face, until a gentle shift of wind returned me to the moment. "The steaks!"

I tuned around in a flurry, yanking the cover up and sloshing my drink.

Val laughed. "You boys are so predictable. I'll get the plates."

We ate and reminisced and were a family again. Sadie gushed about her friends and school and the hopes she had for her teacher. Christopher was less sanguine about school and its exciting possibilities.

"You could always play sports," I said. "It would get you off that computer and outside."

He shook his head. "I don't want to."

"Your old man played football. It's good for you."

He tossed a glance at Val.

"I don't know. Football's dangerous." Val had always been less enthusiastic about sending our son off to compete in a physical contest with other boys who might be larger and meaner than him.

"So is life," I said.

Her frown deepened, and I forced a smile. "But if he doesn't want to, I'm not gonna push it."

"Okay."

The tension ebbed from her face, and she shot me a glance of gratitude. We sat around the table and talked for an hour, catching up on every detail of the kids' lives and the latest gossip from Val's circle of friends. Her closest friend, Julie, was pregnant.

"Is Dom the father?" Dom was Julie's husband.

She gasped. The kids giggled. "Who else would be?"

"That hanger-on that orbits your little girls' club. What's his name?"

"Gill?"

"Gill!" I said it as if the name had been on the tip of my tongue. "I've seen the way they look at each other, and don't tell me she lets any man rub her shoulders like that."

More giggles from the kids.

Val reddened, and I saw I'd chosen unwisely. "Look, Val. I'm just saying; the woman doesn't exactly strike me as the faithful type."

Val glared across the table, mute anger on her face. "Alright kids, time for bed."

"Mom?"

"Mommy!"

"Don't give me any lip. We've had a pleasant time and your dad and I let you play outside for a long time. So let's go." She rose, cast a gunfighter's stare at me, and walked up after them.

I was in the kitchen with scraped plates in neat stacks when Val returned from upstairs.

"What the hell was that shit?"

The good times were over. "What? Julie always was kind of a slut. We both know that."

"But not your fireman buddies. Right?"

I thought of Sam at Thirty-three. "There are plenty of firefighting sluts. Is that what you want to hear?"

"I don't hear you trashing them."

"Because you're not listening. We were just talking about Ollie before..." I thought I saw where this was going.

"Before I became a slut? Is that what you meant to say?"

How had I not seen that? Or had I? "So now I have to tiptoe around your feelings of guilt for eternity? Is that what you're telling me?" I sighed and looked at her in the dark reflection of the kitchen window. "I am trying to forgive you."

"Forgive me?" How could she act like she had nothing to regret?

"Yeah. For fucking your boss in that bed in there." I pointed a wooden spoon toward the master bedroom beyond the living room. "You might still be banging him if I hadn't gotten popped that morning."

She chuckled in self-righteous disbelief. "Oh? And where were you? How had another man become such a big part of my life without you knowing, Lo?"

I put down the spoon and glared.

"Not that it mattered. You didn't a have nice thing to say about anyone, anyway." She laughed again and shook her head. "Scott saw the path I was on. How lonely I was. How much I cried and how withdrawn I'd become. Did you? Or did you care about anything beyond how often you were getting laid?"

We'd all but stopped having sex for our last year under the same roof.

"I'm sorry if I expected faithfulness from my wife."

"Being faithful is about more than cheating, Lo."

A red silence settled over the room, and we glared at each other in the window's reflection. I saw the movement behind her before Christopher's tiny, fragile voice said, "Is everything okay?"

I sagged over the sink and stared into its stainless-steel basin. Val shifted her stance.

"Everything is fine. Fine. Your dad and I are... sorting things out."

I glimpsed both kids in my peripheral vision and tried to put the guilt and shame that muted my anger back on the shelf.

"Yeah." My voice sounded as desperate and empty as Val's. "We're just talking."

The shattered looks on my children's' faces said neither believed us, and I shared an awkward hug with both of them. "Go on upstairs. We'll talk tomorrow."

They nodded, tears in their eyes, and I turned away, tears in mine.

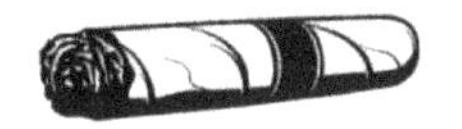

I'd left my shoes by the back door and my keys and wallet in the candy dish in the foyer at the mouth of the stairs. I had donned the former and was retrieving the latter when Val came down, her footfalls heavy, thumping on the treads.

"Well." Her hushed tone held tight to a bitter anger. "That was great. The kids are devastated."

"Are you blaming me?"

"I think we both played our part, but calling me a slut at the dinner table touched it off. Don't you think?"

I stared openmouthed. "Calling you a slut?"

My voice came back to me from the vaulted ceiling, and I cut my losses. "I have to go."

"Yes. I think you do." Val threw the deadbolt and cast the door open.

I stepped onto the porch. The rain had arrived sometime during our dinner. "I don't want this to be the end. We owe it to the kids—"

"Don't you dare hold those babies hostage! Don't you dare! We'll have to figure this out, but I won't have you hold these kids over my head or have you weaponize my guilt like you did today."

My gaze fell on a gold Acura sitting four houses down at the next cross street. The pent-up rage and humiliation roiling within me boiled over, and I stalked across the lawn, Val's voice calling from behind me, "What the hell are you doing?"

I ignored her and strode straight at the Acura, head down, phone held high, the camera recording the parked vehicle so close to the space my wife called home, the place where my children played.

"Diego Ortiz!" I shouted. "Sergeant Diego Ortiz! I see you, Diego Ortiz!"

The pavement behind the Acura flared red, and an upstairs light came on in the neighbor's home to my right. I imagined even more folks had the good sense to keep their lights off. The motor turned over and headlights flared to life. He flicked his brights, and I thought for a moment he'd dart across the lawn and run me down. But he went down the cross street he'd left himself as a getaway and disappeared from view.

I filmed the whole thing, but I never got a good angle on his license plate. I dropped the phone to my side and glared in his wake. "You won't get far, you son of a bitch."

A fresh light came on, my neighbor's porch light. I'd come to a stop in the middle of his yard. Frigid rain drenched my body, but Val's voice made it warm by comparison.

"Lo!"

She stood on our porch, Chris standing at her side, Sadie clinging to the other. I couldn't tell if they were crying, but they both looked terrified. My shoulders sagged in resignation. What had I done?

DEATH ON BEACON

I spent the night tossing and turning and had just drifted off to sleep when the phone rang. I fumbled for it on the nightstand and didn't even look at the ID before answering.

"Hello." My voice was as heavy and leaden as I felt.

It was familiar and brought ill tidings. "I'll be right there."

Manny leaned on the door of his Nissan Titan parked in the street across from his brother's house. A TPD cruiser sat in the same spot the Corolla had occupied a mere two days ago. It was running and condensation had formed on the windows, chilled by the AC.

Manny took his bloodshot eyes from the scene at my approach. I held out a tall styrofoam cup with a plastic lid. "Cafe con leche?"

He offered a weak smile. "Sure. Thanks."

I nodded at his gratitude and offered a Cuban bread stick from the grease-stained white paper bag in my other hand. He shook his head, and I used the truck as a breakfast table.

A metal rattle drew my attention. The American Medical Response crew wrestled an old model stretcher across the home's threshold, a human-shaped Tyvek cadaver bag resting on its thin mattress.

"It's too nice a day for this."

I looked up at the blue sky shining down; the songbirds filling the air. Even Hillsborough Avenue was a whisper. "Yeah."

One of EMTs got into the cab. The other checked with the cop.

"What happened?" I said.

Manny's glance confirmed the obvious.

"You sure?"

He nodded. "So are the cops. Ralph sent me a weird text this morning telling me how sorry he was."

The EMT walked back to the ambulance, and a pink-faced, red-haired cop stepped from his vehicle and crossed the street to us. He wore the same blue-black Tammy had at Thirty-fourth Street. "I'm turning the house back over to you. Sorry for keeping you out but—"

"It's okay, Officer," said Manny. "You had a job to do."

The cop nodded. "I appreciate that, and I'm sorry about your brother."

Manny offered a grateful nod.

"I contacted the funeral home," said the cop. "They'll pick him up after the ME releases the body."

Manny watched the ambulance pull away and nodded again.

"I'll be in my car for a few more minutes doing the paperwork. Let me know if you need anything."

"Thank you, Officer," said Manny.

"Thanks," I said.

Manny let out a long gust of air. "I guess we should go inside."

I put a hand on his shoulder. "If you aren't ready and need something in there, just tell me."

A sad smile slid across his face, and he shook his head. "No. I have to do this."

We crossed the street and lush grass and stepped into the relative dark of the foyer. The table lamp in the museum-piece family room chased the shadows, but it was no match for the grey gloom of the old house. The citrusy fragrance I'd noticed on my previous visit had given way to a stale odor that spoke to the home's age. Manny gazed at the pics that had meant so much to Ralph. "He used to send messages like that all the time. But this one was different. I came right over when he didn't answer the phone."

He took a breath and led me through the pristine room, into the kitchen, and out onto the patio. The couch where he'd sat days ago lay naked. Someone had moved the table to make room for the stretcher and the covers left on the floor out of the way.

A wet stain spread over their lumpy forms and they smelled of fresh urine. The center couch cushion was in the same state. The coffee table that had hosted his dead soldiers was littered with pill bottles. I glimpsed Atenolol, Prozac, and Diazepam among the almost dozen bottles. A half-empty fifth of Scotch stood over the pill bottle graveyard.

A closed photo album stood at the foot of the table. There were no markings or label to identify its purpose. Manny flipped open its cover and came face-to-face with a younger, thinner Ralph, unrestrained joy on his clean-shaven face. He wore a pale blue City of Tampa Fire Department uniform.

Manny smiled. "Ralph was so proud the day they took that picture."

"He looks it."

"Momma and Dad were petrified, but proud, too. They paid for the pictures commemorating his appointment." He set the picture down, the joy still glittering in his eyes. "They did the same for me when I got hired with the county."

"Sounds like you had wonderful parents."

"Yeah." The smile grew distant, then sad. "He was a good brother, too."

"He seemed like a good guy. Troubled, though."

He turned the page. It landed on the *Tribune* front page the day of the fire. *TAMPA FIREFIGHTER KILLED IN OVERNIGHT BLAZE!* It was the same article hanging in Manny's office, the same I'd read during my research.

He turned the page again, and I saw something I hadn't seen. "What are these?"

"Official fire and investigation reports from the original fires. It was easy enough to get if you knew who to pump on the Third

Floor, and after Chelsea Street, Ralph could get whatever he wanted."

Tampa Fire Rescue's headquarters was on the third floor of Station One downtown.

"So he collected his own files?"

Manny nodded. "It became an obsession with him. I tried to steer him away, to get him to move on, but he still lived that day over and over again."

"I saw that on his face when I was here. I'd felt bad for bringing it up."

"Don't do that to yourself. Ralph wasn't one who could let go of things." He gestured toward the house. "Just look at this place, if you need proof."

I nodded.

"I love my family, but I owe it to them for this gift of life they gave me to live it. You know?"

A heavy silence settled over us, and he wiped his eyes. "Damn!"

"May I?" I held the book up.

"Sure."

I moved it to the bar, and flipped through reports on yellowed paper. I stopped at one. It was the same *Tribune* pic from the Ybor Untouchables article, the one with Ortiz and Price standing feet apart. This pic fit into his view of the fire.

"Mean something to you?" Manny was looking over my shoulder again.

"Maybe."

"That's Price, isn't it?"

"That's Price."

"The Ybor Untouchables?"

We shared a grin. Reporters.

"You think I could borrow this book?" I said. "I'd like to take some time to go over these reports."

"Help yourself. I'd like it back, though."

"You'll get it the way I found it."

I closed the book and set it aside.

"You really think the fire that put your father in the hospital is linked to those fires, don't you?"

I thought of the pic of Ardendorff and Townsend. Ortiz's link to all these cases and my suspicion that he was in on Walker's bullshit arrest right after Chelsea Street.

"I do, Manny. I really do."

PRICE'S PIECE

The First United Methodist Church of Plant City stood tall and proud against the pale blue sky of a morning burning its way into afternoon. The stark white columns holding up the matching portico and cupola conspired with the dull red of the temple's brick walls to make First United Methodist one of the most beautiful and distinguished churches in a town of beautiful, distinguished churches.

I stood at the base of the wide, red-tiled stairway sipping on cold café con leche, listening to the muffled notes of lyrical worship that proclaimed the end of the service. Ushers cast open the three white double doors at the top of the stairs and a crowd in its Sunday best streamed across the thresholds into the sunshine. They filtered down the stairs and past me on their way to their restaurant of choice for a late breakfast or early lunch. A few tossed curious glances my way, but none gave voice to whatever was on their mind.

I looked upon them with admiration. It was refreshing to see people worship in suits and dresses in the T-shirt era of faith.

The minister appeared on the portico, saying his goodbyes and shaking hands. So did his deacons. They wore long, white albs and blue stoles. They offered hugs, handshakes, and "God bless yous" to the departing. None of them noticed me, and all returned to the church once the crowd had dissipated. I gave them a few seconds' lead and ascended the steps, resting a hand on one of the outer bannisters that was done in the same white-trimmed brick as the rest of the chapel.

I found two of them in the sacristy shedding their vestments and placing them back in the wardrobe for next Sunday or perhaps the evening service.

"I think we're going to Fred's," Price was saying. "If we hurry, we can still get breakfast."

"Yeah," said his companion, a tall, paunchy black man with close-cropped hair. He was draping his stole over the neck of a hanger. "Sue and I just might join you."

"I hope I don't make you late, Chief."

Both men stopped and looked toward my voice.

Price's face broke into a broad grin that contrasted with the dark suspicion in his eyes.

"Captain!" His voice proclaimed a delight for all to hear. "Jake, allow me to present to you Logan Walsh, one of my captains. Captain Walsh, this is Jacob Fowler, a fellow deacon here at the church."

We exchanged pleasantries, and Fowler thanked me for my service.

I offered an awkward smile and told him it was my privilege.

"Well," he said to Price, "I'll see you at Fred's."

I waited until the goodbyes were all said, and Fowler had left us the room. "Your pal Ortiz paid me a visit last night."

"Who?"

"Diego Ortiz. Sergeant Diego Ortiz from the '98 Arson Task Force. Your partner the day you busted Elias Walker."

All pretense of a smile fell, and his eyes darted toward the doorway through which Fowler had disappeared. "I don't know who you could mean."

I handed him the pic I'd run off from the article. "The Diego Ortiz standing six short feet from you in this picture. Surely a man of your vanity remembers the heady days of the Ybor Untouchables."

He kept his composure and returned the picture. "There were dozens of people on that task force."

"But not dozens who rousted vagrants with you. Not dozens who made a key arrest in the fires days after Chelsea Street. Only one man fits that bill."

Dead eyes looked from a still face. I thought one more good blow might shatter the façade. "You know, he busted my client and is looking very good for the burglary and arson in my father's shop. If it turns out you've steered this investigation away from him in any way, your previous affiliation, no matter how innocent, is going to look very bad."

"If I speak to anyone, it won't be you."

"Well, be careful who you do speak to. I went to SO's IA with my suspicions, with that evidence you accused me of hoarding, and

Davis Carlyle was dragging Pops out of that fire fourteen hours later."

He studied me. "HCSO?"

"HCSO."

Thirty seconds passed before he spoke. "What do you want to know?"

I leaned on the wall behind me. "Tell me about Elias Walker."

He harrumphed at that. "What's to tell? After Jay got killed, the heat was really on to jail a suspect. Any suspect would do. Something to show we were really digging into this case."

I nodded.

"So we went out in pairs, all the overtime we could handle. I got teamed up with Ortiz. He was a big up-and-comer with the PD and was following the task force to the spotlight."

I wondered if he even noticed the hypocrisy in his condescension.

"We were out patrolling, and Ortiz comes across this vagrant... Walker... We both knew the guy. We'd seen him a dozen times patrolling those streets."

"And each of those times, you knew better than to think he could be your man."

"He was carrying lighter fluid in his jacket pocket."

"He was carrying it, or you 'found' it."

Price flushed. "Don't you dare attack my integrity! Don't you dare! He was carrying it. I watched Ortiz pull it out of his pocket myself."

"And what did Walker have to say for himself?"

"He said it was for cooking. He said he always kept a little for cooking."

"And?"

Price's reluctance filled the tiny chamber. "It was a tiny bottle, one of those Zippo deals."

I nodded. "The kind for refilling lighters."

Another pause. "Yes."

One of the few facts I'd retained from my brief glance at Ralph's investigatory reports came back to me. "Wait, a minute. The spectrometer report from the fires cited gasoline as the common accelerant."

"I argued that very point, but Ortiz said the guy could be using what he had on hand."

"So this serial arsonist mastermind who's successfully burned down sixty-plus homes without getting caught was winging it? Was that your partner's logic?"

"I didn't say he was persuasive."

"But it didn't stop you from claiming your fifteen minutes of fame, did it?"

He hid behind that calm mask of his. "The intent was never for Walker to be the torch, but to send a message to both the public and our arsonist. We were out there. Finch hoped we could scare the guy underground or get him to move on before the next fatal fire."

"And fuck the guys he'd burned up, huh?"

Price cast a horrified glance at the door. "This is a church, man! My church! I'll not tolerate that kind of language here."

"Okay. What about the guys, your guys, your firefighters, who got burned up on Chelsea Street? No justice for them?"

"It was a complicated situation. There was more to consider than getting retribution."

"So you made no genuine effort to catch the actual torch?"

His still mask studied me with incredulity. "The people needed reassurance that we were on the case. It was a delicate time for the department."

"Department? You mean careers. The career of the fire chief. The career of the mayor. The..." The mayor! The same mayor who was the current mayor. The same mayor who was running for governor. The same mayor who announced his candidacy about the time Bobby Lee started bragging about a payday. I tried to keep the realization from my face. "And what happened with Walker?"

"The state attorney held onto it for a few weeks, but there was no case. We couldn't put Walker on the scene of any of these fires and couldn't match his lighter fluid to any of the accelerants used in the blazes. He walked."

"Quietly."

Price shrugged. "The fires stopped, the union turned toward the next contract negotiation, and everyone moved on."

I remembered Ralph DeSoto. Not everyone. "You did, too. Right up to fire marshal."

"Yes, I made fire marshal."

"Straight from captain."

"It's hardly the first time."

"But it would be the first time such an appointment wasn't purely political."

Price ground his teeth.

"I guess that's the reward you get for playing ball."

"I had a duty to the department and the chief. And when the time came to replace my predecessor, Chief Finch remembered. That could be a valuable lesson for you, Captain."

I glanced at the wardrobe, the rack of gowns and stoles and the other holy implements scattered about the room. "You know, Deacon, I'm sorry for cursing in this hallowed place, but lying in here to protect a murderer or cover up your own sins? That's a whole different level of sacrilege."

He offered no protest of innocence.

"Oh, one last thing. I'm due back to work tomorrow. I'm going to be putting in for an EOT with Connie Haskins. She's a medic, and she acts captain. I expect that arrangement to be approved per the contract." I waited for an answer he wouldn't give and pushed into the nave.

A FIREFIGHTER'S WAKE

"To Ralph!" A broad-shouldered character with a silver mane hoisted his beer.

"To Ralph," replied the chorus from the room.

The mourners clinked glasses and drank as one. Better than fifty active and retired firefighters had come to Rick's on the River on hours' notice to celebrate a haunted brother claimed by a job that was part drug, part abusive lover. They surrounded Manny, each offering him a drink and each telling him how much they missed Ralph.

Buddy Lewis, a tall, gangly retired district chief with the city, was telling a story. He placed a giant comforting hand on Manny's back. His words were a slurred by beer and washed in and out with the crowd noise, but decades of giving orders on chaotic firegrounds carried his voice through the din: "... was captain on Engine Sixteen and Ralphie was my firefighter. Brand spanking new." He took a sip and scratched at a long beard I doubted had been more than trimmed since his retirement. "Well, he makes the mistake of asking me what we do about dogs. Because he's afraid of them. Right?"

Manny smiled and nodded. "He never liked dogs."

Lewis brandished a smile that helped make him a likable legend in the firefighting community. "Well, one day we go out on this aid call with Rescue Four to this frequent flier and this falling down wood-frame shack is surrounded by a rusting chain-link fence with a bad dog sign hanging by metal twine. Ralph gives me this look like 'Are we goin' in there?' I looked at him and said, 'Boy, you get your ass in there same as if it was on fire.'"

Chuckles went around the room.

"Ole Ralphie, he's a real trooper, takes a deep breath and pushes through the gate. This fuckin' dog is barking and barking, locked in the same room it always is. Shaking the bedroom door, snorting and sniffing under the crack. We move the patient out to the front porch and do our thing and send her off with rescue. So. we're packing up, and Ralph is talking about how much he appreciated me moving out here to the porch and how that dog really wanted our ass. He's rolling the BP cuff up and bends over to put it back in the 747." An old-school orange-and-white plastic EMS tackle box.

"I nod at Kenny Meuze and crouch close to Ralph. Kenny starts running and shouts. 'Holy shit, man, the dog!'" Lewis holds up one of those talon-like hands, still powerful-looking in his seventies. "I start barking and snarling and grab a handful of his ass." A gust of laughter rose from all of us, and Lewis continued with his story, tears glistening in his hazel eyes. "That fuckin' kid. Screamed like no man I've ever heard. And I don't know how he did it, but he crushed our 747 and ran right through the porch banister."

The laughter resumed. I smiled and sipped on a bourbon, the only alcohol of the evening I would allow myself.

"We spent the rest of the afternoon fixing her damn porch and went down to supply next shift to pilfer a new box." The laughter died, and we all remembered as one Ralph was dead.

"To Ralph!" someone said.

"To Ralph," came the reply, and dozens of drinks were upended. Uber was gonna make some money tonight.

I found my way out into the overflow and sat at one of the wooden picnic tables that looked out at the river. Two wooden spines struck out into the water, docks stretching off either side to form slips for boats to park. Three boats were moored there at this late hour.

"We're losing too many like this." A thick man with square hands and a beard looked over from the next table, a dark ale frosting in front of him.

I thought again of the abusive relationship first responders have with their vocation. "We are. Damned if I know what to do about it, though."

This was the second Bay Area firefighter lost to suicide and fourth or fifth first responder this year.

"Get the word out, I guess. Don't be such a lone wolf."

I nodded as if that was possible in an industry that demanded steady composure in the face of the worst this world offered.

"Of course, the last time I saw a firefighter tell his chief he was having issues, the chief questioned his fitness for duty." I sipped at my bourbon. "Can't make much progress that way."

"It isn't any different in the city." He reached across the aisle between us. "Cam Sessions."

I took it. "Lo Walsh."

"Mr. CSI himself."

I smiled. "Hardly."

He gestured at the bench next to me. "May I?"

I moved over to make room, and Sessions took the seat. We clinked our glasses and drank to Ralph. He took three good belts. I finished the last drops in my tumbler.

"Word is you're looking into the Seminole Heights fires."

"I'm looking into an assault and arson that left my father in TGH's ICU."

"And that has taken you to these arsons?"

"It's looking that way. You on the job back then?"

"I was, a truckie on Aerial One, got TDYed captain for a good part of that time." The fire department borrowed the term TDY from the military: Temporary Duty. Someone TDYed was usually acting above their normal grade at an assignment until a permanent replacement could fill it or the person for whom they were filling it returned. "Saw some shit back then."

He said it as if everything to pass between now and then was child's play.

A thirty-footer puttered up the river on its way home. "I keep hearing about how this arson spree was the most open secret in the city back then."

"The city?" Sessions chuckled. "You mean the fucking state, though the Gainesville fires were definitely getting more national coverage. Church fires are just so much sexier than abandoned crack houses."

I let him have the floor.

"The mayor came in promising to change Tampa, to revitalize the city. The first thing he did was slash the operating budget of the fire department while giving extra to the cops. Then, he announces all these city projects for the greater Seminole and Tampa Heights areas. Road improvements, new street signs, fancy new lights to create ambiance. All kinds of city tax breaks for investors willing to help gentrify the place. He sold it by promising more revenue through the increase in property valuations and subsequent tax boon."

"And people took to it?"

Sessions shrugged. "The people who mattered did."

"And when was this?"

"What do I look like? A historian? Right before the fires."

"So the mayor announces this urban renewal thing and someone starts lighting houses?"

"Yep! And boy, were we burning 'em down! Sometimes two or three a night. Plus our normal workload. And we weren't exactly slow back then."

Maybe everything from then on had been child's play. "So you guys thought it was a profit job from jump street?"

"What other conclusions could you draw? I mean, what are the odds, right? The mayor wants to gentrify a couple of our 'classic' neighborhoods and the abandoned eyesores start burning to the ground overnight. We all knew."

"Was there any speculation of who it was?"

He chuckled at that. "As if a bunch of flunky firemen could know such a thing."

I probed my theory. "It sure is convenient that they didn't catch anyone until after Chelsea Street."

Sessions' face grew hard with bitterness.

"*Convenient.*" The word was a curse on his lips. "The union really let us down on that one."

He took another pull from his beer, and I thought he might drop the matter, but he said, "They were all up in arms over Jason and Ralph until the Silver camp offered reconciliation. They pushed the vagrant narrative; said we should get Aerials Four and Nine back up in tribute to their sacrifice." Another long, angry pause stretched. "Only took 'em three administrations and twelve years to get Nine. Sad."

Tampa's powerful mayor system created a challenge for the firefighter's union. Each election cycle saw a divided union with opposing factions supporting different candidates. When the election was over, those who backed the winner were well-situated to promote, especially to the Third Floor. Those who didn't had a harder road with the senior folks having no shot at the coveted admin positions. This cycle repeated every four years and had the effect of turning the body schizophrenic and splitting its political power.

"Then Pedro went down for drug possession and the rest was history."

My head snapped to look at him. "What?"

Sessions looked at me. "Pedro. What was his name. Medea, Medina, something like that. Cuban refugee reporter working the crime beat in Seminole Heights. Good dude. He got busted with five keys of coke in a routine traffic stop, and that was that."

The chill in my blood turned the humid August night to winter. How many times did they go to that well? "TPD did the bust?"

He took a swig and nodded. "Sure did. Last I heard, he was at Rayford doing twenty. He's probably out by now, but his reporter days are over."

I pulled my notepad from my pocket and scribbled the name. Pedro Medea/Medina? "And this Pedro? He smelled a rat?"

"Yeah. He was on it. Hung out at the stations sometimes. Never tried to use anything we said as quotes, just chatted us up to get our thoughts. He used to say they would lead him to the place where he could ask questions."

"Smart."

"He was."

"Did you know him to have any evidence on these fires?"

"Nothing I knew anything about. You can ask him, if he's around."

"I'll look him up, thanks."

I had Manny to his Carrolwood home by 3:30. He looked out at his house through the windshield. "Man, that was really great. The guys, they really loved Ralph. You know?"

"They sure did."

"All old guys, though."

"I noticed that." Active duty firefighters showed up in respectable numbers, but retirees outnumbered them two-to-one.

"I'm thinking about getting out."

I frowned and nodded my understanding.

"I'm serious," he said. "It just isn't the same anymore."

"Pops says the same thing."

"Come on, Lo. You see it, too. Don't you?"

I remembered Lewis's story about Ralph and the dog and imagined the paperwork and investigation that would demand today. And if the rookie's feelings had gotten hurt, it would ruin careers at the very least, might get people fired. "I see it. Can't get away with the shit we used to."

"Isn't that that truth?" He gripped my arm and leaned close. "You get him, Lo. Hear me? You get the bastard who did this. Whatever you need from me, you let me know."

"I might take you up on that."

He squeezed my arm and staggered into the night. I stayed long enough to make sure he was in the house and backed out onto the quiet residential street.

THE KING MAKER

I cleared the bed at 9:30 am with five-and-a-half of the best hours' sleep I'd had in days. The chief approved Haskins's EOT, which was good because I planned to take family leave and dare Garrison to come at me had it not been. I went to the gym, had worked out and showered by 11:15, and was at TGH by noon.

The swelling in Pops' brain was going down, but the doctors gave him another couple of days before trying to wake him. I sat at his side, held his hand, and told him all about the latest in the case to catch his attacker. He offered nothing, and I frowned at the withered shell of a man he was becoming.

"I'm getting close, Pops," I told him. "I'm getting very close." The nurse came in and shooed me while they bathed him. I rose. "I love you, Pops."

I rode to the ground floor, crossed the parking garage under the ER and north toward the nurse's "smoking lounge," a bench that looked north across Hillsborough Bay at the built-up waterfront stretching east and west of river's mouth.

Steady streams of traffic moved over the Platt Street Bridge in the shadow of Tampa's small but beautiful skyline. A pair of mid-rise condos stood two hundred yards apart on Bayshore, dwarfing the sprinkle of coconut palms rising around them. The buildings cast blurred reflections of beige and yellow pastels on a glassy bay made blue by a cloudless sky. The Davis Island Bridge stretched from my left to the mainland, blocking my view of Bayshore's most scenic and famous section with its beautiful joggers and balustraded seawall.

The sun was blinding, and I turned the brightness on my laptop as high as it would go and bent the lid to shade the screen. I found a pose that worked, linked up with my cell for internet access, and dove into the *Tampa Tribune* archives. Pedro Media/Medina was in the bylines of dozens of stories written about burglaries in Seminole Heights, a carjacking in Tampa Heights, and the problem of drunk and disorderlies in Ybor. I also found his stories about the fires. Meticulous research supported the well-structured pieces. I'd read most of them in my research, but none shed any light on who he thought was setting these fires.

There was nothing about his arrest in the *Trib*. I had to move over to the *St. Pete Times*, and even that was a blurb buried on page eight of the metro section. The top of the tiny square read: *Beat Reporter Busted for Drugs*.

> *Tampa Police Department arrested freelance reporter Pedro Medina on Saturday on charges of drug possession. Patrol officers stopped Medina for a traffic vi-*

> *olation when they spotted evidence of drugs "in plain view." Further investigation revealed a large quantity of cocaine in his car. They arrested Medina, and he is now held on fifty-thousand-dollar bond.*

That was the entire story. There was no follow-up, no details, no mention of his *Tribune* ties. Nothing. The world moved on without another thought of poor Pedro. The Florida Department of Corrections database included a mugshot, demographics, and a list of convictions: Possession with intent to distribute.

Sessions was wrong about his sentence. They gave him a hundred and eight months. Fifteen years, plus another sixty months of probation. He got out in '08 after doing half his sentence. Seven-and-a-half years!

I rubbed my eyes and gazed out at the tranquil water. A yacht puttered away from the river mouth. How many lives had this guy wrecked protecting his masters? The bigger question was, who were his masters? Pedro might hold the answers to that.

I googled Pedro Medina and found him without too much trouble. He was a local YouTuber and influencer who did feel-good videos about life in Tampa. I watched a few and recognized an older, fatter, thinner-haired version of the man in the mugshot. His dark eyes danced, and his accented voice proclaimed his love of life and the Tampa Bay Area. I decided by his third "Happy Tampa Day" video this man who'd spent so much of his life in prison on a bad rap was a better man than I or a phenomenal actor.

YouTube listed the email account linked to his profile. I sent him a message.

Pedro,

My name is Logan Walsh. I'm investigating several crimes that seem related to Diego Ortiz. I know you're innocent and would love to help you clear your name. Let's meet and discuss what I know. Please email me if interested.

Logan Walsh

It wasn't a masterpiece in communication, but I lived with it.

I read reports on Silver's political life. He served a pair of terms as South Tampa's District Four rep on the council and then another as the District One at-large councilman before his first stent as mayor in '92. South Tampa was our old-money district. It included the island on which I was sitting, Hyde Park, and SoHo neighborhoods. A person had to get to the gates of MacDill Air Force Base south of Bay-to-Bay Boulevard to get into anything resembling working poor in South Tampa. It was the epicenter of wealth and political influence in the city and suggested to me Ole Monte hadn't pulled himself up by his bootstraps as a lad.

The rest was as Sessions had described. Silver spent his first term cutting budgets and eliminating positions in the city. He shuttered Aerials Nine and Four and cut the engine staffing from four to three. He implemented a city-wide hiring freeze. Though he sponsored a bond that funded new positions and equipment for the police department. He secured the annexation of what would become New Tampa by daisy-chaining University of South Florida to wealthy landowners in that section of the county, adding to the city landmass by a quarter or third.

The promise to revitalize the city's interior dominated his campaign for a second term, raise property values, and make Tampa a place "unsafe for criminals." It worked. The public elected him in a landslide, and he went right to work on his plan to revitalize Seminole Heights: new roads, new lampposts, huge tax breaks for those investing in the region. That was early '97. Two months later, the first of the suspected Seminole Heights fires broke out on Highlands.

I was reading about his campaign when I came across a quote that froze me in my seat. *"I think Monte has what it takes to turn this town into a beacon on the hill, and I'm grateful to be part of the team to put him there," said Silver's campaign manager Bo Richardson.*

Richardson! It was a common name, but... I looked up Bo Richardson and found what I was looking for at once.

Local Man Finds Niche in Politics.

A local Tampa man has become one of the up-and-comers in state and local politics. He has helped mayors and state representatives from up and down the I-4 corridor seek and find office. "I'm 21-and-1" says Richardson with a catlike smile on his face. "We weren't sure how all this was going to work when we first started out, but my family has a long tradition of caring about Florida and what happens in this great state." The interview was a rare one for the normally reclusive man behind the curtain.

"I like to think we've made a difference here and there and helped bring prosperity and success back to this state after all it's been through." And they have. Much of the success of Florida's resurgence as one of the leading powerhouses in the union is because of the men and women Richardson has helped put into office. Perhaps none is more important than Monte Silver, three-time mayor of Tampa and leading contender for the governor's mansion.

"We're especially proud of what Monte has done with his time as mayor here in Tampa and look forward to seeing what he can do as the governor of this great state."

Monte Silver is considered by many to be the savior of Tampa with his unprecedented expansion of the city's borders and his Seminole Heights revitalization project in the late nineties. "Sure, he led the way," said Richardson, "but it was the citizens of Tampa who really turned this place around."
We asked him if he might look to do for the entire nation what he'd accomplished here in the city. Bo simply smiled and said, "Let's win Talley first."

The pic was familiar; it was an older version of the man standing with Drew Richardson in his collage of Tampa's who's who. I looked back at the water and cursed myself for missing this piece. There was, I supposed, a reason people left this kind of thing to the cops. I continued my search and found what I was looking for, a business name and address. Time to go.

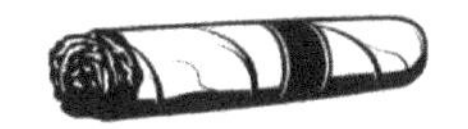

Bayshore Political Group wasn't on Bayshore at all, but in a spacious two-story wood-framed bungalow on Horatio less than a mile from Mandy Drexler's office. I pulled past the hanging wood sign in the shrubbery filling the circular drive, parked under the awning, and crossed the paving stone driveway into the house-turned-campaign-headquarters.

Someone had torn down the partition walls on the first floor, leaving a great room that reminded me of a hotel lobby. A fan the size of an airplane propeller hung from the vaulted ceilings, circulating the conditioned air. A soft spritz breathed the salty aroma of the ocean into the chamber. The furniture contrasted with his brother's office in that it looked both used and practical, designed for comfort and style. Periodicals from *Barron's* to *Tampa Bay Events* covered the coffee table. A glance at the cover suggested they weren't talking about the barbecues in Drew Park or College Hill.

A blonde receptionist looked up from behind a massive oak desk. "Captain Walsh?" The question took me off guard. The smile on her face suggested it was supposed to. "Mr. Richardson is expecting you. Go right up."

"I will. Thanks."

She was back on her computer doing something more worth her time than talking to me before I took my first step. The wide wooden stairs creaked underfoot, the matching dark wood railing smooth under my hand. I reached the top and paused in the doorway before me.

The office was not what I expected. It felt more like a lounge or sitting room than a work space. There was no desk taking up the center of the floor. Plush leather couches gathered in a loose circle around the dark wood wet bar to my left. Elegant-looking bottles stood at attention behind the gold-handled glass doors of a cabinet. A pair of crystal decanters sat on either side of the bar, each containing a golden-brown liquid. The gathering area left plenty of space in the room's center for a giant throw rug and nothing else.

Rows and rows of floor-to-ceiling bookshelves lined the wall to my right. A comfortable red leather chair sat in the corner where an antique pullout tabletop stood ready for use.

"Most people wear that look when they first walk in here." Bo Richardson stood in the threshold of French doors cast open to the Florida sun. He was tall and lean, harder-looking than his huskier brother. He wore a white Panama suit over a pale-yellow shirt and blue tie. I wondered if I might not have interrupted him in the middle of shooting a commercial for the Florida tourism bureau.

"Nice place you have here."

Richardson's friendly smile broadened. "It is, isn't it?"

He held up the glass in his hand. "Juice? Made fresh from our family's groves."

"I'm surprised you have any left after turning so many into subdivisions."

He drew a long sip. "We kept a few."

The distant *swish* of traffic blew in through the open doors and something flickered through his eyes. Admiration? Annoyance? "Diego is quite cross with you, but I must say that stunt you pulled at his hair-brained traffic stop… fucking brilliant."

"Is Diego the one who told you I was coming?"

"I have many ways of knowing what goes on in this city, Captain Walsh."

"I'm not on duty."

"Lo."

"Walsh will do."

His smile grew stiff below narrowed eyes. "I hear you fire department–types don't make much in the course of your duties."

"We do okay."

"Sure, until the old lady takes half of everything, plus alimony and child support. Then where are you gonna be?"

"That's my business."

His condescending smile suggested I'd just lost a measure of his respect. "Of course."

Another long pause passed. "I could use a man of your talents in this business. Knowing things about the opposition is huge, and you have shown quite the aptitude for gathering information."

"I chose the fire department to do something that made it possible to look at myself in the mirror. Taking your blood money doesn't blend with those values."

His smile became all teeth. "Don't make the mistake of thinking I care at all about you and your little investigation. I like your style and think you could be a valuable tool, but you have won no leverage with me. You've been beneath my notice to this point, and, trust me, you don't want to be on my radar, Mr. Walsh. That is a dangerous place to be. For you. For your wife. For those darling kids of yours. Do you understand what I'm saying?"

Rage and terror flooded into my body, and I trembled from the adrenalin. "You touch my—"

"Don't do that. This is chess, Mr. Walsh. You're playing checkers. You are playing well, I grant you, but your pieces can't do the same things mine can."

I thought of all the money, all the Diegos, and all the other options a man of his wealth had at his disposal. He'd burned half this town for profit while the city fathers looked the other way. I wilted.

Bo Richardson saw the doubt in my eyes and his smile broadened. "See, you are a smart man. Go back to your life putting out fires and picking up little old ladies. It's safer and better for your family."

I glared, helpless to speak, powerless to act. I retreated, chased by the fears for my wife and kids.

A SHOWING

"And you can even see the water from your southern windows." Mandy Drexler's voice carried down the staircase and echoed around the empty home, giving the place a hallowed feel. The creaking, clattering report of footsteps upstairs told me the same rich, dark wood that covered the foyer, living room, and dining room floored the entire home.

I stood at the base of the stairs and looked left through the dining room toward the kitchen. An empty pot rack hung above a marble top island covered with business cards, but no one else waited on Mandy's attention. I took that as a good sign.

"It's a great place to raise a family," she was saying. "And the schools... it's South Tampa. Right?"

A voice replied, male, but I couldn't make out his words.

Mandy laughed. "Well, the Academy isn't far from here."

I'd known a few girls to come out of the Academy of the Holy Names, but had never considered them special for it. On the other hand, they often considered themselves very special.

It went on that way for a while, Mandy talking up the neighborhood, the proximity to Bayshore, and the worth of the home. She never discussed the low price. I assumed that was because all pretense of thriftiness was dead in this market, especially in one of the most prestigious neighborhoods in the city. They moved to the top of the stairs and Mandy verified my suspicions. "I won't lie. There's a lot of interest in this home, and it'll go fast."

Their footfalls on the treads were close and filled the empty mini-mansion, one creaking thump at a time. "I just thin…"

I smiled at her.

Her silent stare was noticeable, but she continued her pitch with brief hesitation. "Think about it. It could be under contract by morning. I don't have to tell you how this market is."

The targets of her pitch were off the Ken and Barbie casting sheets. The man's broad-shouldered body wore a soft-yellow golf shirt and Bermuda shorts bought at Banana Republic. His tan looked real, and his swept-back brown hair was going blond from sun exposure. Her blonde might've come from a bottle, but it was a good bottle, and complemented a wasp-waisted body with wide hips and ample bosom. I imagined him piloting a boat around Tampa Bay with her sunbathing in a bikini on the bow.

They tossed me a curious glance that held a trace of wariness. Whether that was from Mandy's reaction or something in my appearance, I couldn't say. Either way, they didn't seem to like what they saw.

"Mr. Walsh!" Mandy tried to sound excited, but her voice skewed into nervous. "I hadn't expected to see you!"

I forced a smile. “I thought I’d swing by and look the place over.”

“Of course.” Mandy’s smile looked ready to shatter into a million pieces, but she held it together long enough to bid Ken and Barbie adieu.

They promised to be in touch and shot me a final, troubled glance. I returned their gesture with a nod and smile, and Mandy closed the door behind them. She stole a glance through the peep hole and spun on me. “What are you doing here?”

“I just walked out of Bo Richardson’s office. You know old Bo.”

“I know of him.”

I tossed a quick smile at her. “He’s kinda pissed at me.”

“Well, he has friends, lots of them. And lots and lots of lawyers.”

“I know. Diego set up my client. I think he planned to do the same to me. Of course, that was better than what he did to my pops and Townsend. So maybe I should be grateful.”

“I don’t know what you’re talking about.”

“Stop it,” I said. “You’re telling me you didn’t know they were burning down those homes, that they were making money hand over fist by driving down the property values of the poorest in the city so they could buy in at rock bottom and turn a buck selling them at a premium when the mayor’s program turned the local market around. You can’t tell me you didn’t notice a dead firefighter on the front page of every paper in the city.”

“Yes, I noticed! Of course I did! Do you think that’s what I wanted? To kill some fireman? To burn people out of their homes for profit? You think that’s why I got into real estate?”

“I think you got into real estate to make money.”

"I did. But not like that."

"Is that why you bought some of those properties yourself?"

She turned her face.

"I've done the research. You were the owner of record on homes in the Seminole and Tampa Heights areas in ninety-seven. The property appraiser says you made quite a tidy profit."

"Yes, I bought a few of the homes, early in the project, and, yes, once I was in, I made my money, but it was two homes. Two measly little cracker shacks."

"Two cracker shacks that brought you almost two hundred Gs in profit between them. That seems like a pretty good return, if you ask me."

"I didn't know!" Her scream echoed through the empty house. Drexler looked around the room in horror, as if someone might hear her. She leaned close and whispered, "I didn't know they were burning the houses. Not at first."

"But you didn't report them, and you didn't quit."

She laughed. "I'd just bought two investment homes. Where the hell was I supposed to go? What was I supposed to do?"

"The police. The fire department. The state fire marshal."

"And go the way of Kinsey? No thanks."

It was hard to argue against that. "It's not too late, you know."

"I know. That's why I don't like you being here."

"You can make a difference, Mandy."

"Maybe I don't want to make a difference. Maybe I'm happy breathing."

I pulled the pic I'd found on the internet. "That might be what you say now, but I don't think it's what this girl would say. This is you, isn't it?"

It was a pic I found during my deep dive into Silver's political history. The pic dated back to his first failed bid to win governor. He stood center stage in the photo, flanked by the Brothers Richardson. A woman barely in frame wore a deep frown and belonged more at a funeral than a campaign fundraiser for an up-and-coming politician.

"Where did you get that?" Her voice was hoarse with fear.

"Article in the *Times*."

"I don't want to talk to you."

"Mandy—"

"We're not friends and you don't know me, so stop talking and leave."

Muffled voices from the stoop were the only warning of approaching people before the door behind me opened.

Mandy looked past me and broke into a broad grin glued together by force of will. "Abby!" She leapt from the stairs and threw out her arms.

Abby was a young, raven-haired girl dressed in an Ann Taylor skirt suit over a white blouse. The two embraced and chattered with another couple, older and more distinguished, but cut from the same spool as Ken and Barbie.

I put my head down and found my way out. No one noticed.

THE CUBA LIBRE

I made it back to my car and stared north at the residential bliss of Willow Avenue. A thick canopy of oaks covered the quiet street flanked by manicured lawns and spacious, comfortable homes whose modest appearance belied the price they could command on the market. The reason for that was in my mirror. Hillsborough Bay and Bayshore Boulevard were a mere half-a-block away, the water crystal blue from the waning afternoon.

I'd never cared for this part of town. Not because the people here were bad or that it was artificial, but because it was a place where I never belonged. I never saw the allure of paying three times what a home was worth because you could throw a rock and hit the water from your front yard. Maybe I was jealous, but it was easier to understand the attraction looking out at a scene that would have inspired Norman Rockwell.

None of my tails had made an appearance, but I couldn't take for granted they weren't there. Diego had friends, probably bent cops like him. That meant they were old hands at surveillance and might be watching me through binoculars or with a drone. I resisted the urge to check the skies and reached for my keys. The chirping of my phone stopped me mid-motion. I had an email.

It was from Pedro Medina. *Cuba Libre, northwest corner of Columbus Drive and Matanzas. 9:00 pm.*

The Cuba Libre bar was new construction. The owners had splashed scenes of the old country across its smooth, tilt slab walls. A mural of Havana before the Castro days adorned the southern wall looking out at Columbus Drive. A scene of men and women working in the sugarcane fields bedecked the east wall, a call back to the name of the bar and the rum it contained.

The smell of Latin food filled the humid air, mingling with the murmuring chatter from inside. I pushed through the swinging door and stepped into a full bar made up in the motif of old Cuba. A sign on the vestibule wall to my right displayed a slashed-through hammer and sickle. The top read Cuba Libertad. What I could see of the floor was plank wood, but dozens of guests obscured the view. A Cuban flag hung over the bar suspended to the to the ceiling at the corners.

The interior walls were the same as the outside: murals of Cuba's 1950's prime looked across a crowded floor at a top-down view of the great city as if through the eye of a soaring bird.

A man in a red-and-orange Guayabera shirt waved from the bar.

I threw up my hand and moved his direction.

Pedro was bigger than I'd expected. Six one or two and two sixty-five, but he wore it well.

"Mr. Medina?"

The man stooped over a plate of ropas vieja over rice. He looked up with chipmunk cheeks and wiped his mouth on a ruby napkin. "Logan Walsh," he said through the napkin.

"Yes."

He extended an enormous hand.

I took it and accepted the seat he offered me. "This your place?"

"Technically, it's the wife's."

He held up the brown bottle in front of him in salutation to someone behind the bar. I glanced back and saw an older Latina with bleached blonde hair and a black tube top. She flashed Pedro a grin and returned to watching the crowd.

He took a heaping bite of the food before him and spoke around it without looking up. "She took a payout as a middle school Spanish teacher and turned this place into a lifelong dream."

I nodded in appreciation. "It's quite the dream."

He paused his eating and something dark and fearful rippled across his features. "Yeah."

I let the crowd fill the heavy silence between us.

"So, you tell me you can prove they railroaded me. That right?"

I ordered a rum and coke from a hot Latina barmaid. "That's right."

Pedro studied me with world-weary brown eyes. "What do you know about it?"

"I know the guy who arrested you for drugs pulled the same stunt on my client a few short weeks ago. I know he tried to pull that shit on others, that he killed a biker who he'd hired to burn half the city down in an arson-for-profit scheme. I know he killed a firefighter and put my father in the hospital."

Pedro raised an eyebrow and nodded. Perhaps he was impressed. Perhaps he was humoring me. "And how much of this can you prove?"

"I—well, I'm still working on that part."

"Working." His smile was rueful. "You know who's pulling the strings on your little conspiracy?"

"I talked to Bo Richardson this morning."

Pedro chuckled. "Richardson." The word was poison on his tongue. "Gotta hand it to them. They had a great thing going. Then they killed Jason." Not that firefighter. Not even firefighter so-and-so, but Jason. "I thought that would get them. But I'd underestimated their influence."

"So, it was Silver."

"It was all of them. They were printing money. Crushing home values, clearing out the worst of the homes, while they used the boosted policing to displace the vagrants out of the Heights and out of the city. It was damn near perfect."

"How did you get on to them, then?"

He shot me a grin that said I knew the answer to that question. "Everyone knew. The firemen. The cops. Hell, half the neighborhood could add two and two and get four. The fires striking when the mayor was pushing urban renewal? When big money was poisted to enter the neighborhood? You didn't have to be able to prove shit to know what was going down."

"But you had proof. You were getting close, or Ortiz would never have framed you."

Pedro nodded. "Yeah. I had a source. He fed me some documents that showed a TPD beat cop, a real cop, not a posing thug like Ortiz, had rousted Townsend. He caught Townsend skulking around an abandoned house."

The revelation hit me in the solar plexus. "They had him? When?"

He shrugged. "March or April of ninety-eight."

"Months before Chelsea Street."

He nodded again. "Yep. But they found nothing on him but a lighter. If he had any flammables, he ditched them on the run."

"So what happened?"

"You tell me."

"Someone buried it."

Pedro pointed at the ceiling in a gesture that would have given me a prize on a game show. "Bingo. When Engine Five got burned on Chelsea Street, they tried to blame it all on Walker. Townsend's arresting officer came to me. He provided copies of the arrest report and street intel notes. He'd made them as an insurance policy against his superiors if the investigation ever went to shit."

"And when it did, he took it to you."

"Yes."

"Why didn't you run the story?" I'd spent the intervening hours since leaving Willow Avenue reading up on Pedro's work.

"My editor. She wanted more." He shrugged. "So, I started leaning on Townsend. I don't know what happened. Either he went to Diego or Diego found out through police channels. Whatever it was, Townsend was dead before I could get a statement and my source in the department got spooked. Next thing I knew, I was getting pulled over ten blocks from my home in West Tampa, and was prison-bound for the next hundred and twenty months."

"And your paper didn't back you?"

"I was freelance, and I was ruffling the feathers of some pretty established reporters. Me going to prison helped some important people at the *Trib*."

I could see that. "Damn."

"Yeah, damn."

I took a sip of my drink. "So what do you have left of that file?"

"You think I kept that shit?" He laughed. "They took it in the search of my home files, no record, no official comment."

"And you didn't file to get them back."

He laughed again. "Get them back? They ruined my life. I stood alone against the great state of Florida on nothing but my word that the man currently running the city was involved in an arson scam that had killed a firefighter. No evidence. No source. No support from my editor. Oh, and a lawyer telling me I should plead or go to a public defender because I couldn't afford him for trial."

I thought of Benny Taylor and his counsel to Bobby Lee. Fucking lawyers. "What about now? You ready to set things back to rights?"

Another laugh. "Are you stupid? Did you not hear a thing I said?" He gestured around the bar. "I have a new life. A wife who loves me, who stuck with me through a seven-year prison term. I'm not risking that now. I go back to prison. It'll be for good... or maybe I'll have a fire like your father."

I wasn't the only one who'd done my research.

"Maybe the city inspectors show up and close this place on some bullshit health code violation. Maybe they attack Maribel's liquor license, or maybe we just get jacked one day and end up a footnote in the unsolved files of Tampa's rising murder rate." He shook his head. "No. I'm out. I brought you here to warn you. To get you out of this game before it eats you the way it ate me... before it's too late."

I tried to see his warning as the ramblings of a bitter old man, broken by years in prison, but they sounded a lot more like wisdom.

"They're vulnerable," I said. "That's why they attack the loose ends."

"Maybe," said Pedro. "But they aren't as vulnerable as you are, as I am. Take it from a man who knows. Let this go. No good can come of it."

I nodded. "One last question. Who was your source in the police department?"

Pedro's look of frustrated exasperation was the only answer I got.

I stepped out into the parking lot. My phone was ringing. I recognized the number. "How you doing, Manny?"

"Hanging in there."

I stopped in the grass lot that was fast becoming a dirt lot and watched the evening traffic pass on Columbus.

"I wanted to call and find out if you wanted a chance to see Silver face-to-face, maybe chat with his inner circle?"

"Oh?"

"Yeah. I have a ticket to his last big fundraiser before the primary. It's a fifteen-hundred-a-plate dinner at the Tampa Bay Yacht and Country Club."

I glanced back at the Cubans cutting sugar cane and listened to the muffled chatter and music from within. "Yeah, I don't know, Manny. I just... I'm meeting a lot of resistance out here."

"What do you mean?"

"I mean... I'm out of options and under threat. I don't know how much farther I can take this. You know?"

"I see." His voice was hard and sharp.

"I'm sorry, man."

"I'm sorry, too."

TWO AWAKENINGS

I spent sleepless hours pondering my next move. Every path so far was a dead end. No one wanted to come clean, because they were too involved or too scared. I'd checked the polls. Silver was ahead and stood poised to sweep the upcoming primary with good matchups against his likely opponent in the general. He was winning, and his brand of power would soon be in the governor's mansion. How many lives would that ruin? How much greater would his reach be then? I tried not to think about it.

I considered Pedro's warning. How the city would come after his wife's liquor license, or the health department would shut her place down. Could they do that? Would they? What had happened to his source? Could I find him? I didn't see how. That was twenty-plus years ago. He would be retired by now, assuming they let him finish his career after his notes ended up in Pedro's possession.

Then there was my crumbling marriage. How could I keep Val and the kids in my life with this craziness? Didn't I have enough to worry about without taking on lost causes? I couldn't control everything or bend the world to my will. I had to live within its rules. "Give me the courage to change those things I can change, the strength to endure those I cannot, and the wisdom to know the difference."

I wrestled with this notion until I drifted into a fitful sleep.

I awoke the next morning to sunlight shining through my window and birds chirping outside. Today was the day they would try to wake Pops. I cleared the bed, put the finishing touches on the house, restoring it to its pre-break-in status, and called Val. She answered on the third ring.

"Hello?"

"Hey."

Frigid silence crossed the miles between us.

"I wanted you to know," I said, "that I'm sorry about the other night. I wasn't trying to be passive aggressive, and I shouldn't have said that about Julie."

"Is that supposed to mean something to me, Lo?"

Old rage brewed within me. I quenched it by changing my approach. "I'm trying, here, Val."

"Are you?"

I gripped the phone. "I called to apologize as a show of good faith."

"A show of good faith." Her flat voice was incredulous. *"That's you all over. Thinking you control everything. The rest of us just dance to your little beat."*

I thought of the tune she'd been calling with Scott, but said, "My behavior is all I can change."

"That's right, and it can't change history. It can't change the past. And it can't change Saturday night, no matter what you do, Lo." Her voice trembled with pain. *"And I don't know that I can stay with a man who's always put me and the kids second."*

Her words put a spear through my heart and a firebrand in my belly.

"Is that what you tell yourself? That you're some kind of victim? It's pretty shitty of you to sit there and blame me for your infidelity, while you enjoyed the lifestyle I worked so hard to provide."

"You heard what Rachael said. You're not supposed to throw that in my face."

"No, she said I have to decide if your betrayal is something I can get over or not, and decide about our future based on that."

"If you can't forgive me for one mista—"

"One mistake repeated several times a week for eight months, Val! I caught you in our own bed." The sight of them returned to me: their flesh pressed together, her husky moans urging him on. My voice grew hoarse with pain. "You'd still be doing it if I hadn't come home by surprise that morning."

Only our breathing sounded on the line for long moments. The energy had left the fight and my helplessness returned. The hope

I'd clung to when dialing the phone had faded to black, leaving me numb and empty. "I gotta go."

I clicked off and stared at the particleboard wall of my mobile home. I really couldn't bring her back.

"His swelling is largely reduced, and we'll now see what kind of function he's retained." Doctor Rajagopal's warm compassionate eyes and tender voice kept that competent knowledge I appreciated so. "I will not hazard a guess as to how he is going to do, but if he doesn't wake up in the next day or two, we'll do an EEG and see where we are at that point."

I nodded. "Thank you, Doctor. I can't tell you what your work has meant to me and my father."

Rajagopal smiled. "You are very kind, Mr. Walsh. I really wish the best for you both."

She left us alone, and I took my seat next to him.

"Well, Pops, it's all up to you now." I took his hand and looked up at the heart monitor above his head. Everything I could read looked great, but that wouldn't matter if he didn't wake up. "You were so right about them. This fucking guy. It goes all the way to the mayor's office... soon to be the governor. He's ended so many lives already, destroyed even more. Everyone's afraid of him. I can't get anyone to stand up to him, to help me build a case, to give me any insight into his weaknesses or vulnerabilities.

"His fucking enforcer... the same asshole who put you in here... is a bent cop. He pulled me over and threatened me. I think he was gonna set me up, but shit didn't go as he planned. He was at the house the night Val had me over, watching us." The memory of that night and all its failures churned in my head.

"I also thought letting this go would save my marriage, that it would show Val I could put the family before my other responsibilities, but Val's too far gone. Or maybe it's me. Maybe I really can't get past what she did."

Sometimes I thought I should just swallow my pride and let her have whatever affair she wanted, as long as we didn't destroy the kids' lives by breaking up our family. I froze and looked at my father.

"Is that why you stayed with Mother? For me? For the family?"

If so, was I happier for that? Did I think I turned out better than if my parents had created two halves from a broken family rather than keep the unhealthy cycle they had going? Would my kids? I thought there was a better way, but it would take both of us.

"I'm sorry, Pops. I never understood how hard it was for you, but Val and I are gonna have to be a proper family. We're gonna have to mend our fences or go our separate ways. I can't take the path you did."

His hand squeezed mine, and I looked into his open eyes. A blossom of joy bloomed in my chest, and we beamed smiles at each other, even if his was weak and lopsided.

A HOSPITAL VISIT...

"Go on, he won't break."

Christopher and Sadie gaped at the frail shell of a man Pops had become as a bed-ridden vent patient. He held his right arm out, and they rushed to him, letting him kiss their heads and stroke their hair. They cried. I gulped down the lump in my throat and wiped a renegade tear from my right eye.

Pops caught me and grinned. He looked good, even if he was still skeletal. The nurses had bathed and shaved him, and he held onto that sharp look of the sixty-eight-year-old who chased down bail jumpers. It was good to see. Dan had interviewed him first thing this morning, but Pops's memory of that day was gone, and he couldn't recall anything about his attacker.

His new room had more space than the cubby he'd occupied in the unit. He'd had a roommate, but the hospital discharged the man this morning. The curtain was open to an empty bed, clean and crisp with made sheets. Even the view was better. I could see the water and part of the convention center if I craned my neck.

It didn't take long for the kids to get antsy. No one designed hospitals to entertain children, especially children of the new millennia.

"Dad, can we go to McDonald's?" asked Christopher.

"In a bit, son. I want to talk to your grandfather. Why don't you go out to that big waiting room and watch TV for a few?"

Both kids nodded and rushed toward the door in a hurried walk. I stopped them before they reached the threshold. "Only if you behave out there."

They smiled as if they didn't know what I was talking about. I returned the gesture with the weary pleading look of a father who didn't want this day to be ruined by having to be dad the disciplinarian.

"Gray al derval." Pops's garbled words brought hope to my chest and broke my heart at the same time.

I forced a smile. "What?"

His face contorted with frustration. "Grey al voderval."

Traumatic brain injury and strokes were different ways to get to the same place: brain damage. He read my incomprehension and wrote on the grease board provided by the nurse. It was a struggle because the left half of his body didn't cooperate with his broken mind. *They are wonderful.*

I smiled. "They are."

"Get oor gundrul."

I smiled the way you smile at a foreigner whose accent is too thick to understand.

Pops recognized that look and wrote: *It's not your fault.*

"Thanks, Pops, but it's not that simple. I—she."

"Mog gest Bawery."

I stared.

He scribed: *Not just Valerie.*

"I know. I could have done better."

He slammed a fist down on the meal table laid over his belly. "Grambammit, goo boo nect gre getrnel zhe vrald."

His garbled words were indecipherable, but his message seemed clear. "I love you, Pops. I'm not taking the blame for this. And I'm not being as forgiving as it seems." I wasn't. I seethed over her behavior. "But there is a vast difference between accepting an unpleasant truth and accepting responsibility for the actions of others—"

"Mo! Mo! Mo!" He scribbled on the whiteboard with fury and proffered it to me. You do not control others. Not me. Not your mother. Not Valerie. And not Silver. NOT SILVER!!!

I read the message twice, three times, and realized he wasn't trying to change the way I saw my marital crisis, but something bigger. Richardson and Silver didn't sic Ortiz on us because I'd asked a few uncomfortable questions. They targeted us because the evidence they'd killed Kinsey to hide had fallen into our hands. That's why Pops was in the hospital. I was already a loose end. So was my family. Neither time nor distance would change that.

But right now, Silver was vulnerable. Right now was my chance. If I didn't seize it with both hands and take the calculated risk of going toe-to-toe with this bastard, I would lose my leverage and the situation would get beyond any means to protect myself. These bastards would bide their time, waiting for the spotlight to shift, to Tallahassee for instance, before taking another, better-aimed shot. But, evenutaly, this would be back in my life.

I looked at Pops. "I have to go."

Pride lit Pops's smile. "Ro bekkem gun."

...AND A PARTY

I took the kids to McDonald's and willed myself not to rush them, focusing on the moment. My failing relationship with Val and encounters with Ortiz had proven these weren't things I could take for granted. We had a blast. Christopher was his usual loyal son self, and Sadie babbled about the latest episode of some show Val let her watch.

The Kinsey Case might not work out. But if it didn't, I would have this moment, this perfect time, to take to eternity or prison with me.

Val was cold at the drop-off, but I said nothing about it. We both had baggage to deal with, but I had other, more imminent problems.

"Manny!" I was still in the driveway when I called. "Please tell me you still have that ticket to Cinderella's ball."

"I kept it, but I thought you were giving up the chase." The accusation in his voice cut, but I didn't blame him.

"I've reconsidered. Are you in?"

I was in the car and backing out of the drive before he responded. *"It's after three The fundraiser starts at seven."*

"I can make it."

I felt his doubt through the line. *"If I do this and you fold the way you did yesterday ..."*

"You'll be fucked," I said. "I won't fold."

"Okay. But we can't meet at the union hall."

"Netpark?"

"What time?"

I glanced at my phone. "Four-thirty?"

"Four-thirty."

The Tampa Yacht and Country Club lived amidst an ancient oak hammock on Ballast Point, at the end of a long drive that was more Savannah, Georgia, than Tampa, Florida, but that image dissipated when I emerged from the tunnel of heavy branches, thick foliage, and great drapes of Spanish moss. The floor-to-ceiling windows of the pristine white building looked out from behind crepe myrtles and short dark green palms. A darkening blue sky looked down from above, foretelling another fiery Florida sunset.

I pulled my Corolla into line with the newest Beemers, Audis, and Teslas, its faded primer-grey paint and fresh coat of yellow oak pollen standing out among all the high-gloss finishes and freshly detailed vehicles. The valet gave me the same suspicious look security had given me when I appeared at the entrance, but the invitation identifying me as a delegate for the firefighter's union seemed to settle everything in their minds. I stepped from the car, and he hesitated. I handed him a twenty from the company till, and he decided it worth the risk.

The car drove away to a lot beyond the view of the driveway. I straightened the ill-fitting prom tux I'd rented in a cash arrangement that wasn't quite Sacino's company policy and risked the job of the teenager who appropriated it. The pants were ready for our next hurricane's storm surge, and the wool hugging my shoulders screamed in protest.

I crossed the driveway in front of a Rolls. A hard-faced security guard stood at the door with hands crossed at his waist. He smiled and nodded at the collection of pretty people, but his face was less welcoming at the sight of me. "You have an invitation, sir?"

I pulled the pass from my pocket. He took it and studied my face. "This is for Manny DeSoto. You aren't Manny DeSoto."

I produced my Fire Department ID that still identified me as Driver Engineer Logan Walsh. "No, sir, his brother died. I'm an understudy."

The scowl he offered could only live on the face of a cop. "That right? Well, you ain't on the list, friend."

"But 2294 is on the list. Come on, man, help a brother out. You see the ID. I'm an active firefighter. You wanna search me for a weapon? Call the union president? I'll wait."

He frowned and moved his head. "Go, but don't fuck around in there."

I accepted my invitation and ID. “I wouldn’t dream of it.”

The inside was a life beyond my dreams. High ceilings, plush carpet, and ornate furniture. Knots of Tampa’s wealthiest and most powerful gathered with drinks in hand, eating from plates of hors d’oeuvres. The men were all bronze, doing their best imitation of Adonis. Some were better at it than others. The appearance of the women was more universal: absolute unrestrained beauty. There were a few older wife-types and one or two matrons of power, but most were off-the-shelf trophy wives who either kept their faces and bodies youthful or got traded in for a newer model.

The event was being held in the White Room, and that was where most of the crowd had congregated. I spied the Brothers Richardson before they spotted me, which was a good thing because I didn’t think they’d be as trusting as the cop at the door. They stood by the bar close to a pair of French doors that were cast open to the waning summer afternoon, reds, oranges, and pinks coloring nature’s cottony ceiling over Tampa Bay.

I retreated from the room and flagged down a passing waitress. I my gaze stayed on the brothers, and I ordered a drink as expensive as some car payments I’d made. The ebbing and flowing crowd moved about the Richardsons, but they never left my sight for more than a snatched second or two. The men were all smiles and in good spirits, talking about who-knew-what and enjoying this night of celebration with their man in the homestretch to the governor’s mansion.

The waitress found me and brought the drink. I took it and plopped a ten-dollar tip on her tray, unsure of the protocol here.

She had the good grace or the self-interest not to correct me. I drew my first sip and froze: Mandy approached the pair; her face furrowed with concern. The men took her in, their smiles falling as if struck. She spoke. They listened.

Drew spoke first, his motions animated and angry. Bo placed a hand on his shoulder and offered that appeasing crocodile smile. People passed between us, and I had a desperate fear they would move to a private room, or my view would get blocked for good. But they came back into sight. More placating from Bo and agitated anger from Mandy. I sipped and watched, wishing I could get closer, but I didn't dare.

Someone interrupted the conversation, and Bo turned to him. He shooed Mandy and took a mic offered by the newcomer. He did the customary blow and tap on the diaphragm. The sound filled the room. *"Attention, everyone. Attention. I'm happy to report Mayor Silver is on final approach in his boat and will join us momentarily."*

The roaring applause hurt my ears, and the crowd filtered into the White Room. I filtered with them and found a place in the back behind one of the larger patrons. He obstructed my line of sight with the Richardsons, but I had a good view of the bay beyond the windows. A forty-footer cut the water, the sunset casting it in a slanted orange glow that turned the gorgeous craft heavenly.

The sound of its motor carried through the open doors on the sea breeze. The loud *toot* of an air horn set off a round of cheers from the outdoor crowd. I kept my low profile, and watched the boat pull up and dock. It took only moments to get the beast tied off, and a gangway deployed. Silver appeared at the top of the ramp, less lean but more polished than I'd remembered. His smooth, bronze complexion accentuated a perfect white smile I could see from a hundred yards. He turned that smile on the people and waved at the energized crowd.

The Richardsons stepped out to meet him and were the first to put their hands in his. Private words passed between them, but there was no sign of the tense anger they'd shared with Mandy. Silver pointed and waved at someone in the throng, and the entourage moved to the room, surrounded by suited bodyguards wearing TPD lapel pins.

One stood out among the others: Diego. His dark eyes searched the crowd, his expression serious and uncompromising. He was one of the mayor's bodyguards! As a sergeant, he was probably its head. That's why he looked familiar. I had seen him in the background when the mayor gave speeches!

"Son of a bitch!" My voice was low, but it still drew startled, condescending gazes.

I smiled at them. "Sorry."

The mayor and the Brothers Richardson stepped into the room, all smiles and waves. The meet and greet had begun. People funneled past him offering their salutations, and the concern and energy Sliver projected to each of the glad handers after a long day at the office was remarkable. He exchanged words, shook hands, touched shoulders, and held eye contact as if his very life depended on what they had to say. I suppose his political life did.

"Okay! Okay, folks!" Bo's voice boomed through the PA. *"Thank you for your support. The mayor appreciates each and every one of you, but we are all famished. Are we not?"*

Shouts of agreement rose from hundreds of throats and the line that had formed dispersed to return to their seats.

I'd been easing my way up trying to get closer, and knew it was now or never. I strode upstream against the dispersing throng and blundered into Diego. He was ordering the crowd to disperse with the tolerant restraint of a man who had the authority to make people do something but couldn't afford to piss them off. "Come on, folks," he said. "Move along. The faster you find your seats, the faster..."

I smiled at his daunted gaze and stepped around him.

He grabbed my arm.

"I need to speak to you, Mayor." I kept my voice loose, but urgent. Engine company captains had experience commanding people, too.

Diego shifted in a way that promised to make me part of the carpet. I had seconds.

"I was Bobby Lee Kinsey's skip tracer. He told me all kinds of things before you murdered him." I kept my voice low enough not to be heard but loud enough to make it clear refusing me would create a scene in his inner sanctum.

Diego wrenched my arm, and his foot reached past my instep.

"Let him go, Diego."

The cop stopped but kept his hold.

Silver's smile broadened, but the dark look in his eyes broached no compromise. "I said leave him be."

I flashed him a smile I was certain to pay for later. "Yeah, Diego. Leave me be."

Diego gave my arm a last twist and released me. The pretty people were taking their seats, though we were the center of attention, even if our words were inaudible over the salacious murmur of intrigue.

An easy politician's smile of perfect white teeth stretched across Silver's face, but black eyes of doom glared from behind the veneer. "What can I do for you, Mr. Walsh?"

"You know who I am."

"Your name has made the rounds."

I tossed a cocky smile to the Richardson brothers. "I'm sure I've caused more trouble than they've let on."

A tick caused a glitch in the matrix of his smile, and he glanced at the Richardsons.

Drew's frown was a mixture of angry resentment and shamed humiliation. Bo's resembled his boss's, dangerous eyes over a plastic smile.

Silver hid behind an artificial laugh and spoke in that smooth, urbane lilt. "I'm afraid I don't know what you mean."

"Oh, you're afraid, alright. And since your boys have spent so much time trying to show me how you could get to me where I lived, I thought it only right to show you I could do the same." I looked around the room. "Though for all its extravagance and beauty, I prefer my own class of losers."

"Is that all?"

"No. My TFR brothers, Jason Acres and Ralph DeSoto? You're gonna pay for them and my father. All of you."

Silver's dark eyes narrowed, and the corner of his mouth fell, turning his expression into a scowl of pure hatred. "Diego, please show Mr. Walsh out. And don't leave any marks."

The right side of Ortiz's face stretched in a wolf's smile. "Come, Captain."

I resisted his push, and said to Silver, "Oh, this conversation is already on social media. If something were to happen to me, it might create a lot of unpleasant questions in your homestretch run for the governor's mansion."

Silver's eyes swept past me to the crowd. He remembered to smile, and said in a loud voice, "Thank you so much for your support."

He waved to me as if I was the adoring press and strode past me to his table.

Diego and one of his gang led me out a side exit behind the bar, past the storage room, and an employee lounge. They struck in a tiled hallway with beige vinyl on the walls. The blow took me in the kidney and sent an angry pulse of pain through my back and into my groin. I fell to one knee and caught a foot in the balls. I had no control of the grunt that escaped my throat or the warm stain that spread across my crotch.

"Jesus," said Diego's partner. "He pissed himself."

The realization offered me no reprieve. They landed blows across my back, into my gut and other soft sections of my body.

Diego forced me to my feet to face his partner, a pug-faced north European with a pink complexion and veiny nose. He landed stout blows on my gut and slapped the side of my head with an open hand. A voice interrupted him.

“Hey, I...” It was the cop from the front door, the one who’d told me not to fuck up. He was coming through another door with my car keys in his hand and froze at the sight before him. He saw me and his dark eyes grew small with rage, but his glance at Ortiz over my shoulder and his partner before me was worse. “What the hell are you two doing?”

“Our jobs, Jack,” said Ortiz. “Maybe you should have done yours.”

His face flushed, and he cast a death stare at me. “You had to fuck around. Didn’t you?” Then he looked at his compatriots. “But we’re not doing this.”

“Silver said—“

“I don’t care if the fucking president himself told you to mash his guts. We’re not thugs, Diego.”

“You mean Sergeant.”

Jack reached for the phone in his jacket pocket. “I mean, either of you lands one more blow. And I’ll call IA right here, right now. Maybe I’ll take a few pics or record a little video for posterity. What do you think Silver would say about that so close to the election?”

The arms holding me in the full nelson went slack, and I crumpled to the dirty tile.

“I expect your transfer papers on my desk first thing in the morning, Jack.” Ortiz and his partner left.

I looked up at Jack and smiled.

He returned the gesture with a scowl. “Don’t you dare thank me. You just fucked up my world with your bullshit.”

I nodded and let him help me from the floor.

“Did you piss yourself?”

I grunted. This evening had started with such potential.

PISSING BLOOD

I drove home gripping the car door. My core was an aching lump of bruised meat and battered organs that shuddered and spasmed when I moved wrong, when I shifted my weight, and when I breathed too much. It took most of an hour to cover the distance between Ballast Point and my home in Seffner.

I lurched from the car, a knot of twisted flesh that might never straighten out again. The slow, ginger crawl up the metal treads to my door helped, but the pain never left. I fumbled with the keys, searching for the one that would let me pass. The door gave, and I stepped into a dark room. I flicked the kitchen light on and leaned against the closed door behind me to let the throbbing pain recede.

I clicked on the window shaker, fumbled through the dark to the bathroom, and flicked on the light. I filled the toilet bowl with urine that was a lovely shade of orange and climbed into the shower. The hot water felt great on my skin, rubbing away my hurts and soaking into my battered flesh. I leaned against the stall and let it massage me until it went cold. I gave my body as quick a soaping as I could manage and shut off the water before it lost all trace of heat.

I wrapped myself in a towel and looked into the mirror. Welts marked my pink cheeks and bags held my blue-grey eyes, but I was otherwise no worse to behold.

My phone rang. It was an 813 number I didn't recognize. "Walsh."

"I hope you're proud of yourself." The indignant voice was familiar, but I couldn't place it among all the people who had cause to be angry with me.

"Oh? Have I done something to merit pride?"

"You're fucking right, you have! You just set this local back ten years." Jamie Dreyfus, the union president.

"Oh, sorry about that. Did you know you're breaking bread with a man who killed a firefighter for profit?"

"What? Bullshit!"

"You really should talk to Manny."

"You mean the VP who violated Mayor Silver's trust by handing you his fucking invitation? I'll pass."

I didn't have time for this. "Read it in the paper, then."

He was threatening my membership when I hung up.

I almost didn't read the text message, thinking it would be Dreyfus, but it was a different, unfamiliar number.

That was quite the demonstration you put on. I don't think Monte saw it coming at all. :) I'd like to see you tomorrow night at the same house we last met. 9:00 PM. Mandy D.

Maybe tonight wasn't a total waste, after all.

See you then.

RENDEZVOUS ON WILLOW

The day had progressed to afternoon before I awoke in agony and struggled to roll out of bed. My piss was still orange, and I considered a trip to the ER, but I hadn't bled to death yet and there was work afoot. So I settled for a round of Tylenol and promised myself to drink lots of water and cranberry juice.

I pulled up to the house at 8:47 pm. The afternoon storms had passed through, leaving the streets wet and quiet. A salt breeze off the bay *swished* through the trees in gusts, but the neighborhood was otherwise silent. I watched the wood-framed Victorian through the expended raindrops that fell from the windblown canopy.

It was dark and still. No one was in the driveway. No one parked in the street. It had occurred to me from the beginning this could be a setup. I frowned, reached into the glove compartment, and pulled out my .38. I checked the load and safety and slid it into the hip holster I wore under the tail of an ancient fire department windbreaker with the lettering scraped off.

I flipped the interior light switch so it would stay black when I opened the door and eased myself up and out with wobbly arms and legs. I pulled an unmarked pill bottle from my pocket and downed a pair of the Tylenol dry.

A rare coolness with low humidity made the early August night feel more like late April or early May. I took another careful look at the dark street, taking in the few lighted windows and noting all the cars: no gold Acuras, no mysterious figures sitting behind steering wheels, and no fogged windows. All good signs, but none of them meant anything about this was safe.

I eased the door closed and cursed myself for not parking farther away and walking. But no one had ambushed me, and it was too late for that now. I walked to the front of the car, bracing myself on the hood, and crossed in front of it. Wet leaves and wet strands of blown moss covered the lush grass and concrete walk to the front steps.

Mandy opened the door at my approach and allowed me to pass into a dark, shadow-strewn home. The wood floor boomed under my feet. The crypt-like echoes proclaimed the home to be as empty as it was dark. But smart men never trusted such proclamations. The empty house was a different landscape at night. One of hard shadows and slanted light. The latter played on Mandy's face, turning her terrified pallor into something phantasmic.

I forced a smile. "You get a buyer yet?"

Mandy's lips turned up at the corners, but it was no proper grin. "A couple. I think we're gonna get twenty percent above asking price."

She bolted and locked the door and glanced out the window at the rain-dampened streets.

I got right to business. "I saw you there last night. You and the Richardsons were having a bit of a row."

Mandy nodded. "They didn't like being told their world was getting ready to fall apart."

"You were there to warn them about me."

She glanced out the windows again and moved toward the stairs. "I told them the Seminole Heights shit was heating up again, and I didn't think it was going to go away this time."

I thought of the body language and the setting. "You were asking for hush money."

"Yes. Enough to get out of here and never come back to this town again." She glanced over my shoulder at the closed door. "Monte is scared."

"Monte?"

She glared at the sarcasm in my voice. "So I know him? That doesn't make me one of his conspirators."

"Is this the part where I say I understand, and no one could blame you for the path of destruction you profited from?"

"I had nothing to do with that. The original plan was to buy the homes on the cheap and double their value when Silver's urban renewal started. But people got greedy."

"Drew."

Mandy chuckled. "It was everyone. Drew said they were just run-down old buildings. No one would miss them. Artie said we were bringing dignity back to the Heights." She shook her head.

"No one was supposed to get hurt, and it was only supposed to happen the couple of times, just enough to drop our entry price."

"But the property values kept plummeting."

Mandy nodded. "And we were buying the whole place up for peanuts as the mayor funneled public monies for all his pet projects renovating the area and cleaning up the neighborhood."

"Until Chelsea Street."

She sighed and glanced at the door. "They were terrified. The dead fireman brought a ton of eyes onto the situation, but we had an out."

"Silver."

Mandy nodded. "He had handpicked people with the police and fire departments who'd helped protect their operation at least once."

I remembered what Pedro said about Townsend getting kicked free without charge or paperwork. "So you found a vagrant to pin it on."

"The vagrant," she said. "Apparently, his people knew this guy, and that he carried stuff on him for cooking fires. They picked him up and tied it into a neat bow. Afterwards, Drew showed his appreciation to us all. He made Ardie the CEO of B&D Construction. Made me president B&D Realty, and paid me a lot of money to go away. Called it a severance package."

"And Kinsey?"

She shrugged. "I told you. I just brokered the deals."

"And made a lot of commission money... plus bonuses... and your profit on the two homes."

"I wa—" She looked over my right shoulder at the door. Her eyes grew wide, and her mouth froze. I darted to my left and reached for my hip. The motion felt slow and was pure agony for my beaten innards.

The loud *clack* of a suppressed gunshot and the tinkle of a breaking pane of glass preceded the *zip* of the bullet that passed through the space I'd just occupied.

Mandy yelped and crumpled backward onto the stairs.

I tumbled toward the shadows and safety of the partition between the dining room and the foyer, my battered body screaming with every bump and twist and roll.

Clack! Clack! Clack! Thuds and *cracks* of bullets striking plaster or wood accompanied each shot.

Clack! Clack! But the reports didn't translate to more plaster dust or wood slivers.

I threw myself into the spacious dining room and hugged the hardwood floor. I had trouble with the .38 and rolled against the pain to draw down on the door. *Pop! Pop!* The explosion of my pistol was blinding and deafening in contrast to my would-be assassin's, but the slugs would be just as deadly. They took glass out of the bottom pane of the window and punched a hole in the front door.

No more shots came my way. I looked through the window behind me: empty. The gunshots left my ears ringing and too damaged to pick up on subtle noises. The entire house reeked of the acrid smell of cordite. I struggled to my knees and peeked through the white tulle curtains shrouding the living-room window and glimpsed a man darting across the street and running up Willow. I checked on Mandy and found why those two extra rounds hadn't shattered plaster or splintered wood.

She'd spilled on the wooden stairs, her arms and legs splayed in unnatural poses. At least one round found the center of her chest, giving birth to a red blossom on her white blouse. Horrified shock lived in her wide, unseeing eyes. Or maybe it was just my own reflected in what I saw.

She had no carotid. I considered searching her belongings, but decided they weren't going anywhere. I dared not call TPD, and I still didn't know what to think of Donner. That left only one choice. I holstered my gun, popped the remote earpieces into my right canal, and hit the autodial on my phone.

HERO TO ZERO IN RECORD SPEED

Dan answered the phone on the second ring. *"Lo?"*

"I told you." I interrupted him with an auctioneer's cadence, telling him about the conspiracy, the murder, and my impending chase.

The Acura streaked east on the next block north.

"What? What? Slow down."

I crossed the yard to the curb and took the hood in a pained baseball slide. The pocket rivet in my jeans gouged the paint, and I grimaced. So much for my imitation of the Duke boys.

I forced my aching body into the car and slammed the door. "No time! Call someone and tell them about the murder and the chase. The suspect is a TPD cop on the mayor's bodyguard detail." I started the car and screeched onto Willow, fishtailing on the wet streets.

I had driven the hundred and fifty feet north to Morrison and broke into a sloppy, skidding turn that almost took me into the high curb before Dan found his voice. *"A rogue Tampa cop who works directly for the mayor. Jesus!"*

"Yeah. Do you have someone at state you can trust?"

"State fire marshal guys, but they won't have any authority at a murder scene deep in the city."

I cursed; he was right. "Well, get someone, because I don't know if this guy has friends on the department who might help cover his ass."

I banked a right on Edison and came to a rolling stop at Bayshore.

Ortiz had already made the turn and was accelerating on the curving boulevard toward downtown. I followed, darting across the two lanes of westbound Bayshore and merging in front of a delivery box truck, who slammed his brakes and swerved. He hit nothing, and no one hit him, but I could see the gestures, even if only in my mind.

I raced past South Boulevard and built-up speed. The palm trees in the median and the concrete streetlamps passed faster with each one. Ortiz was out of sight, and I spared glances down each of the side streets, hoping I wouldn't see his taillights. Then I glimpsed him coming out of the curve at Innman, the gathering speed turning balustrades from the Bayshore seawall solid.

We screamed under the Davis Island Bridge, making the final curves to downtown and passing the *Jose Gasparilla's* dock Formula One–style. Ortiz hit the Platt Street Bridge and caught air seconds ahead of me. His brake lights were bright under the faux tunnel that ran under the Tampa Convention Center Parking

Garage. I made my own rabbit hop and landed on the wet metal decking.

The *vrrm* of the metal passed in the space of a heartbeat, and I was on Channelside Drive. I passed under the garage, but Ortiz accelerated toward the Amalie Arena and the aquarium, leaving an amber light at Franklin Street. It turned red and a white Altima pulled into the intersection, a purple Uber sign in his window. I laid on the horn, swerved left.

The Corolla ran up on the empty sidewalk, squeezing between the front of his stopped car and the steel light pole. I found the road, engine revving and tires squealing, but I'd lost ground. I remembered what Tammy said about him being an instructor in all the practical skills and wondered if I wasn't risking my life and the lives of all these people for nothing.

No! There was evidence in that car. I had to keep up. He couldn't be allowed to get rid of it. I pushed the accelerator, zipping past Amalie Arena, swishing between the palm trees and through the gorge of fresh concrete and steel that had sprouted up in the last decade.

Ortiz's taillights disappeared in the bend by Channelside Plaza. I hit the same subtle turn and watched his brake lights flash as he made the jog for the roundabout in front of the aquarium. He made the turn look easy, The aquarium's erector set glass dome loomed close in the night sky. I took the same curve too fast, fishtailing and powersliding into the wide, empty traffic circle.

The stunt didn't go unnoticed. The blue and red strobes of a police cruiser brought the night to life. I accelerated away, hoping to put enough room between me and the patrol car to avoid having to stop, but I wouldn't be able to ignore him for long. We raced north on Channelside to the Adamo leg of State Road 60 and swung east toward Brandon.

The cop behind me was slow to get on my tail, but he was eating up the wet pavement fast. This wouldn't take long. I took the turn on Adamo better than I'd taken the circle and accelerated with all the power my poor little Corolla could muster. I was approaching Nineteenth Street by the time the cop behind me turned off Channelside, but his turn was smooth and his acceleration even on the wet street.

Ortiz was skidding into a sharp turn on Twenty-first, headed south toward the Leroy Selmon and the Twenty-second Street Causeway. He was slipping away, and I was going to jail. The cop behind me was gaining, and I was already guilty of eluding.

"Fuck it." I followed him into his turn and made the S curve that passed under the Selmon. I didn't see the crash, but I saw the gasoline tanker stopped in the middle of the intersection, the steam from Ortiz's shattered radiator, and the broken concrete light pole still shuddering on the ground.

I slid to a precarious halt on the damp asphalt and left my car almost before it stopped. The cop's siren was screaming in my ear, and I waited to hear the order to put my hands up, but I was already getting my bruised body up to a sprint. I scanned the scene and determined Ortiz had hit a light pole. No wires were down. No hazards beyond the traffic were present, until I realized that wasn't steam from under his hood.

The acrid-sweet smell of burning car hit my nostrils the moment before Ortiz's screams touched my ears. A *whoof* of blossoming flame rose from the engine compartment and the distant scent of fire became a yellow flicker under the crumpled hood. Flames belched from the tented metal and black smoke poured into the cool Tampa Bay air, an oil slick on the midnight blue sky.

The smoke was choking, already biting my lungs, and stinging my eyes. The rising plume veiled Ortiz's flailing form, but glimpses of his wide-eyed terror and the horror in his terrified shrieks told of a man about to burn to death. "Walsh! Walsh! You have to help me! I broke my leg, and I can't open the door."

I thought of Pops lying in his store as it burned down around him and the poetic justice of this man burning alive in a crash of his own making.

"Walsh, I'm burning up! You're a fucking firefighter; you can't do this to me!"

But he was wrong. I could do this. Couldn't I? I'd seen a lot of horrible things and tried to imagine taking pleasure as this evil man burn alive and sagged.

"Walsh!"

I cursed and tried the door. The impact had jammed it. I gritted my teeth and stuck my head inside to assess the situation. I reached down and pulled his legs. They moved, and he screamed.

"I told you it's broken!"

But it wasn't pinned, and that's what I needed to know.

The siren behind me died.

I stood for a fresh breath of air, gulped down six or seven lungfuls, and leaned into the car. Ortiz and I were nose-to-nose. "I'm gonna get you out of here, but it's gonna hurt like a motherfucker."

The heat was setting in, and Ortiz was coughing and gagging. A ripple of doubt passed through me, and I had a premonition of watching him burn alive in front of me. I groped in the smoky darkness and found the lever to roll the seat backward, then found the one that lay him back. Ragged coughs chopped down Ortiz's screams.

I tried to steal a small breath and got hot, angry smoke for my effort. Sputtering coughs rose from my throat. I fumbled across his body for the seat belt and unbuckled it. My right hand groped my hip and my knife from its holster and flipping it open. I pulled the belt as tight as I could and cut the longest piece I could manage.

The cop appeared, pinning me against the door and sending shockwaves of pain through my broken body. "Put your hands behind your back!"

"I'm an off-duty firefighter. I can get him out, but I need your help."

"Do what he says, Hobbes!"

The cop looked into the compartment. "Sarge?"

I motioned with my head. "Can you take out that back window?"

Diego was desperate. "Do it!"

The cop eased up on me, and I resumed tying the ends of the nylon seatbelt together. The smoke coming out of the car was gaining volume and speed. We were running out of time. Hobbes deployed his ASP and shattered the back glass in two strokes. I considered laying my jacket over the back lid, but there was no time. I lay on the lid and stuck my face in the deadly plume.

"Lift your arms."

"Wha?"

"Lift your goddamned arms!"

He did. I looped the strap over him. "Put them down."

A yellow glow rolled across the floorboard. Ortiz screamed. I pulled the strap below him to form a bight and fed the bight from the piece running over his chest through to form a harness. I tugged and pulled, but my battered innards couldn't stand the strain.

Ortiz screamed, and I repositioned so I was kneeling one knee on the back deck, one foot on the back seat. I pulled again, tugging with all my might. He moved, but not much. Oily smoke flowed around me in a black stream of super-heated poison.

"Help! Help me!" I said to Hobbes. More sirens closed from all directions. Blue and red flashed all over the wet street.

Hobbes grabbed the strap.

I looked at him. "One, two, three."

We pulled as one, and Ortiz lifted from his seat. A second tug got him over the back bench. Horse agonized screams erupted with every pull.

I climbed out, gritting against the pain. "One more time!"

We pulled as one, and Ortiz flopped out onto the back deck. More cops rushed up and helped pull him from the car while others buried my face into the asphalt and clasped my hands behind my back. “Get the gun!” I said. “There’s a gun in the car! It was used to kill a woman in South Tampa.”

From hero to zero in record speed.

TWENTY-SECOND AND DURHAM

I'd always heard that police cruisers smelled of vomit, but the only thing I smelled was the caustic scent of burning plastic.

TFR Engine Six arrived out of the south and stretched a line to the car fire. Engine and Rescue Four arrived out of the north and worked on Ortiz.

Four's captain, a pleasant-faced man with blond hair poking from under a crooked helmet, walked over and peered into the cruiser. His open bunker coat hung loose, exposing the white T-shirt with a slash of soot across the belly. "You alright?"

I looked at my surroundings. "All things considered."

"You have some sooty snot there. Looks like you took a lot of smoke."

"Not the first time."

Narrow-eyed curiosity tempered his pleasantness. "Okay. If you don't need anything. I'm gonna head back to the other fella."

"Nothing at all, Captain."

He nodded again, the curious suspicion in full possession of his features, and walked back the way he'd come.

They'd already knocked the fire down and Six had the hood up, making sure it stayed that way. They put Ortiz in the back of the rescue. The captain from Six walked over and handed the tied-off seatbelt to the captain on Four. They chatted over the belt, turned to me as one, and crossed the pavement.

Four's captain offered the tool for my inspection. "You did this?"

"Guilty."

"Which agency do you work for?"

"The county. I'm a captain on a Brandon engine company."

The two men exchanged looks; the fire department gossip machine was winding up.

"You know that guy you saved was an off-duty TPD cop?"

I doubted he would thank me for it. "Yeah, I know."

Rescue pulled out behind them, banking a U-turn on the empty street. They ran emergency, and I wondered if Ortiz had taken more smoke than I thought.

"I'm Ryan Cleese," said Four's captain. "That's Ronnie Garcia."

"Lo Walsh."

We exchanged nods, and they glanced toward the hands cuffed at my back. I offered nothing, wondering how long it would take this tale to make it around the city and into the county. It depended on how many rescues were at TGH and how quickly these guys got back to quarters, but this would be the news at the shift-change in every fire station in Tampa, unincorporated Hillsborough, and all the neighboring communities.

"You sure you don't want transported?" said Cleese.

"I'm sure."

"We'd like to take a look at you and get a refusal and all that."

"Sure. Cap. Whatever you need."

Engine Four's crew looked me over. They gazed at my throat, listened to my lungs, and took an EKG. The woman I took to be the driver looked over the readings and proclaimed me to be in survivable health. I refused transport and signed her release.

They took it and left me to Hobbes' tender mercies. Soot streaked his pecan face, and I wondered what mine must've looked like. "How are you, Mr. Walsh?"

"The jury is still out on that." Bad choice of words.

He smiled as if we were old friends. "Care to tell me why you and your pal were drag racing all over my streets?"

I glanced at the evidence he'd collected from the passenger's seat of Ortiz's car. The silenced pistol that was secured and bagged. "We weren't drag racing."

"Okay, what were you doing?"

"Your homicide division is either on the scene of or en route to a shooting on Willow." I bobbed my head toward the the bagged automatic. "That's your murder weapon."

Hobbes frowned. "Are you saying the guy you pulled out of that car was the trigger man?"

"And that's all I'm prepared to say right now."

His expression darkened. Whether it was from anger at me or frustration with the situation, I couldn't say. "You mind if I look through your car?"

"Sure," I said. "As soon as you get a warrant."

This time, I was the source of his ire. "Wait here."

He secured the gun in the trunk and disappeared among the flashing blue and red and white lights. Officers began roping off the scene with yellow crime scene tape. I guessed a case of road-rage and reckless driving had gotten an upgrade.

It took an hour or more for the detective to show up. When he did, he carried a tall Styrofoam cup of coffee and a weary expression I recognized from all-night structure fires and late-night extrications. The man looked to be early thirties, maybe late twenties, with skin the color of coal and a white smile that was as bright and friendly as his walnut eyes were warm and welcoming. He squatted to be at eye level with me; the pale grey Brooks Brothers two-piece didn't ride or bunch on his lean frame. He wore no tie over his black shirt and shoes more appropriate for a boardroom than a crime scene. He offered me the cup of coffee and noticed the cuffs.

"Oh! I'm sorry." He set the coffee on the roof of the car and searched his blazer pockets. Right pocket, left pocket. "You will not try to escape if I release you, will you, Captain?"

His tenor carried a Caribbean lilt, but I couldn't have said if it was Haitian or Jamaican or something else altogether.

"I'm no threat."

"Dat's good to hear." He touched his breast pocket and pressed against his trouser pockets before he came back to his left blazer pocket and offered a satisfied smile. His manicured hands produced a single handcuff key. "Would you please stand?"

He helped me to my feet and worked the key, releasing the cuffs with the watch-winding *vrrip* unique to the instruments. They opened, releasing my wrists their steel grip, and I realized how uncomfortable I'd truly been. I rubbed my chaffed skin, stretched my battered muscles, and resumed my seat.

The detective offered me the coffee.

I took it and grinned. "What about you? You look like you could use this more than I could."

His smile and tilt of head had a familiarity that suggested us old friends. "Is that anything to say to a man who just brought you coffee?"

I accepted it and took a long whiff. "Cuban."

He nodded. "Mine is in the car. Drank it already."

"This'll ruin my sleep tonight."

"Do you really think sleep is in your future tonight?"

I took a sip. Café con leche. It wasn't sweet enough, but it was good. "Not really."

He offered a hand. "Jean Francois Mondesir."

I took it. "Lo Walsh."

"Yes, Captain Walsh of the Hillsborough County Fire Rescue. Yes?"

"Yes."

"So, maybe you tell me how a firefighter like you ends up chasing a policeman like him." He motioned over his shoulder at the wrecked and burned Acura.

"He killed someone."

"Tell me about that."

I shrugged. "You should have detectives on the scene by now. Maybe they should tell you about it."

His easy smile betrayed none of the anger or frustration I'd have expected from my answer. "Might be I come from there. Might be I know things. I just want to hear it from your mouth."

I took a long drink of coffee and considered my options. It was tempting to talk to this easygoing cop so eager to be my friend. That made him anything but. On the other hand, I had nothing to hide, and the sooner I made him happy, the sooner I could go home and to bed.

A new vehicle arrived out of the north. I recognized it as the HCFR on-duty investigator's black pickup. Two men got out. They had a brief exchange with the cop on the perimeter. He pointed our way. The newcomers flashed their IDs, and the cop scribbled in his notepad. It was Dan and Donner. I kept my mouth shut for the moment.

Mondesir followed my gaze, and I stole a glimpse of the ruthless predator behind the mask. He stepped away to intercept the men out of earshot. They had a brief exchange and returned to me together.

"We are going to continue this at the station," said Mondesir. The affable buddy cop was now all business. He produced the cuffs and offered me a look that was equal parts apology and accusation. It said, *"We had a good thing going, but your friends had to ruin it."*

I let him cuff me again and sat back in the cruiser.

BIG BLUE

The Tampa Police Department Headquarters was a blue ten-story mid-rise that took up a block of Madison between Franklin and Florida. And it was every bit the gaudy eyesore a person might expect from such a building built in the sixties. Hobbes pulled into the garage through a steel roll-up door on the Florida side and parked by a reserved spot closest to the main entrance.

He helped me from the car and up the concrete steps into a building with worn carpet and aged ceiling tiles one would expect of a place the city had given up on. The smell of coffee and industrial cleaner was prominent, but it didn't cover up the smell of dying structure I recognized from fire stations kept past their usefulness.

They re-cuffed me with my hands in front of my body and led to a classic interrogation room with a chair, a table, and nothing else. The smell of coffee wasn't as prevalent here, leaving the cleaner to compete with dying building. Dying building won standing up.

The door opened, and Mondesir led Dan and Donner into the room. The amiable smile he'd worn on Twenty-second and Durham was a distant memory. Neither Dan nor Donner looked any happier. Each carried a manila file folder, and they sat across from me.

Mondesir recorded the incident number, the date, and the interrogating officers for the record, and offered the first smile since Twenty-second Street. "Hello again."

"A shame about the coffee."

"Isn't it, though?"

He asked basic questions: my name, profession, and residence. He asked if my activities tonight were related to my capacity as a fire company captain with Hillsborough County Fire Rescue. "No."

"Were you engaged in any private work associated with your bondsman or private investigator's license?"

"No."

He offered that calm smile. "This sounds like quite a story, eh, Captain?"

"It has its ups and downs."

"I hope you will share it with us."

I glanced at Dan and Donner and knew this to be the moment I should say no. "If it'll help."

"Fantastic!" His excitement brought the Caribbean accent out of him, or perhaps that was part of the routine. "So, tell me how you ended up chasing Diego Ortiz through downtown Tampa this evening."

I told him the entire story, and all three scribbled furiously. Each stopped me at least once to ask clarifying questions, but it was Mondesir who resumed the interrogation. "So, you say you went there at the victim's behest. Yes?"

"That's right."

"And you met her. And she told you this fantastic tale about a series of fires..." he consulted his notes... "twenty-five years ago?"

"It was mostly confirmation of stuff I'd already uncovered."

"And this conspiracy involves her old real estate company, the then and current mayor, and it's all tied to one of your bail jumper from last month?"

"A bail jumper murdered on SO's watch less than twenty-four hours after being returned, yes, sir."

"And you, a firefighter with no law enforcement experience, took this case on to bring justice to those who did this?"

"No. I did it because they burned my father's store with him in it."

"Let us run through that again."

I did.

They all nodded and took dutiful notes as I told them the tale of how Diego attacked Pops and left him to burn alive. I told them how I came to run the fire and the forcible entry conditions I'd found as the first-in engine. I told them how the marks on the steel door suggested a Rabbit Tool and how firefighters and law enforcement were the only ones who had regular access to them, calling upon Dan to verify my comments.

He nodded. "The five-inch spread and uniform pressure is highly suggestive of such a tool."

"And you didn't come to me with any of this," said Donner.

"I came to you, and my father was in ICU twelve hours later."

Donner had no response to that.

"Let's come back to tonight," said Mondesir. "You said Miss Drexler called you—"

"Texted me."

"Texted you"—he glanced at his Tag Huer—"yesterday morning wanting to meet you at this home she had been showing."

"Yes."

"Why there?"

I shrugged. "Neutral site. Maybe she felt safe there. You'd really have to ask her."

He nodded. "And that's when Mr. Ortiz shot at you and missed at point-blank range."

I was Captain Walsh, and Diego was Mr. Ortiz. This Mondesir was good. "Miss Drexler looked over my shoulder and got a... a startled expression."

"And you just jumped out of the way."

"Twenty years on the street teaches you to read situations and take decisive action," I said. "Either way, forensics will back that story. The slugs in Miss Drexler and the wall where he tried to shoot me will match the silenced pistol recovered from his seat. The slug in the door... if it's still there... will match mine."

"You mean the gun found in his seat after you went in there on your rescue attempt?"

"Doesn't really qualify as an attempt when you pull the guy out. Does it?"

Mondesir smiled.

"And," I continued, "why save his life if I killed Drexler? Wouldn't this be an easier story for me to sell if he was dead?"

It was the first time Mondesir was speechless. He glanced at the other two. "You have anything?"

They both shook their heads.

"We'll be back," said Mondesir.

And they were. All. Night. Long.

Mondesir came back in with a partner, a woman named Cynthia. She went through the same story, and I told the same tale, answering with as much honesty and recall as I could manage.

They left and Maury Booth and Rochelle Nixon, two detectives from the Internal Affairs Division, stepped in to ask me about Ortiz. I told them how he'd been conducting off-the-clock surveillance on me, and how I'd seen him at Mandy Drexler's office that first time I'd interviewed her. We discussed how he showed up at my house in Plant City the night of my failed make up attempt with Val, and how I'd been roughly handled by him and another member of the detail at the Tampa Bay Yacht and Country Club. I told her how a stand-up officer named Jack almost caught them.

I told them how my investigation led me to suspect he was the torch who attacked my father, again citing the probable use of the Rabbit Tool to make entry, something he could easily borrow from this building or Thirty-fourth Street. We even discussed his connection to the arson task force from the nineties and report of how he cut Townsend loose as a suspect months before he would kill him in a shootout.

They listened, took notes, and left business cards. It was the first time I thought my story was being taken seriously. "Thank you both."

I put my head down and fell into a deep sleep, but the *clack* of the door opening drew me to consciousness. Mondesir and Dan strode into the room wearing weary smiles. "Well, Mr. Walsh. You are free to go."

I tried the words out in my head before daring to speak. "Free to go?"

"That's right." Mondesir wore a broad smile on his dark face. "You are free to go."

I rubbed my eyes and wiped drool from the table. "That's great, but don't you have my car?"

"Impounded. Yes. We can get you an Uber."

"I'll take him." Dan smiled at me. "It's not too far out of the way."

"Thanks."

I didn't see Donner, but Dan told me on the ride back to Seffner that Donner was off mobilizing a task force. They'd found my files and computer in the car and started salivating like dogs when they discovered all the details I'd left out.

"Silver's going down." He stared east through the windshield toward the rising sun and spoke as if it had already happened. "Chief Price is already on the interview list and is scheduled to make a statement Monday."

"Price?"

He nodded. "I heard about your little conversation."

"At the church."

Dan laughed. "Is that where you chased him down?"

I nodded.

"Well, he changed my directives that afternoon, instructing Mason to give me and Robbie Stewart full access to our counterparts and HCSO."

"That's how Donner came into the picture tonight."

"Yeah. I had little choice on that, but after being with him a while, I thought him clean."

"So, how did Ortiz find out about Pops having the video?"

"We're just guessing here, but they found his name on a records' request."

I closed my eyes. "The requests for the body cam video of Kinsey's arrest."

"Yeah. We suspect that put you on the radar. Ortiz found out you were Kinsey's bondsmen and did the math. But we're still investigating."

"Dammit!"

"You had no way of knowing."

But I had a way of knowing. I'd underestimated him from the beginning.

Dan pulled into the park. "Get some rest. I suspect you'll be on admin leave until they clear you completely, but don't quote me on that."

I got out of the truck and nodded. "I won't. Thanks, Dan."

"Thank you, brother," he said. "Weren't for you, that corrupt shithead might be on his way to the governor's mansion."

"Now it'll be another corrupt shithead."

He blew out a soft chuckle. "Man, don't you know it?"

I closed the door, and he wheeled around the park, leaving me for a long morning of reports and meetings before he could go home.

FAMILY

We were in the Corolla crossing the Davis Island Bridge under a Chamber of Commerce sky.

"He's going to always be that way?" Sadie's voice trembled with despair.

"Not necessarily the way he is now. But Pops has a lot of therapy ahead of him."

"Like what you and Mommy did?"

I smiled and glanced in the mirror at Sadie. "This is a different kind of therapy. Think of it as more a type of school where he has to relearn how to think and talk and use his body."

"Sounds terrible." Christopher's voice was bleak.

Val and I had quite an argument over this. She'd wanted to protect the kids from what had happened to Pops, to pretend everything was fine and that he was fully recovered and doing great. I held firm in my demand that we take them to see him as he was because he was likely to have some level of disability for the rest of his life, and he could always have a setback that killed or further paralyzed him.

She'd relented, but her wrath would be blood red when the kids returned glum and depressed. I hated it, but what could I do besides forbid them from ever seeing their grandfather again?

"It's gonna be a hard road for sure, but facing this stuff is part of growing up. And I couldn't bear to deprive you kids of your grandfather for the rest of his life because he was hurt. That wouldn't be fair to you or him. Would it?"

"No." Neither child seemed happy about it.

We pulled into the parking garage and climbed nine levels before finding a spot. I slipped into a parking spot that was six inches narrower than it needed to be and looked at the kids. "Okay, put on your brave faces, and we'll do something special after this."

"McDonald's?" Christopher's voice clung to hope.

I frowned. "Maybe something outdoors on a day like today. School starts next week, you know."

Moans rose from both throats, and I grinned.

We descended to the third floor and crossed the pedestrian bridge to the hospital. We found his room after some searching.

"Hey, hey!" His words came out garbled but intelligible.

"Hey, Pops! How are you?"

"Breet, begu?"

I studied him, unsure how to ask, and he wrote: *Great and you?*

I smiled and looked at the kids. "Fantastic! Tell Pops where you guys are staying tonight!"

"Dad's trailer!" Sadie's enthusiasm didn't take all the sting out of "Dad's" not "our," but when compared to two weeks ago, it was an unqualified win.

I held my hands in demonstration, and Pops beamed a lopsided smile. The sight warmed and broke my heart at once, but he ended the spell by waving and pointing with his good arm and shouting garbled words beyond understanding. I followed his gaze to the TV. Bay News 9 had a red breaking banner across the bottom of the screen: *The Bayshore Political Group has released a statement.*

He fumbled with the remote. I helped him and got the volume up. The field reporter was standing in front of a familiar house about a mile from Mandy Drexler's office. *"... ayor Silver is suspending his campaign for personal and health reasons. This from a representative of Bayshore Political Group."*

They cut to video showing a young man who bore the Richardson look standing at a podium on the water, maybe the Tampa Bay Yacht and Country Club. *"Mayor Silver is grateful for the support he's getting from all his constituents over these bogus and slanderous accusations and looks forward to being vindicated in both criminal and civil court. But the stress this has caused him and the attention it has stolen from his message have left him little choice but to suspend his campaign at this time."*

A reporter was asking if he would also resign as mayor, but the younger Richardson walked away answering no questions.

The anchor broke in. *"How is this tied to the Infamous Five we've heard so much about?"*

The Infamous Five was the name being given to five of the mayor's eight-member bodyguard detail.

"Well, we don't know much, but we do know agents of the FDLE and FBI have served warrants on the mayor's home and office, as well as his campaign headquarters at the Bayshore Political Group behind me. We have retained the affidavits and believe the John Doe 'with extensive knowledge of the mayor's operations' to be to be based on information provided by the former head of the mayor's bodyguard detail and the ringleader of these rogue cops, Sergeant Diego Ortiz of Tampa. Sergeant Ortiz was arrested last week on charges of murdering forty-nine-year-old Amanda Drexler, a realtor from Tampa. It is believed she was killed to prevent her from—"

I turned it off.

"My son the hero."

"Mother! I didn't know you were coming."

"Coming? I was here. Wasn't I, darling?" She never called Pops by his name, but that didn't keep the giddy glee from his face.

"Gah yhats," he said with that gravelly incoherence.

Both kids offered tepid greetings, and she replied with, "Hello, children. I need your father for a minute."

I followed her into the hallway, grateful she wanted to talk. I'd spent so long judging hers and Pops's relationship, and I had decided it wasn't my place to take sides. "How are you, Mother?"

"Truth be told, I'm distraught, positively distraught."

"What happened?"

She leaned forward and lowered her voice to a whisper. "They are letting your father go! Discharging him!"

I saw this a lot at work. "Well, Mother, they can't keep him forever. Once patients get as healed as they're likely to, they cut them loose. It's the only way to have room for new patients."

"I know that!" Her tone accused me of being silly. "But they want to send him home with me. Either that or put him in a home that will positively break us!" She sighed. "I just don't know what to do."

Rage boiled inside me, my conciliatory conversation about judgement forgotten. "Why don't you get Jimmy Connors to help you take care of him?"

"You..." I thought for a moment she would curse, but she lowered her voice to a harsh whisper. "I thought with your medical training you could help."

"Me? I live in a trailer, and I'm gone for twenty-four hours at a time. Don't you think that would be a little hard on Pops?"

"I could find someone to come help him on the days you were gone."

My mother the giver. "As long as it isn't too much trouble."

She perked up, either oblivious to or ignoring my sarcasm. "No trouble. I have just the person in mind."

Mother pranced into the room, took her clutch I hadn't seen sitting on the green vinyl chair, and strode from the room. "You folks be good, now." She pecked Pops on the forehead and was gone.

I stood in the doorway, listening to her retreating footfalls in a storm of anger and guilt.

Pops read my face and sagged.

I smiled and stepped toward him. "How would you like to stay at my place, Dad?"

He looked at me with hurt eyes, and I hoped it wasn't from anything they'd seen in me. I squeezed his shoulder and nodded. "It'd be great to have you. Just like those long stakeouts waiting for some skip to show up someplace he didn't belong."

Pops smiled at that, and the kids smiled, too. And for the first time in a long time, I think I had showed them what it really meant to be family.

Your Reservations are Waiting

Did you like *Tampa Heat*?

Well, don't let the story end there.

Join the *Firehouse Kitchen Table Newsletter* and get a *Tampa Heat* novella, *Temple Terrace Badger Game*, free. What else should you expect from your membership? You'll get updates on personal appearances, releases, and sales. But there'll also be backstory and the real Tampa history that inspired this novel.

In fact, joining from this link will give you a special email post into the historic arson spree that inspired this tale.

Is that cool or what?

Click on the link here or scan the QR code on the following page to reserve your seat and get all the cool goodies that go with it.

Thanks

~Thad

Afterword

The idea for this story went through many ideations.

I first came up with the concept when a colleague talked about chasing skips and doing PI work in the 48 hours between shifts. I was already writing on my off days and immediately saw the uniqueness of such a story and how it could fit within the established tropes of the hard-boiled PI, a genre I've always loved.

But I was still a lowly firefighter, with years left in my career. I wasn't eager to incur the wrath of the administration for depicting an unflattering truth or storyline they might see as bad for the department.

I first considered setting these tales in a fictitious agency, but discarded the plan.

The whole point of this nuanced story was authenticity and realism.

How could I do that with a fictitious department? How would I maintain Tampa as the focal point and still keep to the genuineness I sought? No, this wouldn't do.

I considered making Lo a City of Tampa firefighter.

This idea had longer legs, but died a quick death for two important reasons. One: I know dozens, probably scores of Tampa firefighters, but relatively little about its inner workings and specific culture. And, Two: There was no way this Hillsborough County firefighter was going to write a book about a firefighting PI and give the "glory" to his department's mostly beloved, but often rival, big brother.

So, I "stayed in my lane" for the next fifteen years, writing some very cool, but very safe sci fi and fantasy as T. Allen Diaz.

But now I'm retired. I have no constraints.

I can write without pressure from above and follow whatever stories I like.

So, here I am, writing cool hard-boiled detective fiction set in an often forgotten city, tailor-made for these kinds of stories. And I'm having a blast. I hope you'll stay with me.

Because I have big plans.

~Thad

ABOUT THE AUTHOR

Thad Diaz was a Tampa Bay firefighter for twenty-five years. He wrote sci-fi and fantasy under the name T. Allen Diaz, but he's always been a fan of hard-boiled mysteries. So, when a fellow employee told him how he spent his off days chasing bail-jumpers, Diaz knew there was a story in that.

Now that he no longer rides the fire truck or works for the county, he can tell that story without reservations or concerns for his career. The *Cigar City Case Files* are based in Tampa and occur in actual or fictionalized places tailored to this great city, making the most of its glorious beauty and gritty underbelly as only a native can.

Diaz still lives in the Tampa Bay area with his wife, two of his kids and a house full of dogs. *Tampa Heat* is only the first in a series that he hopes will span into the double digits. Follow him online and join his email list for the Tampa Heat prequel, River Rat today.

Milton Keynes UK
Ingram Content Group UK Ltd.
UKHW010637041223
433752UK00006B/386